MATHIAS
SANDORF

JULES VERNE

MATHIAS SANDORF

DESSINS PAR L. BENETT

MATHIAS SANDORF

Jules Verne

ROH
PRESS

Mathias Sandorf
By Jules Verne

Set from George Hanna's Original Translation, with slight adjustments, modifications and restorations
Sampson, Low, Marston, Searle and Rivington Edition
London 1889

Illustrations by Léon Benett
As appeared in *Voyages Extraordinaires*
J Hetzel Edition, Paris 1885

ROH Press
First paperback edition
Copyright © 2007 by ROH Press

For information visit:
www.rohpress.com

Cover design: Adapted from Léon Bennet original

ISBN: 978-0-9782707-0-4

Printed in the United States of America

CONTENTS

PART I

PART II

PART III

PART IV

PART V

TO ALEXANDRE DUMAS,

I dedicate this book to you while dedicating it also to the memory of that genius of a storyteller who was Alexandre Dumas, your father. In this work, I have tried to make of *Mathias Sandorf* the *Monte Cristo* of the *Extraordinary Voyages*. I ask you to accept this dedication as a testimony of my deepest friendship.

JULES VERNE

Reply from M. A. Dumas,
June 23rd, 1885

My dear friend,

I am very touched by the thought of dedicating *Mathias Sandorf* to me, which I will begin to read upon my return, Friday or Saturday. You were right, in your dedication, to associate the memory of the father to the friendship of the son. No one would have been more charmed than the author of *Monte Cristo*, in reading your brilliant, original, and engaging adventures. There is between the two of you a literary kinship so obvious that, in terms of literature, you are more his son than I am. I have loved you for a long time and I delight in being your brother.

I thank you for your persevering affection and return it warmly.

ALEXANDRE DUMAS

The carrier pigeon

PART I

CHAPTER I

THE CARRIER PIGEON

Trieste, the capital of Illyria, consists of two towns of widely dissimilar aspect. One of them – Theresienstadt – is modern and well-to-do and squarely built along the shore of the bay from which the land it occupies has been reclaimed; the other is old and poor and irregular, straggling from the Corso up the slopes of the Karst, whose summit is crowned by the picturesque citadel.

The harbour is guarded by the mole of San Carlo, with the merchant shipping berthed alongside. On this mole there may at most times be seen – and very often in somewhat disquieting numbers – many a group of those houseless and homeless Bohemians whose clothes might well be destitute of pockets, considering that their owners never had, and to all appearance never will have, the wherewithal to put into them.

Today, however – it is the 18th of May, 1867 – two personages slightly better dressed than the rest are noticeable amongst the crowd. That they have ever suffered from a superabundance of florins or kreutzers is improbable, unless some lucky chance has favoured them – and they certainly look as though they would stick at nothing that might induce that chance to come.

One of them calls himself Sarcany, and says he hails from Tripoli. The other is a Sicilian, Zirone by name. Together they have strolled up and down the mole at least a dozen times, and now they have halted at its furthest end and are gazing away to the horizon, to the west of the Gulf of Trieste, as if they hoped to sight the ship bringing home their fortune.

"What time is it?" asked Zirone, in Italian, which his comrade spoke as fluently as he did all the other tongues of the Mediterranean.

Sarcany made no reply.

"What a fool I am!" exclaimed the Sicilian. "It's the time you're hungry after you've had no breakfast!"

There is such a mixture of races in this part of Austria-Hungary that the presence of these two men, although they were obviously strangers to the place, provoked no attention. And besides, if their pockets were empty, no one had reason to think so, thanks to their long brown capes, which reached even to their boots.

Sarcany, the youngert of the two, was about five and twenty, and of middle height, well set up, and of elegant manners and address. Sarcany, however, was not his baptismal name, and, probably, he had never been baptized, being of Tripolitan or Tunisian origin; but though his complexion was very dark, his regular features proclaimed him to be more European than African.

If ever physiognomy was deceptive, it was so in Sarcany's case. It required a singularly keen observer to discover his consummate astuteness in that handsome face, with its large dark eyes, fine straight nose, and well-cut mouth shaded by the slight moustache. That almost impassable face betrayed none of the signs of contempt and hatred engendered by a constant state of revolt against society. If, as physiognomists pretend – and they are not infrequently right – every rascal bears witness against himself in spite of all his cleverness, Sarcany could give the assertion the lie direct. To look at him no one would suspect what he was and what he had been. He provoked none of that irresistible aversion we feel towards cheats and scoundrels; and, in consequence, he was all the more dangerous.

Where had Sarcany spent his childhood? No one knew. How had he been brought up, and by whom? In what corner of Tripoli had he nestled during his early years? To what protection did he owe his escape from the many chances of destruction in that terrible climate? No one could say – maybe not even himself; born by chance, helped on by chance, destined to live by chance! Nevertheless, during his boyhood he had picked up a certain amount of practical instruction, thanks to his having to knock about the world, mixing with people of all kinds, trusting to expedient after expedient to secure his daily bread. It was owing to this and other circumstances that he had come to have business relations with one of the richest houses in Trieste, that of the banker, Silas Toronthal, whose name is intimately connected with the development of this history.

Sarcany's companion, the Italian, Zirone, was a man faithless and lawless, a thorough-paced adventurer, ever ready at the call of him who could pay him well, until he met with him who would pay him better, to undertake any task whatever. Of Sicilian birth, and in his thirtieth year, he was as capable of suggesting a villainy as of carrying it into effect. He might have told people where he had been born, had he known; but he never willingly said where he lived, or if he lived anywhere. It was in Sicily that the chances of Bohemian life had made him acquainted with Sarcany. And henceforth they had gone through the world, trying *per fas et nefas* to make a living by their wits. Zirone was a large, bearded man, brown in complexion, and black of hair, taking much pains to hide the look of the scoundrel which would persist in revealing itself in spite of all his efforts. In vain he tried to conceal his real character beneath his exuberant volubility, and, being of rather a cheerful temperament, he was just as talkative about himself as his younger companion was reserved.

Today, however, Zirone was very moderate in what he had to say. He was obviously anxious about his dinner. The night before, fortune had been unkind to them at the gambling-table, and the resources of Sarcany had been exhausted. What they were to do next neither knew. They could only reckon on chance, and as that Providence of the Beggars did not seek them out on the mole of San Carlo, they decided to go in search of it along the streets of the new town.

There, up and down the squares, quays, and promenades on both sides of the harbour leading to the grand canal which runs through Trieste, there goes, comes, throngs, hastens, and tears along in the fury of business a population of some seventy thousand inhabitants of Italian origin whose mother-tongue is lost in a cosmopolitan concert of all the sailors, traders, workmen, and officials who shout and chatter in English, German, French, or Slav. Although this new town is rich, it by no means follows that all who tread its streets are fortunate. No! Even the wealthiest could hardly compete with the foreign merchants – English, Armenian, Greeks, and Jews – who lord it at Trieste, and whose sumptuous establishments would do no discredit to the capital of Austria-Hungary. But, beyond these, how many are the poorer folks wandering from morning to night along the busy streets, bordered with lofty buildings closed like strong rooms, where lie the goods of all descriptions attracted to this free port, so happily placed at the farthest corner of the Adriatic! How many there are, breakfastless and dinnerless, loitering on the quays, where the vessels of the wealthiest shipping firm of the Continent – the Austrian Lloyds – are unloading the treasures brought from every part of the world! How many outcasts there are, such as are found

Sarcany and Zirone remained silent

in London, Liverpool, Marseilles, Havre, Antwerp, and Leghorn, who elbow the opulent ship owners, thronging round the warehouses, where admittance is forbidden them, round the Exchange, whose doors will never open for them, and everywhere round the Tergesteum, where the merchant has planted his office and counting-house and lives in perfect accord with the Chamber of Commerce!

It is admitted that in all the great maritime towns of the old and new world there exists a class of unfortunates peculiar to these important centres. Whence they come we know not; whither they go we are equally ignorant. Amongst them the number of unclassed is considerable. Many of them are foreigners. The railroads and the steamers have thrown them in, as it were, on to a dust heap, and there they lie, crowding the thoroughfares, with the police striving in vain to clear them away.

Sarcany and Zirone, after a farewell look across the gulf to the lighthouse on St. Theresa Point, left the mole, passed between the Teatro Communale and the square, and reached the Piazza Grande, where they talked for a quarter of an hour in front of the fountain which is built of the stone from the neighbouring Karst Hill, and stands by the statue to Charles VI.

Then they turned to the left and came back. To tell the truth Zirone eyed the passers-by as if he had an irresistible desire to feed on them. Then they turned towards the large square of Tergesteum just as the hour struck to close the Exchange.

"There it is, empty – like we are!" said the Sicilian with a laugh, but without any wish to laugh.

But the indifferent Sarcany seemed to take not the slightest notice of his companion's mistimed pleasantry as he indulged in a hungry yawn.

Then they crossed the triangle past the bronze statue of the Emperor Leopold I. A shrill whistle from Zirone – quite a street boy's whistle – put to flight the flock of blue pigeons that were cooing on the portico of the old Exchange, like the grey pigeons in the square of Saint Mark at Venice.

Then they reached the Corso, which divides new from old Trieste. A wide street destitute of elegance, with well patronized shops destitute of taste, and more like the Regent Street of London or the Broadway of New York than the Boulevard des Italiens of Paris. In the street a great number of people; but of vehicles only a few, and these going between the Piazza Grande and the Piazza della Legna – names sufficiently indicating the town's Italian origin.

Sarcany appeared insensible to all temptation, but Zirone as he passed the shops could not help giving an envious glance into those he had not the means to enter. And there was much there that looked inviting, particularly in the provision shops, and chiefly in the *"birrerie,"* where the beer flows more freely than in any other town of Austria-Hungary.

"There's rather more hunger and thirst about in this Corso," said the Sicilian, whose tongue rattled against his parched lips with the click of a castanet.

Sarcany's only reply to this observation was a shrug of his shoulders.

They then took the first turning to the left, and reached the bank of the canal near the Ponto Rosso – a swing bridge. This they crossed, and went along the quays, where vessels of light draught were busy unloading. Here the shops and stalls looked much less tempting. When he reached the church of St. Antonio, Sarcany turned sharply to the right. His companion followed him in silence. Then they went back along the Corso, and crossed the old town, whose narrow streets, impracticable for vehicles as soon as they begin to climb the slopes of the Karst, are so laid out as to prevent their being enfiladed by that terrible wind, the bora, which blows icily from the northeast. In this old town of Trieste, Zirone and Sarcany, the moneyless, found themselves more at home than among the richer quarters of the new.

It was, in fact, in the basement of a modest hotel not far from the church of Santa Maria Maggiore that they had lodged since their arrival in the Illyrian capital. But as the landlord, who remained unpaid, might become pressing as to his little bill, which grew larger from day to day, they sheered off from this dangerous shoal, crossed the square, and loitered for a few minutes near the Arco di Riccardo.

The study of Roman architecture did not prove very satisfying, and as nothing had turned up in the almost deserted streets, they began the ascent of the rough footpaths leading almost to the top of the Karst, to the terrace of the cathedral.

"Curious idea to climb up here," muttered Zirone, as he tightened his cape round his waist.

But he did not abandon his young companion, and away he went along the line of steps, called by courtesy roads, which lead up the slopes of the Karst. Ten minutes afterwards, hungrier and thirstier than ever, they reached the terrace.

From this elevated spot there is a magnificent view extending across the Gulf of Trieste to the open sea, including the port, with its fishing boats passing and repassing, and its steamers and trading ships outward and homeward bound, and the whole of the town, with its suburbs and farthest houses clustering along the hills. The view had no charms for them! They were thinking of something very different, of the many times they had come here already to ponder on their misery! Zirone would have preferred a stroll along the rich shops of the Corso. Perhaps the luck might reach them here, which they were so impatiently waiting for!

At the end of the steps leading on to the terrace near the Byzantine cathedral of Saint Just there was an enclosure, formerly a cemetery, and now a museum of antiquities. There were no tombs, but odds and ends of sepulchral stones lying in disorder under the lower branches of the trees – Roman stelae, medieval cippi, pieces of triglyphs, and metopes of different ages of the Renaissance, vitrified cubes with traces of cinders, all thrown anyhow among the grass.

The gate of the enclosure was open. Sarcany had only to push it. He entered, followed by Zirone, who contented himself with this melancholy reflection:

"If we wanted to commit suicide, this is just the place!"

"And if someone proposed it to you?" asked Sarcany ironically.

"I'd decline, my friend! Give me one happy day in ten, and I ask no more!"

"It shall be given you – and something more as well."

"May all the saints of Italy hear you, and heaven knows they're counted by the hundred!"

"Come along," said Sarcany.

They went along a semicircular path between a double row of urns and sat themselves down on a large Roman rose-window, which had fallen flat on the ground.

At first they remained silent. This suited Sarcany, but it did not suit his companion. And after one or two half-stifled yawns, Zirone broke out with:

"This something that we've been fools enough to wait for is a long time coming."

Sarcany made no reply.

"What an idea," continued Zirone, "to come and look for it among these ruins! I'm afraid we're on the wrong track, my friend. What are we likely to find in this old graveyard? Even the spirits abandon this place once they shed their mortal carcasses. When I join them I shall not worry about a dinner that's late, or a supper that never comes! Time to go."

It fell into the grass

Sarcany, deep in thought, with his looks lost in vacancy, did not move.

Zirone waited a few minutes without saying anything. Then his habitual loquacity urged him to speak.

"Sarcany," he said, "do you know in what form I should like this something to appear? In the form of one of those cashier people from Toronthal's with a pocket-book stuffed full of banknotes which he could hand over to us on behalf of the said banker with a thousand apologies for keeping us waiting so long."

"Listen, Zirone," answered Sarcany, knitting his brows, "for the last time I tell you that there's nothing to be hoped for from Silas Toronthal."

"Are you sure of that?"

"Yes, he gave a definite refusal to my last demands; all the credit I have with him is exhausted."

"That is bad."

"Very bad, but it is so."

"Good, if your credit is exhausted," continued Zirone, "it's because you've had the credit! And to what is that due? To your having many times placed your zeal and intelligence at the service of his firm in certain matters of delicacy. Now, during the first months of our stay in Trieste, Toronthal did not show himself too stingy in money matters. You still must have some hold over him, if you threatened him..."

"What was to be done has already been done," replied Sarcany, with a shrug, "and you cannot go to him for a meal! No! I have no hold over him now; but I may have and shall have, and when that day comes he shall pay me capital and compound interest for what he's refused me to-day! I fancy his business is under a cloud, and that he's mixed up in several doubtful things. Several of those failures in Germany, at Berlin and Munich, have had their effect in Trieste, and Silas Toronthal seemed rather upset when I saw him last. Let the water get troubled, and when it is troubled..."

"Quite so," exclaimed Zirone, "but meanwhile we have only water to drink! Look here, Sarcany, I think you might try one more shot at Toronthal! You might tap his cash-box once more, and get enough out of it to pay our passage to Sicily by way of Malta."

"And what should we do in Sicily?"

"That's my business. I know the country, and I can introduce you to a few Maltese, who are a very tough lot, and with them we might do something. If there's nothing to be done here, we might as well clear out, and let this wretched banker pay the cost. If you know anything about him, he would rather see you out of Trieste!"

Sarcany shook his head.

"It cannot last much longer, you'll see. We've come to the end now," added Zirone.

He rose and stamped on the ground with his foot, as if it were a stepmother unwilling to help him. At the instant he did so he caught sight of a pigeon feebly fluttering down just outside the enclosure. The pigeon's tired wings could hardly move, as slowly it sank to the ground.

Zirone, without asking himself to which of the hundred and seventy-seven species of pigeons now known to ornithological nomenclature the bird belonged, saw only one thing – that the species it belonged to was edible.

The bird was evidently exhausted. It had tried to settle on the cornice of the cathedral. Not being able to reach it, it had dropped on to the roof of the small niche which gave shelter to the statue of St. Just; but its feeble feet could not support it there, and it had slipped on to the capital of a ruined column.

Sarcany, silent and still, hardly followed the pigeon in its flight, but Zirone never lost sight of it. The bird came from the north. A long journey had reduced it to this state of exhaustion. Evidently it was bound for some more distant spot; for it immediately started to fly again, and the trajectory curve it traced in the air compelled it to make a fresh halt on one of the lower branches of the trees in the old cemetery.

Zirone resolved to catch it, and quietly ran off to the tree. He soon reached the gnarled trunk, climbed up it to the fork, and there waited motionless and mute, like a dog pointing at the game perched above his head.

The pigeon did not see him, and made another start; but its strength again failed it, and a few paces from the tree it fell into the grass.

To jump to the ground, stretch out his hands, and seize the bird was the work of an instant for the Sicilian. And quite naturally he was about to wring its neck, when he stopped, gave a shout of surprise, and ran back to Sarcany.

"A carrier pigeon!" he said.

"I'd say its carrying days are over," replied Sarcany.

"Perhaps so," said Zirone, "and all the worse for those waiting for the message."

"A message!" exclaimed Sarcany. "Wait, Zirone, wait! Give him a reprieve!"

And he stopped his companion, who had again caught hold of the neck. Then he took the tiny packet, opened it, and drew forth – a cryptogram.

The message contained only eighteen words arranged in three vertical columns, and this is what it said:

ihnalz	zaemen	ruiopn
arnuro	trvree	mtqssl
odxhnp	estlev	eeuart
aeeeil	ennios	noupvg
spesdr	erssur	ouitse
eedgnc	toeedt	artuee

There was nothing to show whence the message came, or whither it was being sent. Only these eighteen words each composed of an equal number of letters. Could they be made into sense without the key? It was not very likely – unless by some very clever decipherer!

And yet the cryptogram could not be indecipherable!

The characters told him nothing, and Sarcany, who was at first much disappointed, stood perplexed. Did the message contain any important news, and, above all, was it of compromising nature? Evidently the precautions had been taken to prevent its being read, if it fell into other hands than those for whom it was intended. To make use of neither the post nor the telegraph, but the extraordinary means of the carrier pigeon showed that it must refer to something it was desired to keep secret.

"Perhaps," said Sarcany, "there lies in these lines a mystery that'll make our fortune."

"And then," answered Zirone, "this pigeon will represent the luck that we've been running after all the morning! And I was going to strangle it! Anyhow, it's important to keep the message, and we can cook the messenger."

"Not so fast, Zirone," interrupted Sarcany, who again saved the bird's life. "Perhaps the pigeon may tell us whither it was bound, providing, of course that the person who ought to have the message lives in Trieste."

"And then? That won't tell you how to read the message, Sarcany."

"No, Zirone."

"Nor to know where it came from."

"Exactly. But of two correspondents I shall know one, and that may tell me how I am to find the other. So, instead of killing this bird, we'll feed it, restore its strength, and help it reach its destination."

Trieste - The mole of San Carlo

"With the letter?" asked Zirone.

"With the letter – of which I am going to make an exact copy, and that I shall keep until the time comes to use it."

And Sarcany took a notebook from his pocket, and in pencil he made a careful facsimile of the message. Knowing that in most cryptograms it was important not to alter in the least the form and arrangement, he took great care to keep the words exactly in the same order and position and at the same distances as in the document. Then he put the facsimile in his pocket, the message in its case, and the case in its place under the pigeon's wing.

Zirone looked on. He did not share in the hope that a fortune was to be made out of the mystery.

"And now?" he asked.

"Now," answered Sarcany, "do what you can for the messenger."

The pigeon was more exhausted by hunger than fatigue. Its wings were intact, without strain or breakage, and showed that its temporary weakness was due neither to a shot from a sportsman nor a stone from a street boy. It was hungry – it was thirsty; that was all.

Zirone looked about, and found on the ground a few grains of corn, which the bird ate greedily. Then he quenched its thirst with a few drops of water, which the last shower had left in a piece of ancient pottery. So well did he do his work that in half an hour the pigeon was refreshed and restored, and quite able to resume its interrupted journey.

"If it's going far," said Sarcany, "if its destination is beyond Trieste, it does not matter to us if it falls on the way, for we shall have lost sight of it, and it will be impossible for us to follow. But if it's going to one of the houses in Trieste, its strength is sufficient to take it there, for it'll only have to fly for a couple of minutes or so."

"Right you are," replied the Sicilian, "but how are we to see where it drops, even if it's in Trieste?"

"We can manage that, I think," answered Sarcany. And this is what they did.

The cathedral consists of two old Roman churches, one dedicated to the Virgin, one to Saint Just, the patron saint of Trieste. It is flanked by a very high tower, which rises from the angle of the front, and is pierced with a large rose window beneath which is the chief door. This tower commands a view over the plateau on Karst Hill, and over the whole city, which lies spread as on a map below. From this lofty standpoint they could see down on the roofs of all the houses, even on to those clustering on the nearer slopes of the hill that stretched away to the shore of the gulf. It was therefore not impossible to follow the pigeon in its flight, and recognize the house on which it found refuge, provided it was not bound for some other city of the Illyrian peninsula.

The attempt might succeed. It was at least worth trying. They only had to set the bird at liberty.

Sarcany and Zirone left the old cemetery, crossed the open space by the cathedral, and walked towards the tower. One of the ogival doors – the one under the dripstone beneath St. Just's niche – was open. They entered, and began to ascend the stairs, which led to the roof.

It took them two or three minutes to reach the top. They stood just underneath the roof, and there was no balcony. But there were two windows opening out on each side of the tower, giving a view to each point of the double horizon of hills and sea.

Sarcany and Zirone posted themselves at the windows, which looked out over Trieste towards the northwest.

The clock in the old sixteenth-century castle on the top of the Karst, behind the cathedral, struck four. It was still broad daylight. The air was clear, and the sun shone brightly on the waters of the Adriatic, and most of the houses received the light with their fronts facing the tower. Thus far, circumstances were favourable.

Sarcany took the pigeon in his hands; stroked it, spoke to it, gave it a last caress, and threw it free.

The bird flapped its wings, but at first it dropped so quickly that it looked as though it was going to finish its career of aerial messenger with a cruel fall.

The excitable Sicilian could not restrain a cry of disappointment.

"Wait! All is not yet lost!" said Sarcany.

The pigeon had found its equilibrium in the denser lower air, and, making a sudden curve, flew off towards the northwest.

Sarcany and Zirone followed it with their eyes.

In its flight there was no hesitation. It went straight to its home, which it would have reached an hour earlier had it not been for its compulsory halt among the trees of the old graveyard.

Sarcany and his companion watched it with the most anxious attention. They asked themselves if it was going beyond the town – and then all their scheming would come to naught.

It did nothing of the kind.

"I see it! I see it!" said Zirone, whose sight was of the keenest.

"What you have to look for," said Sarcany, "is where it stops, so as to fix the exact spot."

A few minutes after its departure the pigeon settled on a house with one tall gable rising above the rest, in the midst of a clump of trees, in that part of the town near the hospital and public garden. Then it disappeared into a dormer window opening on to the mansard, which was surmounted by a weather vane of wrought iron that ought to have been the work of Quentin Matsys – if Trieste had been in Flanders.

The general direction being ascertained, it would not be very difficult to find the weather vane and gable and window, and, in short, the house inhabited by the person for whom the cryptogram was intended.

Sarcany and Zirone immediately made their way down the tower, and down the hill, and along the roads leading to the Piazza della Legna. There they had to lay their course so as to reach the group of houses forming the eastern quarter of the city.

When they reached the junction of two main roads, the Corsa Stadion leading to the public garden, and the Acquedotto, a fine avenue of trees leading to the large brewery of Boschetto, the adventurers were in some doubt as to the true direction. Should they take the right or the left? Instinctively they turned to the right, intending to examine, one after the other, every house along the avenue above which they had noticed the vane among the trees.

They went along in this manner, inspecting in turn every gable and roof along the Acquedotto, but found nothing like the one they sought. At last they reached the end.

"There it is!" exclaimed Zirone.

And there was the weather vane swinging slowly on its iron spindle above a dormer window, round which, were several pigeons.

There was no mistake. It was the identical house to which the pigeon had flown.

The house was of modest exterior and formed one of the block at the beginning of the Acquedotto.

Sarcany made inquiries at the neighbouring shops, and learnt all he wished to know.

The house for many years had belonged and been inhabited by Count Ladislas Zathmar.

"Who is this Count Zathmar?" asked Zirone, to whom the name meant nothing.

"He is the Count Zathmar!" answered Sarcany.

"But perhaps if we were to ask him..."

"Later on, Zirone; there's no hurry! Take it coolly, and now to our hotel!"

15

Sarcany and Zirone followed it with their eyes.

"Yes, it's dinnertime for those who have got something to dine on!" said Zirone bitterly.

"We may not dine tonight, but it's possible we shall dine tomorrow," answered Sarcany.

"With whom?"

"Who knows? Perhaps with Count Zathmar!"

They walked along quietly – why should they hurry? – and soon reached their modest hotel, still much too rich for them seeing they could not pay their bill.

What a surprise was in store! A letter had arrived, addressed to Sarcany.

The letter contained a note for 200 florins, and these words – nothing more:

> Enclosed is the last money you will get from me.
> It's enough to pay your passage to Sicily. Go, and
> let me hear no more of you.
>
> SILAS TORONTHAL

"Capital!" exclaimed Zirone, "The banker thinks better of it just in time! Assuredly we need never despair of those financial folks!"

"That's what I say," said Sarcany.

"And the coin will do for us to leave Trieste."

"No! Not just yet!"

Trieste: The Grande Canal

CHAPTER II

COUNT SANDORF

The Magyars settled in Hungary towards the end of the ninth century of the Christian era. They now form a third of the population – more than five millions in number. Whence came they – Spain, Egypt, or Central Asia? Are they descended from the Huns of Attila or the Finns of the North? A disputed question, and of little consequence! One thing is very obvious, that they are neither Slavs nor Germans, and have no desire to become so.

They still speak their old language – a language soft and musical, lending itself to all the charm of poetical cadence, less rich than the German, but more concise, more energetic; a language which between the fourteenth and sixteenth centuries took the place of Latin in the laws and edicts, and became the national tongue.

It was on the 21st of January, 1699, that the Treaty of Carlowitz gave Hungary and Transylvania to Austria. Twenty years afterwards the Pragmatic Sanction solemnly declared that the States of Austria-Hungary were thenceforth indivisible. In default of a son, the daughter was to succeed to the crown according to the rule of primogeniture. And it was in accordance with this new statute that in 1749 Maria Theresa ascended the throne of her father, Charles VI, the last of the male line of the House of Austria.

The Hungarians had to yield to superior force; but a hundred and fifty years afterwards people were still to be met with amongst all ranks of society who refused to acknowledge either the Pragmatic Sanction or the Treaty of Carlowitz.

At the time this story opens there was a Magyar of high birth whose whole life might be summed up in these two sentiments, the hatred of everything German, and the hope of giving his country her ancient independence. Although still young, he had known Kossuth, and although birth and education separated them on important political questions, he could not fail to admire the patriot's nobility of heart.

Count Mathias Sandorf lived in one of the comitats of Transylvania, in the district of Fagaras. His old castle was of feudal origin. Built on one of the northern spurs of those Eastern Carpathians, which form the frontier between Transylvania and Wallachia, the castle rose amid the rugged scenery in all its savage pride – a stronghold that conspirators could defend to the last.

The neighbouring mines, rich in iron and copper ore, and carefully worked, yielded a considerable income to the owner of the Castle of Artenak. The estate comprised a part of the district of Fagaras, and the population exceeded 72,000, who, all of them, townsfolk and country folk, took pains to show that for Count Sandorf they felt untiring devotion and unbounded gratitude in return for the constant good he had done. This castle was the object of particular attention on the part of the Chancery of Hungary at Vienna, for the ideas of the master of Artenak were known in high quarters, and anxiety was felt about them, although no anxiety was betrayed about him.

Sandorf was then in his thirty-sixth year. He was rather above the middle height, and of great muscular strength. A well-shaped, noble-looking head rose above his broad, powerful shoulders. Of rather dark complexion, and square in feature, his face was of the pure Magyar type. The quickness of his movements, the decision of his speech, the firm, calm look of his eyes, the constant smile on his lips, that unmistakable sign of good-nature, a certain playfulness of gesture and speech: all went to show an open, generous disposition. It has been said that there are many resemblances between the French and Magyar characters. Sandorf was living proof of the truth of this observation.

One of his most striking peculiarities is worth noting. Although Count Sandorf was careless enough of what concerned only himself, and would pass lightly over any injury which affected him alone, he had never forgiven, and never would forgive an offence of which his friends were the victims. He had in the highest degree the spirit of justice and hatred of treachery, and hence possessed a sort of impersonal implacability, being by no means one of those who leave all punishment in this world to Heaven.

Mathias Sandorf had been highly educated. Instead of confining himself to the life of leisure his fortune opened out to him, he had energetically followed his tastes, and been led to the study of medicine and the physical sciences. He would have made an excellent doctor, had the necessities of life forced him to look after the sick. He was content to be a chemist in high repute amongst the learned. The University of Pesth, the Academy of Sciences at Presburg, the Royal School of Mines at Chemnitz, and the Normal School at Temesvar, had all counted him among their most assiduous pupils. His studious life had improved and intensified his natural gifts. In short, he was a man in the fullest acceptation of the term. And he was held to be so by all who knew him, and more especially by his professors in the different schools and universities, who continued their interest in him as his friends.

Formerly the castle of Artenak had been all gaiety, life, and movement. On this rugged ridge of the Carpathians the Transylvanian hunters had held their meetings. Expeditions, many and dangerous, were organized, in which Count Sandorf sought employment for those instincts of battle, which he could not gratify on the field of politics. He kept himself out of the political stream, watching closely the course of events. He seemed only to care about a life spent between his studies and the indulgences that his fortune allowed him.

In those days the Countess Rena Sandorf was still alive. She was the soul of these parties at Artenak. Fifteen months before this history begins, death had struck her in the pride of her youth and beauty, and all that was left of her was a little girl, who was now two years old.

Count Sandorf felt the blow cruelly. He was inconsolable. The castle became silent and deserted. From that day, under the shadow of profound grief, its master lived as if in a cloister. His whole life was centred in his child, who was confided to the charge of Rosena Lendeck, the wife of the count's steward. This excellent woman, who was still young, was entirely devoted to the sole heiress of the Sandorfs, and was to her quite a second mother.

During the first months of his widowhood, Sandorf never left his castle of Artenak. He thought over and lived amongst the remembrances of the past. Then the idea of his country reduced to an inferior position in Europe seized upon him. For the Franco-Italian war of 1859 struck a terrible blow at the power of Austria. Seven years afterwards, in 1866, the blow was followed by one still more terrible, that of Sadowa. It was no longer Austria bereft of her Italian possessions; it was Austria conquered on both sides, and subordinated to Germany; and to Austria, Hungary felt she was bound. The Hungarians – there is no reasoning about such a sentiment, for it is in their blood – were humiliated in their pride. For them the victories of Custozza and Lissa were no compensation for the defeat of Sadowa.

21

Count Sandorf, during the year which followed, had carefully studied the political outlook, and recognized that a separatist movement might be successful. The moment for action had then come. On the 3rd of May of this year, 1867, he had embraced his little daughter, whom he had left to the tender cares of Rosena Lendeck, and, leaving his castle of Artenak, had set out for Pesth, where he had put himself in communication with his friends and partisans, and made certain preliminary arrangements. Then a few hours later he had gone to Trieste to wait for events.

There he became the chief centre of the conspiracy, and thence radiated all its threads collected in his hands. In this town the chiefs could act with more safety and freedom in bringing their patriotic work to an end.

At Trieste lived two of Sandorf's most intimate friends. Animated by the same spirit, they were resolved to follow the enterprise to its conclusion. Count Ladislas Zathmar and Professor Stephen Bathory were Magyars of good birth. Both were a dozen years older than Sandorf, but were almost without fortune. One drew his slender revenues from a small estate in the comitat of Lipto, belonging to a circle beyond the Danube; the other was a professor of Physical Science at Trieste, and his only income came from his lecture fees.

Ladislas Zathmar lived in the house, discovered on the Acquedotto by Sarcany and Zirone – an unpretending place, which he had put at the disposal of Mathias Sandorf during the time he was away from Artenak, that is to say, till the end of the projected movement, whenever it night be. A Hungarian, Borik, aged about fifty-five, represented the whole staff of the house. Borik was as much devoted to his master as Lendeck was to his.

Stephen Bathory occupied a no less unpretending dwelling on the Corso Stadion, not far from Count Zathmar's. Here his whole life was wrapped up in his wife and his son Peter, then eight years old.

Stephen Bathory belonged, distantly but authentically, to the line of those Magyar princes who in the sixteenth century occupied the throne of Transylvania. The family had been divided and lost in its numberless branches since then, and people may perhaps think it astonishing that one of its last descendants should exist as a simple professor of the academy at Presburg. Whatever he might be, Stephen Bathory was a scientist of the first rank – one of those who live in retirement, but whose work renders them famous. *Inclusum labor illustrat*, the motto of the silk-worm, might have been his. One day his political ideas, which he took no pains to conceal, rendered it necessary for him to resign, and then he came to live at Trieste as professor unattached.

It was in Zathmar's house that the three friends had met since the arrival of Count Sandorf – although the latter ostensibly occupied an apartment in the Palazzo Modello on the Piazza Grande. The police had no suspicion that the house in the Acquedotto was the centre of a conspiracy, which counted numbers of partisans in all the principal towns.

Zathmar and Bathory were Sandorf's most devoted auxiliaries. Like him, they had seen that circumstances were favourable to a movement, which might restore Hungary to the place she desired in Europe. They risked their lives; they knew, but that they cared little about. The house in the Acquedotto had thus become the rendezvous of the chiefs of the conspiracy. Numbers of partisans, summoned from different points of the kingdom, came there to take their measures and receive their orders. A service of carrier pigeons was organized, and established rapid and safe communication between Trieste and the chief towns of Hungary and Transylvania when it was necessary to send what could not well be confided to the post or telegraph. In short, every precaution had been taken, and the conspirators had not as yet raised the least breath of suspicion. Besides, as we know, correspondence was carried on in cipher, and on such a plan that unless the secret was known, absolute security was obtained.

Three days after the arrival of the carrier pigeon, whose message had been intercepted by Sarcany, on the 21st of May, about eight o'clock in the evening, Zathmar and Bathory were in the study, waiting the return of Mathias Sandorf. His private affairs had recently compelled the count to return into Transylvania and to Artenak; but he had taken the opportunity of consulting with his friends at Klausenburg, the capital of the province, and he was to get back this very day, after sending them the dispatch of which Sarcany had taken the duplicate.

During the time Sandorf was away, other correspondence had been exchanged between Trieste and Buda, and many letters in cipher had arrived by pigeon post. And Zathmar was even now busy in working out the real meaning of one of these cryptographic epistles by means of a "grating."

The dispatches were devised on a very simple plan – that of the transposition of the letters. In this system every letter retained its alphabetical value, that is to say, *b* meant *b*, *o* meant *o*, etc. But the letters were successively transposed in accordance with the openings of a grating, which, laid on the message, only allowed such letters to appear as were to be read, and hid all the others.

These gratings are an old invention, but having been greatly improved by Colonel Fleissner, they seem now to offer the best and surest means of obtaining an indecipherable cryptogram. In all the other systems of inversion – be they systems with an invariable base, or a simple key in which each letter is always represented by the same letter or sign; be they systems with a variable base, or a double key in which the alphabet varies with each letter – the security is incomplete. Experienced decipherers are capable of performing perfect prodigies in such investigations, either with the aid of the calculation of probabilities, or by merely trying, and trying, until they succeed. All that has to be done is to find out the letters in the order of their repetition in the cryptogram – *e* being that most frequently employed in English, German, and French, *o* in Spanish, *a* in Russian, and *e* and *i* in Italian – and the meaning of the text is soon made clear. And there are very few cryptograms based on these methods, which defy investigation.

It would appear, therefore, that the best guarantee for indecipherability is afforded by these gratings, or by ciphered dictionaries – codes, that is to say, or vocabularies in which certain common words represent fully formed sentences indicated by the page number. But both these systems have one grave drawback: they require absolute secrecy on the part of those that use them, and the greatest care that the books or apparatus should never get into undesirable hands. Without the grating, or the code, the message will remain unread; but once these are obtained, the mystery vanishes.

It was then by means of a grating – that is to say, a piece of card, cut out in certain places – that the correspondence between Sandorf and his accomplices was carried on; but as an extra precaution, in case the gratings should be lost or stolen, every dispatch after being deciphered was destroyed. There thus remained no trace of this conspiracy in which the greatest noblemen and magnates of Hungary were risking their lives, in conjunction with the representatives of the middleclass and the bulk of the people.

Zathmar had just burnt his last dispatch, when there came a quiet knock at the study door.

It was Borik introducing Count Mathias Sandorf, who had walked up from the nearest railway station.

Zathmar immediately rose to greet him.

"Your journey, Mathias?" asked he with the eagerness of a man who wished at the outset to find that all was well.

"It was a success, Zathmar," answered Sandorf. "I have no doubt of my Transylvanian friends, and we're certain of their assistance."

"You let them have the dispatch which came from Pesth three days ago?" asked Bathory.

"Yes," said Sandorf. "Yes. They have all been cautioned, and they are all ready. They will rise at the first signal. In two hours we shall be masters of Buda and Pesth, in half a day we shall get the chief comitats on both sides of the Theiss, and before the day is out we shall have Transylvania and the rest. Eight million Hungarians will have regained their independence!"

"And the Diet?" asked Bathory.

"Our supporters form the majority," answered Sandorf. "They'll form the new Government and take direction of affairs. All will go regularly and easily, for the comitats, as far as their administration goes, depend very little on the Crown and their chiefs have the police with them."

"But what of the palatine and the council at Buda?" continued Zathmar.

"They'll be neutralized before they can act."

"And unable to correspond with the Hungarian Chancery at Vienna?"

"Yes, all measures have been taken for our movements to be simultaneous, and thus ensure success."

"Success!" said Bathory.

"Yes, success!" answered Count Sandorf. "In the army all of our blood, all of Hungarian blood, are for us! Where is the descendant of the ancient Magyars whose heart will not beat at the sight of the banner of Rodolph and Corvinus?"

And Sandorf uttered the words in a tone of the purest patriotism.

"But," continued he, "neglect nothing that will prevent suspicion! Be prudent, we cannot be too cautious! You've heard of nothing suspicious at Trieste?"

"No," replied Zathmar. "Nothing is spoken of but the works at Pola, for which the greater part of the workmen have been engaged."

In fact for fifteen years the Austrian Government, with a view of the possible loss of Venetia – a loss now realized – had been thinking of founding at Pola, at the southern extremity of the Istrian Peninsula, an immense arsenal and dockyard, so as to command all that end of the Adriatic. In spite of the protests of Trieste, whose maritime importance would thereby be lessened, the works were being pushed on with fever-

Ladislas Zathmar and Stephen Bathory in the study

ish ardour. Sandorf and his friends had thus some justification for their opinion that Trieste would join them in the event of a separatist movement being started in the city.

Up to the present the secret of the conspiracy in favour of Hungarian autonomy had been well kept. Nothing had occurred to cause the police to suspect that the chief conspirators were then assembled at the unpretending house in the Acquedotto.

Everything seemed to have been done to make the enterprise a success; and all that remained was to wait for the moment of action. The cipher correspondence between Trieste and the principal cities of Hungary and Transylvania had almost ceased. There were now few messages for the pigeons to carry, because the last measures had been taken. As money is the soul of war, so it is of conspiracies. It is important that conspirators have ample funds when the signal of uprising is given. And on this occasion the supply would not fail them.

We are aware that, although Zathmar and Bathory could sacrifice their lives for their country, they could not sacrifice their fortunes, inasmuch as their pecuniary resources were but meagre. But Count Sandorf was immensely rich, and, in addition to his life, he had brought his whole fortune to the help of the cause. For many months, through the agency of his steward, Lendeck, he had mortgaged his estates, and thereby raised a considerable sum – more than two million florins.

But it was necessary that this money should always be at call, and that he could draw it at any moment. And so he had deposited it in his own name in one of the banks of Trieste, whose character was above suspicion. This bank was Toronthal's, of which Sarcany and Zirone had been talking in the cemetery on the hill.

The circumstance was fraught with the gravest consequences, as will be seen in the course of this history. Something was said about this money at Sandorf's last interview with Zathmar and Bathory. He told them that it was his intention to call on Toronthal, and give him notice that the cash might be wanted immediately.

Events had so progressed that Sandorf would soon be able to give the expected signal from Trieste – more especially as this very evening he discovered that Zathmar's house was the object of very disquieting surveillance.

About eight o'clock, as Sandorf and Bathory went out, one to go home to the Corso Stadion, and the other to his hotel, they noticed two men watching them in the shadows and following them at such a distance and in such a way as to avoid detection.

Sandorf and his companion, in order to see what this might mean, boldly marched straight on to these suspicious characters, but before they could reach them they had taken flight and disappeared round the corner of St Antonio's Church, at the end of the canal.

CHAPTER III

TORONTHOL'S BANK

"Society" in Trieste, is almost non-existent. Between different races, as between different castes it is seldom found. The Austrian officials assume the highest position, and take precedence according to their ranks in the administrative hierarchy. Generally these men are distinguished, well educated, and well meaning; but despite their authority, they are underpaid and unable to compete with the merchant and banking classes. As entertainments and receptions are rare among the rich and the parties given by the officials are almost all unambitious, the wealthy have taken to displaying their wealth in other manners. They travel about the streets in the finest carriages and attended the theatre dressed in the most extravagant fashions, their wives proudly displaying their diamonds from the balconies of the Armonia or the Teatro Comunale.

Amongst these opulent families, the most renowned was that of the banker Silas Toronthal. The master of that house, whose credit extended beyond the borders of the Austro-Hungarian Empire, was then in his thirty-seventh year. He occupied, with Madame Toronthal, who was several years his junior, a mansion in the Acquedotto.

Silas Toronthal was reputed to have been rich – a reputation he well deserved. Numerous successful speculations on the Stock Exchange, a brisk business with the Austrian Lloyds and other large companies, and the issuing of several important loans from his bank had, or ought to have, brought huge sums into his coffers. Hence his household was conducted on a scale of considerable splendour.

Nevertheless, as Sarcany had said to Zirone, there was a possibility that the affairs of Silas Toronthal were slightly embarrassed – at least at the time. Seven years before, when the funds were shaken by the Franco-Italian war, he had received a severe blow, and more recently the disastrous campaign which ended at Sadowa had sent down the prices on every Exchange in Europe, more especially on those of Austria-

Hungary, and chiefly those of Vienna, Pesth, and Trieste. The necessity of providing the large amounts then drawn out on the current accounts not improbably caused him serious inconvenience. But when the crisis had passed, he doubtless recovered himself, and if what Sarcany had said was correct, it must have been his recent speculations only which had led him into difficulties.

During the last few months a great change had come over Toronthal. His whole look had altered without his knowledge. He was not, as formerly, master of himself. People had noticed that he no longer looked them in the face, as had been his custom, but rather eyed them askance. This had not escaped the notice of Madame Toronthal, a confirmed invalid, submissiveness itself, who knew very little about his business matters.

And if some disaster did menace Toronthal, it must be admitted that he would get very little sympathy. He had many customers, but few friends. The high opinion he held about his position, his native vanity, the airs he gave himself on all occasions, had not done him any good. And above all the people of Trieste looked upon him as a foreigner because he was born at Ragusa, and hence was a Dalmatian. No family ties attached him to the town to which he had come fifteen years before to lay the foundations of his fortune.

Such then was the position of Toronthal's bank. Although Sarcany had his suspicions, nothing had occurred to give rise to a rumour that it was in difficulties. Its credit remained unshaken. And Count Sandorf, after realizing his investments, had deposited with it a considerable sum on condition that it should always be available at twenty-four hours' notice.

It may seem surprising that a connection of any sort should have been formed between a bank of such high reputation and such a very dubious character as Sarcany. It had existed, nevertheless, for two or three years. Toronthal had had a good deal of business with the Regency of Tripoli, and Sarcany had been employed as a kind of broker and general confidential agent, entrusted with the disposal of certain wine and other gifts under circumstances in which it was not always desirable that the Trieste banker should appear in person. Having been engaged in these and other rather suspicious schemes, Sarcany got his foot, or rather his hand, into the bank; and continued to carry on a sort of system of extortion on Toronthal, who was not, however, quite at his mercy, inasmuch as no proof existed of their mutual dealings. But a banker's position is one of extreme delicacy. A word may ruin him. And Sarcany knew how to take advantage of him.

But Toronthal knew what he was about. He had parted with certain sums, which had been dissipated in the gambling houses with the recklessness of an adventurer who takes no thought of the future and then Sarcany becoming too importunate, the banker suddenly drew his pursestrings, and, refused further credit. Sarcany threatened; Toronthal remained firm. And he was safe in doing so after all, for Sarcany had no proofs, and no one would believe him.

This was the reason that Sarcany and his comrade Zirone, found themselves at the end of their resources, and without even the wherewithal to leave the town, and seek their fortune elsewhere. And we know how Toronthal came to their help with sufficient funds to enable them to return to Sicily, where Zirone belonged to one of the secret societies. The banker thus hoped to get rid of the Tripolitan, and hoped never to see or hear of him again. He was doomed to disappointment in this, as in most other matters.

It was on the evening of the 18th of May that the two hundred florins had reached the adventurers at their hotel.

Six days afterwards, on the 24th of the same month, Sarcany presented himself at the bank, and demanded to see Silas Toronthal; and so much did he insist, that he was at length received.

The banker was in his private office, and Sarcany carefully closed the door as soon as he had been introduced.

"You again!" exclaimed Toronthal. "What are you doing here? I sent you, and for the last time, quite enough to help you leave Trieste! You will get nothing more from me, whatever you may say or do! Why have you not gone? I'll take steps to put a stopper on you for the future! What do you want?"

Sarcany received the broadside very coolly. He was quite prepared for it. His attitude was what it had always been of late in his visits to the banker – insolent and provoking.

Not only was he master of himself, but he was quite serious. He had stepped up to a chair, without being invited to sit down, and waited until the banker's bad temper had evaporated, before he replied.

"Well, why don't you speak?" continued Toronthal, who, after hurriedly striding to and fro, had sat down.

"I'm waiting till you're calm," Sarcany replied quietly, "and I'll wait as long as is necessary."

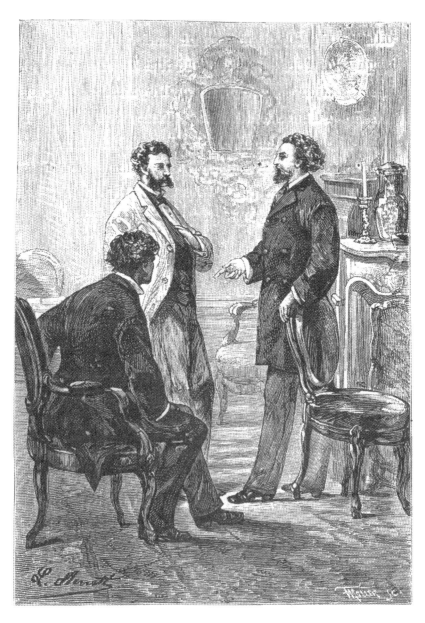

"Our supporters form the majority," answered Sandorf

"What does it matter whether I'm calm! For the last time, what do you want?"

"Silas Toronthal," answered Sarcany, "I have a little business to propose to you."

"I do not want to talk business with you!" exclaimed the banker. "There is nothing in common between you and I; and I only expect to hear that you are off from Trieste today forever."

"I expect to leave Trieste," answered Sarcany, "but I do not like to go until I've repaid you what I owe!"

"You repay me? You?"

"Yes, repay you, interest, capital, without saying anything of the..."

Toronthal shrugged his shoulders at this unexpected proposition.

"The sums I have advanced," he said, "are charged to profit and loss, and are written off! I consider we are clear. I want nothing from you, and I am above such trifles."

"And if it pleases me to remain your debtor?"

"And if it pleases me to remain your creditor?"

Toronthal and Sarcany looked at each other, then Sarcany shrugged and continued – "These are only phrases, and there is nothing in phrases. I repeat, I come to bring you some very important business."

"And suspicious business, too, I daresay?"

"Well, it's not the first time that you've come to me..."

"Words, nothing but words!" said the banker.

"Listen," said Sarcany. "I'll be brief."

"And you had better."

"If what I am going to tell you does not suit you, say so, and I'll go!"

"From here, or from Trieste?"

"From here and from Trieste."

"Tomorrow?"

"This evening!"

"Speak, then!"

"Well, then, this is it," said Sarcany. "But," added he, looking round, "you're sure no one can hear us?"

"You would like our interview to be secret, then?" asked the banker ironically.

"Yes, Silas Toronthal, for you and I hold in our hands the lives of important personages."

"You do, perhaps. I do not!"

"Well, then, listen. I'm on the track of a conspiracy. What its object is I do not yet know. But after what has happened on the plains of Lombardy, after the business at Sadowa, all that is not Austrian is against Austria. And I have reason to think that a movement is afoot in favour of Hungary by which we can profit."

Toronthal, as his only reply, contented himself with saying:

"I have nothing to get out of your conspiracy."

"Perhaps not."

"But how?"

"By denouncing it!"

"Explain!"

"Listen."

And Sarcany told him of all that had happened in the old cemetery, of the carrier pigeon, of the intercepted message – of which he had taken a facsimile – and of how he had found out the bird's destination. He added that for five days he and Zirone had been watching the house; how the same people met there every night, not without great precautions; of other pigeons that had gone away, and others that had come; of how the house was guarded by an old servant, who carefully inspected all who approached; of how Sarcany and his companion had been obliged to act with circumspection to evade the attention of this old man; and of how, during the last few days, he was afraid he had raised suspicions.

Toronthal began to listen more attentively to what Sarcany told him. He asked himself if it were true, and what gain he could get out of it. When the story was told, when Sarcany for the last time affirmed that there was a conspiracy against the State, and that something could be made out of revealing its existence, the banker asked the following questions:

"Where is this house?"

"No. 89, Avenue de Acquedotto."

"To whom does it belong?"

"To a Hungarian gentleman."

"What is the Hungarian gentleman's name?"

"Count Ladislas Zathmar."

"And who are the people that visit him?"

"Two chiefly; two of Hungarian birth."

"One is?..."

"A professor of this town. His name is Stephen Bathory."

"The other is?..."

"Count Mathias Sandorf."

Toronthal made a start of surprise, which did not escape Sarcany. He had easily found the three names by following Bathory to the Corso Stadion and Sandorf to the Palazzo Modello.

"You see, Toronthal," continued Sarcany, "these are the names I have no hesitation in giving you. You see I am not playing with you."

"All that is very vague!" replied the banker, who evidently wished to know more before committing himself.

"Vague?" said Sarcany.

"Yes! To begin with, you have no material proof!"

"And what is this, then?"

The copy of the message was placed in Toronthal's hands. The banker examined it, not without curiosity. But its cryptographic words gave no sign of sense to him, and there was nothing to prove that they were of the importance that Sarcany asserted. If he had any interest in the affair, it was merely in so far as it affected his customer, Count Sandorf, and with him nothing could occur to make him uneasy, unless it came to pass that he desired to draw out at short notice the funds deposited in the bank.

"Well," said he at length, "my opinion still is that it's very vague."

"Nothing seems clearer to me, on the contrary," answered Sarcany, whom the banker's attitude in no way dismayed.

"Have you been able to decipher this letter?"

"No, but I know how to do so when the time comes."

"And how?"

"I have had something to do with such matters before," said Sarcany, "and a good many ciphered dispatches have passed through my hands. From a careful examination of that one, I see that its key does not depend on a number or a conventional alphabet, which attributes to a letter a different meaning to its real meaning. In this letter an *s* is an *s*, a *p* is a *p*; but the letters are arranged in a certain order, which order can be discovered by a grating."

Sarcany, as we know, was right. That was the system that had been used for the correspondence. We also know that it was the most indecipherable one that could be found.

"Be it so," said the banker. "I do not deny but what you are right; but without the grating you cannot read the message."

"Evidently."

"And how will you get the grating?"

"I do not know yet," answered Sarcany, "but rest assured I shall get it."

Trieste

"Really! Well, if I were in your place, Sarcany, I should give myself a good deal of trouble to do so!"

"I shall take the trouble that is necessary."

"To what end? I should content myself with going to the police and handing them the message."

"I'll do so," replied Sarcany coldly, "but not with these simple presumptions. What I want before I speak are material, undeniable proofs. I intend to become master of this conspiracy – yes! Absolute master of it, to gain advantages from it, which I ask you to share! And who knows even if it may not be better to join the conspirators instead of taking part against them?"

Such language did not astonish Toronthal. He well knew of what Sarcany was capable. But if Sarcany did not hesitate to speak in this way, it was because he, too, knew of what Toronthal was capable. His conscience was elastic enough for anything. Sarcany knew him of old, and suspected that the bank had been in difficulties for some time, so that this conspiracy, surprised, betrayed, and made use of, might come to its aid. Such was Sarcany's idea.

Toronthal, on the other hand, was seeking to join in with his old broker. That there did exist some conspiracy against the Austrian Government, and that Sarcany had discovered the conspirators, he was inclined to admit. This house of Ladislas Zathmar, with the secret meetings, this ciphered correspondence, the enormous sum held at call by Sandorf: all began to look very suspicious. Very likely Sarcany was right. But the banker was anxious to do the best he could for himself, and sound the matter to the bottom, and would not yet give in. So he contented himself with saying:

"And when you have deciphered the letter – if you ever do – you will find it only refers to private affairs of no importance, and consequently there will be no profit for you – or me!"

"No!" said Sarcany, in a tone of the deepest conviction. "No! I'm on the track of a serious conspiracy, conducted by men of high rank, and I add, Silas Toronthal, that you doubt it no more than I do."

"Well, what do you want?" asked the banker.

Sarcany rose, and, in a lower tone, looking straight at Toronthal, replied, "What I want is this: I want admission to Count Zathmar's house, on some pretext yet to be found, so that I can gain his confidence. Once there, where nobody knows me, I shall get hold of the grating and decipher this dispatch, which I can then make use of to further our interests."

"Our interests? Why do you want to mix me up in the affair?"

"Because it is well worth the trouble, and you will gain something out of it."

"And could not you do that by yourself?"

"No! I have need of your help."

"Explain."

"To attain my end I want time, and while I'm waiting I want money. I have none."

"Your credit is exhausted here, you know!"

"Well, you'll open another."

"What good will that do me?"

"This. Of the three men I've spoken to you about, two are poor – Zathmar and Professor Bathory – but the third is immensely rich. His possessions in Transylvania are considerable. You know that if he is arrested as a conspirator, and found guilty, his goods will be confiscated, and the greatest part of them will go to those who discovered and denounced the conspiracy! You and I, Silas Toronthal! We go shares!"

Sarcany was silent. The banker made no answer. He was thinking if it were worthwhile to join in the game. He was not the man to personally compromise himself in an affair of this nature; but he felt that his agent would be man enough to act for both. If he decided to join in the scheme, he knew well how to make a treaty, which would hold his man at his mercy, and enable him to remain in the dark. He hesitated, for all that. Good! To get all, what did he risk? He need not appear in this odious affair, and he would reap the profit – enormous profit – which would get the bank on a sound footing again.

"Well?" asked Sarcany.

"Well? No!" answered Toronthal, frightened at having such an associate, or, to use the proper word, such an accomplice.

"You refuse?"

"Yes – I refuse – besides, I do not believe in the success of your schemes."

"Take care, Toronthal," said Sarcany, in a threatening tone, which he could not restrain.

"Take care? And of what if you please?"

"Of what I know of certain transactions..."

"Clear out!" answered Toronthal.

"I shall know how to compel you..."

"Go!"

At the moment there came a gentle knock at the door. As Sarcany quickly stepped to the window the door opened, and the messenger said in a loud voice,

"Count Sandorf will be glad if Mr. Toronthal will give him a few moments' conversation."

Then he retired.

"Count Sandorf!" exclaimed Sarcany.

The banker was anything but pleased for Sarcany to know of this visit. And he also foresaw that considerable difficulty would result from the count's unexpected arrival.

"And what does Count Sandorf do here?" asked Sarcany ironically. "You, then, have something to do with the conspirators at Count Zathmar's! I'd wager I've been talking to one of them!"

"Again I tell you to go."

"I shall not go, Toronthal, and I shall find out why Count Sandorf comes to your banking-house!"

And he stepped into a cupboard leading out of the office and shut the door.

Toronthal was about to call and have him turned out, but he thought better of it.

"No!" he muttered, "After all, it's better Sarcany should hear all that goes on!"

The banker rang for the messenger, and requested him to admit the count.

Sandorf entered the office, replied coldly, as was his wont, to the obsequious inquiries of the banker, and seated himself in a chair, which Toronthal brought forward.

"I did not know, count, that you were in Trieste, so that you call unexpectedly; but it's always an honour for the bank to receive a visit from you."

"Sir," replied the count, "I'm one of your least important customers, and I never have much business, as you know. But I have to thank you for having taken charge of the money that I have with you."

"Count," observed Toronthal, "I would remind you that that money is on current account here, and that you are losing all interest for it."

"I know," replied Sandorf. "But I do not wish to make an investment with your house; it's left simply on deposit."

"Quite so, count, but money is dear just now, and it does not seem right that yours should remain unproductive. A financial crisis threatens to extend over the whole country. The position is not an easy one in the

"Have you been able to decipher this letter?"

interior. Business is paralyzed. Many important failures have shaken public credit, and I'm afraid others are coming."

"But your house, sir, is safe enough," said Sandorf, "and on very good authority I know that it has been but little affected by these failures."

"Oh! Very little," answered Toronthal, with the greatest calmness. "The Adriatic trade keeps us going with a constant flood of maritime business that is wanting to the Pesth and Vienna houses, and we have only been very slightly touched by the crisis. We have nothing to complain of, count, and we do not complain."

"I can only congratulate you, sir," answered Sandorf. "By-the-by, with regard to this crisis, is there any talk of political complications in the interior?"

Although Sandorf had asked the question without appearing to attach any importance to it, Toronthal regarded it with rather more attention. It agreed so well, in fact, with what he had just heard from Sarcany.

"I do not know of anything," said the banker. "And I have not heard that the Austrian Government has any apprehension on the subject. Have you, count, any reason to suppose that something is – ?"

"Not at all," replied Sandorf, "but in banking circles things are frequently known which the public does not hear of till afterwards. That is why I asked you the question, leaving it to you to answer or not, as you felt inclined."

"I have heard nothing in that way," said Toronthal, "and, besides, with a client like you, count, I should not think it right to remain silent if I knew anything, as your interests might suffer."

"I'm much obliged to you," answered Sandorf, "and, like you, I do not think there is much to fear either at home or abroad. I'm soon going to leave Trieste on urgent private affairs for Transylvania."

"Oh! You are going away?" asked Toronthal quickly.

"Yes, in a fortnight, or perhaps later."

"And you'll return to Trieste?"

"I do not think so," answered Sandorf. "But before I go, I have some business to settle. My accounts for the castle of Artenak must be put in order. I have received a quantity of notes from my steward, farm rents and forest revenue, and I have not the time to check them. Do you know of any accountant, or could you spare one of your clerks, to do it for me?"

"Nothing easier."

"I should be much obliged."

"When shall I send him to you, count?"

"As soon as possible."

"To what address?"

"To my friend, Count Zathmar, whose house is No. 89, in the Acque-dotto."

"It shall be done, count."

"It will take ten days or more, I should think, and when the accounts are in order, I shall leave for Artenak. I shall be glad, therefore, if you will have the money ready, so that I can draw."

Toronthal at this request could not restrain a slight movement, which, however, was unnoticed by Sandorf.

"What date do you wish to draw?"

"The eighth of next month."

"The money shall be ready."

And Count Sandorf rose, and the banker accompanied him to the door of the anteroom.

When Toronthal re-entered his office he found Sarcany, who greeted him with, "Within two days I must get admission to Count Zathmar's house in the character of this accountant."

And Toronthal answered, "Yes, you must indeed."

CHAPTER IV

THE CIPHER

Two days afterwards Sarcany was installed in the house of Ladislas Zathmar. He had been introduced by Silas Toronthal, and on his introduction had been received by Count Sandorf. The banker and his agent had become accomplices, the object of their schemes being the discovery of a secret which might cost the chiefs of the conspiracy their lives, and the result, as the price of their information, a fortune falling into the pocket of an adventurer, that it might find its way into the strong box of a banker who had reached the point of being unable to honour his engagements.

A formal agreement had been drawn up between Toronthal and Sarcany, according to which the expected profit was to be shared equally. Sarcany was to have sufficient to enable him and his companion, Zirone, to live comfortably at Trieste, and to meet all outgoings and expenses. In exchange, and as a guarantee, he had handed over to the banker the facsimile of the message which contained – there could be no doubt – the secret of the conspiracy.

It may perhaps be said that Sandorf was imprudent in acting thus. Under such circumstances to introduce a stranger into the house where such important matters were in hand, on the very eve of a rising of which the signal might be sent at any moment, might seem an act of strange imprudence. But the count had not acted thus without being obliged.

It was necessary that his personal affairs should be put in order now that he was about to enter on a perilous adventure in which he risked his life, or at least his exile, if he was obliged to fly in the event of failure. Besides, the introduction of a stranger into Zathmar's house appeared to him calculated to prevent suspicion. He fancied that for some days – and we know that he was not mistaken – there had been spies in the Acquedotto; spies who were no other than Sarcany and Zirone. Were

Trieste: The Stock Exchange

the police of Trieste keeping their eyes on his friends and him, and their proceedings? Sandorf might well think so and fear so. If the meeting place of the conspirators, hitherto so obstinately kept hidden, seemed to him to be suspected, what better means of baffling suspicion could be devised than to admit within it an accountant merely busying himself with accounts. How could the presence of a clerk be dangerous to Zathmar and his guests? In no way. There was no longer any interchange of ciphered correspondence between Trieste and the other towns of Hungary. All the papers relating to the movement had been destroyed. There remained no written trace of the conspiracy. The measures had been taken that were intended to be taken. Count Sandorf had only to give the signal when the moment arrived. So that the introduction of a clerk into the house, which the Government might have under surveillance, was calculated to allay all suspicion. That is to say, the reasoning was just and the precaution good, had the clerk been any one else than Sarcany, and his introducer any other than Silas Toronthal.

Sarcany was a past-master in duplicity, and took full advantage of the gifts be possessed – that open face, with its frank, clear expression, and honest, straightforward look. Count Sandorf and his two companions could not but be taken with him – and they were taken with him. In no way did he show or learn that he was in the presence of the chiefs of a conspiracy to raise the Hungarian race in revolt against the Germans. Mathias Sandorf, Stephen Bathory, and Ladislas Zathmar seemed at their meetings to be only occupied with discussions on art and science. There was no secret correspondence; there were no mysterious comings and goings about the house. But Sarcany knew what he wanted. The chance he wanted was sure to come in time, and he waited for it.

In entering Zathmar's house, Sarcany had but one object in view – to possess himself of the grating that would enable him to decipher the cryptogram; and as no ciphered dispatch arrived at Trieste, he began to ask himself if, for prudential reasons, the grating had been destroyed. This would be rather annoying for him, as all the scaffolding of his scheme was based on his being able to read the letter brought by the pigeon.

Thus as he worked at putting in order the accounts of Mathias Sandorf, he kept his eyes open; he watched, he spied. Admission to the room where the meetings took place between Zathmar and his companions was not forbidden him. Very often he worked there all alone; and then his eyes and his fingers were occupied in quite other tasks than making calculations or casting figures. He ferreted among the papers; he opened the drawers by means of skeleton keys made him by Zirone, who was quite an adept in such matters. And all the time he kept a strict watch on Borik, with whom he seemed somehow to be quite out of sympathy.

For five days Sarcany's search was useless. Each morning he came with the hope of succeeding; each evening he returned to his hotel without having discovered anything. He feared he was going to fail after all in his treacherous enterprise. The conspiracy – if there were a conspiracy, and he could not doubt that there was one – might come to a head at any moment before it had been discovered, and consequently before it had been reported. "But rather than lose the benefit of a discovery, even without satisfactory proofs, better inform the police," said Zirone, "and give them a copy of the letter."

"That is what I'm going to do if necessary," said Sarcany.

Of course Toronthal was kept informed of all that went on. And it was not without difficulty that the impatience of the banker was duly curbed.

Chance came at last to his assistance. On the first occasion it brought him the message, and now it came to him to show him how the message could be deciphered. It was the last day of May, about four o'clock in the afternoon. Sarcany, according to his custom, was going to leave Zathmar's house at five. He was greatly disappointed that he had advanced no further than on the first day, and that the work he had been doing for Count Sandorf was approaching its end. When the task was finished, he would evidently be dismissed with thanks and rewards, and he would have no chance of again entering the house.

Zathmar and his two friends were not at home. There was no one in the house but Borik, and he was busy on the ground floor. Sarcany, finding himself free to do as he liked, resolved to go into Count Zathmar's room, which he had not yet been able to do, and there search everything he could. The door was locked. Sarcany with his skeleton keys soon opened it and entered.

Between the two windows opening on to the street there was a writing desk, whose antique shape would have delighted a connoisseur in old furniture. The shut down front prevented any one inspecting what was inside.

It was the first time Sarcany had the chance of getting near this piece of furniture, and he was not the man to waste his opportunities. To rummage its different drawers he only had to force the front! And this he did with the aid of his instruments, without the lock being injured. In the fourth drawer, under a pile of papers, was a kind of card cut into curious holes. The card caught his attention at once. "The grating!" he said. He was not mistaken. His first idea was to take it with him, but on reflection he saw that its disappearance would awake suspicion if Count Zathmar noticed it had gone. "Good," said he to himself, "as I copied the message, so I'll copy the grating, and Toronthal and I can read the dispatch at our ease."

The grating was merely a square of card about two and a half inches long divided into thirty-six equal squares. Of these thirty-six equal squares arranged in six horizontal and vertical lines like those on a Pythagorean table of six ciphers, twenty-seven were shaded and nine were open – that is to say, nine squares had been cut out of the card and left nice openings in different positions. Sarcany had to be careful to take the exact size of the grating, and the exact position of the nine blank squares. And this he did by tracing the grating on a sheet of white paper, and marking on his copy a small cross which he found on the original, and which seemed to distinguish the top side. As he traced the grating on his paper he found that blanks occupied the places of squares 2, 4, and 6 in the first line, of 5 in the second line, of 3 in the third line, of 2 and 5 in the fourth line, of 6 in the fifth line, and of 4 in the sixth line, exactly as shown in the annexed diagram, wherein the open squares represented unshaded, and which is an accurate portrait of the grating of which Sarcany and Toronthal made such dastardly use.

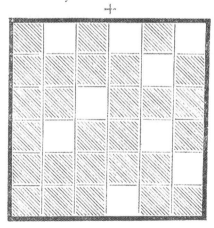

By means of this grating, which it would be easy to copy using a piece of ordinary card, Sarcany felt that he would have no difficulty in deciphering the facsimile of the message then in Toronthal's possession; and so he put back the original grating among the papers, as he had found it, left Zathmar's room, left the house, and returned to his hotel.

A quarter of an hour afterwards Zirone beheld him enter the room with such a triumphant air that he could not help exclaiming, "Hallo!

The banker accompanied him to the door of the anteroom.

What is up? Take care of yourself! You are not so clever in hiding your joy as you are your grief, and you'll betray yourself, if..."

"Shut up," answered Sarcany, "and to work without losing a moment."

"Before we eat?"

"Before we eat."

And then Sarcany picked up a card of moderate thickness. He cut it according to his tracing so as to obtain a grating of the exact shape of his copy, not forgetting the little cross, which showed the right end uppermost. Then he took a rule and divided his rectangle into thirty-six squares, all of equal size. Then of these thirty-six squares nine were marked as they appeared on the tracing, and cut out with the point of a penknife so as to show through them, when applied to the message, whatever signs or letters were to be read.

Zirone sat facing Sarcany, and watched him as he worked. He was deeply interested in the performance, because he thoroughly understood the system of cryptography employed in the correspondence.

"Now that is ingenious," he said, "highly ingenious, and may be of some use! When I think that each of those empty squares may perhaps hold a million florins..."

"And more!" said Sarcany.

The work was at an end Sarcany rose and put the cut card into his pocket-book.

"The first thing tomorrow morning I call on Toronthal," he said.

"Keep an eye on his cash-box."

"If he has the message, I have the grating!"

"And this time he'll have to give it up."

"He will give it up."

"And now we can eat?"

"We can eat."

"Come on then."

And Zirone, always blessed with a healthy appetite, did full justice to the excellent steak he had, according to his custom, previously ordered.

In the morning – it was the 1st of June – at eight o'clock, Sarcany presented himself at the bank, and Toronthal gave orders for him to be shown to his office immediately.

"There is the grating," was all that Sarcany said as he laid the card on the table.

The banker took it, turned it round and round, jerked his head first to one side, then the other, and did not seem at all to share in the confidence of his associate.

"Let us try it," said Sarcany.

"Well, we'll try it."

Toronthal took the facsimile of the message from one of the drawers in his desk and laid it on the table.

It may be recollected that the message was composed of eighteen words, each containing six letters – the words being quite unintelligible. It was obvious that each letter ought to correspond with a square of the card; and consequently that the six first words of the message, composed of thirty-six letters, must have been obtained by means of the thirty-six squares.

And in the grating the arrangement of the blank squares had been so ingeniously thought out, that for every quarter turn – that is, for the four times the blank squares changed their position – they came in a different place.

It will be seen that this must be so; for if at the first application of the grating to white paper the figures 1 to 9 are inscribed in each blank space, and then, after a quarter turn, the figures 10 to 18, then, after another quarter turn, the figures 19 to 27, and then, after another quarter turn, the figures 28 to 36, it will be found that no square has two numbers, and that each of the thirty-six squares is filled in. Sarcany very naturally began on the six first words of the message, intending to make four successive applications of the grating. He then thought of treating the next six, and then the six finals in the same way, and thus use up the eighteen words of the cryptogram.

It need scarcely be said that Sarcany had told Toronthal what he intended to do, and that the banker had approved of the plan.

Would the practice confirm the theory? Therein lay all the interest of the experiment.

The eighteen words of the message were these:

ihnalz	*zaemen*	*ruiopu*
aruuro	*trvree*	*mtgssl*
odxhnp	*estlev*	*eevarl*
aeeeil	*ennios*	*noupvg*
spesdr	*erssur*	*ouitse*
redguc	*tocedt*	*artuee*

At first they set to work to decipher the six words. To do this Sarcany wrote them out on a sheet of white paper, taking care so to space the letters and lines as to bring each letter under one of the squares of the grating. And this was the result

i	h	n	a	l	z
a	r	u	u	r	o
o	d	x	h	n	p
a	e	e	e	i	l
s	p	e	s	d	r
e	e	d	g	n	c

Then the grating was placed over the letters so that the little cross was on top, and then through the nine openings there appeared the nine letters shown below, while the other twenty-seven were hidden:

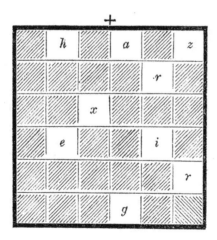

Then Sarcany made a quarter turn from left to right so as to bring the side with the cross to the right. And these were the letters that appeared through the spaces:

51

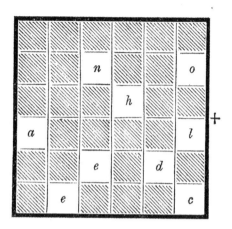

At the third attempt the letters visible were these:

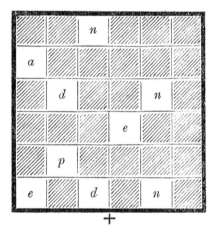

To the astonishment of Toronthal and Sarcany, none of these combinations gave any sense. They endeavoured to read them consecutively in the order they had been obtained, but they proved as meaningless as the dispatch itself. Was the message to remain undecipherable?

The fourth application of the grating resulted thus:

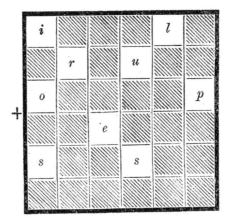

which was as obscure as the others.

In fact the four words which had been discovered were:

hazrxeirg
nohaledec
nadnepedn
ilruopess

And these meant – nothing.

Sarcany could not conceal his rage at such a disappointment.

The banker shook his head, and remarked, in a slight tone of irony:

"Perhaps that is not the grating!"

Sarcany simply writhed in his chair.

"Let us try again!" he said.

"Try again!" said Toronthal.

Sarcany, having mastered his nervous agitation, began experimenting on the six words forming the second column of the message. Four times did he apply the grating; and these are the four meaningless words that he obtained:

amnetnore
velessuot
etseirted
zerrevnes

This time Sarcany threw the grating on to the table with an oath.

In curious contrast Toronthal kept quite cool. He was carefully studying the words hitherto obtained, and remained deep in thought.

He fancied that for some days there had been spies in the Acquedotto

"Confound all gratings and all who use them!" exclaimed Sarcany, rising.

"Sit down," said Toronthal.

"Sit down?"

"Yes; and finish the last column."

Sarcany gave Toronthal a look. Then he sat down, took the grating, and applied it to the last six words of the message, as he had done to the others. He did it mechanically, as though he took no interest in what he was doing.

And the words given by the four applications of the grating were:

uonsuoveu

qlangisre

imerpuate

rptsetuot

That was all. The words were as meaningless as the others.

Sarcany, enraged beyond all bounds, took the paper on which he had written the barbarous words, which the grating had yielded, and was about to tear it into tatters, when Toronthal stopped him.

"Do not get excited," he said.

"Eh!" exclaimed Sarcany, "what can you do with an insoluble logogriph like that?"

"Write all those words in a line, one after the other," said the banker.

"And why?"

"To see."

Sarcany obeyed; and he obtained the following:

hazrxeirgnohaledecnadnepednilruopessamnetnorevelessuotetseirtedzerrevnesuonsuoveuq langisreimerpuaterptsetuot

The letters had scarcely been written before Toronthal snatched the paper from Sarcany, read it, and gave a shout. It was the banker now who lost his head. Sarcany thought he had gone mad.

"Read!" said Toronthal, holding out the paper to Sarcany. "Read!"

"Read!"

"Yes! Don't you see that, before they used the grating, Count Sandorf's correspondents wrote the letter backwards?"

Sarcany took the paper, and this is what he read, proceeding from the last letter to the first:

Trieste: The Lloyd's Building

"Tout est pret. Au premier signal que vous nous en-
verrez de Trieste, tous se leveront en masse pour
l'independance de la Hongrie. Xrzah."

"And the four last letters?" he asked.

"An agreed upon signature, or something to fill up," said Toronthal.

"Oh, then! 'All is ready. At the first signal you send us from Trieste,
all of us will rise together for the independence of Hungary.' That's it,
isn't it? Well, we've got them at last!"

"But the police haven't got them!"

"That is my business."

"You'll act with great secrecy?"

"That is my business," said Sarcany. "The Governor of Trieste shall
be the only person to know the names of the two honest patriots who
have nipped in its bud this conspiracy against the Austrian Empire!"

And as he spoke, the mockery of each tone and gesture betrayed the
true feeling with which he uttered the words.

"And now I have nothing else to do," said the banker.

"Nothing," answered Sarcany, "except to take your share of the
profit."

"When?"

"When the three heads fall, they should be worth a million apiece."

Toronthal and Sarcany bid each other adieu. If they wished to gain
anything out of the secret that chance had handed them, they must be
quick and denounce the conspirators before the plot broke out.

Sarcany returned to Zathmar's house as if nothing had occurred, and
went on with the accounts. His work was nearly finished. Count Sandorf, in thanking him for the zeal he had shown, told him that he should
not require his services after the next eighteen days.

To Sarcany's mind this meant that about that time the signal was to be
given from Trieste to the chief Hungarian towns.

He continued therefore to watch with the greatest care, but so as to
give rise to no suspicion, all that took place in Zathmar's house. And he
played his part so well, he seemed so imbued with liberal ideas, and had
taken so little pains to hide the invincible repulsion he said he felt for
the Germans, that Sandorf had thought of giving him a post later on,
when the rising should have made Hungary a free country. It was not so
with Borik, who had never got over the first feeling of dislike with
which the young man had inspired him.

Sarcany neared his triumph.

It was on the 9th of June that Count Sandorf had agreed with his friends to give the signal, and the 8th had come.

But the informer had been at work.

In the evening, about eight o'clock, the police suddenly entered Zathmar's house. Resistance was impossible. Count Sandorf, Count Zathmar, Professor Bathory, Sarcany himself, who made no protest, and Borik were secretly arrested.

CHAPTER V

EVENTS BEFORE, DURING AND AFTER THE TRIAL

Istria, which became part of Austria-Hungary in accordance with the treaty of 1815, is a triangular peninsula, of which the isthmus forms the base. This peninsula extends from the Gulf of Trieste to the Gulf of Quarnero; and along its coastline are several harbours. Amongst others, almost at the extreme southern point is Pola, which the Government were then forming into a dockyard and arsenal of the first rank.

The province, more especially on its western coast, is still Italian, and even Venetian in its customs and language. The Slavic element still struggles with the Italian element, and the German element has some difficulty in maintaining its influence.

There are several important towns on the coast and in the interior. Amongst these are Capo d'Istria and Pirano, whose population is almost entirely employed in the salt works at the mouths of the Risano and Corna-Lunga; Parenzo, the headquarters of the Istrian Diet and the residence of the bishop; Rovigno, rich in its olive trees; and Pola, where tourists find interest in the superb monuments of Roman origin, and which is destined to become the most important military port in the Adriatic.

But neither of these towns has the right to call itself the capital of Istria. The place that bears that title is Pisino, situated almost in the centre of the triangle, and thither, unknown to them, the prisoners were about to be taken after their secret arrest.

At the door of Zathmar's house a post-chaise was waiting. The four prisoners entered it, and two of the Austrian police, who were put in charge during the journey, took their places beside them. They were thus prevented from exchanging a word, which might in any way compromise them or lead to a mutual understanding before their appearance in the dock.

An escort of twelve mounted gendarmes, commanded by a lieutenant, took up their positions in front, behind, and at the doors of the carriage; and ten minutes afterwards they were out of the town. Borik was taken direct to the prison at Trieste, and there put into solitary confinement.

Where were the prisoners going? In what fortress of the Austrian Government were they to be lodged, since the castle at Trieste was not to receive them? Count Sandorf and his friends would have been glad to know, but they tried to discover in vain.

The night was dark. By the light of the carriage lamps only the first rank of the mounted escort could be seen. The pace was rapid, Sandorf, Bathory, and Zathmar remained motionless and silent in their corners; Sarcany did not seek to break the silence, either to protest against his arrest, or to ask why the arrest had been made.

After leaving Trieste the post-chaise made a bend, which took it obliquely towards the coast. Count Sandorf, amid the noise of the trotting horses and the jingling sabres, could hear the distant murmur of the surf on the rocks along the shore. For a moment a few lights shone out in the night, and almost immediately disappeared. This was the small town of Muggia, which the post-chaise had just passed without halting. Then Sandorf noticed that the road lay into the interior.

At eleven o'clock the chaise stopped to change horses. It was only at a farm, where the horses were waiting ready to be harnessed. It was not a post-station.

The escort resumed its journey. The carriage passed along a road among the vineyards where the vines interlaced themselves in festoons to the branches of the mulberry trees. The road was flat, and the carriage made rapid progress. The darkness now grew more profound, for heavy clouds, brought up by a violent sirocco from the southeast, covered the sky; and although the windows were let down from time to time to admit a little fresh air – for the nights are warm in Istria – it was impossible to distinguish anything, even close at hand. Although Sandorf and his friends noted every incident on the road, the direction of the wind, and the time elapsed since their departure; they could not discover the direction in which the carriage was travelling. The object was doubtless to keep it as secret as possible, so that their place of confinement should not be known to the public.

About two o'clock in the morning they again changed horses. As at the first change, the halt did not last five minutes.

Count Sandorf thought he could make out in the gloom a few houses at the end of a road, as though on the extreme outskirt of a town.

This was Buje, the chief place of a district situated about twenty miles south of Muggia.

As soon as the horses were put to, the lieutenant spoke a few words to the postillion in a low tone, and the chaise set off at a gallop.

About half-past three o'clock the day began to dawn. An hour later the position of the rising sun would have shown them the direction in which they were going, but the police shut down the shutters, and the interior of the carriage was plunged into complete darkness.

Neither Count Sandorf nor his friends made the least observation. It would not have been replied to; that was quite certain. The best thing to do was to submit and wait.

An hour or two afterwards – it was difficult to reckon how the time went – the post-chaise stopped for the last time, and the change of horses was very quickly performed at Visinada.

As they left here, all that could be noticed was that the road had become very hard. The shouts of the postillion, the cracking of his whip, incessantly urged the horses forward, and the shoes rattled on the hard stony ground of a mountainous region. A few hills with little clumps of greyish trees could be made out on the horizon. Two or three times the prisoners heard the sounds of a flute. They came from the young shepherds who were playing their curious tunes as they gathered together their flocks of black goats; but this afforded no sufficient indication of the country the prisoners were passing through. That had to be found out without seeing it.

About nine o'clock the chaise went off in quite a different direction. Unless they were mistaken, they were descending rapidly after having reached the highest point of their journey. The speed was much increased, and occasionally the wheels had to be skidded.

In fact, after leading through the hilly country commanded by Mont Maseru, the road drops down obliquely as it approaches Pisino. Although the town is very much above sea level, it seems to be in a deep valley, to judge from the neighbouring hills. Some distance before it is reached, the campanile above the houses picturesquely grouped on the hillside becomes visible.

Pisino is the chief place of the district, and contains about 24,000 inhabitants. It is situated almost in the centre of the peninsula, and, particularly at fair time, a large business is done among the mixed population of Morlaques, Slavs of different tribes, and even Tsiganes, who flourish there.

Sarcany put back the original grating among the papers

The capital of Istria is an old city, and has retained its feudal character. This strikingly appears in the ancient castle, which towers above several more modern military establishments where the administration of the Government is carried on.

It was in the courtyard of this castle that the post-chaise stopped on the 9th of June, about ten o'clock in the morning, after a journey of fifteen hours. Count Sandorf, his two companions, and Sarcany left the vehicle, and a few minutes afterwards were shown into separate vaulted cells.

Although they had had no communication with each other, and had not been able to exchange ideas in any way, yet Sandorf, Zathmar, and Bathory were all engaged in pondering over the same subject. How had the secret of the plot been discovered? Had the police come on the track by chance? There had recently been no correspondence between Trieste and the Hungarian and Transylvanian towns. Was there a traitor in the camp? But who could be the traitor? Confidence had been placed in none. There were no papers to fall into a spy's hands. All the documents had been destroyed. Had they rummaged the most secret corners of the Acquedotto they would have found not a single suspicious note! And that is what had happened. The police had discovered nothing – except the grating, which Zathmar had not destroyed in case he wanted it for future use. But unhappily the grating was serious evidence, for it was impossible to explain its use except as a means of ciphered correspondence.

In fact everything rested on the copy of the message that Sarcany, with Toronthal's connivance, had handed over to the Governor of Trieste after having made out its real meaning. But unfortunately that was quite enough to make good the accusation of conspiring against the State; and it had been decided to bring Count Sandorf and his friends before a special tribunal, a military tribunal, which would proceed in military fashion.

Sarcany's game was a deep one, and he played it with the coolness and deliberation that distinguished him. He had allowed himself to be arrested, to be convicted, if need be, on the understanding that he should receive a pardon; and in this way he hoped to disarm suspicion.

Sandorf was completely deceived by him – and who would not have been? – and resolved to do his utmost to clear him of the charge. It would not be difficult, he thought, to show that Sarcany had taken no part in the conspiracy, that he was merely an accountant only recently introduced into Zathmar's house to arrange certain private matters which in no way had reference to the plot. If needful, he would call Silas Toronthal to testify to the young man's innocence. There could be no doubt, therefore, that Sarcany would be found innocent of having been either a principal or accessory, in the event of the prosecution being persisted in.

The Austrian Government knew nothing of the conspiracy beyond what they heard at Trieste. The conspirators in Hungary and Transylvania remained absolutely unknown. There was no trace in existence of their complicity in the plot. Sandorf, Bathory, and Zathmar need have felt no anxiety on this head. As far as they were concerned they had made up their minds to deny everything until some material evidence was produced. In that case they knew that their lives were forfeit. Others would one day take up the movement that had now proved abortive. The cause of independence would find new leaders. If they were convicted, they would avow what had been their hopes. They would show the object at which they had aimed, and which one day would be attained.

It was not without some reason that Count Sandorf and his two friends thought that the action of the police had been much restricted in the matter. At Buda, at Pesth, at Klausenburg, in all the towns in which the rising was to take place at the signal from Trieste, inquiries had been made in vain. That was why the Government had arrested the chiefs so secretly at Trieste. They had sent them to Pisino, and desired that nothing should be known of the matter, in the hope that something would happen to betray the senders of the cipher message. The hope was not realized. The expected signal was not given. The movement was stopped for a time at least. The Government had to content itself with trying Sandorf and his companions for high treason.

The inquiries took several days; and it was not till the 20th of June that the proceedings began with the examination of the accused. They were not even confronted with each other, and were only to meet before their judges.

The chiefs of the Trieste conspiracy were, as we have said, to be tried before a court-martial. The proceedings before such a court never take long, the trial is conducted very quickly, and there is no delay in the execution of the sentence.

It was so in this matter.

On the 25th of June, the court-martial met in one of the lower rooms of the fortress of Pisino, and the accused were brought before it. The proceedings did not take very long, and nothing startling was discovered.

The court opened at nine o'clock in the morning. Count Sandorf, Count Zathmar, and professor Bathory, on the one side, and Sarcany on the other, saw each other for the first time since their imprisonment. The clasp of the hand which Sandorf and his friends interchanged as they met, gave yet another proof of their unanimity. A sign from Zathmar, and Bathory gave Sandorf to understand that they left it to him to speak for them. Neither would undertake the defence. All Sandorf had done up till then had been done well. All that he thought fit to say to the judges would be well said.

The hearing was a public one, in the sense that the doors of the room were open. But few persons were present, for the affair had not yet transpired; and the spectators, some twenty in number, belonged to the staff of the castle.

The identity of the accused was first proved. Then, immediately afterwards, Sandorf asked the president the name of the place which he and his companions had been brought for trial, but no reply was given to the question.

The identity of Sarcany was likewise established. He still did nothing to distinguish his case from that of his companions.

Then the facsimile of the message handed over to the police was produced; and the accused were asked if they remembered receiving the original. They replied that it was the duty of the prosecution to prove that they received it.

At this reply the grating, which had been found in Zathmar's desk, was produced.

Sandorf and his companions could not deny that the grating had been in their possession. They did not try to. To such material evidence, there was no reply. The application of the grating permitted the cryptographic letter to be read, and the letter must consequently have been received.

And thus they learnt how the secret of the conspiracy had been discovered, and the basis on which the prosecution was originated.

From this time forward question and answer passed rapidly, and clearly told the story.

Sandorf denied nothing. He spoke on behalf of his two friends. A movement intended to bring about the separation of Hungary from Austria, and the autonomic reconstitution of the kingdom of the ancient Magyars had been organized by them. Had they not been arrested, it would shortly have broken out, and Hungary would have reconquered

Count Sandorf, Count Zathmar, Professor Bathory, Sarcany himself, who made
no protest, and Borik were secretly arrested

its independence. Sandorf claimed to be the chief of the conspiracy, and insisted that his fellow prisoners were merely his agents. But Zathmar and Bathory protested against this contention, and claimed the honour of having been his accomplices, and desired to share his fate.

When the president interrogated the prisoners as to their dealings with others, they refused to reply. Not a name was given.

"You have now three heads," said Sandorf, "and that must be enough for you."

Three heads only, for Sandorf then set himself to exculpating Sarcany, a young clerk employed in Count Zathmar's house on the recommendation of Silas Toronthal.

Sarcany could only confirm what Sandorf stated. He knew nothing of the conspiracy. He had been greatly surprised to learn that in this quiet house in the Acquedotto a plot was in progress against the safety of the State. If he had made no protest when he was arrested, it was because he had no idea what it was all about.

Neither Count Sandorf nor Sarcany had any difficulty in proving this – and it is probable that the court had already made up its mind in the matter. At the suggestion of the judge advocate the charge against Sarcany was there and then abandoned.

By two o'clock in the afternoon the pleadings were all over, and the sentence was given without even an adjournment.

Count Mathias Sandorf, Count Ladislas Zathmar, and Professor Stephen Bathory were found guilty of high treason against the State and sentenced to death.

The prisoners were to be shot in the courtyard of the castle.

The execution was to take place within forty-eight hours. Sarcany was to be kept in custody until the closing of the gaol books, which would not take place until after execution of the sentence.

By the same judgment all the possessions of the prisoners were confiscated.

The prisoners were then removed.

Sarcany was taken back to the cell he occupied at the bottom of an elliptic corridor on the second floor of the donjon. Sandorf and his two friends, during the last hours of life that remained to them, were quartered in a large cell on the same level, exactly at the end of the major axis of the ellipse, which the corridor made. The secret was now known. The condemned were to be left together until their execution.

This was a consolation, even a pleasure for them, when they found themselves alone and allowed to give way to feelings, which they could not at first restrain.

"My friends," said Sandorf, "I am the cause of your deaths! But I have nothing to ask pardon for! We worked for the independence of Hungary! Our cause was just! It is our duty to defend her! It is an honour to die for her!"

"Mathias," said Bathory, "we thank you for having associated us with you in the patriotic work, which would have been the work of all your life..."

"As we are associated with you in death!" added Zathmar.

Then, during a momentary silence, the three gazed round the gloomy cell in which they were to spend their last hours. A narrow window some four or five feet high, cut through the thick wall of the donjon, let in a certain amount of light. There were three iron bedsteads, a few chairs, a table and a shelf or two, on which were a few articles of crockery.

Zathmar and Bathory were soon lost in thought.

Sandorf began to walk up and down the cell.

Zathmar was alone in the world, had no family ties and no near relations. There was only his old servant, Borik to mourn for him.

It was not so with Bathory. His death would not only prove a blow to himself. He had a wife and son, whom it would reach. That wife and child might even die! And if they survived him, how were they to live? What was to be the future of a penniless woman and her eight-year-old child? Had Bathory possessed any property, how much of it would remain after a judgment, which directed it to be confiscated, and sentenced him to death?

As for Sandorf, all his past life returned to him! His wife came to him! His little daughter came – a child, just two years old, now left to the care of the steward. And there were his friends whom he had led to ruin! He asked himself if he had done well, if he had not gone farther than his duty towards his country required. Would that the punishment had fallen on him alone, and not upon those that were innocent!

"No! No! I have only done my duty!" he said to himself. "My country before all, and above all!"

At five o'clock a warder entered the cell, placed the dinner on the table, and went out again without saying a word. Sandorf would have liked to know in what fortress he was kept a prisoner, but as the president of the court-martial had not thought fit to answer the question it was quite certain that the warder would not give the information.

The prisoners hardly touched the dinner, which had been prepared for them. They passed the rest of the day talking on various matters, in the hope that their abortive movement would one day be resumed. Very often they returned to the incidents of the trial.

"We now know," said Zathmar, "why we have been arrested, and how the police discovered us from that letter which they came across."

"Yes, Ladislas," said Sandorf, "but into whose hands did that message, which was one of the last we received, at first fall, and who copied it?"

"And when it was copied," added Bathory, "how did they read it without the grating?"

"The grating must have been stolen," said Sandorf.

"Stolen! and by whom?" asked Zathmar. "The day we were arrested it was still in the drawer in my desk, whence the police took it."

This was, indeed, inexplicable. That the letter had been found on the pigeon, that it had been copied before being sent to its destination, that the house where the person to whom it was addressed had been discovered: all that could be explained. But that the cryptographic dispatch could have been deciphered without the grating by which it had been formed was incomprehensible.

"And besides," continued Sandorf, "we know that the letter was read, and it could not have been read without the grating! It was this letter which put the police on our traces, and it was on it that the whole charge was based."

"It matters very little, after all," answered Bathory.

"On the contrary, it does matter," said Sandorf. "We may have been betrayed! And if there has been a traitor – not to know..."

Sandorf suddenly stopped. The name of Sarcany occurred to him; but he abandoned the thought at once without caring to communicate it to his companions.

Far into the night Sandorf and his companions continued their conversation on all that was unintelligible with regard to these matters.

In the morning they were awakened from sound sleep by the entry of the warder. It was the morning of their last day but one. The execution was fixed to take place in twenty-four hours from then.

Bathory asked the warder if he might be permitted to see his family.

The warder replied that he had no orders on the subject. It was not likely that the Government would consent to give the prisoners this last

The chaise set off at a gallop

consolation, inasmuch as they had conducted the affair throughout with the greatest secrecy, and not even the name of the fortress, which served them as a prison had been revealed.

"If we write letters, will they be forwarded?" asked Sandorf.

"I'll bring you paper, pens, and ink," replied the warder, "and I promise to deliver your letters to the Governor."

"We're much obliged to you," said Sandorf. "If you do that, you do all you can! How shall we reward you?"

"Your thanks are sufficient, gentlemen," said the warder, who could not conceal his emotion.

He soon brought in the writing materials. The prisoners spent the greater part of the day in making their last arrangements. Sandorf said all that a father's heart could prompt in his instructions regarding his baby girl, who would soon be an orphan; Bathory all that a husband and father could think of in bidding a loving farewell to his wife and son; Zathmar all that a master could say to an old servant who remained his only friend.

But during the day, although absorbed in their writing, how many times did they stop to listen! How many times did they seek to discover if some distant noise was not coming along the corridors of the donjon! How many times did it seem to them as though the door of their cell had opened, and that they were to be permitted one last embrace of wife, son, or daughter! That would have been some consolation! But, in truth, the pitiless order deprived them of this last adieu and spared them the heart-rending scene.

The door did not open. Doubtless neither Madame Bathory nor her son, nor the steward, Lendeck, to whose care Sandorf's daughter had been given, knew any more where the prisoners had been taken to after their arrest than Borik in his prison at Trieste. Doubtless, also, neither knew of the doom in store for the conspirators.

Thus passed the earlier hours of the day. Occasionally Sandorf and his friends would talk for a while. Occasionally they would be silent for some time, and then the whole of their lives would be lived over again in their memories with an intensity of impression quite supernatural. It was not with the past, as affecting the past that they were entirely concerned; the recollections seemed all to shape themselves with a view to the present. Was it, then, a prescience of that eternity which was about to open on them, of that incomprehensible and incommensurate state of things which is called the infinite?

Bathory and Zathmar abandoned themselves without reserve to their reveries, but Sandorf was invincibly dominated by an idea, which had taken possession of him. He could not doubt that there had been treachery in this mysterious affair. For a man of his character to die without punishing the traitor, whoever he was, without knowing even who had betrayed him, was to die twice over. Who had got hold of this message to which the police owed the discovery of the conspiracy and the arrest of the conspirators? Who had read it, who had given it up, who had sold it, perhaps? Pondering over this insoluble problem, Sandorf's excited brain became prey to a sort of fever. And while his friends wrote on, or remained silent and motionless, he strode about, uneasy and agitated, pacing the floor of his cell like a wild beast shut up in a cage.

A phenomenon – strange, but not unintelligible in accordance with acoustical law – came at last to his aid and whispered the secret he had despaired of discovering.

Several times he had stopped short as he turned at the angle, which the dividing wall of the cell made with the main wall of the corridor, on to which the different cells opened. In this angle, just where the door was hinged, he seemed to hear a murmur of voices, distant and hardly recognizable. At first he paid no attention to this, but suddenly a name was pronounced – his own – and he listened intently. At once he detected an acoustical phenomenon, such as is observable in the interiors of galleries and domes, or under vaults of ellipsoidal form. The voice, travelling from one point of the ellipse, after following the contour of the walls without being perceptible at any intermediate point, is plainly heard at the other focus. Such is the phenomenon met with in the crypts of the Pantheon, in Paris, in the interior of the dome of St. Peter's, at Rome, and in the whispering gallery at St. Paul's, in London. The faintest word uttered at one focus of these curves is distinctly heard at the focus opposite.

There could be no doubt that two or more persons were talking either in the corridor or in a cell situated at the end of the diameter, the focal point of which was close to the door of the cell occupied by Sandorf.

By a sign he called his two companions to him. The three stood listening.

Fragments of phrases distinctly reached their ears; phrases broken off and dying away as every now and then the speakers moved from and towards the point whose position determined the phenomenon.

And these are the phrases they heard at different intervals:

"Tomorrow, after the execution, you'll be free."

"And then we'll share Count Sandorf's fortune..."

"Without me you'd never have deciphered that message."

"And without me, if I hadn't taken it from the pigeon, you'd never have got hold of it..."

"Well, no one would suspect that the police owe..."

"Even the prisoners have no suspicion."

"Neither relatives nor friends are coming to see them."

"Until tomorrow, Sarcany"

"Until tomorrow, Silas Toronthal."

Then the voices fell silent, and they heard the sound of a door being shut.

"Sarcany! Silas Toronthal!" exclaimed Sandorf. "That's where it came from!"

He looked at his friends and was quite pale. His heart stopped beating in the grip of the spasm. His eyes dilated, his neck stiffened, his head sank back to his shoulder: everything showed that his energetic nature was in the grasp of terrible anger, excited to its furthest extreme.

"Those two! The scoundrels! Those two!" he repeated with a roar.

Then he collected himself, looked round him, and strode across the cell.

"Escape! Escape!" he exclaimed. "We must escape!"

And this man, who would have walked bravely to death a few hours later, this man who had never even thought of making an effort for his life, this man had now but one thought to live, to live to punish those two traitors, Sarcany and Toronthal!

"Yes! To be revenged!" exclaimed Bathory and Zathmar.

"To be revenged? No! To do justice!"

All Count Sandorf was in those words.

A few minutes afterwards they were shown into separate vaulted cells

CHAPTER VI

THE DONJON OF PISINO

The fortress of Pisino is one of the most curious specimens of those formidable buildings, which arose in the Middle Ages. It has a fine feudal aspect. It only wants the knights in its vaulted halls and the ladies in their long brocaded robes and pointed bonnets at its arched windows, and the archers and crossbowmen on its machicolations, its battlemented galleries, its mangonels at the embrasures, its portcullis, and its drawbridges. The stonework is still intact; but the governor with his Austrian uniform, the soldiers with their modern weapons, the warders and turnkeys who no longer wear the particoloured costume, half yellow and half red, of the old days, strike a false note in the midst of all this magnificence of the past.

It was from the donjon of this fortress that Count Sandorf was endeavouring to escape during the last hours before his execution. A mad attempt, no doubt, for the prisoners did not even know in what part of the donjon their prison lay, nor anything of the country across which they would have to journey after their escape.

And perhaps it was fortunate that their ignorance was complete in the matter. Had they known more, they might have recoiled before the difficulties, to say nothing of the impossibilities of such an enterprise.

It is not that this province of Istria offers no favourable chances for an escape, for no matter what direction the fugitives took, they would reach the seacoast in a few hours. It is not that the streets of Pisino are so carefully guarded that there is a risk of being arrested at the very first step. But to escape from the fortress, and particularly from the donjon occupied by the prisoners, had up to then been considered impossible. Even the idea had never occurred to anyone.

The situation and exterior arrangement of the donjon in the fortress of Pisino were as follows: The donjon occupies one side of the terrace with which the town here ends. Leaning over the parapet of this terrace, the eye plunges into a deep ravine, whose rugged sides, covered with thick entanglements of creepers, are cut down perpendicularly. Nothing overhangs the wall; there is not a step to enable any one to ascend or descend; not a fence to halt at; not a prominence to seize hold upon in any part of it; nothing but the uncertain lines, smooth, rubbed, and irregular, which mark the oblique cleavage of the rocks. In a word, it is an abyss, which attracts, fascinates, and never gives back anything that drops into it.

Above this abyss rises one of the sidewalls of the donjon, pierced with a few windows giving light to the cells on the different floors. Were a prisoner to lean out of one of these openings, he would recoil with terror, lest vertigo drag him into the void below! And if he fell, what would be his fate? His body would be dashed to pieces on the rocks at the bottom, or it would be carried away by the torrent whose current during flood is irresistible.

This abyss is the Buco, as it is called in the district. Through it runs a river known as the Foiba. This river finds its only outlet in a cavern, which it has gradually cut out of the rocks, and into which it falls with the impetuosity of a tide-race or a whirlpool. Where does it go as it passes under the town? No one knows. Where does it reappear? Of this cavern, or rather this channel, bored in the schists and clays – no one knows the length, the height, or the direction. Who can say what thousands of angles, what forests of pillars supporting the enormous substructure of the fortress and entire city its waters are dashed against in their course? Many bold explorers, when the water level has been neither too high nor too low, have taken a light boat and endeavoured to descend the Foiba through the gloomy tunnel, but the arches have been too low, and have soon interposed an impracticable obstacle. In fact, nothing was known of this subterranean river. Perhaps it was lost in some still deeper cavern, and perhaps it entered the Adriatic below the tidemark.

Such, then, was the Buco, of which Count Sandorf did not even know the existence; and as the only escape was by the window of his cell, which opened above the Buco, he would be almost as certain to meet his death there as if he stood in front of the firing party on the morning of his execution.

Zathmar and Bathory waited but for the time to act, ready to remain behind, if necessary, and sacrifice themselves to help Count Sandorf, or ready to follow him if their flight would not hamper his.

"We'll all three go," said Sandorf. "Wait till we get out before we separate!"

Eight o'clock then struck from the clock in the town. The prisoners had only twelve hours to live.

Night began to close in – a night, which promised to be very dark. Thick, almost motionless, clouds unrolled themselves cumbrously across the sky. The atmosphere was heavy, almost unbreathable, and saturated with electricity. A violent storm was coming on. Lightning had not yet passed between these masses of vapour, heaped around like so many accumulators, but distant growlings were heard along the summits of the hills that encircle Pisino.

Under such circumstances there was some chance of success, if an unknown gulf had not gaped beneath the feet of the fugitives. In a dark night they might not be seen. In a wild night they might not be heard.

As Sandorf had instantly recognized, flight was only possible through the window of the cell. To force the door, to cut into its strong planks of oak, all bound and ironed, was not to be dreamt of. Besides, the step of a sentinel resounded on the flags of the corridor. And once the door was cleared, how were they to find their way through the labyrinth of the fortress? How were they to pass the portcullis and drawbridges, at which there were always so many men on guard? On the side of the Buco there was no sentinel; but the Buco was a better defence to the face of the donjon than a cordon of sentries.

Sandorf then went to the window and examined it, to see if they could squeeze through.

This window was exactly three and half feet wide and two feet high. The gap widened as it ran outwards through the wall, which hereabouts was nearly four feet thick. A solid crossbar of iron guarded it. It was fixed in the side near the interior opening. There were none of those wooden boards, which allow the light only to enter from above, for they would have been useless, owing to the position of the opening. If then the crossbar could be removed or displaced, it would be easy to get through the window, which was not unlike an embrasure in a fortress wall.

But once the passage was free, how were they to make the descent down the perpendicular side? By a ladder? The prisoners had not one and could not make one. By the bedclothes? They had only the heavy woollen counterpanes thrown on the mattresses, which lay on the iron frames fixed to the wall. It would have been impossible to escape by the

"You have now three heads," said Sandorf, "and that must be enough for you."

window, if Count Sandorf had not noticed a chain, or rather an iron rope, hanging outside, which might aid them to escape.

The cable was the lightning conductor fixed to the crest of the roof above the side of the donjon, the wall of which rose straight from the Buco.

"Do you see that cable?" said Count Sandorf to his two friends. "You must have the pluck to use it, if you want to escape!"

"The pluck we have," said Zathmar, "but have we the strength?"

"What does it matter?" replied Bathory, "If strength fails us, we shall die an hour or two sooner that is all!"

"There's no need to die, Stephen," said Sandorf. "Listen to me, and you also, Ladislas; do not miss any of my words. If we possessed a rope, we should not hesitate to hang ourselves outside the window, so that we might slip down it to the ground. Now this cable is better than a rope, because its rigidity will render its descent much easier. Like all lighting conductors, there's no doubt but that it's fastened to the wall with staples. These staples will be fixed points on which our feet may find a rest. There's no swinging to dread, because the cable is fixed to the wall. There's no vertigo to fear, because it's night and you'll see nothing. Once through the window, with courage and sangfroid, we'll be free. It's possible we may risk our lives, but it gives us ten chances to one; whereas, if we wait till the morning, and our keepers find us here, it's hundreds upon hundreds to one that we will die!"

"Be it so," replied Zathmar.

"Where does the cable end?" asked Bathory.

"In a well probably," answered Sandorf, "but certainly outside the donjon, and we'll take advantage of it. I do not know. I only see one thing at the end of it, and that is liberty – perhaps!"

Count Sandorf was right in his supposition that the lightning conductor was fastened to the wall by staples at equal distances. The descent would thus be easy, for the fugitives could use the staples as stepping-stones to keep them from sliding down too swiftly. But what they did not know was that when it left the crest of the plateau on which rose the wall of the donjon, the iron cable became free, floating, abandoned in the void, and its lower end plunged into the waters of the Foiba then swollen by recent rains. Where they reckoned on finding firm ground at the bottom of the gorge was foaming torrent, leaping impetuously into the caverns of the Buco. If they had known this, would they then have recoiled from their attempted escape? No.

"Death for death," said Sandorf. "We may die after doing all we can to escape death."

The first thing was to clear the passage through the window. The crossbar that obstructed it would have to be removed. How was this to be done without a pair of pincers, a wrench, or any other tool? The prisoners had not even a knife.

"The rest will not be difficult," said Sandorf, "but that may prove impossible! To work!"

And he climbed up to the window, seized the crossbar vigorously with his hand, and felt that it would not require such a very great effort to pull it down.

The iron bars, which formed it, were loose in their sockets. The stone, split away at the edges, did not offer very much resistance. Probably the lightning conductor, before it was repaired, had been in inferior condition for its purpose, and electric sparks had been attracted by the iron of the crossbar, and had acted on the wall; and how powerful such influence would be we are well aware. This may have been the cause of the breakages round the sockets into which the ends of the bars were thrust, and of the decomposition of the stone, which was reduced to a sort of spongy state, as if it had been pierced by millions of electric points.

This explanation was given by Stephen Bathory as soon as he noticed the phenomenon.

But it was not explanation, but work that was wanted, and that without losing a moment. If they could manage to clear the extremities of the bars after forcing them backwards and forwards in their sockets, so as to knock off the angles of the stone, it might be easy to push the ironwork out of the embrasure, which widened as it went outwards. The noise of the fall was not likely to be heard amid the long rollings of the thunder, which were going on almost continuously in the lower strata of the clouds.

But we shall never get that ironwork out with our hands," said Zathmar.

"No!" answered Sandorf. "We ought to have a piece of iron, a blade..."

Something of the sort was necessary; there could be no doubt. Friable as the wall might be round the sockets, the nails would be broken, and the fingers worn till they bled in trying to reduce it to powder. It could never be done without some hard point or other.

Sandorf looked round the cell, which was feebly lighted from the corridor by the small fanlight over the door. Then he felt the walls, on the chance of a nail having been left in them. He found nothing. Then it occurred to him that it would not be impossible to take off one of the legs of the iron bedsteads, which were fixed to the wall. The three set to work, and soon Bathory called to his companions in a whisper.

The rivet of one of the metal laths forming the latticework of the bed had given way. All that was necessary was to seize hold of this by the free end and twist it backwards and forwards until it broke off.

This was soon done. Sandorf thus obtained a thin piece of iron, about an inch wide and five inches long, which he wrapped round the end with his silk cravat, and with it he began to clear away the four sockets.

This could not be done without some noise. Fortunately the rumbling of the thunder prevented the noise from being heard. During the intervals of silence Sandorf stopped, to resume his task as soon as the storm began again. The work advanced rapidly.

Bathory and Zathmar took up their positions near the door and listened, so as to stop him when the sentry went by.

Suddenly a "Sh-sh-sh" escaped from Zathmar's lips.

The work instantly stopped.

"What's the matter?" asked Bathory.

"Listen," answered Zathmar.

His ear was again at the focus of the ellipsoidal curve, and again there was evident the acoustical phenomenon which had told the prisoners the secret of the treachery.

These are the fragments of speech which were caught at short intervals:

"Tomorrow ... set ... liberty ..."

"Yes ... books closed ... and ..."

"After the execution ... I shall rejoin my comrade, Zirone, in Sicily."

"Yours has been a short visit to the donjon of ..."

Evidently Sarcany and a warder were engaged in conversation. Further, Sarcany had pronounced the name of a certain Zirone, who was mixed up in the whole affair. Sandorf made a careful note of the new name.

Unfortunately the last word, which would have been so useful for the prisoners to know, did not reach them. At the end of the last sentence a

Sandorf climbed into the embrasure

violent clap of thunder took place, and while the electricity followed the lightning conductor, a shower of sparks escaped from the strip of metal that Count Sandorf held in his hand. Had it not been for the silk with which he held it he would probably have been affected by the discharge.

And so the last word, the name of the donjon was lost in a loud peal of thunder. The prisoners could not hear it. Had they known in what fortress they were confined, and through what district they would have to make their way, how much greater would have been the chances of an escape attempted under such difficult circumstances!

Count Sandorf resumed his task at the window. Three out of the four sockets were already scraped away sufficiently to allow the ends of the crossbar to be moved out of them. The fourth was then attacked by the light of the dazzling flashes, which constantly illumined the sky.

At half past ten o'clock the work was done. The crossbar was clear of the walls, and could be slipped out of the embrasure. It only had to be pushed forward and dropped on the outside of the wall. And this was done as soon as Zathmar heard that the sentry had reached the far end of the corridor.

The crossbar was moved along the embrasure. It fell over and vanished.

At the moment there was a lull in the storm. Sandorf listened to hear when the heavy frame struck the ground. He heard not a sound!

"The donjon is built on a high rock which rises from the valley," remarked Bathory.

"The height does not matter!" answered Sandorf. "There can be no doubt that the lightning conductor reaches the ground, because that is necessary for it to be of any use. And so we shall reach the ground without the risk of a fall."

The reasoning was right, as a rule, but it was wrong in this instance, for the end of the conductor was plunged in the waters of the Foiba.

The window being clear, the moment for escape had come.

"My friends," said Sandorf, "this is what we had better do. I am the youngest, and, I think, the strongest. It is my place therefore to be the first to go down this iron rope. In case of some obstacle, which is impossible for us to foresee, preventing my reaching the ground, I may have strength enough to climb back to the window. Two minutes after I have gone, Stephen, you get out of the window and follow me. Two minutes after him, Ladislas, you come the same way. Once we've reached the foot of the donjon, we'll act according to circumstances."

"We'll obey you, Mathias," answered Bathory. "We'll do what you tell us to do; we'll go where you tell us to go. But we do not like you taking the greatest share of the danger on yourself…"

"Our lives are not worth as much as yours," added Zathmar.

"They're worth quite as much in the face of an act of justice which has to be done," answered Count Sandorf. "And if one of us alone survives, he'll be the one to perform that act! Shake hands, my friends!"

And then, while Zathmar went to watch at the door of the cell, Sandorf climbed into the embrasure. A moment afterwards he was hanging in the air. Then, while his knees gripped the iron rope, he slid down, hand under hand, feeling with his feet for the staples on which to rest.

The storm burst forth again with extraordinary violence. It did not rain, but the wind was terrific. Flash overlapped flash. The zigzags crossed and crossed above the donjon, attracted by its isolated position and its towering height. The point of the lightning rod gleamed with pallid brilliancy as the electricity streamed off in a long spear point of flame, and the cable shook and swung with the furious lashing of the storm.

The risk that was run in hanging on to this conductor, through which the electricity was travelling, to lose itself in the waters of the Buco, was terrible. Had the apparatus been in perfect condition there would have been no danger of a stroke, for the extreme conductibility of the metal compared to that of the human body, which is very much less, would have preserved the daring man who was suspended from it. But if the point of the conductor were blunted, or there were any solution of continuity in the cable, or a rupture occurred at any spot below, a stroke was quite possible due to the meeting of the positive and the negative; and this without a lightning flash, owing to the tension of the accumulation in the defective apparatus.

Count Sandorf was fully aware of the danger to which he was exposed. A sentiment more powerful than that of the instinct of preservation made him brave it. He slipped down slowly, cautiously, through the electric emanations, which enveloped him as in a mist. His foot sought each staple down the wall, and for an instant he paused, and as a blinding flash illumined the abyss beneath him he tried, but in vain, to discover its depth.

When Mathias had descended about sixty feet from the window, he found a firm resting-place. It was a sort of ledge a few inches wide, which marked the beginning of the base of the wall. The lightning conductor did not end here, it went down lower, and – unknown to the fugitive – from this point downwards it was unfastened and floated free, sometimes skirting the rocky wall, sometimes swinging in mid-air, sometimes scraping against the rocks, which overhung the abyss.

Count Sandorf stopped to recover his breath. His feet rested on the ledge, his hands grasped the iron cable. He saw that he had reached the first course of the masonry of the donjon. But how far he was above the valley he could not estimate. It must be very deep, he thought.

In fact a few large birds, dazed with the blinding brilliancy of the lightning, were flying round him with heavily flapping wings, and instead of rising sank out of sight beneath his feet. Hence he must be on the brink of a precipice which fell away, deep down below him.

As the birds disappeared he heard a noise above, and by the light of a vivid flash he saw a confused mass detach itself from the wall.

It was Stephen Bathory escaping from the window. He had grasped the conductor and was slowly slipping down to join Count Sandorf. Mathias waited for him, his feet firmly planted on the narrow ledge. There Stephen could wait while he continued the descent.

In a few minutes both were standing on the narrow stonework.

As soon as the thunder ceased for an instant they could speak, and hear each other.

"And Ladislas?" asked Sandorf.

"He will be here in a minute."

"Nothing wrong aloft?"

"Nothing."

"Good! I'll make room for Ladislas; and you, Stephen, wait till he reaches you."

"Agreed."

A tremendous flash seemed to envelope them in flame. It seemed as though the electricity coursing through the cable had penetrated their nerves. They thought they had been struck.

"Mathias! Mathias!" exclaimed Bathory, under an impression of terror that he could not master.

"Be cool! I'm going down! You'll follow!" was Sandorf's reply.

And already he had seized the cable, with the intention of slipping to the first staple below, where he intended to wait for his companion.

Suddenly there were shouts from above. They seemed to come from the window of the cell. Then these words rang out:

"Save yourselves!"

It was Zathmar's voice.

A tremendous flash seemed to envelope them in flame.

Immediately a bright light shot from the wall, followed by a sharp report. This time it was not the cable broken by a lightning flash, which lit up the gloom; it was not the roar of the thunder, which resounded in the air. A gun had been fired, a chance shot probably from one of the embrasures of the donjon. It was just as much a signal to the guard as if a bullet had been aimed at the fugitives. The escape had been discovered.

The sentry had heard some noise. He had called five or six of the warders and entered the cell. The absence of two of the prisoners had been immediately discovered, the state of the window showed how they had escaped. And Zathmar rushing to the window had given the alarm.

"Poor fellow!" exclaimed Bathory. "To desert him, Mathias! To desert him!"

A second time there came the discharge of a gun. The report mingled with the roll of the thunder.

"Heaven have pity on him!" said Sandorf. "But we must escape – we must, to avenge him! Come, Stephen, come!"

It was time. Other windows on the lower storey of the donjon were being opened. New discharges lighted them up. Shouts were heard. Perhaps the warders could run round the base of the wall and cut off the retreat of the fugitives! Perhaps they might be shot!

"Come!" exclaimed Sandorf for the last time.

And he slid down the iron cable, which Bathory grasped immediately after him.

Then they saw that the rope hung loosely over the abyss. Resting-places, staples, there were none. They were swinging wildly at the end of the rope, which cut their hands as it slipped through them. Down they went, with their knees chafing and bleeding, without the power to stop themselves as the bullets whistled past.

For a minute, for eighty feet and more, they glided down – down – asking themselves if the abyss in which they were engulfed were really bottomless. Already the roar of the raging waters below them could be heard. Then they understood that the lightning conductor led down into the torrent. What was to be done? To climb back to the base of the donjon they could not; their strength was unequal to the task. And death for death, it was better to chance that which waited for them in the depths below.

Suddenly there came a fearful clap of thunder and an intense electric glare. Although the conductor was not struck, yet the tension of the electricity was such that the iron rope grew white as a platinum thread beneath the discharge of a battery or pile.

Bathory uttered a cry of despair and let go.

Sandorf saw him pass, almost touching him, with his arms wide open.

And then he let go the iron rope, which glowed in his hands, and he fell more than forty feet into the torrent of the Foiba, which foamed along at the foot of the unknown Buco.

CHAPTER VII

ALONG THE FOIBA

It was about eleven o'clock. The clouds had begun to dissolve in drenching showers. Mingled with the rain there fell huge hailstones, which shot into the waters of the Foiba and rattled over the rocks down its sides like the stream of lead from a machine gun. The firing from the embrasures had ceased. Why waste ammunition on the fugitives? The Foiba would only give them up as corpses – if even it did that.

As soon as Count Sandorf fell into the torrent he found himself swept helplessly into the Buco. In a few moments he passed from the intense light with which the electricity filled the ravine into the profoundest darkness. The roar of the waters had taken the place of the roll of the thunder. For into that impenetrable cavern there entered none of the outside light or sounds.

"Help!"

There was a cry. It was Stephen Bathory. The cold of the water had called him back to life, but he could not keep himself afloat, and he would have been drowned had not a vigorous arm seized him as he was sinking.

"I'm here! Stephen! Don't be afraid!"

Count Sandorf was by his side, holding him with one hand while he swam with the other.

The position was critical. Bathory could hardly move his limbs. They had been half-paralyzed by the stroke. Although the pain of his burnt hands had been sensibly lessened by their plunge into the cold, the sense of inertia into which he had been thrown did not allow of his using them. Had Sandorf abandoned him for a moment he would have been drowned; and yet Sandorf had enough to do to save himself.

There was the complete uncertainty as to the direction, which this torrent took, the place it ended, the river or sea into which it flowed. Had even Sandorf known that the river was the Foiba the position could not

have been more desperate than if he knew what became of its impetuous waters. Bottles thrown into the entrance of the cavern had never
come to sight again in any stream on the Istrian peninsula, perhaps from
their having been broken against the rocks in their course, perhaps from
having been swept below into some mysterious rift in the earth's crust.

The fugitives were carried along with extreme rapidity – and thus
found it easy to keep on the surface. Bathory had become unconscious.
He was quite helpless and motionless in the hands of Sandorf, who
fought well for both, but felt that all would soon end in his sinking from
sheer exhaustion. To the danger of being dashed against some projecting rock, or the side of the cavern, or the hanging prominences of the
roof, there was added that of being sucked down in one of the whirlpools which foamed in many a corner where a sharp angle of the bank
gave the current a sudden curve. Twenty times were Sandorf and his
friend seized in one of these liquid suckers and irresistibly drawn to its
centre in the manner of the Maelstrom. Then they would be spun round
by the gyratory movement, and then thrown off from the edge like a
stone from a sling as the eddy broke.

Half an hour went by under such circumstances with death imminent
each minute and each second. Sandorf, endowed with superhuman energy, had not yet yielded in despair. He rejoiced that his companion was
almost senseless. Had he retained the instinct of self-preservation he
would struggle, and then Sandorf would be obliged to leave him to his
fate, or both would be overwhelmed.

Nevertheless, the state of affairs could not continue very long. Sandorf's strength began to fail him. Every now and then as he supported
Bathory's head, his own would sink back into the liquid pillow. Suddenly
respiration became difficult. He gasped for breath, he was choking, he
was wrestling with asphyxia. Often he had to leave go of his companion,
whose head sank instantly; but invariably he managed to grip him again,
and that amid the wild racing of the waters which shouldered back and
piled on each other by the occasional narrowing of the channel, thun-
dered along in foam.

At last Count Sandorf thought that all was lost. Bathory slipped from
his grasp. He tried to rescue him. He could not. He had lost him; and he
himself was dragged down to the torrent's bed.

A violent shock nearly broke his shoulder. He stretched out his hand
instinctively. His fingers closed on a clump of roots, which were swimming by.

The roots were those of a tree trunk being brought down by the torrent. Sandorf fastened on to this raft and dragged himself back to the surface of the Foiba. Then while he grasped the roots with one hand he sought for his companion with the other. A moment afterwards Bathory was seized by the arm and after a violent effort hoisted on to the trunk, where Sandorf took his place beside him. Both were for a time saved from the danger of drowning, but they had bound up their destiny with that of their raft, and given themselves over to the caprices of the rapids of the Buco.

Sandorf had not lost his consciousness for a moment. He made it his first care to make sure that Bathory could not slip from the tree. By excess of precaution he placed himself behind him, so as to hold him in his arms. In this position he kept watch for the end. At the first glimpse of light that penetrated the cavern he would see what the waters were like as they emerged. But there was nothing as yet to show that they were near the end of this wonderful stream.

However, the position of the fugitives had improved. The tree was about twelve feet long, and the spreading roots were now and then struck against the projections. If it were not subjected to a very violent shock its stability in spite of the irregularities of the stream seemed to be assured. Its speed could not be less than nine miles an hour, being equal to that of the torrent that bore it.

Sandorf had recovered all his coolness. He tried to revive his companion, whose head rested on his knees. He found that his heart still beat, but that his breathing was difficult. He bent over and tried to breathe a little air into his lungs. Would that the preliminaries of asphyxia had not injured him without hope of relief!

Soon Bathory made a slight movement. More marked expirations came from his parted lips.

At last a few words escaped from his mouth.

"My wife!... My son!... Mathias!"

His whole life was in those four words.

"Stephen, do you know me? Do you know me?" asked Sandorf, who had to shout to make himself heard above the wild tumult with which the torrent filled the vaults of the Buco.

"Yes... Yes... I know you! Speak!... Speak! Give me your hand!"

"We're no longer in immediate danger," replied Count Sandorf. "We're on a raft. To where, I cannot say, but at least we can rest."

"Mathias! And the donjon?"

Pisino and the Foiba

"It's already far off! They'll think we met our deaths in the torrent; and never dream of pursuing us. Wherever this torrent leads, whether a river or the open sea, we shall get there alive! Do not lose heart, Stephen! I'll look after you. Rest some more and recover your strength, you'll have need of it soon enough. In a few hours we shall be safe! We shall be free!"

"And Ladislas?" murmured Bathory.

Mathias Sandorf did not reply. What could he say? Zathmar, after giving the alarm from the window, must have been seized, so that flight was impossible, and now under strict guard could in no way be helped by his friends.

Stephen's head fell back. He had not the physical strength to master his torpor. But Sandorf watched over him, ready for anything, even to abandon the raft, if it happened to crash up against the rocks, which in the midst of the profound darkness were impossible to avoid.

It was nearly two in the morning when the speed of the current, and consequently that of the tree, began to slow. Evidently, the channel was getting wider, and the waters, finding a freer passage between the walls, were travelling at a more moderate pace. It was not unreasonable to expect that the end of the subterranean pass was close at hand.

But if the walls were widening, the roof was closing in on them. By raising an arm, Count Sandorf could skim the surface of the irregular schists that stretched above his head. Frequently there came a grating noise as the roots of the tree ground against the roof. Then the trunk would stagger as it recoiled from some violent collision and swing off in a new direction. And then it would drift across the stream, and twist and writhe till the fugitives feared they would be wrenched away. That danger over – after it had been experienced several times – there remained another of which Sandorf coolly calculated the consequences. What was to happen if the roof continued to close down? Already his only way of escape was to fall backwards the instant his hand felt a projecting rock. Would he have to take to the stream? As far as he was concerned, he might attempt it; but how could his companion keep afloat? And if the channel kept low for a long distance how were they to come out of it alive? How indeed – and was death to be the end after so many escapes from death?

Sandorf, energetic as he was, felt his heart wrung with anguish. He saw that the supreme moment was approaching. The tree's roots ground against the overhanging rocks more violently; and at times the top of the trunk was driven so deeply into the current that the water entirely covered it.

"But," said Sandorf, "the outlet cannot be far off."

And then he looked to see if some vague streak of light did not filter into the darkness ahead. By this time was the night advanced enough for the darkness outside to have lifted? Was the lightning still flashing beyond the Buco? If so a little light perhaps would show itself in this channel, which threatened to get too small to hold the Foiba. But there was nothing. Nothing but absolute darkness and roaring waters of which even the foam remained black!

Suddenly there was a terrific shock. By its forward end the tree had dashed against an enormous pendant from the roof. As it struck it completely turned over. But Sandorf did not let go of it. With one hand he desperately clung to the roots, with the other he held his companion. And the tree sank, and with it the men sank into the mass of waters, which then filled the channel to the roof.

This lasted for nearly a minute. Sandorf felt that he was lost. Instinctively he stopped breathing, so as to economize the little air that remained in his lungs.

Suddenly through the liquid mass, although his eyes were closed, he felt the impression of a vivid light. A lightning flash it was, followed by the noise of thunder.

It was the light at last.

The Foiba had emerged from the subterranean channel and was flowing in the open. But whither was it flowing? On what sea coast was its mouth? That was still the insoluble question – a question of life or death.

The trunk of the tree had floated to the surface again. Bathory, by a strong effort was dragged up and took his place at the end. Then Sandorf looked before him, around him, above him.

Up stream, a dark mass was being left behind. This was the huge cliff of the Buco in which the underground channel opened, which gave passage to the waters of the Foiba. Day was already showing itself, by the scattered streaks of light overhead, vague as the nebulae, which the eye can only just see on a winter's night. From time to time a few pale lightning flashes lighted up the background amid the dull roar of occasional thunder. The storm was slowly going or else dying away.

To the right, to the left, Sandorf threw a glance of keen anxiety. He saw that the river flowed between two high cliffs, and that its speed was terrific.

They were in a rapid, which was taking them along amid all its races and eddies. But above their head now was the infinite, and no longer the narrowing vault with its ledges threatening each instant to crush them. But there was no bank on which they could set foot, no slope on which they could disembark. Two steep high walls shut in the narrow Foiba, and it was really the old channel with its vertical walls, but without its roof of stone.

The last immersion had greatly revived Bathory. His hand had sought Sandorf's, who clasped it as he whispered:

"Saved!"

But had he a right to use the word "saved", when he did not even now where the river ended or what country it traversed, or when they would be able to abandon their raft? Such, however, was his energy that he sat upright on the tree and three times shouted to the world aloud:

"Saved! Saved! Saved!"

Who could hear him? No one on those rocky cliffs, whose boulders and schists had not mould enough to bear even a bramble. The country hidden by the high banks would be sought by no human being – a desolate country through which the Foiba runs imprisoned like an artificial canal between its rocky walls. Not a brook flows in to feed it. Not a bird skims its surface, not even a fish ventures into its too rapid waters. Here and there huge rocks rise in its bed and their parched summits show that the watercourse with all its violence is nothing but a sudden overflowing due to heavy rain. At ordinary times the bed of the Foiba is simply a deep ravine.

The only danger now was lest the tree should be hurled on to the rocks. It avoided them of itself as it kept in the middle of the currents, which swept round them. But it was impossible to check its speed to get to shore in case a suitable landing place was noticed.

An hour passed and no immediate danger appeared. The final flashes had died out in the distance, and the storm only manifested itself by the heavy thundering which reverberated among the lofty clouds whose long narrow bands streaked the horizon. Day was breaking and the grey was rising over the sky that had been cleared by the tumult of the night. It was about four o'clock in the morning.

Stephen lay in Sandorf's arms.

A distant report was heard towards the southwest.

"What is that?" asked Sandorf, who was still on the lookout. "Is that a gun announcing that a harbour is open? If so we cannot be far from the

Bathory was seized by the arm

sea. What port can it be? Trieste? No, for there is the east, where the sun is rising! Can it be Pola, at the extreme south of Istria? But then..."

A second report was now heard, and this was almost immediately followed by a third.

"Three cannon shots," said Sandorf. "That is the signal for an embargo placed upon ships that are outward bound. Has that anything to do with our escape?"

He might fear so. Assuredly the authorities would neglect nothing to keep the fugitives from getting away from the coast.

"Heaven help us!" murmured Sandorf.

And now the lofty cliffs, which shut in the Foiba, began to shorten. Nothing could be seen of the country. Sudden bends marked the horizon and bounded the view a few hundred feet away. To take the bearings was impossible.

The much-widened riverbed, silent and deserted, allowed the current to flow more slowly. A few trees brought down by the stream were floating near them. The June morning was quite chill. In their wet clothes, the fugitives shook till their teeth chattered.

Towards five o'clock the cliffs had given place to long, low banks, and the country on each side was flat and naked. The Foiba had widened to about half a mile, and become a stretch of stagnant water, which might be called a lagoon, if not a lake. In the distance towards the west, there were a few vessels. Some at anchor, some with their canvas set waiting for the breeze; and these seemed to show that the lagoon was a haven cut well back into the coast. The sea then was not far off, and there would be no difficulty in finding it. But it would not be prudent to seek shelter with the fishermen. To trust themselves in their power, supposing they had heard of the escape, would be to chance being handed over to the Austrian gendarmes, who were probably now scouring the country.

Sandorf knew not what to do, when the tree struck against a stump on the left side of the lagoon and stopped dead. The roots got entangled with a clump of brushwood and the tree swung round parallel with the bank as if it had been a boat under the control of a steersman.

Sandorf got ashore, and looked around. He wished to make sure that no one saw him.

As far as he could see there was no one, fisherman or otherwise, within sight on the lagoon.

And yet within a hundred yards of him there was a man stretched at full length on the sand who could see both him and his companion.

Sandorf, thinking all was safe, went back to the tree, lifted his companion in his arms and laid him on the bank. He knew nothing of where he was or where he was to go.

In reality this sheet of water, which serves as the mouth of the Foiba, is neither a lagoon nor a lake, but an estuary.

It bears the name of the Leme Canal, and it communicates with the Adriatic by a narrow creek between Orsera and Rovigno, on the western side of the Istrian peninsula. But it was not known before this voyage that its waters came from the Foiba, and were brought through the gorge of the Buco during heavy rains.

A few paces from the bank there was a deserted hut, and Sandorf and Bathory after a short rest took shelter in it. There they stripped, and waited while the sun dried their clothes. The fishing vessels were leaving the Leme Canal, and as far as they could see the place was deserted.

The man who had been watching them since they landed now got up, and carefully noted the position of the hut. And then he disappeared round a knoll and made off towards the south.

Three hours afterwards Sandorf and his companion resumed their clothes. They were still damp, but it was necessary to move on.

"We must not stay too long in this hut," said Bathory. "Do you feel yourself strong enough to start?" asked Sandorf.

"I'm almost exhausted with hunger!"

"Let us try to reach the coast! There we may perhaps procure something to eat and something to take us to sea. Come, Stephen!"

And they left the hut, evidently suffering more from hunger than fatigue.

Sandorf's intention was to follow the southern bank of the Leme Canal until he reached the sea. The country was deserted, it is true, but quite a number of streams intersected it on their way to the estuary. This watery network along the banks is nothing more nor less than a vast sponge, and the mud is impassable, so that the fugitives had to strike southwards obliquely, easily keeping their course by the sun, which had now risen. For two hours they kept on without meeting a human being, and without finding anything to satisfy the hunger that was devouring them.

Then the country became less arid. They found a road running east and west, which boasted a milestone that gave no indication as to the region across which they were feeling their way like the blind. There were, however, some hedges of mulberry trees, and farther on a field of sorghum, which enabled them to allay their hunger, or rather to cheat the wants of their stomachs. The sorghum chewed and even eaten, and the refreshing mulberries, might perhaps be enough to keep them from fainting from exhaustion before they reached the coast.

But if the country was inhabited, if a few fields showed that the hand of man was employed about them, the fugitives had to be careful how they met the inhabitants.

About noon five or six foot-passengers appeared on the road. As a matter of caution Sandorf thought he and Bathory had better get out of sight. Fortunately an enclosure round an old ruined farm lay some fifty yards to the left. There, before they had been noticed, he and his companion took refuge in a kind of dark cellar where in the event of any one stopping at the farm they ran little risk of discovery if they waited till the night.

The foot-passengers were peasants and salt-marsh workers. Some were driving a flock of geese, doubtless to market at some town or villa, which could not be very far from the canal. Men and women were clothed in Istrian style, with the jewels, medals, earrings, breast crosses, and filigree pendants, which ornament the ordinary costume of both sexes. The salt-marsh workers were more simply dressed, as with sack on back and stick in hand they marched along to the salterns in the neighbourhood, or perhaps even to the important establishment at Stagnone or Pirano in the west of the province.

Some of them stopped when they reached the farm, and rested for a little on the doorstep. They talked in a loud voice, not without a certain animation, but only of things concerning their trade.

The fugitives leant against the corner and listened. Perhaps these people had already heard of the escape and were talking about it. Perhaps they were saying something, which might reveal in what part of Istria they then were.

Not a word passed on the subject. They could only continue to guess.

"If the country people say nothing about our escape it's a fair inference," said Sandorf, "that they've not yet heard of it."

"That," said Bathory, "would go to prove that we're some distance from the fortress. Considering the rapidity of the torrent which kept us underground for more than six hours, I'm not surprised at that."

"That must be it," said Sandorf.

A couple of hours passed, and then some salt-workers, as they passed the farm without stopping, were heard talking about the gendarmes they had met at the gate of the town. What town? They gave it no name.

Two steep high walls shut in the narrow Foiba

This was not very reassuring. If gendarmes were about, it was probable that they were scouring the country in search of the fugitives.

"But," said Bathory, "considering how we escaped, they might well believe us dead, and never think of pursuit."

"They'll believe we're dead when they find our bodies," answered Sandorf.

There being no doubt that the police were afoot, and in search of them, they decided to stay till night. Although they were tortured with hunger, they dared not leave their retreat, and they were wise.

About five o'clock the tramp of a small troop of horse was heard along the road.

Sandorf, who had been out to the gate of the enclosure, hurriedly rejoined his companion and dragged him into the darkest corner of the cellar. There they hid themselves under a heap of brushwood, and remained motionless.

Half a dozen gendarmes headed by a sergeant were coming along the road towards the east. Would they stop at the farm? Sandorf anxiously asked. If they searched the place they could not fail to find them.

They halted. The sergeant and two of the men dismounted, while the others remained in the saddle, and received orders to search the country along the canal and then to return to the farm, where the rest would meet them at seven o'clock.

The four gendarmes moved off immediately. The sergeant and the two others picketed their horses, and sat down to talk. From the corner of the cellar the fugitives could hear all that passed.

"Yes, we shall go back to the town this evening and get the orders for tonight," said the sergeant in reply to one of the men. "The telegraph may bring us fresh instructions from Trieste."

The town in question was not Trieste; that was one point of which Count Sandorf made a note.

"Are you not afraid," said the second gendarme, "that while we're looking about here the fugitives may have got down the Quarnero Canal?"

"Yes, that's possible," answered the first gendarme, "for they might think it safer than here."

"No matter," said the sergeant, "they risk being found nonetheless, for the whole coast is being scoured from one end to the other."

Second fact worth noting: Sandorf and his companion were on the west coast of Istria, that is to say, near the Adriatic shore, and not on the banks of the opposite canal which runs out at Fiume.

"I think they are having a look round the salt-works at Pirano and Capo d'Istria," said the sergeant.

"They might hide there easily and get on board a vessel crossing the Adriatic and bound for Rimini or Venice."

"They had much better have waited patiently in their cell," said one of the gendarmes philosophically.

"Yes," added the other, "sooner or later they'll be caught, if they have not fished them up out of the Buco! That would finish it, though, and we should not have to trot about the country in all this heat."

"And who says it hasn't finished it?" replied the sergeant. "Perhaps the Foiba has been the executioner, and when it's in flood the wretched men could not have chosen a worse road out of the donjon of Pisino."

The Foiba then was the name of the river, which had carried off Count Sandorf and his companion! It was the fortress of Pisino to which they had been taken after their arrest, and there they had been imprisoned, tried, and sentenced! It was from its donjon that they had escaped! Count Sandorf knew this town of Pisino well! He had at last fixed on this point, which was so important for him to know; and it would no longer be by chance that he would cross the Istrian peninsula, if flight was still possible.

The conversation of the gendarmes did not stop here; but in these few words the fugitives had learnt all they wished to know – except, perhaps, the name of the town by the canal on the Adriatic coast.

Soon the sergeant got up, and walked about the enclosure, watching if his men were returning to the farm. Twice or thrice he entered the ruined house, and looked into the rooms, rather from professional habit than suspicion. He even came to the door of the cellar, and the fugitives would certainly have been discovered if the darkness had not been so great. He even entered it, and tossed about the brushwood in the corner with his scabbard, but without reaching those beneath. At this moment Sandorf and Bathory passed through almost the whole gamut of anguish.

They had resolved to sell their lives dearly if the sergeant reached them. To throw themselves on him, profit by his surprise to deprive him of his arms, to attack him two to one, to kill him or make him kill himself, they had fully made up their minds.

At this moment the sergeant was called out, and he left the cellar without noticing anything suspicious. The four gendarmes sent off to search had just returned to the farm. Despite all they could do they had not come across any traces of the fugitives in the district between the coast and the canal. But they had not come back alone – a man accompanied them.

He was a Spaniard employed in the salt-works in the neighbourhood. He was returning to the town when the gendarmes met him. As he told them that he had been all over the country between the town and the salt-works, they resolved to bring him to the sergeant. The man had no objection to go with them.

The sergeant asked him if he had noticed any strangers in the salt-works.

"No, sergeant," said the man, "but this morning, about an hour after I left the town, I saw two men who had just landed at the point along the canal."

"Two men, do you say?" asked the sergeant.

"Yes, but as in these parts we thought the execution at Pisino took place this morning, and had heard nothing about the escape, I did not pay much attention to the men. Now I know what has occurred I should not be surprised if they were the two you want."

"What's your name?" asked the sergeant.

"Carpena, I'm employed at the salt-works."

From the corner of the cellar Sandorf and Bathory could hear almost every word of this conversation, which affected them so nearly. They however failed to catch the man's name.

"Could you recognize these two men you saw this morning?"

"Yes, probably!"

"Well, you can come and make a declaration, and put yourself at the disposal of the police."

"I'm at your orders."

"Do you know there's a five thousand florins reward for the discovery of the fugitives?"

"Five thousand florins!"

"And the hulks for him who harbours them!"

"You don't say so!"

"Go," said the sergeant.

The Spaniard's news had the effect of sending off the gendarmes. The sergeant ordered his men to mount, and as night had fallen he started for the town, after having thoroughly searched the banks of the canal. Carpena at the same time set out, congratulating himself that the capture of the fugitives would be worth so much to him.

Sandorf and Bathory remained in hiding for some time before they left the cellar, which had served them for a refuge. Their thoughts ran as

"Two men, do you say?" asked the sergeant.

follows: As the gendarmerie were on their traces, as they had been seen and were likely to be recognized, the Istrian provinces were no longer safe for them, and they must leave the country as soon as possible, either for Italy on the other side of the Adriatic, or across Dalmatia and the military frontier.

The first plan offered the best chances of success, providing they could possess themselves of a vessel, or prevail on some fisherman to land them on the Italian coast. And this plan they adopted.

Hence about half-past eight o'clock, as soon as the night was dark enough, Sandorf and his companion, after leaving the ruined farm, started off towards the southwest so as to reach the Adriatic coast. And at first they were obliged to keep to the road to avoid being lost in the marshes of the Leme.

But did not this unknown road lead to the town, which it put into communication with the heart of Istria? Were they not running into great danger? Undoubtedly, but what else could they do?

About half-past nine the vague outline of a town appeared about a quarter of a mile ahead in the darkness; and it was not easy to recognize it.

It was a collection of houses clumsily built in terraces on an enormous mass of rock, which towered over the sea above the harbour cut back into the re-entering angle on one of its sides. The whole was surmounted by a high campanile, whose proportions were much exaggerated in the gloom.

Sandorf had quite decided not to enter the town, where the presence of two visitors would soon be known. He tried therefore to pass round the walls so as to reach one of the points on the coast if possible.

But this they did not do without being followed for some distance by the same man who had already seen them on the Leme Canal – the same Carpena whose information they had heard given to the sergeant of gendarmerie. In fact as he went home and thought over the reward that had been offered, the Spaniard left the road so as to watch it better, and chance, luckily for him, but unluckily for them, again put him on the track of the fugitives.

Almost at the same moment a squadron of police came out from one of the gates of the town and threatened to bar the way. They had only just time to scramble out of sight, and then to hurry at full speed towards the shore by the side of one of the walls.

Here they found a fisherman's hut, with its little windows lighted up and its door open. If they could not find a refuge here, if the fisherman refused to receive them, they were lost.

To seek refuge was to risk everything, but the time had gone by for hesitation. Sandorf and his companion ran towards the door of the hut, and stopped on the threshold. Inside was a man mending his nets by the light of a ship's lantern.

"My friend," asked Count Sandorf, "can you tell me the name of this town?"

"Rovigno."

"And to whom are we speaking?"

"Andrea Ferrato, the fisherman."

"Will Andrea Ferrato consent to give us a night's lodging? "

Andrea Ferrato looked at them, advanced towards the door, caught sight of the squadron of police at the end of the wall, divining doubtless who they were that asked his hospitality and understood that they were lost if he hesitated to reply.

"Come in," he said.

But the two fugitives did not move.

"My friend," said Sandorf, "there are five thousand florins reward for whoever will give up the prisoners who escaped from the donjon of Pisino!"

"I know it."

"There are the hulks," added Sandorf, "for him who harbours them."

"I know it."

"You could deliver us to..."

"I told you to come in; come in, then!" answered the fisherman.

And Andrea Ferrato shut the door as the squadron of police came tramping past the hut.

CHAPTER VIII

THE FISHERMAN'S HUT

Andrea Ferrato was a Corsican, a native of Santa Manza, a little port in the arrondissement of Sartene, situated at the back of the southern point of the island. This port and Bastia and Porto Vecchio are the only ones that open on to that monotonous eastern coast of which the sea has gradually destroyed the capes, filled up the gulfs, effaced the bays, and devoured the creeks.

It was at Santa Manza, on that narrow portion of the sea between Corsica and the Italian mainland, and often among the rocks of the straits of Bonifacio that Andrea Ferrato followed his trade as a fisherman. Twenty years before he had married a young girl of Sartene. Two years afterwards they had had a daughter who was christened Maria. The fisherman's calling is a rough one, particularly when to the fishing for fish there is added the fishing for coral, which has to be sought for at the bottom of the most dangerous channels in the strait. But Andrea Ferrato was bold, robust, indefatigable, and clever with the net as with the trawl. His business prospered. His wife, active and intelligent, ruled the little house at Santa Manza to perfection. Both of them knew how to read, write, and calculate, and were fairly educated, if we compare them with the hundred and fifty thousand who cannot write their names which statistics now reveal to exist out of the two hundred and sixty thousand inhabitants of the island.

Besides – perhaps on account of this education – Andrea Ferrato was very French in his ideas and feelings, although he was of Italian origin, like the majority of the Corsicans. And at that time this had occasioned some animosity against him.

The canton, in fact, situated at the southern extremity of the island, far from Bastia, far from Ajaccio, far from the chief centres of administration, is at heart very much opposed to everything that is not Italian or Sardinian – a regrettable state of things that we hope to see the end of as the rising generation becomes better educated.

Hence, as we have said, there was more or less latent animosity against the Ferratos. In Corsica animosity and hatred are not very far apart. Certain things occurred which embittered this animosity. One day Andrea, driven out of all patience, in a moment of anger killed a well-known vagabond who was threatening him; and he had to seek safety in flight.

But Andrea Ferrato was not at all the man to take refuge in the *maquis*, to live a life of daily strife as much against the police as against the companions and friends of the deceased, to perpetrate a series of revenges, which would end by reaching his own people. Resolving to expatriate himself, he managed to leave Corsica secretly, and reached the Sardinian coast. When his wife had realized their property, given up the house at Santa Manza, sold the furniture, the boat, and the nets, she crossed over and joined him. They had left their native land forever.

But the murder, although it was justifiably committed in self-defence, weighed on Andrea's conscience. With the somewhat superstitious ideas due to his origin, he greatly desired to ransom it. He had heard that a man's death is never pardoned till the day when the murderer saves another life at the risk of his own. He made up his mind to save a life as soon as an occasion presented itself.

Andrea did not remain long in Sardinia, where he would easily have been recognized and discovered. Energetic and brave, although he did not fear for himself he feared for those who belonged to him, he feared that the reprisals of family on family might reach them. He merely waited till he could go without exciting suspicion, and then sailed for Italy, where, at Ancona, an opportunity offered for him to cross the Adriatic to the Istrian coast, of which he availed himself.

And that is the story of why the Corsican had settled at Rovigno. For seventeen years he had followed his trade as a fisherman – and had become as well off as he had been. Nine years afterwards a son was born to him, who was named Luigi. His birth cost his mother her life.

Andrea Ferrato now lived entirely for his daughter and his son. Maria, then aged eighteen, acted as mother to the little boy of eight. And except the deep and constant grief for the loss of his wife the fisherman of Rovigno was as happy as he could be in his work and the consciousness of having done his duty. He was respected throughout the district. He was ever ready to help, and his advice was always valuable. He was known to be clever at his trade. Among the long ridges of rocks, which guard the Istrian shore, he had no reason to regret the Gulf of Santa Manza or the Straits of Bonifacio. He had become an excellent pilot in those parts where the same language is spoken as in Corsica. From his pilotage of the ships between Pola and Trieste he earned almost as much as from his fishing. And in his house the poor were not forgotten, and Maria did her best in works of charity.

But the fisherman of Santa Manza had never forgotten his vow: a life for a life! He had taken one man's life. He would save another's.

That was why, when the two fugitives presented themselves at his door, guessing who they were, knowing the penalty to which he was exposing himself, he had not hesitated to say to them, "Come in," and adding in his thoughts, "And may Heaven protect us all!"

The squadron of police passed the door and did not stop. Sandorf and Bathory could thus fancy they were safe – at least for that night.

The hut was built not in the town itself, but about five hundred yards from its walls, below the harbour and on a ridge of rocks, which commanded the beach. Beyond, at less than a cable's length was the sea, breaking on the sands and stretching away to the distant horizon. Towards the southwest there jutted out the promontory whose curve shuts in the small roadstead of Rovigno.

It had but four rooms, two at the front and two at the back, but there was a lean-to of boards in which the fishing and other tackle was kept. Such was the dwelling of Andrea Ferrato. His boat was a balancello with a square stern about thirty feet long, rigged with a mainsail and foresail – a description of boat well adapted for trawling. When she was not in use she was moored inside the rocks, and a little boat drawn up on the beach was used in journeying to and from her. Behind the house was an enclosure of about half an acre, in which a few vegetables grew among the mulberry and olive trees and the vines. A hedge separated it from a brook about six feet broad; and beyond was the open country.

Such was this humble but hospitable dwelling to which Providence had led the fugitives; such was the host who risked his liberty to give them shelter.

As soon as the door closed on them, Sandorf and Bathory examined the room into which the fisherman had welcomed them.

It was the principal room of the house, furnished in a way that showed the taste and assiduity of a careful housekeeper.

"Would you like something to eat?" asked Andrea.

"Yes, we're dying of hunger!" answered Sandorf. "We've had no food in twelve hours."

"Go and sleep, gentlemen. No one knows you're here."

"You understand, Maria?"

And in a minute Maria had put on the table some salt pork, some boiled fish, a flask of the local wine of the dry grape, with two glasses, two plates, and a white tablecloth. A "veglione," a sort of lamp with three wicks fed with oil, gave light in the room.

Sandorf and Bathory sat down to the table: they were quite exhausted.

"But you?" said they to the fisherman.

"We've had our meal!" answered Andrea.

The two famished men devoured – that is the proper word – the provisions, which were offered with such simplicity and heartiness.

But as they ate they kept their eyes on the fisherman, his daughter and his son, who sat in a corner of the room and looked at them back without saying a word. Andrea was then about forty-two, a man of severe and even sad expression, with a sunburned face, black eyes, and a keen look. He wore the dress of the fishermen of the Adriatic, and was of active, powerful build.

Maria – whose face and figure recalled her mother – was tall, graceful, pretty rather than handsome, with bright black eyes, brown hair, and a complexion lightly tinted by the vivacity of her Corsican blood. Serious by reason of the duties she had fulfilled from her childhood, having in her attitude and movements the serenity a reflective nature gives, everything about her showed an energy that would never fail, no matter in what circumstances she might be placed. Many times she had been sought in marriage by the young fishermen of the country, but in vain. Did not all her life belong to her father and the child who was so dear to him?

That boy Luigi was already an experienced sailor – hardworking, brave and resolute. Bareheaded in wind and rain he accompanied Andrea in his fishing and piloting. Later on he promised to be a vigorous man, well trained and well built, more than bold, even audacious, ready for anything and careless of danger. He loved his father. He adored his sister.

Count Sandorf had been keenly examining these three, united in such touching affection. That he was among people he could trust he felt sure. When the meal was finished, Andrea rose and approaching Sandorf said:

"Go and sleep, gentlemen. No one knows you're here. Tomorrow we can talk."

"No, Andrea Ferrato, no!" said Sandorf. "Our hunger is now appeased! We've recovered our strength! Let us leave the house this instant, where our presence is so dangerous to you and yours."

111

"Yes, let us leave," added Bathory. "And may Heaven reward you for what you've done!"

"Go and sleep; it's necessary," said the fisherman. "The beach is watched tonight. An embargo has been put upon all the ports on the coast. You can do nothing now."

"Be it so, if you wish it," answered Sandorf.

"I wish it."

"One word only. When was our escape known?"

"This morning," answered Andrea. "But there were four prisoners in the donjon of Pisino. You are only two. The third, they say, was set free."

"Sarcany!" exclaimed Sandorf, immediately checking the movement of anger that seized him as he heard the hated name.

"And the fourth?" asked Bathory, without daring to finish the sentence.

"The fourth is still living," answered Ferrato. "His execution has been put off."

"Living!" exclaimed Bathory.

"Yes," answered Sandorf ironically. "They're keeping him till they've got us, to give us the pleasure of dying together."

"Maria," said Ferrato, "take our guests to the room at the back, but do not take a candle. The window must not show from without that there's a light in the room. You can then go to bed. Luigi and I will watch."

"Yes, father," answered the boy.

"Come, sirs," said the girl.

A moment afterwards Sandorf and his companion exchanged a cordial handshake with the fisherman. Then they passed into the chamber, where they found two good mattresses of maize on which they could rest after so many fatigues.

But already Andrea had left the house with Luigi. He wished to assure himself that no one was prowling round the neighbourhood, neither on the beach nor beyond the brook. The fugitives could then sleep in peace till the morning.

The night passed without adventure. The fisherman had frequently been out. He had seen nothing suspicious.

In the morning of the 18th of June, while his guests were still asleep, Andrea went out for news into the centre of the town and along the wharves. There were many groups talking over the events of the past day. The placard stuck up the evening before relating the escape, the penalties incurred and the reward promised, formed the general subject of conversation. Some were gossiping, some detailing the latest news, some repeating the rumours in vague terms, which meant nothing in particular. There was nothing to show that Sandorf and his companion had been seen in the neighbourhood, nor even that there was any suspicion of their presence in the province. About ten o'clock, when the sergeant and his men entered Rovigno, after their night expedition, a rumour spread that two strangers had been seen twenty-four hours before on the Leme Canal. The district from there to the sea had been searched for them in vain. There was not a vestige of their visit. Had they then reached the coast, possessed themselves of a boat, and gone to some other part of Istria, or had they crossed the Austrian frontier? It would seem so.

"Good," said one of the men. "There are five thousand florins saved to the treasury."

"Money that might be better spent than in paying rascally informers!"

"And they have managed to escape!"

"Escape? Yes. And they're safe on the other side of the Adriatic."

From this conversation, which took place among a group of peasants, artisans and shopkeepers, who were standing in front of one of the placards, it seemed that public opinion was rather in favour of the fugitives – at least among the people of Istria who are either Slavs or Italians by birth. The Austrian officials could hardly count on treachery.

But they were doing all they could to recover the fugitives. All the squadrons of police and companies of gendarmerie had been afoot since the evening, and an incessant exchange of dispatches was taking place between Rovigno, Pisino, and Trieste.

When Andrea returned home about eleven o'clock, he brought back the news, which was thus rather favourable than otherwise.

Sandorf and Bathory had had their breakfast taken them into their room by Maria, and were finishing it as he appeared. The few hours' sleep, the good food, and the careful attention had entirely recovered them from their fatigues.

"Well, my good friend?" asked Count Sandorf as soon as Andrea closed the door.

"Gentlemen, I do not think you have anything to be afraid of at present."

"But what do they say in the town?" asked Bathory.

"They're talking a good deal about two strangers who were seen yesterday morning when they landed on the bank of the Leme Canal – and that concerns you."

A few fishermen were on the beach

"It does concern us," answered Bathory. "A man, a salt-worker in the neighbourhood, has seen and reported us."

And Andrea Ferrato was told of what had passed at the ruined farm while they were in hiding.

"And you do not know who this informer was?" asked the fisherman.

"We did not see him," replied Sandorf, "we could only hear him."

"That's a pity," said Ferrato. "But the important thing is that they've lost trace of you, and if it's supposed that you have taken refuge in my house I do not think anyone would betray you. A promise made is binding in these parts."

"Yes," answered Sandorf, "and I'm not surprised at it. A fine lot of fellows are the people of these provinces! But we have to do with the Austrian officials, and they won't leave a stone unturned to retake us."

"There is one thing in your favour," said the fisherman, "and that's the pretty general opinion that you've already crossed the Adriatic."

"And would to Heaven they had!" added Maria, who had joined her hands as if in prayer.

"That we shall do, my dear child," said Sandorf in a tone of entire confidence, "that we shall do, with Heaven's help..."

"And mine, count," replied Andrea. "Now I'm going on with my work as usual. People are accustomed to see us getting our nets ready on the beach, or cleaning up the balandello, and we must not alter that. Besides, I must go and study the weather before I decide what to do. You remain in this room. Do not leave it on any pretext. If necessary you can open the window on to the yard, but remain at the back of the room, and do not let yourselves be seen. I'll come back in an hour or two."

Andrea then left the house, accompanied by Luigi, and Maria busied herself with the housework as usual.

A few fishermen were on the beach. As a matter of precaution he went and exchanged a few words with them before beginning on his nets.

"The wind is pretty steady now," said one of them.

"Yes," answered Andrea, "that last storm cleared the weather for us."

"Hum!" added another," the breeze will freshen towards evening and turn to a storm if the bora joins in with it."

"Good! Then the wind will blow off the land, and the sea won't be so lively among the rocks."

"We shall see!"

"Are you going fishing tonight, Andrea?"

"Certainly, if the weather will let me."

"But the embargo?"

"The embargo is only on big ships, not on coasting boats."

"All the better; for we have got a report that shoals of tunnies are coming up from the south, and there is no time to lose in getting out the madragues."

"Good," said Andrea. "But we shall lose nothing."

"Eh? Perhaps not!"

"No, I tell you, if I go out tonight I shall go after bonicous, out Orsera or Parenzo way."

"As you like! But we'll set to work to get madragues down at the foot of the rocks."

"All right."

Andrea and Luigi then went after their nets stowed away in the out-house, and stretched them out on the sand so as to dry them in the sun. Then two hours later the fisherman came back, having told Luigi to get ready the hooks for the bonicous, which are a sort of fish with brownish-red flesh belonging to the same genus as the tunnies and the same species as the anxides.

Ten minutes later, after a smoke at his door, Andrea rejoined his guests in the room, while Maria continued her work about the house.

"Count," said the fisherman, "the wind is off the land, and I do not think the sea will be rough tonight. The simplest way and consequently the best way to avoid observation is for you to come with me. If you think so, it would be better to get away tonight about ten o'clock. You can then get down between the rocks to the water's edge. No one will see you. My boat will take you off to the balancello, and we can at once put to sea without attracting attention, for they know I'm going out to-night. If the breeze freshens too much I'll run down the coast so as to set you ashore beyond the Austrian frontier, at the mouths of the Cat-taro."

"And if it does not freshen, what are you going to do?" asked San-dorf.

"We'll go out to sea," answered the fisherman, "and I'll land you on the coast of Rimini, or at the mouth of the Po."

"Is your boat big enough for a voyage like that?" asked Bathory.

"Yes, it's a good boat, half-decked, and my son and I have been out in her in very bad weather. Besides, we must run some risk."

"We must run some risk," said Count Sandorf, "our lives are at stake, and nothing is more natural. But for you, my friend, to risk your life..."

"That's my business, count," answered Andrea, "and I'm only doing my duty in wishing to save you."

"Your duty?"

"Yes."

And Andrea Ferrato related that episode in his life on account of which he had left Santa Manza, and told how the good he was about to do would be a just compensation for the evil he had done.

"You are a splendid fellow!" exclaimed Sandorf, much affected by the recital.

Then continuing:

"But if we go to the mouths of the Cattaro or the Italian coast that will necessitate a long absence, which on your part will astonish the people of Rovigno. After you've put us in safety there's no need for you to return and be arrested..."

"Never fear," answered Andrea. "Sometimes I'm five or six days at sea. Besides, that's my business. It's what must be done and it is what shall be done."

So that the only thing to do was to discuss the scheme, which was evidently a good one and easy of execution, for the balancello was quite equal to the voyage. Care would have to be taken in getting on board; but the night was sure to be dark and moonless, and probably with the evening one of those thick mists would come up along the coast, which does not extend far out to sea. The beach would then be deserted. The other fishermen, Ferrato's neighbours, would be busy, as they had said, among their madragues on the rocks two or three miles below Rovigno. When they sighted the balancello, if they did sight her, she would be far out at sea with the fugitives under her deck.

"And what is the distance in a direct line between Rovigno and the nearest point of the Italian coast?" asked Bathory.

"About fifty miles."

"And how long will it take you to do that?"

"With a favourable wind we ought to cross in twelve hours. But you have no money. You'll want some. Take this belt, it's got three hundred florins in it, and buckle it round you."

"My friend..." said Sandorf.

"You can return it later," replied the fisherman, "once you're safe. And now wait here till I come back."

Matters being thus arranged Ferrato went to resume his usual occupations, sometimes on the beach and sometimes about his house. Luigi, without being noticed, took on board in a spare sail provisions for sev-

"What do you want?"

eral days. There seemed no possibility of suspicion that might alter Ferrato's plans. He was even so careful in his precautions as not to see his guests again during the day. Sandorf and Bathory remained in hiding at the back of the room in which the window remained open. The fisherman was to call them when it was time for them to go.

Many of the neighbours came in to have a chat during the afternoon about the appearance of the tunnies and the fishing. Andrea received them in the front room and offered them something to drink as usual.

The greater part of the day thus passed in going backwards and forwards and in talk. Many times the subject of the prisoners cropped up. There was a rumour that they had been caught near the Quarnero Canal on the opposite side of Istria – a rumour that was soon afterwards contradicted.

All seemed working for the best. That the coast was more closely watched than usual by the customhouse men, the police, and the gendarmes was certain; but there would probably be no difficulty in evading the guard when night came on.

The embargo, as we know, had only been put on the long-voyage ships and the Mediterranean coasters, and not on the local fishing boats. The balancello would thus be able to get under sail without suspicion.

But Andrea Ferrato had not reckoned on a visit he received in the evening. This visit was a surprise at the first, and made him anxious, although he did not understand the meaning of the threat until after his visitor's departure.

Eight o'clock was on the point of striking, and Maria was preparing the supper and had already laid the table in the large room, when there came two knocks at the door.

Andrea did not hesitate to go and open it. Much surprised he found himself in the presence of the Spaniard, Carpena.

This Carpena was a native of Almayati, a little town in the province of Malaga. As Ferrato had left Corsica, so had Carpena left Spain, to settle in Istria. There he found employment in the salt-works and in carrying the products of the western coast into the interior – a thankless occupation that barely brought him in enough to live upon.

He was a strong fellow, still young, being not more than five and twenty – short of stature but broad of shoulder, with a large head covered with curly, coarse black hair, and one of those bulldog faces that look as forbidding on a man as on a dog. Carpena was unsociable, spiteful, vindictive, and a good deal of a scoundrel, and was anything but popular. It was not known why he had left his country. Several quarrels with his fellow workmen, a good deal of threatening with one and the other followed by fights and scuffles, had not added to his reputation. People liked Carpena best at a distance.

He, however, had a sufficiently good opinion of himself and his person – as we shall see – and was ambitious of becoming Ferrato's son-in-law. The fisherman, it must be confessed, did not give his overtures a cordial reception. And that will be understood better when the man's pretensions have been disclosed in the conversation that followed.

Carpena had hardly set foot in the room than Andrea stopped him short with:

"What do you want?"

"I was passing, and as I saw a light in your window I came in."

"For what reason?"

"To visit you, neighbour."

"I do not enjoy your company, as you well know!"

"Not usually," answered the Spaniard, "but tonight it will be different."

Ferrato did not understand and could not guess what such enigmatic words meant in Carpena's mouth. But he could not repress a sudden start, which did not escape his visitor, who shut the door behind him.

"I want to speak to you!" said he.

"No! You have nothing to say to me."

"Yes – I must speak to you – in private," added the Spaniard, lowering his voice.

"Come then," answered the fisherman, who during this day had his reasons for not refusing anyone admittance. Carpena, at a sign from Ferrato, crossed the room and entered his bedroom, which was separated only by a thin partition from that occupied by Sandorf and his companion.

One room opened to the front, the other onto the back of the house. As soon as they were alone –

"What do you want of me?" asked the fisherman.

"Neighbour," answered Carpena, "I again come to appeal to your kindness."

"What for?"

"About your daughter."

"Not another word!"

"Listen then! You know that I love Maria, and that my dearest wish is to make her my wife."

And in fact Carpena had for several months been pursuing the girl with his attentions. As may be imagined these were due more to interest than to love. Ferrato was well off for a fisherman, and compared to the Spaniard, who possessed nothing, he was rich. Nothing could be more natural than that Carpena should wish to become his son-in-law; and on the other hand nothing could be more natural than that the fisherman invariably showed him the door.

"Carpena," answered Ferrato, "you've already spoken to my daughter and she's told you: no. You've already asked me and I've told you: no. You again come here today and I tell you: no, for the last time."

The Spaniard's face grew livid. His lips opened and showed his teeth. His eyes darted a ferocious look at the fisherman. But the badly lighted room prevented Ferrato from seeing that threatening physiognomy.

"That's your last word?" asked Carpena.

"That's my last word, if it is the last time you ask me. But if you renew the request you shall have the same reply."

"I shall renew it! Yes! I shall renew it!" repeated Carpena – "if Maria tells me to do so."

"If she tells you to do so!" exclaimed Andrea. "Maria! You know she has neither friendship nor esteem for you!"

"Her sentiments may change after I've had an interview with her," answered Carpena.

"An interview?"

"Yes, Ferrato. I wish to speak to her."

"When?"

"Now! – You understand – I must speak to her – I must – this very night."

"On her behalf I refuse!"

"I wouldn't be so rash," said Carpena, raising his voice. "Take care!"

"Take care?"

"I'll have my revenge!"

"Oh! Take your revenge if you like, or if you dare!" answered Ferrato, who was getting angry in turn. "All your threats won't frighten me! And now get out or I'll throw you out!"

The blood mounted to the Spaniards eyes. Perhaps he thought of attacking the fisherman! But he restrained himself, and making a snatch at the door, he dashed out of the room and out of the house without saying another word.

He had scarcely gone before the door of the other room opened and Count Sandorf, who had lost none of the foregoing conversation, appeared on the threshold. Stepping up to Andrea he said to him in a low voice:

"That is the man that gave the information to the sergeant of the gendarmerie. He knows us. He saw us when we landed on the bank of the Leme Canal. He followed us to Rovigno. He evidently knows that you've sheltered us in your house. So let us be off at once, or we'll all be done for!"

CHAPTER IX

THE FINAL EFFORT OF THE FINAL STRUGGLE

Andrea Ferrato remained silent. He said nothing in answer to Count Sandorf. His Corsican blood boiled within him. He had forgotten the fugitives for whom up to then he had risked so much. He thought only of the Spaniard, he saw only Carpena!

"The scoundrel! The scoundrel!" he murmured at length. "Yes! He knows all! We're at his mercy! I ought to have understood!"

Sandorf and Bathory looked anxiously at the fisherman. They waited for what he was going to say, what he was going to do. There was not an instant to lose. The informer had perhaps, already done his work.

"Count," said Andrea, "the police may enter my house at any moment. That beggar knows or supposes that you're here! He came to bargain with me! My daughter was to have been the price of his silence! He would ruin you to exact his revenge upon me! If the police come you cannot escape, and you will be discovered. Yes! You must go at once!"

"You're right, Ferrato," answered Count Sandorf, "but before we separate, let me thank you for all you've done and all you intended to do..."

"What I intended to do I shall still do!" said Andrea seriously.

"We refuse!" said Bathory.

"Yes, we refuse," added Sandorf. "You're already too deeply compromised as it is! If they find us in your house they'll send you to the hulks. Come, Stephen, we must leave this house before we bring ruin and misfortune on it! Escape, but escape alone!"

Ferrato seized Sandorf's hand.

"Where will you go?" said he. "The police patrol the country night and day, the authorities watch every corner, there's not a spot on the coast that you can get off from, not a footpath across the frontier that's free! To go without me is to go to your death."

"Follow my father," added Maria. "Whatever happens he'll do his duty and try to save you."

"That is it, daughter," said Ferrato. "It is only my duty! Your brother can wait for us in the boat. The night is dark. Before we can be seen we shall be at sea. Good-bye, Maria. Good-bye!"

But Sandorf and Bathory would not let him move. They refused to profit by his devotion. To leave the house so as not to compromise the fisherman, yes! But to embark under his charge and send him to the hulks: no!

"Come," said Sandorf, "once out of the house we shall only have to fear for ourselves."

And by the open window they began to get down into the yard to cross it and escape, when Luigi rushed in. "The police!" he said.

"Adieu!" said Sandorf.

And followed by Bathory he leapt to the ground.

At the same moment the police came running into the front room.

Carpena was at their head.

"Scoundrel!" said Ferrato.

"This is my answer to your refusal," replied the Spaniard.

The fisherman was seized and garrotted. In a moment the police had visited and searched every room in the house. The window opening on to the yard showed the road taken by the fugitives. They started in pursuit.

Sandorf and his companion had reached the hedge, which ran along the stream. Sandorf leaped it at a bound and turned to help over Stephen, when the report of a gun rang out some fifty paces off.

Bathory was hit by the bullet, which only grazed his shoulder, it is true; but his arm remained paralyzed and he could not let his companion seize it to help him.

"Escape, Mathias!" he exclaimed. "Escape."

"No, Stephen, no. We'll die together," replied Sandorf, after trying for the last time to lift his wounded companion in his arms.

"Escape, Mathias!" repeated Bathory. "And live to punish the traitors!"

Bathory's last words were, as it were, a command to Sandorf. To him there fell the work of the three – to him alone. The magnate of Transylvania, the conspirator of Trieste, the companion of Stephen Bathory and Ladislas Zathmar must give place to the messenger of justice.

At this moment the police had reached the end of the yard and thrown themselves on the wounded man. Sandorf would fall into their hands if he hesitated another second.

"Adieu, Stephen, adieu!" he exclaimed.

With a leap he cleared the brook, which ran along by the hedge, and disappeared.

Five or six shots were fired after him; but the bullets missed, and turning aside he ran quickly towards the sea.

The police, however, were on his track. Not being able to see him in the darkness they did not try to run straight after him. They dispersed so as to cut him off not only from the interior but from the town and from the promontory which shelters the Bay of Rovigno.

A brigade of gendarmes reinforced them and were so manoeuvred as to prevent him from taking any other route than that towards the sea. But what could he do there? Could he possess himself of a boat and put out to the open sea? He would not have time and before he could get her clear he would be shot. From the first he saw that his retreat to the east was cut off. The noise of the guns, the shouts of the police and the gendarmes as they approached told him that he was hedged in on the beach. His only chance of escape was to the sea and by the sea. It was doubtless to rush to certain death; but better to find it among the waves than before the firing-party in the courtyard of the fortress of Pisino.

Sandorf then ran towards the beach. In a few bounds he had reached the first small waves that licked the sand. He already felt the police behind him, and the bullets fired at random whistled past his head.

All down this Istrian coast there is a reef of isolated rocks just a little way out from the shore. Between these rocks there are pools filling the depressions in the sand – some of them several feet deep, some of them quite shallow.

It was the last road that was open, and although Sandorf thought death was at the end he did not hesitate to take it.

He raced along, clearing the pools and jumping from rock to rock; but his profile thus became more visible against the less dense darkness of the horizon. And immediately the shouts gave the alarm and the police dashed out after him.

He had resolved not to be taken alive. If the sea gave him up, it would give up a corpse.

The difficult chase over the shaking and slippery rocks, over the viscous wracks and weeds, through the pools where every step might mean

"Escape, Mathias!" repeated Bathory. "And live to punish the traitors!"

a fall, lasted for more than a quarter of an hour. The fugitive was still ahead, but the solid ground was soon to fail him.

He reached the last rocks of the reef. Two or three police were not more than ten yards away; the others were about double as far behind.

Count Sandorf stopped. A last cry escaped him – a cry of farewell thrown to Heaven. Then as a discharge of bullets rained around him, he precipitated himself into the sea.

The police came to the very edge of the rock and saw nothing but the head of the fugitive, like a black point, turned towards the offing. Another volley pattered into the water round the count.

And doubtless one or two bullets reached him, for he sank under the waves and disappeared.

Till day broke the police kept watch along the reef and the beach, from the promontory to beyond the fort of Rovigno. It was useless. Nothing showed that Sandorf had again set foot on shore. It remained undoubted then that if he had not been shot he had been drowned.

But though a careful search was made no body was ever found among the breakers nor on the sands for more than a couple of leagues along the coast. But as the wind was off shore and the current running to the southwest, there could be no doubt that the corpse of the fugitive had been swept out to the open sea.

Count Sandorf, the Magyar nobleman, had then found his grave in the waves of the Adriatic.

After a minute investigation this was the verdict, a very natural one, to which the Austrian Government came.

Stephen Bathory, captured as we have seen, was taken under escort during the night to the donjon of Pisino, there for a few hours to join Ladislas Zathmar.

The execution was fixed for the 30th of June.

Doubtless at this supreme moment Stephen would have a last interview with his wife and child; Ladislas would see his servant for the last time, for permission had been given to admit them to the donjon. But Madame Bathory and her son, and Borik, who had been let out of prison, had left Trieste. Not knowing where the prisoners had been taken, for their arrest had been a secret one, they had searched for them even in Hungary, even in Austria, and after the sentence was announced they could not reach them in time.

Bathory had not the last consolation of seeing his wife and son. He could not tell them the names of those who had betrayed him.

Another volley pattered into the water round the count

Stephen Bathory and Ladislas Zathmar at five o'clock in the evening were shot in the courtyard of the fortress. They died like men who had given their lives for their country.

Toronthal and Sarcany could now believe that they were beyond all chance of reprisal. In fact the secret of their treachery was only known to themselves and to the Governor of Trieste. Their reward was half the possessions of Count Sandorf, the other half, by special favour, being reserved for his heiress when she attained her eighteenth year.

Toronthal and Sarcany, insensible to all remorse, could enjoy in peace the wealth obtained by their abominable treachery.

Another traitor seemed to have nothing to fear. This was the Spaniard Carpena to whom had been paid the reward of 5000 florins.

But if the banker and his accomplice could remain and hold their heads up at Trieste, Carpena under the weight of public reprobation had to leave Rovigno, to live no one knew where. What did it matter? He had nothing to fear, not even the vengeance of Ferrato.

For the fisherman had been arrested, found guilty, and sentenced to imprisonment for life for having sheltered the fugitives. Maria and her young brother Luigi were now left alone to live in misery in the house from which the father had been taken never to return.

And so three scoundrels for mere greed, without even a sentiment of hatred against their victims – Carpena excepted perhaps – one to restore his embarrassed affairs, the others to gain money, had carried through this odious scheme.

Was such infamy to remain unpunished in this world? Count Sandorf, Count Zathmar, Stephen Bathory, these three patriots, and Andrea Ferrato the honest fisherman, where they not to be avenged?

The future will show.

Ragusa

PART II

CHAPTER I

PESCADE AND MATIFOU

Fifteen years after the events narrated in the prologue of this history, on the 24th of May 1882, there was a holiday at Ragusa, one of the chief towns of the Dalmatian provinces.

Dalmatia is a narrow tongue of land lying between the northern Dinaric Alps, Herzegovina, and the Adriatic. It is just large enough to hold a population of four to five hundred thousand, with a little squeezing.

A fine race are these Dalmatians: sober in an arid country, where arable land is rare, proud among the many political vicissitudes they have undergone, haughty towards Austria which gained them by the Treaty of Campo Formio in 1815, and honest towards all; so much so that the country can be called, according to a beautiful expression reported by M. Yriarte, "The land of the lockless doors."

Dalmatia is divided into four circles, and these are subdivided into districts; the circles are those of Zara, Spalato, Cattaro, and Ragusa. The governor general resides at Zara, the capital of the province, where the Diet meets of which many members form part of the Upper House at Vienna

Times are much changed since the sixteenth century, when Uscoques – fugitive Turks at war with the Mussulmans as well as the Christians, with the Sultan as well as the Venetian Republic – were the terror of the sea. But the Uscoques have disappeared, and traces of them are no longer to be found in Carniola. The Adriatic is now as safe as any part of the poetical Mediterranean.

Ragusa, or rather the small state of Ragusa, was a republic even before Venice. It was only in 1808 that a decree of Napoleon united it, the year following to the kingdom of Illyria and made of it a duchy for Marshal Marmont. In the ninth century Ragusan vessels, which ploughed every sea of the Levant, had the monopoly of the trade with the Infidels – a monopoly granted them by the Holy See – and Ragusa in consequence was of great importance among the small republics of southern Europe. In these days Ragusa is famous for still nobler things; and the reputation of its scientists, the renown of its writers, and the taste of its artists had given it the name of the Slavic Athens.

The modern shipping trade must have harbours where there is good anchorage, and water deep enough to receive vessels of large tonnage. Ragusa has no such harbour. The basin is narrow, crowded with rocks at the water level, and hardly large enough to admit small coasters and fishing boats.

Fortunately about a mile and a half to the north on one of the indentations of the bay of Ombola Fumera, a caprice of nature has formed an excellent harbour adapted for all the needs of modern navigation. This is at Gravosa, and the harbour is perhaps the best on the Dalmatian coast. It has water enough even for warships; there are several repairing slips and building yards; and there the large mail boats can put in with which the immediate future is to endow the waters of the world. It follows, therefore, that the road to Ragusa to Gravosa has become a regular boulevard planted with magnificent trees bordered with charming villas, frequented by the population of the town, which in 1882 amounted to from sixteen to seventeen thousand inhabitants.

On this 24th of May, about four o'clock on a beautiful spring afternoon, the Ragusans were crowding in great numbers towards Gravosa. In that suburb – for Gravosa being built at the gates of the town may well be called such – a local fair was in progress with the usual games and sports, travelling booths, music and dancing in the open air, quacks, acrobats, and entertainers, from whose shouts, and songs, and instruments there arose a tremendous uproar along the street and jetties.

For a stranger it afforded an excellent opportunity for studying the various types of the Slavic race and the mixture of Bohemians of all kinds. In addition to the travelling showmen who had come to the fair to make money out of the curiosity of the locals, the country folk and mountaineers had thronged in to take part in the rejoicing. The women were in great numbers – girls from Ragusa, peasants from the neighbourhood, fisherwomen from the coast. Some were in dresses approaching the latest fashions of Western Europe; others were in dresses which varied with each district, at least in detail – white bodices embroidered on the arms and breast, cloaks of many colours, waistbands with thousands of silver pins, (quite a mosaic, in which the colours were as confusing as a Persian carpet), white bonnets over hair tied up with many coloured ribbons, the "okronga" surmounted by the veil which hung down behind like the puksul of the Oriental turban, leggings and shoes fixed to the feet with plaited straw. And with all this elaborate rig-out, a heap of jewels in the form of bracelets, and collars or pieces of silver arranged in a hundred ways as ornaments for the neck, the arms, the breast and waist. Jewellery, too, was conspicuous in the dress of men, whose clothes were edged with bright coloured embroideries.

But among all the Ragusan costumes, which even the seamen of the port wore gracefully, those of the commissionaires – a privileged corporation – were of a kind to attract special notice. These porters were regular Orientals, with turban, jacket, waistcoat, belt, large Turkish trousers and slippers. They would not have disgraced the quays of Galata or the Tophane at Constantinople.

The fair was in full swing. The booths were doing a roaring trade. There was an additional attraction provided which bound to bring a crowd together; this was the launch of a trabacolo, a sort of craft peculiar to the Adriatic rigged with two masts and two sails bent to a yard top and bottom by the upper and lower bolt ropes.

The launch was to take place at six o'clock in the evening, and the hull of the trabacolo, with the shores already cleared away, was only waiting for the key to be knocked out to glide into the sea. But up to the present the mountebanks, wandering minstrels and acrobats had been in full work amusing the public by their talents and agility.

The musicians drew the most spectators, and among them the guzlars or players were the best patronized. Accompanying themselves on their strange instruments, they sang in guttural tones the songs of their country, and they were well worth stopping to hear.

The guzla used by these virtuosos of the street has several strings stretched on a long frame, and scraped with a bow. There is no risk of the singers failing for want of notes, for they go in search of them high and low, as much in their heads as in their chests.

One of the singers – a huge fellow, yellow of skin and brown of hair, holding between his knees the guzla which looked like a cello grown thin – was singing with much mimicry and gesture a canzonet of which the following is almost a literal translation:

"When gay the song comes ringing,
The song of the gypsy girl,
Mark well the look she's flinging
To help the words she's singing!

133

Cape Matifou juggled with his young companion

Oh beware
Of the gypsy girl!

Too far away from her you stay,
And then her love-lit eyes grow tender,
And 'neath their veiling lashes say,
'Come nearer, love - and I'll surrender!"

"When gay the song comes ringing,
The song of the gypsy girl,
Mark well the look she's flinging
To help the words she's singing!
Oh beware
Of the gypsy girl!"

After this the singer with his wooden bowl in his hand went round the ring and made a collection of a few coppers. But the take seemed to be rather poor, and he returned to his place to soften his auditors with the second couplet of his canzonet.

"When the full gaze of her glorious eyes,
Meets yours and all their witchcraft lend her,
Your heart she wins as her rightful prize,
She'll keep it – and she'll ne'er surrender!

"When gay the song comes ringing,
The song of the gypsy girl,
Mark well the look she's flinging
To help the words she's singing!
Oh beware
Of the gypsy girl!"

A man of from fifty to fifty five was listening to the gypsy's song; but being little sensible to such poetical seductions, his purse had hitherto remained unopened; and he was about to move off when the young lady by his side stopped him and said:

"Father, I have no money with me. Will you give that man something?"

And that is why the guzlar received four or five keutzers, which he would not have had without the girl's intervention. Not that her father, who was very rich, was mean enough to refuse alms to a poor foreigner, but simply because he was never moved by human misery.

The father and daughter passed through the crowd towards other booths just as noisy, while the guzla players disappeared into the nearby *osterie,* probably to liquidate their receipts with a few bottles of slivovitz, a type of brandy made from fermented plum juice, much favoured among the locals. Though as strong as any spirit, it slides down their gullets like the sweetest syrup.

But all the open-air artists, singers and mountebanks were not so freely patronized. Among the most deserted were two acrobats who were figuring away on a platform with no spectators to encourage them.

Above the stand was a sheet of canvas in a very bad state of repair, with portraits of wild animals daubed on in distemper, in which in most fantastic outline there could be seen lions, jackals, hyenas, tigers, boars, etc, leaping and disporting themselves in marvellously unreal landscapes. Behind was a tiny arena, railed off with pieces of old canvas which boasted so many holes for the eyes of the indiscreet to look through that they must have seriously diminished receipts. In front on one of the poles was a dilapidated piece of plank as an apology for a signboard. On it these five words were roughly written in charcoal:

PESCADE & MATIFOU
FRENCH ACROBATS

From a physical point of view – and probably from a moral one also – these two men were as different from the other as two human beings could be. They were both natives of Provence, and it was that fact alone that had brought them together to fight the battle of life.

Whence came these queer names? Were they the two geographical points between which curves the bay of Algiers? Yes! And the names fitted them perfectly, as that of Atlas does some giant wrestler.

Cape Matifou is an enormous mamelon, strong and unshakable, which rises at the northeast end of the vast roadstead of Algiers as if to defy the unchained elements and illustrate the celebrated line:

"Its mass indestructible wearied out in time."

And such was the athlete Matifou – an Alcides, a Porthos, a fortunate rival of the Ompdrailles, of Nicholas Creste, and other famous wrestlers who have shone in the arenas of the south.

This giant was more than six feet in height, with a voluminous head, shoulders in proportion, chest like a smith's bellows, and limbs like tree-trunks, with the strength of steel. He was manly strength in all its magnificence, and had he known his age, we should have found, not without surprise, that he had only just entered his twenty-second year. Although this giant was not gifted with striking intelligence, yet his heart was good, and his character was simple and gentle. He knew neither hate nor anger. He would do no one an injury. Seldom, indeed, would he shake the hand that was offered him for fear he should crush it in his own. In his powerful nature there was nothing of the tiger, although he had the strength. And besides at a word, at a sign even from his companion, he would obey, as if he had been the gigantic son of that little slip of a man.

As a contrast, at the western extremity of the Bay of Algiers, Point Pescade, opposite Cape Matifou, is a thin, spare, narrow rocky tongue running out into the sea. From it the name of Pescade was given to this fellow of twenty, who was small, slender, skinny, and of not half the weight of his friend, but supple, active, quick-witted, of inexhaustible good-humour through good and evil fortune, a philosopher in his way, inventive and practical – a regular monkey without the mischief – and indissolubly linked by fate to the enormous pachyderm whom he led through all the phases of a mountebank's life.

Both were acrobats by profession and travelled from fair to fair. Matifou – or Cape Matifou as he was also called – wrestled in the ring, giving all sorts of displays of strength, bending iron bars on his biceps, lifting the heaviest of his audience at arm's length, and juggling with his young companion as if he were a tennis ball. Pescade – or Point Pescade as he was commonly called – gesticulated, sang, played the fool, amused the public by his clownish wit, astonished them by his feats as an equilibrist, at which he was very clever, and mystified them with his conjuring tricks.

But why on this occasion on the quay at Gravosa are these two poor fellows left out in the cold, while the people crowd to the other booths? Why have they taken so little when they are in such great need? It is difficult to say.

Their language, an agreeable mixture of Provencal and Italian, was more than enough for them to make themselves understood. Since their departure from Provence, where they had known no relatives and seemed to have been produced by spontaneous generation, they had wandered about from markets to fairs, living ill rather than well, but still living, and if not dining every day, at least having something for supper

"Come in, gentlemen!" shouted Point Pescade

every night; and that was good enough for them, for, as Point Pescade remarked, "We need not ask for the impossible."

But if the worthy fellow did not ask for it on this occasion, he tried at it nonetheless in his endeavour to get together a dozen spectators before his platform in the hope that they would pay a visit to his miserable arena. But neither his witticisms, to which his foreign accent gave such point, nor his patter which would have made the fortune of a vaudevillist, nor his facial twists which would have drawn a grin from a graven image, nor his acrobatic contortions which were quite prodigies of dislocation, nor the attractions of his grass wig whose goat's-beard tail dusted the hem of his jacket, nor his sallies which were worthy of a Pulcinello of Rome or a Stentarcilo of Florence, had the slightest effect on the public.

And yet they had been performing for the Slavs for many months. After leaving Provence they had crossed Lombardy and Venetia, mounted, it could almost be said, one on the other. Cape Matifou famous for his strength; Point Pescade celebrated for his agility. Their renown had preceded them to Trieste in Illyria. From Trieste they had advanced through Istria, descending on the Dalmatian coast at Zara, Salone, Ragusa, finding it more profitable to advance than to retreat. Behind them they were used up, in front of them their entertainment was new and likely to bring good business. Now, alas! the tour which had never been very good threatened to become very bad, and the poor fellows had but one desire, which they knew not how to realize, to get back to their native land and never come so far away from it again.

But they were dragging a weight behind them, the weight of misery, and to walk many leagues with that weight at their feet was very hard!

But without thinking of the future they had to think of the present that is of the night's supper, which had not yet been earned. They had not a kreutzer in the treasury, if that pretentious name could be given to the corner of the handkerchief in which Point Pescade used to keep the money. In vain he sparred away on his trestles. In vain he shouted despairing appeals into vacancy. In vain Cape Matifou exhibited his biceps on which the veins stood out like the ivy on an old tree! Not a spectator showed the slightest idea of entering the canvas ring.

"Hard to move these Dalmatians!" said Point Pescade.

"As paving stones," remarked Cape Matifou.

"I don't think we shall have any luck today! Look here, Cape Matifou, we shall have to pack up."

"Pack up, where for?"

"You are curious!"

"Tell us."

"Well, I'll think of some place where we're at least sure of one meal a day."

"What place is that, Point Pescade?"

"Oh, it's far, far away – and much farther than very far, Cape Matifou."

"At the end of the world?"

"The world has no end," sententiously replied Pescade. "If it had an end it wouldn't be round! If it didn't turn it would be immovable, and if it was immovable..."

"Well!" asked Cape Matifou.

"Well, it would tumble into the sun in less time than I could juggle a rabbit."

"And then?"

"And then there'll happen what happens to a clumsy juggler when two balls go smash in the air! Crack! Crash, collapse, and the people hiss and want their money back, and you have to give it to them, and tonight we shall have nothing for supper!"

"And so," asked the giant, "if the earth tumbles into the sun we shall have nothing for supper?"

And Cape Matifou fell into infinite perspectives. Seated on a corner of the platform, with his arms crossed on his tights, he began to nod his head like China doll; he said no more, he saw no more, he heard no more. He was absorbed in a most unintelligible association of ideas all mixed up in his mighty noggin. And this is what he felt gape like a gulf in the depths of his being. It seemed to him that he rose high, very high; higher than very high: this expression of Pescade's had struck him as being very appropriate. Then suddenly he was left alone and he fell – into his own stomach – that is to say into emptiness.

It was quite a nightmare. The poor fellow rose on the steps, with his hands extended as if he were blind. A moment later he tumbled on to the platform.

"Eh! Cape Matifou, what's up?" exclaimed Point Pescade, seizing his comrade by the hand and dragging him back.

"Me," answered the giant in confusion. "Me – do you mean?"

"Yes! You!"

"I've been thinking," said Matifou, collecting his ideas – a difficult operation, notwithstanding their number was so inconsiderable. "I've been thinking that it's necessary I should speak to you, Point Pescade!"

"Say on then, my Cape and fear not that I shall not listen! Avaunt, thou public, avaunt."

The giant sat down on the steps, and in his strong arms gently, as if he were afraid of smashing him, drew his companion to his side.

He kept it back – for ten seconds

CHAPTER II

THE LAUNCH OF THE TRABACOLO

"And so this does not do?" asked Cape Matifou.

"What does not do?" replied Point Pescade.

"This business!"

"It might do better, it must be admitted, but it might do worse!"

"Pescade?"

"Matifou!"

"Don't you wish to hear what I'm going to say?"

"I do wish, on the contrary, if it's worth wishing for."

"Well – you ought to leave me," said the giant."

"What do you mean by leaving you? To leave you to yourself?" asked Point Pescade.

"Yes."

"Continue, Hercules of my dreams! You interest me!"

"Yes, I'm sure that if you were alone you'd draw the people! I prevent you. It's my fault that you don't, and without me, you'd be able to..."

"Now, look here, Cape Matifou," replied Pescade seriously.

"You're big, are you not?"

"Yes."

"And tall?"

"Yes."

"Well, big and tall as you are I do not understand how you could manage to hold such a huge stupidity as you've just uttered."

"And why, Point Pescade?"

"Because it's bigger and taller than you are, Cape Matifou! Me to leave you! But if was not here, with whom would you do the juggling?"

"With whom?"

"Who would perform the dangerous jump on to your occiput?"

"I do not know..."

"Or the grand flight between your hands?"

"Booh!" answered the giant, embarrassed by these pressing questions.

"Yes – in presence of a delighted audience, when by chance there is an audience!"

"An audience," murmured Matifou.

"There, shut up," continued Pescade, "just think of earning something for supper tonight."

"I'm not hungry."

"You are always hungry, Cape Matifou," said Point Pescade, opening his companion's enormous jaws with his hands. "I see your canines as big as those of a bulldog! You are hungry, I tell you; and when we have earned half a florin, or a quarter of a florin, you shall eat."

"But you, my little Pescade?"

"Me? A grain of millet will be enough! I don't want to be strong like you, my son. This is how I look at it. The more you eat the more you grow! The more you grow the more you become a phenomenon..."

"Phenomenon – yes!"

"But with me, on the contrary, the less I eat, the more I waste, and the more I waste the more I become a phenomenon! Is that not true?"

"That is true," answered Matifou innocently. "And so, Point Pescade, in my own interest I ought to eat!"

"Just so, my big dog, and in mine I ought not to eat!"

"But suppose there is only enough for one?"

"Then it will be yours."

"But suppose there is enough for two"

"It would still be yours! My dear Matifou, you're worth any two men!"

"Four – six – ten!" exclaimed the giant.

And putting aside the emphatic exaggeration so common to all giants, ancient and modern, Matifou had in truth thrown every wrestler hitherto opposed to him. Two facts were told of him, which showed his prodigious strength. One evening in a circus at Nimes an upright supporting the woodwork began to give way. The cracking caused a good deal of alarm among the spectators who were threatened with being crushed by the fall of the roof or crushed by themselves as they thronged to the door. But Cape Matifou was there. He made a leap to the beam, which was already out of the perpendicular, and as the framework sagged down he held it upon his shoulders as long as it was necessary to allow the audience to disperse. Then with another bound he jumped out, and the same moment the roof collapsed behind him. That was done by strength of shoulder. The following was done by strength of arm.

One day on the plains of Camargue, a bull went mad and escaped from the enclosure and chased and injured several people, and would have done a great deal of damage had it not been for Cape Matifou. The giant ran at the animal, waited for it, and as it lowered its head for the rush he seized it by the horns, and with one twist of his arm laid it on its back with its four hoofs kicking helplessly in the air.

Of his superhuman strength there had been other proofs, but these will serve to show not only Matifou's muscularity, but also his courage and devotion, for he never hesitated to risk his life when he could help his fellows. So that he was as good as he was strong. But that he should lose none of his strength it was necessary, as Pescade had said, that be should eat, and his companion obliged him to eat, stinting himself when there was only enough for one. This night, however, supper – even for one – had not yet appeared above the horizon.

"We're in a fog," said Point Pescade.

And to dissipate it he returned to his jokes and grimaces. He strode along the platform, he gesticulated, he did a few dislocations, he walked on his hands when he did not walk on his feet – having observed that you do not feel so hungry with your head downwards. He began over again, in his half-Provencal, half-Slavic lingo, that perpetual patter of the show booth, which every clown fires off at the crowd.

"Come in, gentlemen!" shouted Point Pescade. "There is nothing to pay till you go out – and then it's only a kreutzer."

But to go out it was necessary to go in, and although five or six people stopped, no one attempted to enter the arena.

Then Point Pescade with a long switch pointed out the ferocious animals depicted on the canvas. Not that he had a menagerie to show the public! But these terrible creatures existed in some parts of Africa and India, and if ever Cape Matifou met them on the road, why they would only make a mouthful for Cape Matifou!

And thus he chattered on, interrupted every now and then by the giant with a bang on the big drum that echoed like a cannon shot.

"The hyena, gentlemen, the hyena that comes from the Cape of Good Hope. Active and sanguinary, you see him clearing the walls of the graveyard on which he preys."

Then turning to the other side of the stand he pointed at a daub of yellow in a clump of blue trees.

"Here you are! The young and interesting rhinoceros only fifteen months old! He came from Sumatra and nearly wrecked the ship he was brought over in by sticking his horn through the hull."

The stranger held out his hand to the giant...

Then to the other end he turned again to show the lion amidst a greenish mass of the bones of his victims.

"Behold, gentlemen! The terrible lion of the Atlas! He lives in the depths of the Sahara, in the burning sands of the desert! When the heat gets too much for him, he hides in the caves! If he finds any water dripping he opens his mouth and drinks it as it drops! And that's why he's called an humidian!"

But all the attractions seemed to fail. Point Pescade shouted in vain. In vain Cape Matifou banged the big drum. Things were growing desperate.

However, a few Dalmatians, powerful looking mountaineers, came at last, and stopped – before the athletic Matifou, and coolly examined him with the air of connoisseurs.

Point Pescade immediately challenged them:

"Walk up, gentlemen! Come in! Now's your time! Grand contest! Man to man! A clear field! Cape Matifou will throw any amateur that honours him with his confidence! A pair of cotton tights as a prize for the conqueror! Are you game, gentlemen?" added Point Pescade, addressing these big fellows who stared at him with astonishment.

But the big fellows did not seem to see the fun of accepting the challenge, and Point Pescade had to announce that as no amateurs were forthcoming the contest would take place between Cape Matifou and himself. "Yes! Skill shall be pitted against strength."

"Walk up! Walk up! Don't all come at once!" vociferated poor Pescade. "You'll see now what you've never seen before! Point Pescade and Cape Matifou locked in combat! The twins of Provence! Yes – twins – but not of the same age, nor of the same mother! Eh? Aren't we like each other – me particularly!"

A young man stopped in front of the platform. He listened gravely to these threadbare pleasantries.

The young man was about twenty-two, or a little older. He was above the middle height. His handsome features, with a certain severity about them, denoted a pensive nature, disciplined probably in the school of suffering. His large black eyes, his beard that he kept short, his mouth rarely accustomed to smile, but clearly cut beneath his silky moustache, proclaimed unmistakably his Hungarian origin and the preponderance of Magyar blood. He was dressed quietly in a modern suit, without any pretence at being in the fashion. His bearing could not be mistaken; the young man was already a man.

He listened, we have said, to the useless patter of Point Pescade. With some sympathy he looked at him showing off on the platform. Having suffered himself he probably could not remain indifferent to the suffering of others.

"Two Frenchmen!" he said to himself. "Poor fellows! They haven't done much today!"

And then the idea occurred to him to constitute himself an audience – an audience that paid. It was only a bit of charity, perhaps, but it was a bit of charity in disguise, and it might be welcome.

So he advanced towards the door – that is towards the piece of canvas, which on being raised gave admittance to the ring.

"Walk in, sir! Walk in!" said Pescade. "We're just going to commence!"

"But – I'm alone..." said the young man good-naturedly.

"Sir," replied Point Pescade proudly, and somewhat chaffingly, "the true artist looks at the quality and not at the quantity of his audience!"

"However – you will allow me?" said the gentleman, taking out his purse.

And he picked out two florins and placed them on a tin plate in a corner of the platform.

"Bravo!" said Pescade.

Then he turned to his companion with –

"To the rescue, Matifou, to the rescue! We'll give him something for his money."

But as he was about to step in, the sole spectator of the French and Provencal arena, stopped abruptly. He had just caught sight of the girl and her father who a quarter of an hour before had been listening to the guzlar. Both he and she had had the same thought and done a charitable action. The one had given alms to the gipsy; the other had given alms to the acrobat.

But, evidently, the meeting in this way was not enough for him – for as soon as he saw the lady he forgot all about the arena and the money he had paid for his place, and dashed off towards the spot where she had again mixed with the crowd.

"Hi! Sir! – Sir!" shouted Pescade. "Your money! We haven't earned it! What's up? Where are you going? Vanished! Sir!"

But he sought to find his "audience" in vain. It had been eclipsed. Then he looked at Matifou, who with his mouth wide open was quite as much astonished as he was.

"Just as we were going to commence," said the giant.

"We are unlucky."

"We'll commence all the same!" said Pescade, running down the steps into the ring.

But at this moment there was a great shouting in the direction of the harbour. The crowd was growing excited and moving towards the seaside; and there was heard above the din the words:

"The trabacolo! The trabacolo!"

The time had come for the launch of the little vessel. The sight, always an attractive one, was of a kind to excite the public curiosity. And the quays where the people had gathered were soon deserted for the yard in which the launch was to take place.

Point Pescade and Matifou saw that there was no chance of an audience at present, and being anxious to find the solitary stranger who had failed to fill their arena, they left it without even stopping to shut the door – and why should they shut it? – and walked off to the yard.

This yard was situated at the end of a point just beyond the harbour, where the beach sloped gradually to the sea. Pescade and his companion after a good deal of elbowing found themselves in the front row of spectators. Never, even on a benefit night, had they had such an audience!

The shores had been cleared away from the trabacolo and she was now ready for the ceremony. The anchor was ready to be let go as soon as the hull entered the water, so as to stop her running too far out into the channel. Although the trabacolo measured only about fifty tons, the mass was considerable enough for every precaution to be taken against accident. Two of the workmen of the yard were on the aft deck near the flagstaff that bore the Dalmatian colours, and two others were forward standing by the anchor.

The trabacolo was to be sent into the water stern first, as is done in all other launches. Her keel resting on the soaped slide was kept in its place by a key. When the key was removed, the boat should begin to slip, and then with increasing swiftness she would rush down the ways into her natural element.

Half a dozen carpenters with sledge mallets were knocking in wedges under the keel forward, so as to increase the speed at which she would take the sea. Everyone followed the operation with the greatest interest amid a general silence.

At this moment from behind the point to the south there suddenly glided into view a yacht. She was a schooner of about three hundred and fifty tons. She was keeping on past the point so as to open the entrance into the harbour. As the breeze was from the northwest she was close-hauled on the port tack, so as to take her straight to her anchorage. Ten minutes after she had been sighted she had come up as rapidly as if she had been looked at through a telescope with a continually lengthening tube.

To enter the harbour the schooner would have to pass in front of the yard where the trabacolo was ready for launching; and as soon as she was sighted it was thought best to suspend operations for a time, and wait till she had gone by. A collision between the two vessels, one broadside on, the other coming at great speed, would have caused a catastrophe on board the yacht.

The workmen, then, stopped driving in the wedges, and the man in charge of the key was told to wait. It would only be for a minute or so. On came the schooner. She could be seen to be getting ready to anchor. Two of the jibs were taken in and the foresail brailed up. But she went on at a good speed under her forestaysail and Spanish reefed mainsail.

All eyes were turned on this graceful vessel whose white sails were now gilded by the oblique rays of the sun. Her sailors in Levantine uniform, with red caps, were running about at their various duties, while the captain, near the man at the helm, gave his orders in a quiet voice.

Very soon the schooner was abreast of the building yard. Suddenly a shout arose. The trabacolo began to move. For some reason the key had given way, and she began to slide the moment the yacht was passing with starboard side towards her.

A collision seemed inevitable. There was neither the time nor the means to prevent it. Nothing could be done. To the cries of the spectators there had come in reply a shout of alarm from the schooner's crew.

The captain put down his helm; but it was impossible for his ship to get by in time to avoid the shock.

The trabacolo was slipping down the ways. A white smoke rose from the friction forward and the stern had already plunged into the waters of the bay.

Suddenly a man jumped out from the crowd. He seized a rope, which hung from the fore part of the trabacolo. But in vain he tried to hold it back at the risk of being dragged away. Close by them was an iron cannon stuck into the ground like a post. In an instant he slipped the rope over it and let it out hand over hand at the risk of being dragged round with it. He kept it back and with superhuman strength he checked it – for ten seconds.

Then the rope broke. But the ten seconds were enough. The trabacolo had plunged into the waves and recovered as from a dive. She shot across the channel, grazing by hardly a foot the schooner's stern, just as the anchor dropped into the depths and brought her sharply up by the tension of the chain.

The schooner was saved.

The hero of this daring manoeuvre was no other than Cape Matifou.

"Well done! Very well done!" exclaimed Point Pescade, running up to the giant, who lifted him in his arms, not to juggle with him, but to embrace him as he always embraced – that is almost to the point of suffocation.

And then the applause resounded from all sides. Five minutes later the schooner had taken up her position in the centre of the harbour; then an elegant whaleboat with six oars brought the owner ashore.

He was a tall man about sixty, with almost white hair and grey beard cut in the Oriental fashion. Large black eyes lit up his face and a curious vivacity displayed itself in his healthily brown face. The most striking thing about him was the air of nobility that distinguished him. As soon as he set foot on shore he walked up to the two acrobats, whom the crowd was greeting and applauding.

The people stood back as he advanced. As soon as he reached Cape Matifou his first action was not to open his purse and take something from it. No! He held out his hand to the giant, and said to him in Italian:

"Thank you, my friend, for what you did."

Cape Matifou was too bashful to notice the compliment.

"Yes! It was good! It was superb!" said Pescade, with all the redundancy of the Provencal idiom.

"You're Frenchmen?" asked the stranger.

"The French of the French!" answered Pescade. "French from the south of France."

The stranger looked at them with feeling and sympathy. Before him were two mountebanks, one of who at the risk of his life had done him a great service; for a collision between the trabacolo and the schooner would have meant several victims.

"Come and see me on board!" he said.

"When?" asked Pescade with a most gracious salute.

"Tomorrow morning."

"Tomorrow morning!" answered Pescade, while Matifou gave sign of consent by nodding his head.

But the crowd had not ceased to surround the hero of the adventure, he would have been carried about in triumph had he not been so large. But Point Pescade, always wide awake, thought he could make some money out of the public excitement. And as soon as the stranger after a gesture of friendship had left for the jetty, he broke out with:

"The match, sirs, the match between Pescade and Cape Matifou. Walk up, gentlemen, walk up. You don't pay till you go out – or you can pay as you come in – just as you please."

This time he was listened to and followed by a public he had never dreamt of before.

The ring was too small! They even had to refuse money!

The stranger passed on, but scarcely had he advanced a step in the direction of the quay when he found himself near the young lady and her father who had been present throughout the scene.

Close by was the young man who had followed them, and to whose salute the father only had given a very haughty acknowledgment.

In this man's presence the stranger experienced a movement he could hardly suppress. It was as if his whole body was repelled, while his eye flashed like lightning.

The girl's father stepped up to him and said:

"You've just escaped a great danger, sir, thanks to the courage of that acrobat."

"Quite so," replied the stranger, whose voice voluntarily or not was masked by emotion.

Then addressing his interlocutor he asked:

"To whom do I have the honour of speaking?"

"To Silas Toronthal of Ragusa," answered the old banker of Trieste. "And may I ask who the owner of the yacht is?"

"Doctor Antekirtt!" replied the stranger.

Then they parted, while shouts of applause were heard from the distant ring of the French acrobats.

And that evening, not only did Cape Matifou have enough to eat, that is to eat as much as four ordinary people, but enough was left for one. And that was enough for the supper of his comrade, Point Pescade.

CHAPTER III

DOCTOR ANTEKIRTT

There are people who give a good deal of employment to Fame – that woman of a hundred mouths whose trumpets blare forth their names towards the four cardinal points of the earth.

This was so in the case of the celebrated Dr. Antekirtt, who had just arrived in the harbour of Gravosa. His arrival had been signalized by an incident, which would have been enough to attract public attention to the most ordinary traveller. And he was not an ordinary traveller.

For several years there had been woven round Dr. Antekirtt a sort of legend in all the legendary countries of the extreme East. Asia from the Dardanelles to the Suez Canal, Africa from Suez to Tunis, the Red Sea along the whole Arab coast, resounded with his name as that of a man of extraordinary knowledge in the physical sciences, a sort of gnostic or taleb who possessed the last secrets of the universe. In earlier times he would have been called an Epiphane; in the countries of the Euphrates he would have been venerated as a descendant of the ancient Magians.

How much of this reputation was undeserved? All that would make the Magian a magician, all that would attribute to him supernatural power. The truth is that Dr. Antekirtt was a man of high education, powerful mind, shrewd judgment, great penetration, and marvellous perspicacity, who had been remarkably served by circumstances. For example, in one of the central provinces of Asia Minor he had been able by a discovery of his own to save a whole population from a terrible epidemic up to then considered to be contagious; and in consequence his fame was unequalled.

One thing that contributed to his celebrity was the impenetrable mystery, which surrounded him. Whence came he? No one knew. What had been his history? None could say. Where had he lived and how? All that was certain about Dr. Antekirtt was that he was adored by the people in Asia Minor and Eastern Africa, that he was held to be a physician of

Point Pescade and Cape Matifou regarded her with no less curiosity…

wonderful skill, that the report of his extraordinary cures had even reached the great scientific centres of Europe, and that his attentions were as freely bestowed on the poorest as on the richest men and pachas of these provinces. But he had never been seen in the west, and for many years his place of residence was unknown; and hence the propensity to regard him as some mysterious avatar, some Hindoo incarnation, some supernatural being curing by supernatural means.

But if Dr. Antekirtt had not yet practiced his art in the principal states of Europe, his reputation had preceded him. Although he had only arrived at Ragusa as an ordinary traveller – a wealthy tourist yachting in the Mediterranean – the news of his arrival had soon spread through the town; and the accident so narrowly prevented by the courage of Cape Matifou had had the effect of still further arousing the public attention.

The yacht would have done credit to the wealthiest and most fastidious of nautical sportsmen. Her two masts without rake and placed well amidships – thus giving her the full benefit of a large mainsail and forestaysail – her long bowsprit with its two jibs, her yards on the foremast, and her powerful spars, were designed for a sail plan that would drive her at immense speed. She was, as we have said, a schooner of about three hundred and fifty tons. Of long, fine lines, neither too broad in the beam, nor too deep in the draught, but of ample stability, she was a craft that in a seaman's hands could be depended on in all weathers. In a decent breeze, either on or off the wind, she could easily reel off her thirteen knots an hour, and would have held her own in a match with any of the crack cruisers of the British clubs.

Her interior fittings were in keeping with her external appearance. The whiteness of her Canadian pine deck, without a knot in its planking, her companions and skylights of teak with their brass work as bright as gold, her beautifully carved helm, her spare spars under their white cases, her taut halyards and running rigging contrasting in colour with her galvanized iron shrouds and stays, her varnished boats hanging gracefully from their davits, the brilliant black of her hull relieved only by a plain gold riband combined to make her a vessel of exquisite taste and extreme elegance.

This yacht is of considerable importance in our story. She was the floating home of that mysterious personage – its hero. Below, luxury strove with comfort. The cabins and saloons were decorated regardless of cost. The carpets and hangings and the rest of the furniture were ingeniously adapted for all the requirements of pleasure navigation; and this was shown not only in the cabins, but even in the pantry where the silver and porcelain services were kept secure from the movement of the ship, in the galley which was a picture of Dutch cleanliness, and in the crew's quarters. The men, numbering about twenty, were dressed like Maltese sailors, with short trousers, sea boots, striped shirts, brown waistbands, red caps, and guernseys – on which in white letters there appeared the initials of the schooner's name and that of her proprietor.

But to what port did this yacht belong? On what register had she been entered? In what Mediterranean country did she lay up for the winter? What was her nationality? No one knew, just as no one knew the nationality of the doctor! A green flag with a red cross in the upper corner, floated at her gaff. And the flags of all nations could be sought through in vain for such an ensign. Nevertheless the officers of the port before Dr. Antekirtt came ashore had had the papers sent to them, and doubtless found them all in due order, for, after the visit of the health officer, they had given her free pratique.

But what was this schooner's name? There was written on her counter in the neatest of gold lettering the solitary word *Savarena*.

Such was the splendid pleasure craft that was now the admired of all in the harbour of Gravosa. Point Pescade and Cape Matifou, who in the morning were to be received on board by Dr. Antekirtt, regarded her with no less curiosity, and with a great deal more emotion than the sailors of the port. As natives of the coast of Provence they were well up in seafaring matters. Point Pescade especially regarded this gem of marine architecture with all the feeling of a connoisseur. And this is what they said to each other in the evening after they had closed their show:

"Ah!" said Cape Matifou.

"Oh!" said Point Pescade.

"Eh, Point Pescade?"

"Who said she wasn't, Cape Matifou?"

And these words doing duty for admirative interjections were as expressive in the mouths of the two acrobats as others much longer could have been.

The *Savarena* was now anchored; her sails were stowed, her ropes were all coiled carefully down, and the awning had been pitched aft. She was moored across an angle of the harbour and thus showed that rather a long stay was in contemplation.

During the evening Dr. Antekirtt contented himself with a short walk in the neighbourhood of Gravosa. While Silas Toronthal and his daughter returned to Ragusa in their carriage, which had waited for them on the quay, and the young man we have mentioned went back down the long avenue without waiting for the end of the fair then in full swing, the doctor strolled about the harbour. It is one of the best on the coast, and at the time contained a considerable amount of shipping of different nationalities. Then after leaving the town he followed the shore of the bay of Ombla Fiumera, which extends for about thirty-six miles to the mouth of the little river Ombla, which is deep enough for vessels of moderate draught to ascend almost to the foot of the Viastiza Mountains. About nine o'clock he returned to the jetty, where he watched the arrival of a large Lloyd mail steamer from the Indian Ocean. Then he returned on board, went down to his cabin, and remained there till the morning.

Such was his custom, and the captain of the *Savarena* – a seaman named Narsos, then in his fortieth year – had orders never to trouble the doctor during his hours of solitude.

It should be said that the officers and crew knew no more of the past history of the owner than outsiders. They were none the less devoted to him, body and soul. Although the doctor would not tolerate the least infraction of discipline, he was very kind and liberal to all. And men were always ready to join the *Savarena*. Never was there a reprimand to give, a punishment to inflict, or a dismissal to effect. It was as though the schooner's crew were all one family.

After the doctor had come aboard all arrangements were made for the night. The lights were got up fore and aft, the watch was set, and complete silence reigned.

The doctor was seated on a large couch in an angle of his apartment. On the table were a few newspapers that his servant had bought in Gravosa. The doctor ran them over carelessly, taking no note of the leaders, but picking out the facts and reading the shipping news, and the fashionable movements. Then he threw the papers down, a sort of somnolent torpor gained upon him, and about eleven o'clock, without calling in his valet, he lay down, though it was some time before he slept.

And if we could have read the thought that especially troubled him, we might have been surprised to find that it found shape in words as, "Who was that young man who bowed to Silas Toronthal on the quay at Gravosa?"

About eight o'clock next morning the doctor appeared on deck. The day promised to be magnificent. The sun was already shining on the mountaintops, which form the background of the bay. The shadows were swiftly retreating to the shore across the surface of the waters. And very soon the sun shone direct on the *Savarena*.

The boat stopped at the starboard gangway – the place of honour

Captain Narsos came up to the doctor to receive his orders, which, after a pleasant greeting, were given him in very few words.

A minute afterwards a boat left the schooner with four men and a coxswain and headed for the wharf, where she was to wait the convenience of Point Pescade and Cape Matifou.

It was a grand day and a grand ceremony in the nomadic existence of these two honest fellows who had wandered so many hundreds of miles away from that beloved Provence they so longed to see.

They were both on the jetty. They had changed their professional costume for ordinary clothes – rather worn, perhaps, but clean; and stood there looking at the yacht and admiring her as before. And they were in particularly good spirits. Not only had they supped last night, but they had breakfasted this morning. A piece of extravagance that could only be explained by their having taken the extraordinary amount of forty-two florins. But do not let it be thought that they had dissipated all their receipts. No! Point Pescade was prudent, and looked ahead, and life was assured them for a dozen days at the least.

"It's to you we owe that, Cape Matifou!"

"Oh! Pescade!"

"Yes, you, you big man."

"Well, yes, to me if you like!" answered Matifou.

The *Savarena*'s boat now came alongside the wharf. The coxswain rose, cap in hand, and hastened to say that he was "at the gentlemen's orders."

"Gentlemen! What gentlemen?" asked Point Pescade.

"Yourselves," answered the coxswain. "You whom Dr. Antekirtt is waiting for on board."

"Good! You see we're gentlemen already!" said Point Pescade.

Cape Matifou opened his huge eyes and twirled his hat in his hands.

"When you're ready, gentlemen!" said the coxswain.

"Oh, we're quite ready – quite ready!" said Point Pescade with a most affable bow.

And a moment afterwards the two friends were comfortably seated on the black rug with red edging which covered the thwart, while the coxswain had taken his place behind them.

Of course the enormous weight of our Hercules brought the boat down four or five inches below her usual load line. And the corners of the rug had to be turned in to prevent their dragging in the water. The four oars dipped, and the boat slipped quickly along towards the *Savarena*.

It must be admitted that the two passengers were rather excited and even shy. Such honours for a pair of mountebanks! Cape Matifou dared not stir. Point Pescade, with all his confusion, could not conceal that cheerful smile which always animated his intelligent face.

The boat passed round the schooner's stern and stopped at the starboard gangway – the place of honour.

The ladder bent beneath Matifou's weight as he went up the side. As soon as he and Pescade had reached the deck they were taken aft to the doctor.

After a cordial "good morning" several formalities and ceremonies had to be gone through before the visitors would consent to sit down. At last they did so.

The doctor looked at them for a moment or two without speaking. His passionless, handsome face impressed them greatly. But there could be no doubting that if the smile was not on his lips it was in his heart.

"My friends," said he, "yesterday you saved my crew and myself from a great danger. I wished to thank you once more for having done so, and that is why I asked you to come on board."

"Doctor," answered Point Pescade, who began to recover some of his assurance, "you're very kind. But what my comrade did any man would have done in his place, if he had had the strength. Wouldn't he, Cape Matifou?"

Matifou gave an affirmative sign, which consisted in shaking his head up and down.

Be it so," said the doctor, "but that's not all, for your companion has risked his life, and I consider myself obliged to him."

"Oh, doctor!" replied Point Pescade, "you'll make my old Cape blush, and it'll never do to let the blood rush to his head."

"Well, my friends," continued the doctor, "I see you do not care for compliments! So I will not insist upon them! However, as every service is worthy of…"

"Doctor!" answered Point Pescade. "I beg pardon for interrupting you, but a good action, as the copybooks say, is its own reward, and we have been rewarded."

"Already! And how?" asked the doctor, who began to think he had been anticipated.

"Undoubtedly!" replied Pescade. "After that extraordinary exhibition of strength on the part of our Hercules the public were anxious to judge for themselves of his powers under more artistic conditions. And so they came in crowds to our Provencal arena. Cape Matifou threw half a dozen of the stoutest mountaineers and strongest porters of Gravosa, and we took an enormous sum!"

"Enormous?"

"Yes, unprecedented in our acrobatic careers."

"And how much?"

"Forty-two florins!"

"Oh! Indeed! But I did not know that!" answered the doctor good-humouredly. "If I had known you were giving a performance I should have made it a duty and a pleasure to be present! You'll allow me then to pay for my seat..."

"This evening, doctor," answered Point Pescade, "If you come to honour our efforts with your presence."

Cape Matifou bowed politely and shrugged up his huge shoulders, "which had never yet bitten the dust," to quote from the verbal programme issued by Point Pescade.

The doctor saw that he could not persuade the acrobats to receive any reward at least of a pecuniary kind. He resolved therefore to proceed differently. Besides his plans with regard to them had been decided on the previous night; and from inquiries he had made regarding the mountebanks he had found that they were really honest men in whom all confidence could be placed.

"What are your names?" asked he.

"The only name I am known by is Point Pescade."

"And yours?"

"Matifou," answered Hercules.

"That is to say Cape Matifou," added Pescade, not without some pride in mentioning a name of such renown in the arenas of the south of France.

"But those are surnames..." observed the doctor.

"We have no others," answered Pescade, "or if we had, our pockets got out of repair and we lost them on the road."

"And – your relations?"

"Relations, doctor! Our means have never allowed us such luxuries! But if we ever get rich, we can easily find them."

"You're Frenchmen? From what part of France?"

"From Provence," said Pescade proudly, "that is to say, we're Frenchmen twice over."

"You are facetious, Point Pescade!"

"That's my trade. Just imagine a clown with a red tail a street jester with a solemn humour. He would get more apples in an hour than he could eat in a lifetime! Yes, I'm rather lively, extremely lively, I must admit."

"And Cape Matifou?"

"Cape Matifou is more serious, more thoughtful, more everything!" said Pescade, giving his companion a friendly pat much as if he were caressing a horse. "That is his trade also. When you're pitching half-hundreds about, you have to be serious! When you wrestle you not only use your arms but your head! And Cape Matifou has always been wrestling – with misery! And he hasn't yet been thrown!"

The doctor listened with interest to the brave little fellow who brought no complaint against the fate that had used him so ill. He saw that he possessed as much heart as intelligence, and wondered what he would have become had material means not failed him at the outset of life.

"And where are you going now?" he asked.

"Where chance leads us," answered Point Pescade. "And it's not always a bad guide, for it generally knows the roads, although I fancy it has taken us rather too far away from home this time! After all, that is our fault. We ought to have asked at first where it was going!"

The doctor looked at them both for a minute. Then he continued:

"What can I do for you?"

"Nothing, sir," answered Pescade, "nothing – I assure you."

"Would you not like very much to go back to Provence?"

At once a light sprang into their eyes.

"I can take you there."

"That would be capital," answered Pescade.

And then addressing his companion he said:

"Cape Matifou, would you like to go back?"

"Yes – if you come, Point Pescade."

"But what should we do? How should we live?"

Cape Matifou knit his brows as was his way when in a fix.

"We can do – we can do..." he muttered.

"You know nothing about it – and neither do I! But anyhow it is our country! Isn't it strange doctor, that fellows like us have a country, that although we have no parents we are born somewhere? It has always seemed queer to me."

"Can you arrange for both of you to stop with me?" asked the doctor.

At this unexpected proposition Pescade jumped up with a start, while Hercules looked on, wondering if he ought to get up too.

'Stop with you, doctor?" answered Point Pescade. "But what good shall we be to you? Exhibitions of strength and activity we are accustomed to, but we can do nothing else! And unless it is to amuse you during the voyage..."

"Listen," said the doctor. "I want a few men, brave, devoted, clever and intelligent, who can help me in my plans. There's nothing to keep you here. Will you join these men?"

"But when your plans are realized..." said Point Pescade.

"You need not leave me unless you like," said the doctor with a smile. "You can stay on board with me. And look here, you can give a few lessons in acrobatics to the crew. But if you want to go back to your country you can do so, and I'll see you do not want for the rest of your lives."

"Oh, doctor!" said Pescade. "But you do not intend to leave us nothing to do! It won't do for us to be good for nothing!"

"I'll give you something to do that'll suit you."

"The offer is a tempting one," said Pescade.

"What is your objection to it?"

"Only one perhaps. You see us two, Cape Matifou and me! We're of the same country, and we ought to be of the same family if we had a family! Two brothers at heart. Cape Matifou could not exist without Point Pescade, nor could Point Pescade without Cape Matifou. Imagine the Siamese twins! You must never separate us, for separation would cost us our lives. We're quite Siamese – and we like you very much, doctor!"

And Point Pescade held out his hand to Cape Matifou, who pressed it against his breast as if he had been a child.

"My friends," said the doctor, "I had no idea of separating you, and I understand that you'll never leave each other."

"Then we can look upon it as arranged if..."

"If what?"

"If Cape Matifou consents."

"Say yes, Point Pescade," answered Hercules, "and you'll have said yes for both."

"Excellent," said the doctor, "then it's agreed, and you'll never, repent it! From this day forward you need do nothing else."

"Oh, doctor! Take care!" said Pescade. "You may be engaging more than you think."

"And why?"

"Can you arrange for both of you to stop with me?" asked the doctor

"We may cost you too much! Particularly Matifou! He is a tremendous eater, and you wouldn't like him to lose his strength in your service."

"I hope he'll double it."

"Then he'll ruin you!"

"He won't ruin me, Point Pescade."

"But he'll want two meals—three meals a day!"

"Five, six, ten if he likes," said the doctor with a smile. "He'll find the table always laid for him."

"Eh! Old Cape!" exclaimed Point Pescade quite delightedly. "You'll be able to grub away to your heart's content!"

"And so will you, Point Pescade."

"Oh! I eat like a bird! But may I ask, sir, will we be going to sea?"

"Quite often, my friend. I have business in all quarters of the Mediterranean. My patients are scattered all over the coast! I'm going to carry on a sort of international practice of medicine! When a sick man wants me in Tangier or in the Balearics when I'm at Suez, am I not to go to him? What a physician does in a large town from one quarter to another, I do from the Straits of Gibraltar to the Archipelago, from the Adriatic to the Gulf of Lyons, from the Ionian Sea to the Gulf of Cadiz! I have other vessels ten times faster than this schooner, and generally you'll come with me in my visits."

"That we will, doctor," said Point Pescade, rubbing his hands.

"Are you afraid of the sea?" asked the doctor.

"Afraid of the sea!" exclaimed Point Pescade. "Children of Provence! Ragamuffins rolling about in the coast boats! No! We're not afraid of the sea, nor of the pretended sickness it yields. We're used to walking about on our hands, heads down and heels in the air, if the ladies and gentlemen who are inclined to be seasick only had a couple of months of that exercise they'd never need to stick their nose in a basin! Walk up! Walk up! Ladies and gentlemen, follow the crowd!"

And Pescade came out with a scrap of his patter as gaily as if he were on the stand in front of his arena.

"That's good, Point Pescade!" said the doctor. "We'll listen to you as long as you like, and I advise you never to lose your cheerful spirits. Laugh, my boy, laugh and sing as much as you like. The future may have such sad things in store for us that we cannot afford to despise happiness as we go."

As he spoke the doctor became serious again, and Pescade who was watching him came to the conclusion that in his past life he had experienced a greater share of grief than usual.

"Sir," said he after a pause, "from today we belong to you body and soul."

"And from today," answered the doctor, "you can take possession of your cabin. Probably I shall remain a few days at Gravosa and Ragusa; but it's as well you should get into the way of living on board the *Savarena*."

"Until you take us off to your country..." added Pescade.

"I have no country," said the doctor, "or rather I have a country, a country of my own, which can become yours if you like."

"Come on, Matifou, then. We'll go and wind up the arm! Be easy. We owe no one anything, and we're not going to offer a composition!"

And having taken leave of the doctor they embarked in the boat that was waiting for them, and were rowed to the quay.

In a couple of hours they had made out their inventory and transferred to some brother showman the trestles, painted canvas, big drum and tambourine which formed the whole assets. The transfer did not take long, and was not very difficult, and the weight of the money realized did not seriously inconvenience them.

But Point Pescade kept back his acrobat's costume and his cornet, and Matifou kept his trombone and his wrestling suit. It would have been too much for them to part with such old friends that reminded them of so many triumphs and successes; and so they were packed at the bottom of the small trunk, which contained their furniture, their wardrobe, and all their belongings.

About one o'clock in the afternoon Matifou returned to the *Savarena*. A large cabin forward had been assigned to them – a comfortable cabin "furnished with everything you can desire," as Pescade said.

The crew gave a cordial greeting to the newcomers who had saved them from a terrible accident, and Point Pescade and Matifou had no occasion to grieve for the food they had left behind them.

"You see, Cape Matifou," said Pescade, draining a glass of good Asti wine, "you can attain anything with good manners. But you must have good manners!"

Cape Matifou only replied by a nod, his mouth was full of a huge piece of grilled ham which accompanied by ten fried eggs very soon disappeared down his throat.

"Ah, the money we'd make," said Point Pescade, "if we could charge people to watch you eat!"

CHAPTER IV

STEPHEN BATHORY'S WIDOW

The arrival of Dr. Antekirtt had caused quite a commotion, not only in Ragusa, but throughout the province of Dalmatia. The newspapers after announcing the schooner's arrival had swooped down on the prey, which promised to yield such a series of sensational articles. The owner of the *Savarena* could not escape the honours and drawbacks of celebrity. His personality was the order of the day. Legend had seized upon him for its own. No one knew who he was, whence he came, or whither he was going. This was just the thing to pique public curiosity. And naturally where nothing is known the field is more open and imagination has more scope.

The reporters, anxious to gratify their readers, had hurried to Gravosa – some of them even went out to the schooner. But the personage about whom rumour was so busy was not to be seen. The orders were precise. The doctor would not receive such visitors. And the answers given to the visitors were always the same.

"Where does the doctor come from?"

"Where he pleases."

"Where is he going?"

"Where he likes."

"But who is he?"

"No one knows, and perhaps he does not know any more than you do!"

Not much to be gained for their readers, from such replies as these! And so they gave the reins to their imagination, Dr. Antekirtt became all they pleased. He became all that these interviewers at bay thought fit to invent. To some he was a pirate chief. To others he was an African king cruising incognito in quest of knowledge. Some affirmed that he was a political exile; others that a revolution had driven him from his country and that he was travelling for purposes of science and art. The readers could take their choice. As to his title of doctor there seemed to be two opinions; in the opinion of some he was a great physician who had effected wonderful cures in desperate cases, in the opinion of others he was a great quack who would find it difficult to produce his diplomas!

Under any circumstances the physicians of Gravosa and Ragusa would have no chance of prosecuting him for the illegal practice of medicine. Dr. Antekirtt maintained a constant reserve, and whenever a patient would have done him the honour to consult him, he invariably declined.

The owner of the *Savarena* took no apartments on shore. He did not even enter any of the hotels in the town. During the first two days after his arrival at Gravosa he hardly got as far as Ragusa. He contented himself with a few walks in the neighbourhood, and two or three times he took with him Point Pescade whose natural intelligence he appreciated.

But if he did not go to Ragusa, one day Pescade went there for him. He had been sent on some confidential errand and these were his replies to the questions asked him when he returned:

"And so he lives in the Stradone?"

"Yes, doctor, that is to say in the best street of the town, he has a house not far from the place where they show visitors the palace of the old doges; a magnificent house with servants and carriages. Quite in the style of a millionaire."

"And the other?"

"The other, or rather the others," answered Pescade, "they live in the same neighbourhood, but their house is up a narrow, winding, hilly street that takes you to houses that are very second rate."

"And their house!"

"Their house is humble, small, dismal-looking outside, but I should think it was all right inside. It looks as though the people that lived there were poor and proud."

"The lady?"

"I didn't see her, and I heard that she hardly ever went out of the Rue Marinella."

"And her son?"

"I saw him, doctor, as he came back to his mother."

"What was he like?"

"He seemed thoughtful and anxious! They say that the young fellow has seen sorrow! And he looks like it!"

"But, Pescade, you've seen sorrow, and yet you do not look like it."

"Physical suffering isn't moral suffering, doctor! That's why I've always hidden mine – and even laughed over it."

After this the doctor stopped his walks about Gravosa. He seemed to be waiting for something that he had not desired to provoke by going to Ragusa, where the news of his arrival in the *Savarena* was, of course, known. He remained on board, and what he was waiting for happened.

On the 29th of May, about eleven o'clock in the morning, the doctor was examining the quays of Gravosa through his telescope, when he suddenly gave orders for the whaleboat to be launched, entered it, and landed at the mole where a man seemed to be watching for him.

"It is he!" said the doctor. "It is really! I recognize him, though he is so changed."

The man was old, and broken down with age, and although he was not more than seventy, his hair was white, and his head was bowed. His expression was sad and weary, and his face received but little animation from the feeble gaze his tears had often hidden. He remained motionless on the quay, never having lost sight of the boat since it left the schooner.

The doctor looked as though he did not see the old man, still less recognize him. He took no notice of his presence. But before he had taken many steps he advanced towards him, and humbly uncovered.

"Dr. Antekirtt?" he asked.

"Yes," answered the doctor, looking at the poor old man whose eyes as they looked at his gave not the slightest sign of recognition.

Then he added:

"Who are you, my friend, and what do you want with me?"

"My name is Borik," answered the old man, "I'm in the service of Madame Bathory, and I've been sent by her to ask you to make an appointment for her to see you."

"Bathory?" repeated the doctor. "Is she the widow of the Hungarian who paid for his patriotism with his life?"

"The same," answered the old man. "Though you've never met her, you do know of her, you are after all, Dr. Antekirtt."

The doctor listened attentively to the old man who kept his eyes on the ground. He seemed to ask if the words contained some hidden meaning.

Then he resumed:

"What does Madame Bathory want with me?"

"For reasons you can understand, she desires to have an interview with you."

169

In a couple of hours they had made out their inventory

"I'll go and see her."

"She would prefer to visit you aboard your ship."

"Why?"

"It's important the interview should be kept secret."

"Kept secret? From whom?

"From her son! It's not desirable that Mr. Pierre should know that Madame Bathory has had a visit from you."

The reply seemed to surprise the doctor; but he did not allow Borik to notice it.

"I prefer to go to Madame Bathory's house," said he. "Can I not do so in her son's absence?"

"You can, doctor, if you can arrange to come tomorrow. Pierre Bathory is going to Zara this evening, and he won't be back for twenty-four hours."

"What does Pierre Bathory do?"

"He's an engineer, but up to the present he hasn't been able to secure an appointment. Ah! Life's been hard for his mother and him."

"Hard!" answered the doctor. "Has Madame Bathory been in want?"

He stopped himself. The old man bowed his head and sighed and sobbed.

"Doctor," said he at last, "I cannot tell you more. In the interview, which she desires, Madame Bathory will tell you all that you should know."

It was evident that the doctor was thoroughly, master of himself to conceal his emotion so successfully.

"Where does Madame Bathory live?" asked he.

"At Ragusa, in the Stradone quarter, at No. 17 in the Rue Marinella."

"Can I see Madame Bathory tomorrow between one and two o'clock in the afternoon?"

"You can, doctor, I'll introduce you."

"Tell Madame Bathory she can expect me at that time."

"I thank you, in her name," replied the old man. Then after some hesitation added:

"You may think," added he, "that she wishes to ask some favour of you."

"And what may that be?" asked the doctor quickly.

"Nothing," answered Borik.

Then, after a humble bow, he walked away down the road from Gravosa to Ragusa.

171

Evidently those last words had been rather a surprise for the doctor. He remained motionless on the quay, looking after Borik as he walked away. And when he returned on board he shut himself up in his room, and remained there during the rest of the day.

Point Pescade and Cape Matifou took advantage of the holiday thus given them. They did themselves the pleasure of visiting the fair as spectators. To say that the active clown was not tempted to remonstrate at the clumsy juggler, or that the powerful wrestler did not burn to take part in the struggle between the athletes is to say what is contrary to the truth. But both remembered that they had the honour of belonging to the crew of the *Savarena*. They remained as simple spectators, and did not spare the bravos when they thought them deserved.

The next day the doctor went ashore a little after noon.

After he had sent the boat back he started along the road from Gravosa to Ragusa – a fine avenue a mile and a quarter long bordered with villas and shaded with trees. The avenue was not as lively as it would be a few hours later, when it would be crowded with carriages and loungers on horse and foot.

The doctor, thinking all the time of his interview with Madame Bathory, followed one of the side streets and soon reached the Borgo Pille, a kind of stone arm, which stretches along the triple line of the fortifications of Ragusa. The gate was open, and through the three walls gave access to the interior of the city.

A splendid paved road is the Stradone, extending from the forgo Pille to the suburb of Plocce after passing straight through the town. It runs along the foot of a hill on which rises quite an amphitheatre of houses. At one end is the palace of the doges, a fine monument of fifteenth century age, with an interior courtyard, Renaissance portico, and semicircular windows whose slender columns are worthy of the best period of Tuscan architecture.

The doctor had not to go as far as this. The Rue Marinella that Borik had mentioned the day before turns off to the left about the middle of the Stradone. If his pace slackened at all it was when he threw a rapid glance at a mansion built of granite whose rich façade and square outbuildings were to the right of him. Through the open gate of the courtyard he could see the master's carriage with superb horses, with the coachman on the box, while a manservant was waiting on the flight of steps under the elegant verandah.

Immediately afterwards a man got into the carriage, the horses came out of the courtyard and the gate closed behind them. This was the individual who three days before had accosted Dr. Antekirtt on the quay at Gravosa; he was the old banker of Trieste, Silas Toronthal.

The doctor, desirous of avoiding a meeting, turned quickly back, and did not resume his journey until the carriage had disappeared at the end of the Stradone.

"Both in the same town!" he murmured. "This is chance; it's not my fault."

Narrow, steep, badly paved, and of poor appearance are the roads, which open on to the left of the Stradone. Imagine a large river with the tributaries on one of its sides all mountain torrents! To secure a little air the houses cluster on the hillside one above the other, and touch one another. Their eyes look into their eyes, if it is allowable so to speak of the windows or dormers that open along their fronts. Thus they mount one over another to the crest of one of the two hills whose summits are crowned by Forts Mincetto and San Lorenzo.

No vehicle could travel there. If the torrent was absent, except on days of heavy rain, the road was nonetheless a ravine, and its slopes and inequalities were only rendered passable by steps and landing-places. There was a great contrast between the modest dwellings and the splendid mansions of the Stradone.

The doctor reached the corner of the Rue Marinella and began to mount the interminable steps, which did duty for the road. He had gone about sixty yards when he stopped in front of No. 17.

There the door opened immediately. Old Borik was waiting for the doctor. He introduced him without saying a word into a room cleanly kept, but poorly furnished.

The doctor sat down. There was nothing to show that he felt the least emotion at finding himself in this house – not even when Madame Bathory entered and said: "Dr. Antekirtt?"

"Yes," said the doctor.

"I should have liked to have saved you the trouble of coming so far and so high!" said Madame Bathory.

"I came to call on you, Madame, and I hope you'll think I am quite at your service."

"Sir," replied Madame Bathory, "it was only yesterday that I heard of your arrival at Gravosa, and I immediately sent Borik to request an interview with you."

"Madame, I'm ready to hear what you have to say."

"I'll retire," said the old man.

The doctor soon reached the Borgo Pille

"No, you can stay, Borik!" answered Madame Bathory. "You're the only friend our family has, and you had better know all I'm going to say to Dr. Antekirtt."

Madame Bathory sat down, and the doctor sat in front of her, while Borik remained standing at the window.

Professor Stephen Bathory's widow was then in her sixtieth year. If her figure was still upright in spite of the burden of age, her white hair and deeply-wrinkled face showed how much she had had to struggle against grief and misery. But she seemed as energetic as ever. In her was apparent the valiant companion and confiding friend of him who had sacrificed his life for what he deemed to be his duty.

"Sir," said she in a voice which betrayed how vainly she was trying to hide her emotion, "you being Dr. Antekirtt, I am under an obligation to you, and I ought to tell you what happened at Trieste fifteen years ago…"

"Madame, being Dr. Antekirtt I can spare you the mournful story. I know it and I may add – being Dr. Antekirtt – that I know what has been your life since the never-to-be-forgotten 30th of June, 1867."

"Will you then tell me," said Madame Bathory, "what is the reason of the interest you take in my life?"

"The interest, Madame, that a man must feel for the widow of a Magyar who did not hesitate to risk his life for the independence of his country."

"Did you know Professor Bathory?" asked the widow.

"I knew him, I loved him, and I reverence all who bear his name."

"Are you then a native of the country for which he died?"

"I am of no country, Madame."

"Who are you then?"

"A dead man not yet gone to his grave," answered the doctor coldly.

Madame Bathory and Borik started at this unexpected reply; but the doctor immediately continued:

"However, Madame, it's necessary that the story that I asked you not to tell should be told by me, for if there are circumstances about it that you know there are others that you do not know, and of these you will not be ignorant much longer."

"Be it so, then, I'm listening."

"Madame," began the doctor, "fifteen years ago three Hungarian nobles became the chiefs of a conspiracy the object of which was to give Hungary her ancient independence. These men were Count Mathias Sandorf, Professor Stephen Bathory, and Count Ladislas Zathmar, three friends united for years in the same hope, three living beings with but one heart.

"On the 8th of June, 1867, the evening before the day on which the signal of the rising was to be given which was to extend through Hungary to Transylvania, Count Zathmar's house at Trieste was entered by the Austrian police. Count Sandorf and his two companions were seized, taken away, and thrown into prison that very night in the donjon of Pisino, and a week or two afterwards were condemned to death.

"A young accountant named Sarcany was arrested at the same time in Count Zathmar's house; he was a perfect stranger to the plot, and was set at liberty after the affair was over.

"The night before the execution an attempt at escape was made by the prisoners who were left together in the same cell. Count Sandorf and Stephen Bathory availed themselves of the lightning conductor and got out of the donjon of Pisino. They fell into the torrent of the Foiba at the moment when Ladislas Zathmar was seized by the warders and prevented from following them.

"Although the fugitives had very little chance of escaping death, for a subterranean stream bore them through the centre of a country they did not even know, they succeeded in reaching the banks of the Leme Canal, near the town of Rovigno, and at Rovigno they found shelter in the house of a fisherman, Andrea Ferrato.

"This fisherman – a brave fellow – had made all preparations to take them across the Adriatic, when out of pure personal revenge, a Spaniard named Carpena, who had discovered the secret of their retreat, gave information to the police of Rovigno. They tried to escape a second time. But Stephen Bathory was wounded and recaptured, while Mathias Sandorf was pursued to the beach, and sunk under a shower of bullets, the Adriatic never giving up his corpse.

"The day after Stephen Bathory and Ladislas Zathmar were shot in the fortress of Pisino. Then, for having given them shelter, the fisherman Andrea Ferrato was sentenced to imprisonment for life, and sent to Stein."

Madame Bathory bowed her head. Sad at heart she had listened without a word to the doctor's story.

"You knew all these details, Madame?" asked he.

"Yes, as you do probably, from the newspapers."

"Yes, from the newspapers," was the reply. "But one thing which the newspapers did not tell the public because the matter was conducted in secret, I happened to learn owing to the indiscretion of one of the warders of the fortress, and that I'll now tell you."

"Proceed."

"Count Mathias Sandorf and Stephen Bathory were found in Ferrato's house owing to their being betrayed by Carpena, the Spaniard. And they were arrested three weeks before in the house at Trieste owing to traitors having informed against them to the Austrian police."

"Traitors!" exclaimed Madame Bathory.

"Yes, Madame, and the proof of the treason was produced at the trial. In the first place these traitors had intercepted a letter addressed to Count Sandorf, which they had found on a carrier pigeon and copied; and in the second place they had managed to obtain a tracing of the grating, which enabled them to read the dispatch. Then when they had read the message they handed it over to the Governor of Trieste. And, doubtless, a share of Count Sandorf's wealth was their reward."

"The wretches! Are they known?" asked Madame Bathory in a voice trembling with emotion.

"No, Madame," answered the doctor. "But perhaps the three prisoners knew them, and would have said who they were had they been able to see their families before they died."

It will be remembered that neither Madame Bathory, then away with her son, nor Borik who was in prison at Trieste, had been able to visit the prisoners in their last hours.

"Shall we never know the names of these wretches?" asked Madame Bathory.

"Madame," answered the doctor, "traitors always end by betraying themselves. But this is what I have to say to complete my story:

"You remained a widow with a boy of eight, almost penniless. Borik, the servant of Count Zathmar, would not leave you after his master's death; but he was poor and had only his devotion to offer you.

"Then, Madame, you left Trieste for this humble dwelling at Ragusa. You have worked, worked with your hands to earn sufficient for your material as well as your mental needs. You wished in fact that your son should follow in science the path that his father had made illustrious. But what an incessant struggle it was, what misery you had so bravely to submit to! And with what respect I now bend to the noble woman who has shown such energy as a mother, and made of her son – a man!"

And as he spoke the doctor rose and a shade of emotion just made itself visible despite his habitual reserve.

The steps of the Rue Marinella

Madame Bathory had nothing to say in reply. She waited, not knowing if the doctor had finished, or if he was going on to relate such facts as were personally known to him and concerning which she had asked for the interview.

"However, Madame," continued the doctor, divining her thoughts, "human strength has doubtless its limits, and as you fell ill and exhausted with such trials you would doubtless have succumbed if an unknown – no! a friend of Professor Bathory – had not, come to your aid. I should never have said anything about this had not your old servant told me of your wish to see me..."

"Quite so," answered Madame Bathory. "Have I not to thank Dr. Antekirtt?"

"And why, Madame? Because during the last five or six years, in remembrance of the friendship which bound him to Count Sandorf and his two companions, and to help you in your work, Dr. Antekirtt has sent you a sum of a hundred thousand florins? Was he not only too happy to put the money at your disposal? No, Madame, it is I, on the contrary, who ought to thank you for having accepted the gift if it was of any help to the widow and son of Stephen Bathory!"

The widow bowed and answered:

"In any case I have to thank you. That is the first object of the visit I wished to make. But there was a second..."

"What is that, Madame?"

"It was – to give you back the money..."

"What, Madame?" said the doctor quickly, "you do not wish to accept it?"

"Sir, I do not think I have any right to the money. I do not know Dr. Antekirtt. I never heard his name. The money may be a sort of alms coming from those whom my husband fought and whose pity is hateful to me. And so I do not care to use it, even for the purpose Dr. Antekirtt intended."

"And – so this money..."

"Is untouched."

"And your son!"

"My son will have nothing, but what he owes to himself."

"And to his mother!" added the doctor, with whom such grandeur of soul and energy of character could not but excite admiration and command respect.

Madame Bathory had risen, and from a desk, which she unlocked, she drew forth a roll of notes, which she handed to the doctor.

"Sir," said she, "take back the money, it's yours, and receive the thanks of a mother as if she'd used it to educate her son!"

"The money no longer belongs to me, Madame!" replied the doctor, refusing it with a gesture.

"I repeat that it has never belonged to me."

"But if Pierre Bathory can use it..."

"My son will find the situation for which he is fit and I can trust him as I can trust myself."

"He will not refuse what his father's friend insists on accepting."

"He will refuse."

"At least, Madame, will you allow me to try?"

"I beg you, do nothing, doctor," answered Madame Bathory. "My son doesn't know I've received this money, and I do not wish him ever to know it."

"Be it so, Madame! I understand your feelings, although I'm a stranger and unknown to you! Yes, I understand and admire them! But I repeat, if the money is not yours, it is not mine."

Dr. Antekirtt rose. There was nothing in Madame Bathory's refusal to annoy him personally and her delicacy only filled him with a feeling of profound respect. He bowed to the widow, and was turning to leave when another question stopped him.

"Sir," said Madame Bathory, "you've told me of some miserable proceedings which sent to their deaths Ladislas Zathmar, Stephen Bathory, and Count Sandorf?"

"I said what was true, Madame."

"But does any one know these people?"

"Yes, Madame."

"Who?"

"God!"

And as he spoke the doctor made a low obeisance and left.

Madame Bathory remained deep in thought. By some secret sympathy, for which she could not account, she felt herself irresistibly drawn towards the mysterious personage who was so mixed up with the events of her life. Would she ever see him again? And if the *Savarena* had only brought him to Ragusa to make this visit, would the yacht go to sea and never return?

The next day's newspapers announced that an anonymous gift of a hundred thousand florins had been made to the hospitals of the town.

It was the gift of Dr. Antekirtt, but was it not also the gift of the widow who had refused it for herself and her son?

CHAPTER V

DIVERSE INCIDENTS

The doctor was in no such hurry to leave Gravosa as Madame Bathory imagined. After endeavouring in vain to help the mother he resolved to try and help the son. If up to then Pierre Bathory had not found the post for which his brilliant acquirements fitted him he would probably not refuse the doctor's offers. To put him in a position worthy of his talents, worthy of the name he bore, was not an act of charity; it was only an act of justice!

But, as Borik had said, Pierre Bathory had gone to Zara on business.

The doctor wrote to him without delay. He wrote that same day. The letter stated that he would be glad to receive Pierre Bathory on board the *Savarena*, having a proposition to make that might interest him.

The letter was posted at Gravosa, and all that could be done then was to wait for the young engineer's return. Meanwhile the doctor continued to live more retired than ever on board the schooner. The *Savarena*, moored in the centre of the harbour with her crew never coming ashore, was as isolated as if she were in the centre of the Mediterranean or the Atlantic.

This was a peculiarity that much exercised the minds of the curious, reporters and others, who had never given up all hope of interviewing the legendary owner, although they had not yet been allowed on board the yacht, which was almost as legendary as himself! As Point Pescade and Cape Matifou occasionally had shore leave they often found themselves quite an attraction to the reporters desirous of obtaining a particle or two of information that might bear working up.

We know that with Point Pescade a certain amount of fun had been introduced on board the schooner, and if Cape Matifou remained as serious as the capstan of which he had the strength, Pescade laughing and singing all day long was as lively as a man-o'-war pennant. When, active as a seaman and agile as a cabin boy, he was not clambering about the spars to the delight of the crew to whom he was delivering a series of lessons on ground and lofty tumbling, he was amusing them by his interminable jokes. Dr. Antekirtt had recommended him to retain his cheerful spirits and he kept them and yet parted with them to others!

We have said above that he and Cape Matifou often had shore leave. They in fact were free to come and go as they pleased. The rest of the crew remained on board; they could go ashore when they liked. And hence the very natural propensity of the curious to follow them and attempt to draw them into conversation. But they could get nothing out of Point Pescade, whether he wished to be silent or to speak, for he had really nothing to tell.

"Who is your Dr. Antekirtt?"

"A famous physician! He can cure all your complaints – even those you're going to take with you to the other world!"

"Is he rich?"

"Hasn't got a halfpenny! I give him his allowance every Sunday!"

"But where does he come from?"

"Why, from no one knows where!"

"And where's that?"

"All I can tell you about it is that it is bordered on the north by something big and on the south by nothing at all!"

Evidently there was not much to be got out of Pescade, and Cape Matifou remained as dumb as a lump of granite.

But although they said nothing to strangers, the two friends, between themselves, often had a talk about their new master. They liked him already, and they liked him very much. Between them and the doctor there was a sort of chemical affinity, a cohesion that from day to day bound them more firmly together.

And each morning they waited to be called into the cabin to hear him say:

"My friends, I have need of you."

But nothing came – to their vexation.

"Is this sort of thing going on much longer?" asked Point Pescade. "It's rather hard to remain doing nothing when you haven't been brought up to it, eh, Cape?"

"Yes, your arms get rusty," answered Hercules, looking at his enormous biceps motionless as the rods of an engine at rest.

"Shall I tell you something, Cape Matifou?"

"Tell me what you like."

"Do you know what I think about Dr. Antekirtt?"

182

"No, but tell me, that'll help me answer you."

"Well, that in his past life there have been things – things! Look at his eyes which every now and then give a glance that almost blinds you like lightning! And when the thunder rolls..."

"It makes a noise."

"Exactly, Cape Matifou, a noise ... and I fancy we shall come in useful at that game!"

It was not without reason that Point Pescade spoke in this way. Although the most complete calm reigned on board the schooner, the intelligent little fellow could not help noticing certain things, which set him thinking. Nothing could be more evident than that the doctor was not a simple tourist on a yacht cruise in the Mediterranean. The *Savarena* was the centre of a web of many threads whose ends were held in the hands of her mysterious owner.

Letters and dispatches seemed to arrive from every corner of the mighty sea whose waters bathe the shores of so many different countries. They came from the French coast, the Spanish coast, the coast of Morocco, of Algeria, and Tripoli. Who sent them? Evidently correspondents occupied on certain matters the gravity of which could not be mistaken – unless they were patients consulting the celebrated doctor by correspondence, which did not seem to be probable.

In the telegraph office at Ragusa the meaning of these messages was a mystery, for they were in an unknown tongue of which the doctor alone seemed to know the secret. And even when the language was intelligible what sense could be made out of such phrases as:

"Almeira. They thought they were on the track of Z. R. False trail now abandoned."

"Recovered the correspondent of H. V. 5 ... Connected with troop K. 3 between Catania and Syracuse. To follow."

"In the Manderaggio, La Valetta, Malta, have verified the passage T. R. 7."

"Cyrene. Wait fresh orders. Flotilla of Antek – ready. *Electric No. 3* under pressure day and night."

"R. 0. 3. Since death. Both disappeared."

And this other telegram containing some special news by means of an agreed upon number.

"2117. Sarc. Formerly a broker. Service Toronth. Ceased connection Tripoli of Africa."

And to nearly all these dispatches there was sent from the *Savarena*:

"Sir," said she, "take back the money, it's yours."

"Let the search proceed. Spare neither money nor trouble. Send new papers."

Here was an exchange of incomprehensible correspondence that seemed to embrace the whole circuit of the Mediterranean. The doctor was not as much at leisure as he wished to appear. Notwithstanding professional secrecy it was difficult to prevent the fact of this interchange of mysterious telegrams from becoming known to the public; and hence a redoubling of the curiosity about the enigmatic physician.

In the upper circles of Ragusa Silas Toronthal was perhaps the most perplexed of men. On the quay at Gravosa he had met the doctor a few minutes after the *Savarena* arrived. During this meeting he had experienced in the first place a strong feeling of repulsion and in the second an equally strong feeling of curiosity, which, up to the present, circumstances had not allowed the banker to gratify.

To tell the truth the doctor's presence had had a disturbing influence on Toronthal, which he could not explain. By preserving the incognito at Ragusa, and continuing the difficulty of access, the banker's desire to see him again had been greatly increased; and several times he had gone to Gravosa. There he had stood on the quay, looking at the schooner, and burning with envy to get on board. One day even he had been rowed out to her, and received the invariable reply:

"Dr. Antekirtt does not see anyone."

The result of all this was that Toronthal felt a sort of chronic irritation in face of an obstacle he could not overcome. And so, at his own expense, he set a detective to watch if the mysterious stranger made any visits in Gravosa or the neighbourhood.

We may judge therefore of the uneasiness with which the banker heard that Borik had had an interview with the doctor, and that the day following a visit had been made to Madame Bathory.

"Who is this man?" he asked himself.

But what had he to fear in his present position? For fifteen years nothing had transpired as to his former machinations. And yet anything referring to the family of those he had betrayed and sold rendered him uneasy. If remorse never troubled his conscience fear occasionally did, and the appearance of this doctor, powerful owing to his fame and powerful owing to his wealth, was anything but reassuring to him.

"But who is this man?" he repeated. "Who is he that comes to Ragusa and visits Madame Bathory? Did she send for him as a physician? What can she and he have in common?"

To this there could be no answer. One thing comforted Toronthal a little, and that was that the visit to Madame Bathory was not repeated.

The banker had made up his mind that cost what it might he would make the doctor's acquaintance. The thought possessed him day and night. By a kind of illusion to which over-excited brains are subject he fancied that he would recover his peace of mind if he could only see Dr. Antekirtt, talk to him and ascertain the motives of his arrival at Gravosa. And he sought about for some way of obtaining an interview.

And he thought he had found it, and in this way. For many years Madame Toronthal had suffered from a languor, which the Ragusan doctors were powerless to overcome. In spite of all their advice, in spite of all the attentions of her daughter, Madame Toronthal was not quite bed-ridden, but she was visibly wasting away. Was her complaint due to mental causes? Perhaps — but no one had been able to discover it. The banker alone was aware that his wife owing to her knowledge of his past life had conceived an invincible disgust at an existence, which filled her with horror. Whatever might be the cause of Madame Toronthal's state of health, which had puzzled the doctors of the town, it seemed to afford the banker the opportunity he desired for entering into communication with the owner of the *Savarena*, and he wrote a letter and sent it off to the schooner by messenger.

"He would be glad," he said, "to have the advice of a physician of such undoubted distinction." Then apologizing for the inconvenience it would occasion to one living in such retirement, he begged Dr. Antekirtt "to appoint a time when he could expect him at his house in the Stradone."

When the doctor received this letter in the morning, he looked first at the signature, and then not a muscle in his face moved. He read the letter through to the last line, and yet nothing showed the thoughts it suggested.

What reply should he give? Should he take advantage of the opportunity to visit Toronthal's house, and become acquainted with his family? But to enter the house even in the character of a physician, would that not embarrass his future action?

The doctor hesitated not a moment. He answered by a very short note, which was handed to the banker's servant. All it said was:

"Dr. Antekirtt regrets that he is unable to attend Madame Toronthal. He does not practice in Europe."

When the banker received this laconic reply he crumpled it in his hands in his vexation. It was evident that the doctor would have nothing to do with him. It was a transparent refusal indicative of a settled plan.

"And then," said he to himself, "if he does not practice in Europe, why did he go to Madame Bathory – if it was in the character of a physician that he went to her? What was he doing there? What is there between them?"

The uncertainty worried Toronthal exceedingly. His life had become a burden to him since the doctor had appeared at Gravosa, and would continue to be so until the *Savarena* had sailed. He said not a word to his wife or daughter about his futile letter. He kept his anxiety to himself. But he did not give up watching the doctor's movements, and kept himself informed of all his proceedings at Gravosa and Ragusa.

The very next day came a new and equally serious cause of alarm.

Pierre Bathory had returned disappointed to Zara. He had not been able to accept the position that had been offered to him – the management of important smelting works in Herzegovina.

"The terms would not suit me." That was all he said to his mother. Madame Bathory did not think it worthwhile to ask why the terms were unacceptable; a look sufficed her. Then she handed him a letter that had arrived during his absence.

This was the letter in which Dr. Antekirtt asked Pierre Bathory to visit him on board the *Savarena* to discuss a proposal he was in a position to make him.

Pierre Bathory handed the letter to his mother. The doctor's offer was no surprise to her.

"I was expecting that," she said.

"You expected this?" asked the young man in astonishment.

"Yes, Pierre! Dr. Antekirtt came to see me while you were away."

"Do you know who this man is then that everybody is talking about at Ragusa?"

"No; but Dr. Antekirtt knew your father, and he was the friend of Count Sandorf and Count Zathmar, and in that character he came here."

"Mother," asked Pierre, "what proof did the doctor give that he was my father's friend?"

"None," answered Madame Bathory, who did not care to mention the hundred thousand florins that she wished to keep secret from all but herself and the doctor.

Ragusa: The Piazza

"And suppose he's some informer, some spy, some Austrian detective?"

"You'll see that."

"Do you advise me to go, then?"

"Yes, that's my advice. We should not neglect a man who is desirous of befriending you for the friendship he bore your father."

"But what has he come to Ragusa for?" asked Pierre. "Has he any business in this country?"

"Perhaps he thinks of doing some. He's supposed to be very rich; it's possible he may be thinking of offering you a post worth accepting."

"I'll go see him and find out."

"Go today then, and at the same time return the visit I'm unable to return myself."

Pierre embraced his mother, and it seemed as he lingered near her as though some secret was choking him, some secret that he dare not tell. What was there then in his heart so sad and serious that he dare not confide it to his mother?

"My poor child," murmured Madame Bathory.

It was one o'clock in the afternoon when Pierre entered the Stradone on his way to the harbour of Gravosa. As he passed Toronthal's house he stopped for an instant – only for an instant. He looked up at one of the wings the windows of which opened on to the road. The blinds were drawn. Had the house been uninhabited it could not have been more shut up.

Pierre Bathory continued his walk, which he had rather slackened than stopped. But his movements had escaped the notice of a woman who was watching on the opposite side of the Stradone.

She was above the usual height. Her age? Between forty and fifty. Her walk? Almost mechanical. This foreigner – her nationality could be easily seen from her brown frizzled hair and Moorish complexion – was wrapped in a dark coloured cloak, with its hood thrown over her headdress ornamented with its sequins. Was she a Bohemian, a Gitana, a Gipsy, an Egyptian, a Hindoo? So many types did she resemble that it was difficult to say. Anyhow she was not asking for charity and did not look as though she would accept any. She was there on her own account, or on the account of somebody else, watching not only what went on at Toronthal's, but also what took place in the Rue Marinella.

As soon as she caught sight of the young man coming into the Stradone and walking towards Gravosa, she followed so as to keep him in view; but so adroitly that he was unaware of her proceedings. Besides he was too much occupied to bother himself with what was taking place behind him. When he slackened his pace in front of Toronthal's, the woman slackened hers. When he started on again, she started on, suiting her pace to his.

Reaching the first gate of Ragusa, Pierre strode through it swiftly, but not swiftly enough to distance the stranger. Once through the gate she found him hurrying on to Gravosa and twenty yards behind him she followed down the avenue.

At the same moment Silas Toronthal was returning to Ragusa in an open carriage, so that he could not avoid meeting Pierre.

Seeing them both the Moor stopped for a moment. Perhaps, she thought, they will have something to say to each other. And so with kindling eyes she slipped behind a neighbouring tree. But if the men were to speak, how could she hear what they said?

They did not speak. Toronthal had seen Pierre twenty yards before he reached him, and instead of replying with the haughty salute he had used on the quay at Gravosa when his daughter was with him, he turned away his head as the young man raised his hat and his carriage drove rapidly on towards Ragusa.

The stranger lost nothing of this little scene: and a feeble smile animated her impassable face.

Pierre, more in sorrow than anger, continued his walk without turning back to look after Toronthal.

The Moor followed him from afar, and might have been heard to mutter in Arabic:

"It's time he came!"

A quarter of an hour afterwards, Pierre arrived on the quays of Gravosa. For a few minutes he stopped to admire the schooner whose burgee was lazily fluttering from the mainmast head.

"Whence comes this Dr. Antekirtt?" he said to himself. "I do not know that flag."

Then addressing himself to a pilot who was standing near he asked:

"Do you know what flag that is?"

The pilot did not know. All he could say about the schooner was that she had come from Brindisi and that all her papers had been found in order by the harbour-master, and as she was a pleasure yacht the authorities had respected her incognito.

Pierre Bathory then hired a boat and was rowed off to the *Savarena*, while the Moor, very much surprised, watched him as he neared the yacht.

In a few minutes the young man had set foot on the schooner's deck and asked if Dr. Antekirtt were on board. Doubtless the order, which denied admittance to strangers, did not apply to him, for the boatswain immediately replied that the doctor was in his room. Pierre presented his card and asked if he could see the doctor. A sailor took the card and disappeared down the companion, which led to the aft-saloon. A minute afterwards he returned with the message that the doctor was expecting Mr. Pierre Bathory.

The young man was immediately introduced into a saloon where only a half-light found its way in through the curtains overhead. But when he reached the double doors, both of which were open, the light from the glass panels at the end shone on him strong and full.

In the half-shadow was Dr. Antekirtt seated on a divan. At the sudden appearance of the son of Stephen Bathory he felt a sort of thrill go through him, unnoticed by Pierre, and these words escaped, so to speak, from his lips:

"Tis he! Tis he!"

And in truth Pierre Bathory was the very image of his father, as the noble Hungarian had been at his age. There was the same energy in his eyes, the same nobleness in his attitude, the same look of enthusiasm for all that was good and true and beautiful.

"Mr. Bathory," said the doctor, rising, "I'm very glad to see you decided to accept my invitation."

And he motioned Pierre to sit down in the other angle of the saloon.

The doctor had spoken in Hungarian, which he knew was the young man's native language.

"Sir," said Pierre Bathory, "I would have come to return the visit you made to my mother even if you hadn't asked me to come on board. I know you're one of those unknown friends to whom the memory of my father and the two patriots who died with him is so dear. I thank you for having kept a place for them in your remembrance."

In thus evoking the past, now so far away, in speaking of his father, and his friends Mathias Sandorf and Ladislas Zathmar, Pierre could not hide his emotion.

"Forgive me," he said. "When I think of these things I cannot help..."

Did he not feel then that Dr. Antekirtt was more affected than he was, and that if he did not reply it was the better to keep hidden what he felt?

"Mr. Bathory," he said after a lengthened pause, "I have nothing to forgive in so natural a grief. You're of Hungarian blood, and what child

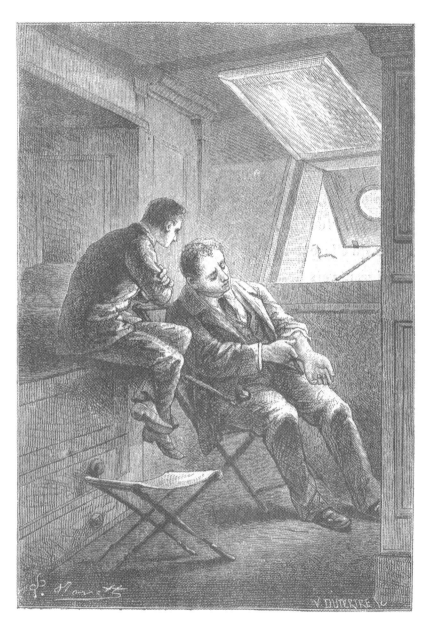

"Yes, your arms get rusty," answered Hercules

of Hungary would become so denaturalized as not to feel his heart ache at such remembrances? At that time, fifteen years ago – yes, already fifteen years have passed – you were still young. You can scarcely remember your father and the events in which he took part."

"My mother is his other self!" answered Pierre. "She brought me up in the creed of him she has never ceased to mourn. All that he did, all he tried to do, all the life of devotion to his people and his country I have learned from her. I was only eight years old when my father died, but it seems that he's still living, for he lives again in my mother."

"You love your mother as she deserves to be loved," said the doctor, "and we venerate her as if she were a martyr's widow."

Pierre could only thank the doctor for thus expressing himself. His heart beat loudly as he listened; and he did not notice the coldness, natural or acquired, with which the doctor spoke, and which seemed to be characteristic.

"May I ask if you knew my father personally?" asked he.

"Yes, Mr. Bathory," was the reply, not without a certain hesitation, "but I knew him as a student knew a professor who was one of the most distinguished men in the Hungarian universities. I studied medicine and physics in your country. I was one of your father's pupils, for he was only my senior by twelve years. I learnt to esteem him, to love him, for I felt that all his teaching was imbued with that spirit which made him later on an ardent patriot, and I only left him when I went away to finish the studies I'd begun in Hungary. But shortly afterwards Professor Stephen Bathory sacrificed his position for the sake of ideas he believed to be noble and just, and no private interest could stop him in his path of duty. It was then that he left Presburg to take up his residence in Trieste. Your mother had sustained him with her advice, and encompassed him with her thoughtfulness, during that time of anxiety. She possessed all the virtues of a woman as your father had all the virtues of a man. You will forgive me for calling up your sorrowful past, and if I have done so it's only because you're not one of those that can forget it!"

"No, sir, no," replied the young man with the enthusiasm of his age, "no more than Hungary can forget the three men who were sacrificed for her – Ladislas Zathmar, Stephen Bathory, and the boldest of the three, Mathias Sandorf!"

"If he was the boldest," answered the doctor, "do not think that his two companions were inferior to him in devotion, in sacrifices, or in courage! The three are worthy of the same respect! The three have the same right to be avenged."

The doctor paused, and then asked if Madame Bathory had told him the circumstances under which the chiefs of the conspiracy had been delivered up, if she had told him that treachery had been at work? But the young engineer had not heard anything.

In fact Madame Bathory had been silent on the subject. She shrank from instilling hatred into her son's life, and perhaps sending him on a false track, for no one knew the names of the traitors. And the doctor thought that for the present he had better maintain the same reserve.

What he did not hesitate to say was that without the odious deed of the Spaniard who had betrayed the fugitives in the house of Ferrato the fisherman, Count Sandorf and Stephen Bathory would probably have escaped. And once beyond the Austrian frontier, no matter in what country, every door would be opened to receive them.

"With me," he concluded, "they would have found a refuge which never would have failed them."

"In what country, sir?"

"In Cephalonia, where I then lived."

"Yes, in the Ionian Islands under the protection of the Greek flag they would have been safe, and my father would be still alive."

For a minute or two the conversation dropped with this return to the past. The doctor broke the silence.

"Our recollections have taken us far from the present. Shall we now talk about it, and especially of the future I have been thinking of for you?"

"I'm ready," answered Pierre. "In your letter you gave me to understand that it might be to my interest..."

"In short, Mr. Bathory, as I'm aware of your mother's devotion during the childhood of her son, I'm also aware that you're worthy of her and after many a harsh experience you've become a man..."

"A man," said Pierre bitterly, "a man who has not enough to keep himself, nor to give his mother a return for what she's done for him."

"That is so!" answered the doctor, "But the fault is not yours. I know how difficult it is for anyone to obtain a position with so many rivals struggling against you. You're an engineer?"

"Yes. I passed out of the schools with the title, but I'm an engineer unattached, and have no employment from the State. I've been seeking an appointment with some manufacturing company, and up to the present I've found nothing to suit me – at least at Ragusa."

"And elsewhere?"

"Elsewhere?" replied Pierre, with some hesitation.

"Yes! Was it not about some business of the sort that you went to Zara a few days ago?"

"I had heard of a situation which a metallurgical company had vacant..."

"And this situation?"

"It was offered to me."

"And you did not accept it?"

"I had to refuse it, because I should have had to settle permanently in Herzegovina."

"In Herzegovina? Would not Madame Bathory have gone with you?"

"My mother would go wherever my interests required."

"And why did you not take the place?" persisted the doctor.

"Sir," said the young man, "at present I have strong reasons for not leaving Ragusa."

And as he made the remark the doctor noticed that he seemed embarrassed. His voice trembled as he expressed his desire – more than his desire – his resolution not to leave Ragusa.

What was the reason for his refusing the offer that had been made?

"That'll make what I was going to offer you unacceptable," said the doctor.

"Should I have to go..."

"Yes – to a country where I'm about to commence some very considerable works, which I should put under your management."

"I'm very sorry, but believe me, as I've made this resolution..."

"I believe you, and perhaps I regret it as much as you. I should have been very glad to have been able to help you, in consideration of my feelings towards your father."

Pierre made no reply. A prey to internal strife he showed that he was suffering – and suffering acutely. The doctor felt sure that he wished to speak, and dared not. But at last an irresistible impulse impelled Pierre towards the man who had shown such sympathy with his mother and himself.

"Sir – sir," said he with an emotion that he took no pains to hide, "do not think it is caprice or obstinacy that makes me refuse your offer. You've spoken like a friend of Stephen Bathory. You'd show me all the friendship you felt for him! I feel it although I've only known you a few minutes. Yes, I feel for you all the affection that I should have had for my father."

"Pierre! My child!" said the doctor, seizing the young man's hand.

In the half-shadow was Dr. Antekirtt seated on a divan

"Yes! Sir!" continued Pierre, "and I'll tell you all! I'm in love with a young lady in this town! Between us there's the gulf, which separates poverty from wealth. But I won't look at the abyss, and perhaps she hasn't seen it! If occasionally I can see her in the street or at the window, it gives me a happiness I haven't the strength to renounce! At the idea that I must go away, and go away for long, I become insane! Ah! Sir! Understand me, and forgive my refusal!"

"Yes, Pierre," answered the doctor, "I understand you and I have nothing to forgive. You've done well to tell me so frankly; and it may lead to something! Does your mother know of what you've been telling me?"

"I haven't said anything to her yet. I have not dared, because in our modest position she would perhaps have the wisdom to deprive me of all hope! But she may have divined and understood what I suffer – what I must suffer."

"Pierre," said the doctor, "you've confided in me, and you're right to have done so! Is the young lady rich?"

"Very rich! Too rich! Yes, too rich for me!"

"Is she worthy of you?"

"Ah! Sir, could I dream of giving my mother a daughter that was not worthy of her?"

"Well, Pierre," continued the doctor, "perhaps the abyss may be bridged!"

"Sir," said the young man, "do not encourage me with hopes that are unrealizable."

"Unrealizable!"

And the tone in which the doctor uttered the word betrayed such confidence in himself that Pierre Bathory seemed as if it were transformed, as if he believed himself master of the present, master of the future.

"Yes, Pierre," continued the doctor, "have confidence in me. When you think fit, and think the time has come, you will tell me the lady's name..."

"Why should I hide it, now? It's Sava Toronthal!"

The effort the doctor made to keep calm as he heard the hated name was as that of a man who strives to prevent himself from starting when lightning strikes at his feet. For an instant – several seconds – he remained motionless and mute.

Then in a voice that betrayed not the slightest emotion he remarked:

"Good! Pierre, good! I must think it over! Let me see..."

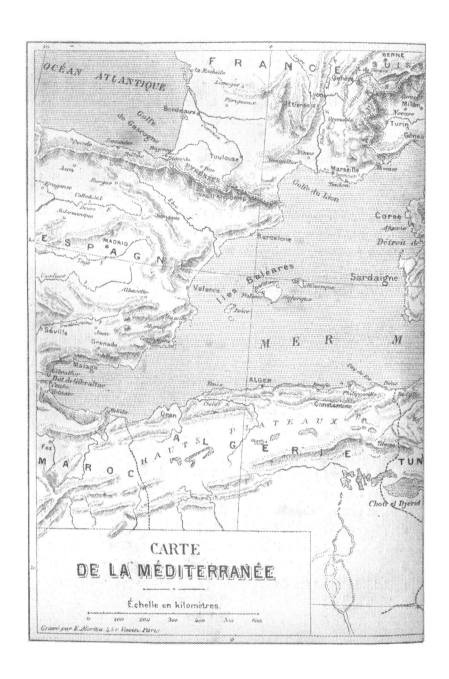

CARTE
DE LA MÉDITERRANÉE

Échelle en kilomètres.

Gravé par E. Morteu 45 r. Vavin. Paris.

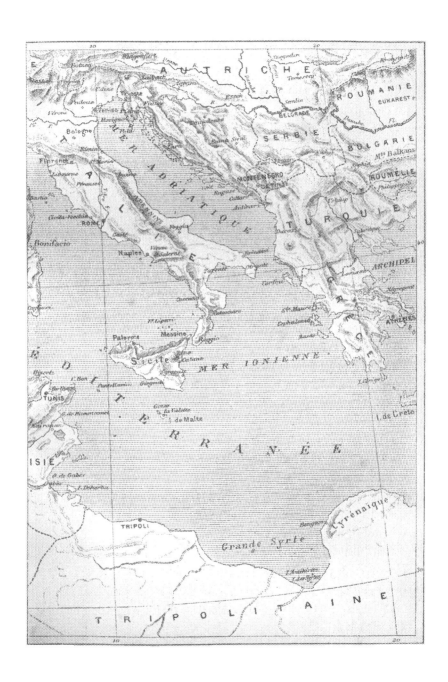

199

"I'll go," interrupted the young man, clasping the hand which the doctor held out to him, "and allow me to thank you as I would have thanked my father."

He left the doctor alone in the saloon, and then gaining the deck he entered his boat, landed at the quay, and returned to Ragusa.

The stranger who had been waiting for him all the time he was on board the *Savarena* – followed him back.

Pierre felt very much happier in his mind. At last his heart had been opened! He had found a friend in whom he could trust – more than a friend, perhaps. To him this had been one of those happy days of which fortune is so stingy in this world.

And how could he doubt it when, as he passed along the Stradone, he saw the corner of the curtain at one of the windows of Toronthal's house slowly rise and suddenly fall!

But the stranger had also seen the movement, and as Pierre turned up the Rue Marinella, she remained motionless at the corner. Then she hurried to the telegraph office and dispatched a message, which contained but one word – and that was:

"Come!"

The address of that monosyllabic message was – "Sarcany, To Be Called For, Syracuse, Sicily."

CHAPTER VI

THE MOUTHS OF THE CATTARO

And so destiny, which plays so predominant a part in the events of this world, had brought together in Ragusa the families of Bathory and Toronthal; and brought them not only to the same town, but to the same quarter of that town – the Stradone. And Sava Toronthal and Pierre Bathory had seen each other, met each other; loved each other! Pierre the son of a man who had been betrayed to death, and Sava the daughter of the man who betrayed him!

As soon as the engineer had left the schooner, the doctor might have been heard to say to himself:

"And Pierre goes away full of hope, hope he never had before, hope that I have just given him!"

Was the doctor the man to undertake a merciless struggle against this fate? Did he feel himself strong enough to dispose of the affairs of humankind at his will? That force, that moral energy, which must be his if he was to succeed in fighting destiny, would it not fail him?

"No! I'll fight against it!" he said. "Such love is hateful, criminal! That Pierre Bathory should become the husband of Toronthal's daughter and one day learn the truth would be to deprive him of all hope of revenge! He could only kill himself in despair! And I'll tell him all if need be! I'll tell him what this family has done to his! At all costs I will break this thing off!"

And in truth such a union did seem monstrous. It will be remembered that in his conversation with Madame Bathory the doctor had told her that the three chiefs of the Trieste conspiracy had been the victims of an abominable scheme which had been brought to light in the course of the trial, and that this had come to his knowledge through the indiscretion of one of the Pisino warders.

And it will also be remembered that Madame Bathory for certain reasons had thought it best to say nothing of this treachery to her son. Be-

201

sides she did not know who the traitors were. She did not know that one of them was wealthy and respected and lived at Ragusa, a few yards away from her in the Stradone. The doctor had not named them? Why? Doubtless because the hour had not yet come for him to unmask them! But he knew them. He knew that Silas Toronthal was one of the traitors and that Sarcany was the other. And if he had not taken her more into his confidence, it was because he reckoned on Pierre's assistance, and wished to associate the son in the retribution with which he was about to visit the murderers of his father.

And that is why he could not say more to the son of Stephen Bathory without breaking his heart.

"It matters little!" he repeated. "I shall break off this match."

Having made up his mind, what did he do? Reveal to Madame Bathory and her son the history of the banker of Trieste?

But did he hold proofs of the treachery? No, for Mathias Sandorf, Stephen Bathory, and Ladislas Zathmar who alone had these proofs were dead. Did he spread through the town reports of this abominable act without first telling Madame Bathory? That would probably have been enough to open an abyss between Pierre and the young lady – an abyss that could not be bridged. But if the secret were divulged would not Silas Toronthal try to leave Ragusa?

But the doctor did not want the banker to disappear. He wanted the traitor to remain ready for the executioner when the day of the execution arrived. And were he to disappear, events might turn out differently to what he had imagined.

After having weighted the question in all its pros and cons the doctor resolved to proceed more vigorously against Toronthal. In the first place it was necessary to get Pierre away from the town where the honour of his name was in danger. Yes! He would spirit him away so that no one could trace him! When he had him in his power he would tell him all he knew about Toronthal and Sarcany his accomplice, and he would associate him in his work. But he had not a day to lose.

It was with this object that a telegram from the doctor brought to the mouths of the Cattaro, south of Ragusa on the Adriatic, one of the swiftest vessels of his fleet. She was one of those huge launches, which served as the forerunners of our modern torpedo boats. Her long steel tube was about forty-four yards in length and seventy tons measurement, had neither mast nor funnel, and carried simply an exterior deck and a steel cage with lenticular scuttles for the steersman who could be securely shut up in it when the state of the sea rendered such precautions necessary. She could slip through the water without losing time or distance in following the undulations of the surge; and having a speed excelling that of all the torpedo boats of the Old or New World could easily travel her thirty miles an hour. Owing to this excessive speed the doctor had been able to accomplish many extraordinary voyages, and hence the gift of ubiquity with which he had been credited, for in very short intervals of time he had been able to run from the farthest corners of the Archipelago to the outermost borders of the Libyan Sea.

There was, however, one striking difference between steam launches and the doctor's boats, and that was that instead of superheated steam it was electricity that furnished their motive power by means of powerful accumulators invented by himself long before the later inventions that have become so famous. In these accumulators he could store the electricity to a practically unlimited extent. These dispatch boats were known as *Electrics*, with merely a number denoting the order in which they had been built. It was *Electric No. 2* that had been telegraphed for to the mouths of the Cattaro.

Having given these orders, the doctor waited for the moment of action, and warned Point Pescade and Cape Matifou that he would soon require their services. It is hardly necessary to say that they were very glad at having at last an opportunity of showing their devotion. One cloud, one only, threw its shadow over the gladness with which they welcomed the doctor's warning.

Point Pescade was to wait at Ragusa to keep watch on the houses in the Stradone and Rue Marinella, while Cape Matifou was to go with the doctor to Cattaro. This was a separation – the first after so many years of misery that they had lived through together – and hence a touching anxiety on the part of Cape Matifou in thinking that he would no longer be near his Little Pescade!

"Patience, old Cape, patience! It won't last! The play's just beginning, and unless I'm mistaken it's a splendid piece they're getting ready for us, and we have an excellent director who's given us both important parts! Believe me; you'll have no reason to complain of yours."

"Think so?"

"I'm sure of it! Ah! No lover's part for you! It's not in your nature, although you're so sentimental! No traitor's part either! You're too big for that! No, you're to be the good genius coming in at the end to punish vice and recompense virtue!"

"Like they do in the travelling booths?" answered Cape Matifou.

The *Electric No. 2* at the mouths of the Cattaro.

"Like they do in the travelling booths! Yes! I can see you in the part, old Cape! At the moment the traitor expects it least you'll appear with your huge hands open, and have only to clasp him in them to bring about the end! Though you may not be on the stage for long, it's a sympathetic part and what cheers from the gallery you'll get during the run!"

"Yes, perhaps so," answered Hercules, "but all the same we must separate."

"For a few days! Only promise me you won't destroy yourself during my absence! Get your six meals regularly and grow! And now clasp me in your arms; or rather pretend to do so as if you were on the stage, else you'll risk stifling me. We must get used to a little play-acting in this world! Now embrace me again, and never forget your little Point Pescade who'll never forget his big Cape Matifou!"

Such was the affecting farewell of these two friends when their separation came; and Cape Matifou was truly sad at heart when he returned on board the *Savarena*. The same day his companion took up his quarters in Ragusa with orders not to lose sight of Pierre Bathory, to watch Toronthal's house, and to keep the doctor informed of all that went on.

During this time Point Pescade should have met in the Stradone with the mysterious stranger who was evidently on a similar mission; and doubtless he would have done so had not the Moor after sending off the telegram left Ragusa for some place further south, where Sarcany could join her. Pescade was thus not interfered with in his operations, and could carry out his instructions with his habitual intelligence.

Pierre Bathory never imagined that he had been so closely watched, nor did he know that for the eyes of the Moor there had now been substituted those of Point Pescade. After his conversation with the doctor, after the avowal he had made, he had felt more confident. Why should he now hide from his mother what had taken place on board the *Savarena?* Would she not read it in his look and even in his soul? Would she not see that a change had taken place in him, and that grief and despair had given place to hope and happiness?

Pierre, then, told his mother everything. He told her who the girl was that he loved, and how it was for her that he had refused to leave Ragusa. His post was of little consequence! Had not Dr. Antekirtt told him to hope?

"That's why you suffered so much, my child," answered Madame Bathory. "May heaven help you and bring you all the happiness we've missed up to now!"

Madame Bathory lived in great retirement in her house in the Rue Marinella. She did not go out except to church with her old servant, for she attended to her religious duties with all the practical and austere piety of her race. She had never heard tell of the Toronthals. Never had she looked at the large mansion she passed on her way to the Church of the Redeemer, which is situated just where the Stradone begins. She therefore did not know the daughter of the old banker of Trieste.

And so Pierre had to describe her and tell what she had said to him when they first met, and how he did not doubt that his love was returned. And all these details he gave with an ardour that his mother was not surprised to find in the tender passionate soul of her son.

But when Pierre told her of the position of the Toronthals, when she found that the young lady would be one of the richest heiresses of Ragusa, she could not conceal her uneasiness. Would the banker consent to his only child becoming a poor man's wife?

But Pierre did not think it necessary to insist on the coolness and even contempt with which Toronthal had always received him. He was content to repeat what the doctor had said to him – how he had told him that he could, that he ought even, have confidence in his father's friend who felt for him a quasi-paternal affection. A fact, which Madame Bathory did not doubt, knowing what he had already wished to do for her and hers. And in the end, like her son and like Borik, who thought it his duty to give his advice, she did not abandon all hope; and there was a trifling gleam of happiness in the humble home in the Rue Marinella.

On the following Sunday Pierre had again the happiness of seeing Sava Toronthal at church. The girl's face, always rather sad in its expression, lighted up when she caught sight of Pierre, as if it had been transfigured. They spoke to each other with their looks, and they understood each other. And when Sava returned home, she bore with her a portion of that happiness she had so clearly read in the young man's countenance.

But Pierre had not again seen the doctor. He waited for an invitation to revisit the schooner. Some days elapsed, but no letter came.

"Doubtless," he thought, "the doctor is making inquiries. He has come or sent to Ragusa to ascertain something about the Toronthals! Perhaps he has been getting an introduction to Sava. Yes! It's not impossible that he's already seen her father and spoken to him on the subject! A line from him, only a word, how happy it would make me – particularly if that word were 'Come!'"

The word did not arrive, and Madame Bathory had some trouble in calming her son's impatience. He began to despair, and now it was her turn to give him hope, although she was not without anxiety. The house in the Rue Marinella was open to the doctor, as he knew, and, even without this new interest he had taken in Pierre, was not the interest he took in the family for whom he had already shown such sympathy enough to attract him there?

And so Pierre after counting the days and the hours had no longer strength to resist. He must, at all costs, again see Dr. Antekirtt. An invincible force urged him to Gravosa. Once on board the schooner, his impatience would be understood; his action would be excused even if it were premature.

On the 7th of June at eight o'clock in the morning Pierre Bathory left his mother without saying anything to her of his plans. He left Ragusa and hurried to Gravosa at such a rate that Point Pescade could hardly keep up with him. As he reached the quay in front of the moorings occupied by the *Savarena* at his last visit he stopped.

The schooner was not in the harbour.

Pierre looked about to see if she had changed her place. He could not see her anywhere.

He asked a sailor who was walking on the quay what had become of Dr. Antekirtt's yacht.

The *Savarena* had sailed the night before, he replied, and he no more knew where she had gone than where she had come from.

The schooner gone! The doctor had disappeared as mysteriously as he had arrived.

Pierre went back to Ragusa in greater despair than ever.

Had an accident revealed to the young man that the schooner had left for Cattaro, he would not have hesitated to follow her. But his journey would have been useless. The *Savarena* reached the mouths, but did not enter them. The doctor accompanied by Matifou went on shore in one of her boats, and the yacht departed for some unknown destination.

There is no more curious spot in Europe, and perhaps in the Old World, than this orographic and hydrographic curiosity known as the mouths of Cattaro. Cattaro is not a river as any one might be tempted to think; it is a town, the seat of a bishop, and the capital of a Circle. The mouths are six bays side by side communicating with each other by narrow channels, which can be sailed through in six hours. Of this string of lakes, which stretch along in front of the mountain, of the coast, the last,

Others cooking a small sheep over a coal fire.

situated at the foot of Mount Norr, marks the limit of the Austrian Empire. Beyond that is the Ottoman Empire.

It was at the entrance of the mouths that the doctor landed, after a rapid passage. There one of the swift electric boats was in waiting to take him to the last of the bays. After doubling the point of Ostro, passing before Castel Nuovo, between the two panoramas of towns and chapels, before Stolivo, before Perasto, a celebrated place of pilgrimage, before Risano, where the Dalmatian costumes begin to mingle with Turkish and Albanian, he arrived from lake to lake at the last bight at the bottom of which is built Cattaro.

Electric No. 2 was moored a few cable lengths from the town on the sleepy gloomy waters which not a breath of air troubled on this fine night in June.

But it was not on board of her that the doctor intended to take up his quarters. For the purposes of his ulterior projects he did not wish it to be known that this swift vessel belonged to him; and he landed at Cattaro and with Cape Matifou accompanying him went off to one of the hotels in the town.

The boat that had brought them was soon lost in the darkness to the right of the harbour up a small creek where it could remain invisible. There, at Cattaro the doctor could be as unknown as if he had taken refuge in the most obscure of the world's corners. The Bocchais, the inhabitants of this rich district of Dalmatia, who are of Slavish origin, would hardly notice the presence of a stranger amongst them.

From the bay it looks as though Cattaro were built in hollows on the side of Mount Norri. The first houses border on a quay, an esplanade won from the sea at the apex of the acute angle of a small lake, which runs deep into the mountain mass. It is at the extremity of this funnel with its splendid trees and background of verdure that the Lloyd mail boats, and large coasters of the Adriatic, run in to unload.

The doctor was busy in search of lodging. Cape Matifou had followed him without even asking where they had landed. It might be in Dalmatia, or it might be in China, but it mattered little to him. Like a faithful dog he followed his master. He was only a tool perhaps, a machine, a machine to turn, to bore, to pierce, which the doctor kept till he thought the time had come to use it.

Having left the quincunxes of the quay they entered the fortifications of Cattaro; then they passed along a series of narrow hilly roads in which is crowded a population of from four to five thousand. As he did so

209

they were closing the Marine Gate – a gate that remains open only till eight o'clock at night except on the arrival of the mail boats.

The doctor soon discovered that there was not a single hotel in the town, and he had to look about for lodgings. At last he found a house, and obtained a room on the ground floor in a sufficiently respectable street. At first it was arranged that Cape Matifou should be boarded by the proprietor, and although the price charged was enormous on account of his enormous proportions, the matter was soon satisfactorily settled. Dr. Antekirtt reserved the right of taking his meals elsewhere in the town.

In the morning, after leaving Cape Matifou to employ his time as he pleased, the doctor walked to the post office for any letters or telegrams that might be waiting for him. There was nothing there, and then he went for a stroll out of the town. He soon found a restaurant patronized by the better class of the inhabitants and Austrian officers and officials who looked upon being quartered here as equivalent to exile, or even to being in prison.

Now, the doctor was only waiting for the moment to act; and this was his plan. He had decided to kidnap Pierre Bathory. But to take him away on board the schooner while she lay at Ragusa would have been difficult. The young engineer was well known at Gravosa, and as public attention had been attracted to the *Savarena*, the affair even if it succeeded would be very much noised about. Further, the yacht being only a sailing vessel, if any steamer went after her from the harbour she would almost be certain to be caught.

At Cattaro, on the contrary, Pierre could be spirited off much more quietly. Nothing would be easier than to get him there. At a word sent from the doctor, there was no doubt but that he would start immediately. He was as unknown at Cattaro as the doctor himself, and once he was on board, the *Electric* could speed off to sea, where he could be told the past life of Silas Toronthal, and Sava's image become effaced by the remembrance of his father's wrongs.

Such was the doctor's very simple plan of campaign. Two or three days more, and the work would be accomplished; Pierre would be separated forever from Sava Toronthal.

Next day, the 9th of June, there arrived a letter from Point Pescade. It reported that there was nothing new at the house in the Stradone, and that Point Pescade had seen nothing of Pierre since the day he had gone to Gravosa twelve hours after the schooner sailed, he had not left Ragusa, and remained at home with his mother. Point Pescade supposed –

and he was not wrong in doing so – that the departure of the *Savarena* had brought about this change in his habits, for as soon as he had found her gone he had gone home looking the picture of despair.

The doctor decided to write next day and invite Pierre Bathory to join him immediately at Cattaro.

But something very unexpected happened to change his plans and allow chance to intervene and lead to the same end.

About eight o'clock in the evening the doctor was on the wharf at Cattaro when the mail steamer – the *Saxonia* was signalled.

The *Saxonia* came from Brindisi, where she had put in to take on board a few passengers. She was bound for Trieste, calling at Cattaro, Ragusa, and Zara, and the other ports on the Austrian coast of the Adriatic.

The doctor was standing near the gangway along which the people came ashore, when in the twilight his attention was monopolized by one of the travellers whose luggage was being brought off to the wharf.

The man was about forty, of haughty even impudent bearing. He gave his orders loudly; and was evidently one of those persons who even when polished show that they have been badly brought up.

That fellow! – Here – at Cattaro!"

The passenger was Sarcany. Fifteen years had elapsed since he had acted as accountant in Zathmar's house. With the exception of his clothes he was still the adventurer we saw in the streets of Trieste at the beginning of this story. He wore an elegant travelling suit with a dustcoat of the latest fashion, and his trunks with their many mountings showed that the old Tripolitan broker was accustomed to make himself comfortable.

For fifteen years Sarcany had lived a life of pleasure and luxury, thanks to the fortune he had acquired from his share of Count Sandorf's wealth. How much was there left of it? His best friends, if he had any, would have been puzzled to say. He had a look of preoccupation, of anxiety even, the cause of which was difficult to discover behind the mask with which he concealed his true disposition.

"Where does he come from? Where's he going?" asked the doctor who did not lose sight of him.

Where he had come from was easily ascertained by asking the purser of the *Saxonia*. The passenger had come on board at Brindisi. Did he come from Upper or Lower Italy? They did not know. In reality he came from Syracuse. On receipt of the telegram from the Moor he had instantly left Sicily for Cattaro.

For it was at Cattaro that the woman was waiting to meet him, her mission at Ragusa having apparently come to an end.

The Moor was there, on the wharf, waiting for the steamer. The doctor noticed her, he saw Sarcany walk up to her, he heard the words she said to him in Arabic, and he understood them:

"It was time!"

Sarcany's reply was a nod. Then after seeing his luggage passed by the customhouse officer, he went off with the Moor towards the right so as to go outside the town.

The doctor hesitated for a moment. Was Sarcany going to escape him? Ought he to follow him?

Turning round he saw Cape Matifou who was standing gaping at the Saxonia's passengers. He beckoned to him and the giant was at his side in an instant.

"Cape Matifou," said he, pointing to Sarcany who was walking away, "Do you see that man?"

"Yes."

"If I tell you to carry him off, will you do so?"

"Yes."

"And you'll give him something to prevent his getting away if he resists?"

"Yes."

"Remember I want him alive!"

Cape Matifou was a man of few words, but he had the merit of speaking to the point. The doctor could depend upon him. What he received the order to do, he would do.

The Moor could be seized, gagged, thrown aside in any corner, and before she could give the alarm, Sarcany would be on board the *Electric*.

The darkness, though it was not very profound, would facilitate matters.

Sarcany and the Moor continued their walk round the town without noticing that they were being watched and followed. They did not yet speak to each other. They did not wish to do so until they reached some quiet place where they could be safe from interruption. They reached the south gate opening on the road, which leads from Cattaro to the mountains on the Austrian frontier.

At this gate is an important market, a bazaar well known to the Montenegrins. Here they have to transact their business, for they are not allowed to enter the town except in very limited numbers and after having left their weapons behind them. On the Tuesday, Thursday, and Saturday of each week the mountaineers come down from Niegons or Cettinge, having walked for five or six hours carrying eggs, potatoes, poultry, and bundles of considerable weight.

This was a Thursday. A few groups whose business had not finished till late had remained in the bazaar intending to pass the night there. There were about thirty of these mountaineers, moving about, chatting and disputing, some stretched on the ground to sleep, others cooking before a coal fire a small sheep impaled on a wooden spit in Albanian fashion.

To this place, as though it was well known to them, came Sarcany and his companion. There it would be easy for them to talk at their case, and even remain all night without having to go in search of lodging. Since her arrival at Cattaro the Moor had not bothered to find other accommodations.

The doctor and Cape Matifou followed them in, one after the other. Here and there a few fires were smouldering and giving but little light. The doctor regretted that he had not put his project into execution on his way from the wharf. But it was now too late. All that could be done was to wait till an opportunity presented itself.

In any case the boat was moored behind the rocks less than 200 yards from the bazaar, and about two cable lengths away lay the *Electric* with a small light at the bow to show where she was moored.

Sarcany and the Moor took up their position in a dark corner near a group of mountaineers already asleep. There they could talk over their business without being understood, if the doctor wrapped in his travelling cloak had not joined the group without attracting their attention. Matifou concealed himself as well as he could and waited, ready to obey orders.

Sarcany and his companion spoke in Arabic, thinking that no one in that place could understand them. They were mistaken, for the doctor was there. Familiar with all the dialects of Africa and the East, he lost not a word of their conversation.

"You got my telegram at Syracuse?" said the Moor.

"Yes, Namir," answered Sarcany, "and I started next day with Zirone."

"Where is Zirone?"

"Near Catania, organizing his new gang."

"You must get to Ragusa tomorrow and you must see Silas Toronthal!"

Sarcany and the Moor took up their position in a dark

"I'll be there, and I'll see him! You're sure you're not mistaken, Namir? The time has come?"

"Yes! The banker's daughter..."

"The banker's daughter!" said Sarcany in such a singular tone that the doctor could hardly prevent himself from giving a start.

"Yes! His daughter!" answered Namir.

"What? He allows her to be made love to without my permission!?!"

"Are you surprised, Sarcany? Nothing is more certain nevertheless! But you'll be even more surprised when you hear who wishes to be the husband of Sava Toronthal."

"Some ruined gentleman anxious for her father's millions."

"No!" replied Namir. "A young man of good birth and no money!"

"And the name of this fellow?"

"Pierre Bathory."

"Pierre Bathory!" exclaimed Sarcany. "Pierre Bathory marry the daughter of Silas Toronthal."

"Be calm, Sarcany. That the daughter of Silas Toronthal and the son of Stephen Bathory are in love with each other is no secret from me! But perhaps Silas Toronthal does not know it."

"Does he not know it?"

"No! And besides he'd never consent."

"I wouldn't be so sure," answered Sarcany. "Toronthal is capable of anything – even of consenting to this marriage if it could quiet his conscience, supposing he has a conscience after these fifteen years. Fortunately I'm here, ready to spoil his game, and tomorrow I shall be at Ragusa."

"Good!" said Namir who seemed to have a certain ascendancy over her companion.

"The daughter of Silas Toronthal marries nobody but me you understand, Namir, and with her I'll get out of my difficulties again."

The doctor had heard all he wanted. It mattered not what else Sarcany had to say to the Moor.

A scoundrel coming to claim a scoundrel's daughter! Heaven had indeed intervened in the work of human justice! Henceforth there was nothing to fear for Pierre, whom this rival was to set aside. There was no use, then, in summoning him to Cattaro, or in attempting to carry off the man who wished to be Toronthal's son-in-law.

"May the wretches marry amongst themselves and become all the same family!" said the doctor. "And then we shall see!"

He left, and beckoned to Matifou to follow him. Matifou had not asked why the doctor wished him to walk off with the *Saxonia*'s passenger, and he did not ask why the attempt was postponed.

The next day, June 10th, at Ragusa, the doors of the principal drawing room at the house in the Stradone were thrown open about half past eight in the evening and a servant announced in a loud tone:

"Mr. Sarcany."

CHAPTER VII

COMPLICATIONS

Fourteen years had elapsed since Silas Toronthal had left Trieste to take up his residence at Ragusa. Being of Dalmatian birth nothing could be more natural than that when he retired from business he should return to his native land.

The traitors had kept their secret well. The price of their treachery had been duly paid. And thereby a handsome fortune fell to the banker and his old Tripolitan correspondent.

After the execution of the two prisoners in the fortress of Pisino, after the flight of Count Mathias Sandorf who had found his death in the waves of the Adriatic, the sentence had been completed by the seizure of their possessions. Of the house and small estate belonging to Ladislas Zathmar nothing remained – not even enough to yield a living to his old servant. Of Stephen Bathory's possessions nothing remained, for he had no fortune and the lessons he gave produced his only income. But the castle of Artenak and its rich dependencies, the neighbouring mines, and the forests on the northerly slopes of the Carpathians were of considerable value. They were divided into two parts, one of which was sold to pay the informers, and the other was placed under sequestration to be restored to the count's heiress when she had attained her eighteenth year. If the child died before then her share was to revert to the State.

The two quarters given to the informers amounted to a little over 1,500,000 florins, and with this huge sum they could do as they pleased.

At the outset the accomplices made up their minds to separate. Sarcany did not care to remain with Toronthal; and the banker had no wish to continue his business relations with him. And so Sarcany left Trieste with Zirone, who not having left him in adversity was not the man to leave him in prosperity. Both disappeared and the banker heard nothing about them for some time. Where had they gone? Probably to some large European city where people did not bother themselves about a man's origin providing he was rich, and cared nothing of how a man had gained his wealth providing he spent it amongst them.

The banker breathed more freely when they left him. He thought he had no more to fear from a man who to a certain extent held him in his power, and who might some time or other use that power. Nevertheless, although Sarcany was rich it was never safe to trust to prodigals of his species, and if he ran through his money what was to prevent his coming back to his old accomplice?

Six months afterwards Toronthal, having cleared off his difficulties, sold his business, and definitely abandoned Trieste for Ragusa. Although there was nothing to fear from the indiscretion of the governor, who was the only person that knew the part he had played in the discovery of the conspiracy, this seemed the safest course for a man who did not wish to lose reputation, and whom an ample fortune assured an easy life wherever he went.

This resolution to leave Trieste was probably further encouraged by a peculiar circumstance – which will be mentioned later on. This circumstance was known only to himself and his wife, and had, but on one occasion only, brought him into connection with Namir, whom we have seen as acquainted with Sarcany.

It was at Ragusa then that the banker had settled down. He had left it very young without either friends or relations. He had quite dropped out of recollection, and it was as a stranger that he returned to the town, which he had not revisited for forty years.

To a rich man appearing under such circumstances Ragusan society gave a hearty welcome. Only one thing was known about him, and that was that he had held a high position at Trieste. The banker sought and found a mansion in the most aristocratic quarter of the town. He engaged a fresh staff of servants and lived an opulent life. He visited and was visited. As no one knew anything of his past life, was he not one of those privileged beings who in this world are called happy?

Toronthal did not suffer much from remorse. Had it not been for the fear that some day his abominable treachery would be discovered there would apparently have been nothing to trouble his existence – except his wife who remained a silent but living reproach to him.

For that unhappy woman, honest and straightforward as she was, knew of the hateful scheme that had sent the three patriots to their deaths. A word escaped from her husband when his affairs were in jeopardy, a hope imprudently expressed that some of Sandorf's money might help him out of his difficulties, some signatures he had had to obtain from his wife, had drawn from him the confession of his share in the Trieste conspiracy.

An insurmountable aversion for the man who was bound to her was the feeling she thereupon experienced – and the feeling was all the keener from her being of Hungarian birth. But as we have said she was a woman of no moral energy. The blow fell on her, and she could not recover from it. Henceforth at Trieste and afterwards at Ragusa she lived apart from her husband, as much as her position permitted. She appeared at the receptions in the house in the Stradone, it was necessary for her to do so, and her husband insisted on it; but when she had played her part as a woman of the world she retired to her apartments. There she devoted herself entirely to the education of her daughter, on whom she had concentrated all her affection, and endeavoured to forget what she knew. To forget, when the man who had acted in this way was living under the same roof with her!

Two years after their removal to Ragusa, the state of things became still more complicated. And if the complication was an annoyance to the banker it was a subject of further grief to his wife.

Madame Bathory, her son and Borik, had also left Trieste to take up their quarters at Ragusa, where they had a few relatives.

Stephen Bathory's widow knew nothing of Silas Toronthal; she did not even know that he and Count Sandorf had ever had business together.

But if Madame Bathory did not know the banker, he knew her. To find himself in the same town, to meet her as he passed by, poor, working to educate her child, was anything but agreeable to him. Had Madame Bathory come to Ragusa before he had made up his mind to live there, he would probably have chosen otherwise. But when the widow came to live at her humble house in the Rue Marinella his mansion had already been bought, he had occupied it, and the position had been definitely accepted. It would not have done to change his residence for the third time.

"We get accustomed to everything!" he said to himself. And he resolved to shut his eyes to this permanent witness to his treachery.

But what was only an unpleasantness for the banker was an incessant cause of grief and remorse to Madame Toronthal. Secretly on several occasions she had tried to send help to this widow who had no other wealth than her work; but the help was always refused like that of other unknown friends.

Cattaro

Then the position became almost insupportable owing to an occurrence, most unforeseen, almost improbable, and even terrible by the complications it might bring about.

Madame Toronthal had concentrated all her affections on her daughter, who was two and a half years' old when at the end of 1867 her husband came to live at Ragusa.

Sava was now seventeen, a beautiful girl, more of the Hungarian than the Dalmatian type. With her dark abundant hair, and bright glowing eyes set deep beneath a somewhat lofty forehead of "psychic form" – if we can appropriately use the term that chirognomists apply more particularly to the hand – with her well-curved mouth, and sweet complexion and her graceful figure rather above the middle height, she was at least certain of never being passed by with indifference.

But that which was most striking about her was the pensive, serious mien that seemed to show she was ever in search of some long-faded remembrance of something, she knew not what, that at once allured and saddened her. On this account it was that she treated with extreme reserve all those whom she met in her father's house, or out of doors.

She was supposed to be the heiress of an enormous fortune which one day would be entirely her own, and was of course much sought after. But although many eligible individuals were introduced in whom all the social proprieties were duly found, she had always refused, under her mother's advice, to give them the slightest encouragement. Toronthal himself had never alluded to the subject of her marriage. Probably the son-in-law he wanted – more for himself than Sava – had not yet come forward.

To finish this portrait of Sava Toronthal we should note a very marked tendency to admire such acts of virtue or courage as were due to patriotism. Not that she took much interest in politics, but in the recital of all that affected her country, in the sacrifices made for it, and in recent examples by which its history had been made illustrious, she took deep interest. And these sentiments were hardly owing to the accident of her birth – for assuredly she did not inherit them from Silas Toronthal – but seemed to have arisen spontaneously in her own noble generous heart.

Would that explain the sympathetic attraction between her and Pierre? Yes! A stroke of ill luck had intervened in the banker's game, and brought these two young people together. Sava was only twelve years old when one day somebody had said in her presence:

"There goes the son of a man who died for Hungary!"

And that was never effaced from her memory.

Both grew up. Sava thought of Pierre long before he had noticed her. She saw him looking so serious, so thoughtful! But if he was poor he could at least work to be worthy of his father's name – and she did not know the whole story.

We know the rest, we know how Pierre Bathory was in his turn attracted and won by a nature which sympathized completely with his own, and how when the girl knew not her real feelings towards him, the young man already loved her with a profound affection that she was soon to share.

All that concerns Sava will have been said when we have described her position in the family.

Towards her father she had always been most reserved. Never had the banker betrayed the slightest feeling of kindness towards her, never had he greeted his daughter with a caress. This coolness between them arose from a complete want of accord on every subject. Sava had for Toronthal the respect a daughter should have for her father – nothing more. He let her do as she liked, he did not interfere with any of her tastes, he placed no limit on her works of charity which his natural ostentation willingly encouraged. In short, on his part there was indifference; on hers there was, it must be confessed, antipathy or rather aversion.

For Madame Toronthal Sava had quite a different feeling. The banker's wife submitted to her husband's control, although he showed her but little deference, but she was kind and good and worth a thousand times more in the honesty of her life and the care of her personal dignity. She was very fond of Sava. Beneath the young girl's shyness she had discovered her real worth; but the affection she felt for her was rather artificial and modified by a kind of admiration, of respect, and even of fear. The elevation of Sava's character, her straightforwardness, and at certain times her inflexibility, might explain this strange form of maternal love. However, the girl returned love for love, and even without the ties of relationship the two would have been deeply attached to each other.

There is therefore nothing to be astonished at in Madame Toronthal being the first to discover what was passing in the mind and heart of Sava. Frequently had the girl spoken of Pierre Bathory and his family without noticing the sorrowful impression that the name made on her mother. And when Madame Toronthal discovered that Sava was in love with the young man:

222

"Heaven wills it then!" was all she murmured.

We may imagine what these words meant, but it is somewhat difficult to understand how the love of Sava for Pierre could make amends for the injury done to the Bathory family.

Madame Toronthal having, however, satisfied herself that it was all in accordance with the designs of Providence, had brought herself to think in her pious, trustful heart that her husband would consent to this union of the families, and so without saying anything to Sava she resolved to consult him on the subject.

At the first words his wife uttered, Toronthal flew into a towering rage which he made no effort to control, and she had to retreat to her apartment with the following threat ringing in her ears:

"Take care, Madame! If ever you dare speak to me again on that subject, I'll make you repent it."

And so what Silas Toronthal called "destiny" had not only brought the Bathory family to live in the same town, but had even brought Sava and Pierre to meet and love one another.

Why, it may be asked, so much irritation on the banker's part? Had he formed any secret designs on Sava, on her future, that were prejudiced by this complication? In the event of his treachery being one day exposed, was it not his interest that the consequences should be atoned for as much as possible? What could Pierre say when he had become Sava Toronthal's husband? What could Madame Bathory do? Assuredly it would be a horrible situation, the victim's son married to the murderer's daughter, but it would be horrible for them, not for him, Silas Toronthal.

Yes, but there was Sarcany, of whom there was no news, but whose return was always possible, a return that might lead to further engagements between the accomplices. He was not the man to forget if fortune turned against him.

Toronthal was, it need scarcely be said, not without anxiety at what was to become of his old Tripolitan agent. He had had no news from him since he left Trieste, fifteen years ago. Even in Sicily, where Sarcany was most likely to be heard of, all inquiries had proved in vain. But he might come back any day, and hence a constant state of terror for the banker until the adventurer was dead! And the news of his death Toronthal would have received with easily intelligible satisfaction! Perhaps then he would have looked upon the possibility of a marriage with Pierre in a somewhat different light; but at present it was not to be dreamt of.

Sava was now seventeen

Toronthal never alluded to the way in which he received his wife when she had spoken to him about Pierre Bathory. He offered her no explanation of his conduct. What he did was to keep a strict watch on Sava, and even to set spies to look after her; and with regard to the young engineer, to behave towards him as haughtily as possible, to turn his head when he met, and to act in every way so as to crush out all hope. And he succeeded only too well in showing that every attempt on his part would be useless.

It was under these circumstances that on the evening of the 10th of June the name of Sarcany was heard across the room in the mansion in the Stradone as the door opened and that individual entered. In the morning Sarcany and Namir had taken the train at Cattaro for Ragusa. Sarcany had gone to one of the chief hotels in the town, dressed himself in the height of fashion, and without losing an hour had hurried round to visit his old friend.

Toronthal welcomed him, and gave orders that they were not to be disturbed. How did he take this visit? Was he master enough of himself to conceal his true feelings at the reappearance? Was Sarcany as imperious and insolent as formerly? Did he remind the banker of promises made and engagements entered into years before? Did they speak of the past, the present, or the future? What they said we know not, for their interview was secret.

But this was its result.

Twenty-four hours afterwards, a rumour was afloat which might well startle society at Ragusa. Every one was talking of the marriage of Sarcany – a wealthy Tripolitan – with Sava Toronthal.

Evidently the banker had had to yield to the threats of the man who could destroy him by a word. Neither his wife's prayers nor Sava's horror availed anything against the father who claimed to dispose of his daughter as best suited his convenience.

One word only as to Sarcany's interest in the marriage – an interest he had not thought it worthwhile to hide from Toronthal. Sarcany was now ruined. The fortune, which had been sufficient to help Toronthal out of his difficulties, had hardly been enough to keep the adventurer during the fifteen years. Since his departure from Trieste Sarcany had run through Europe, living in the height of extravagance, and the hotels of Paris, London, Berlin, Vienna, and Rome had never had windows enough for him to throw the money through to gratify his fancies. After a career of pleasure he had taken to gambling to finish his ruin, and had visited nearly every famous gaming haunt on the Continent.

Zirone had, of course, been his constant companion, and when the money had been run through they had returned together to the east of Sicily and waited till an opportunity offered to resume the connection with the banker of Trieste. Nothing could be simpler than that he could restore his fortunes by marrying Sava, the sole heiress of the rich Silas Toronthal – who could refuse him nothing.

In fact no refusal was possible, and no refusal was attempted. Perhaps after all between the two men there was still something hidden concerning the problem they were seeking to solve, which the future would reveal!

However, a very clear explanation was required from Sava by her father. What would she do?

"My honour depends on the marriage," said Silas Toronthal, "and the marriage must take place."

When Sava took back the reply to her mother, she nearly fainted in her daughter's arms and burst into tears of despair.

Toronthal had then told the truth!

The wedding was fixed for the 6th of July.

We can imagine what a life had been led by Pierre during these three weeks. His misery was dreadful. A prey to impotent rage, sometimes he remained at home in the Rue Marinella; sometimes he escaped from the accursed town, and his mother feared he would never return.

What consolation could she offer him? While no marriage was talked of, while Pierre Bathory was repulsed by Sava's father, some hope did remain. But with Sava married came a new abyss – an abyss that could not be bridged. Dr. Antekirtt in spite of his promises had abandoned Pierre. And besides, she asked herself, how could the young lady who loved him, and whose energetic nature she knew, how could she agree to this union? What was the mystery in this house in the Stradone, which brought such things about? Pierre would have done better to leave Ragusa to accept the situation which had been offered him abroad, to go far away from Sava if they were going to hand her over to this stranger, this Sarcany! Despair had in truth entered the house which a ray of happiness had brightened but for a few days.

Point Pescade kept constant watch, and was one of the first to discover what was going on.

As soon as he heard of this new marriage between Sava Toronthal and Sarcany he wrote to Cattaro. And as soon as he heard of the pitiable state to which the young engineer was reduced he sent off the news to the doctor.

The only reply was for him to continue his observations, and to keep Cattaro thoroughly informed of all that happened.

As the 6th of July approached Pierre's state became worse. His mother could not keep him quiet. How could they possibly make Toronthal change his plans? Was it not evident from the haste with which it had been declared and fixed that the marriage had been decided on for some time, that Sarcany and the banker were acquaintances of old date, that the "rich Tripolitan" had some peculiar influence over Sava's father?

Pierre Bathory wrote to Toronthal eight days before the date fixed for the wedding. His letter received no reply.

Then Pierre tried to speak to the banker in the street. He did not succeed in meeting him. Pierre then sought him at his house. He was not allowed to cross the threshold. Sava and her mother remained invisible. There was no possibility of communicating with them.

But if Pierre could not see Sava nor her father he very often ran against Sarcany. To the looks of hate with which he greeted him Sarcany replied with looks of disdain. Pierre then thought of insulting him, of provoking him to fight. But why should Sarcany accept a meeting, which he had every inducement to refuse?

Six days went by. Pierre in spite of the entreaties of his mother, and the prayers of Borik, left the house in the Rue Marinella on the evening of the 4th of July. The old servant attempted to follow, but soon lost sight of him. Pierre hurried on at a venture, as if he was mad, along the most deserted streets of the town and by the side of the walls.

An hour afterwards they brought him home – dying. He had been stabbed in the upper part of the left lung.

There seemed to be no doubt that in a paroxysm of despair he had committed suicide.

As soon as Point Pescade heard of the misfortune he ran to the telegraph office.

An hour later the doctor received the news at Cattaro.

It would be difficult to describe the grief of Madame Bathory when she found herself in the presence of her son, who had perhaps but a few hours to live. But the mother's energy steeled itself against the woman's weakness. To work, first: to weep, afterwards.

A doctor was sent for. He arrived in a few minutes, he examined the wounded man, he listened to the feeble intermittent breathing, he probed the wound, he bandaged it, he did all that his art told him – but he gave no hope.

227

Fifteen hours afterwards the case was aggravated by the occurrence of considerable haemorrhage, and respiration, becoming hardly apparent, threatened soon to end.

Madame Bathory was on her knees by the bedside praying to God not to take away her son. The door opened.

Doctor Antekirtt walked in and approached the bed.

Madame Bathory would have rushed towards him. He stopped her with a gesture.

Then he went to Pierre, and carefully examined him without uttering a word. Then he looked at him long and fixedly. As if some strange magnetic power shot forth from his eyes to the very brain where thought was lingering for a moment before it finally left, he seemed to fill that brain with his own life, with his own will.

Suddenly Pierre half rose towards him. His eyelids lifted. He looked at the doctor. He fell back inanimate.

Madame Bathory threw herself on her son, gave one scream and fainted in Borik's arms.

The doctor closed the eyes of the corpse; then he rose, left the house, whispering as he did so the old phrase from the Indian legend:

'Death destroyeth not, it only rendereth invisible.'

CHAPTER VIII

A MEETING IN THE STRADONE

The death made a good deal of noise in the town, but no one suspected that Sarcany and Silas Toronthal were in any way concerned in it.

It was on the morrow, the 6th of July, that the marriage was to take place.

Neither Madame Toronthal nor her daughter heard anything about the death, precautions having been taken by Toronthal and his destined son-in-law to keep it from their ears.

It had been agreed that the wedding should be a very quiet one. As an excuse it was given out that Sarcany's family were in mourning. This was hardly in accordance with Toronthal's usual love of show, but he thought it better that no more fuss than necessary should be made. The newly married couple were to remain a few days at Ragusa, and then leave for Tripoli, where Sarcany it was said usually lived. There would therefore be no party in the Stradone, either for the reading of the settlements or after the religious service, which was to immediately follow the civil ceremony.

During the day, while the last preparations were being made at the Toronthals', two men strolled along the opposite side of the Stradone.

One was Cape Matifou, the other Point Pescade.

The doctor had brought Matifou back with him to Ragusa. His presence was no longer necessary at Cattaro and the two friends, the "twins," as Pescade said, were supremely happy at seeing one another again.

As soon as the doctor had reached Ragusa he had made his first appearance in the Rue Marinella, then he had retired to a quiet hotel in the suburb of Plocce, where he waited until the wedding had taken place in furtherance of his plans.

Next morning he had again visited Madame Bathory and helped to put Pierre in his coffin. He had then returned to his hotel, having sent Pescade and Matifou to keep watch on the Stradone.

And although Pescade was all eyes and ears, that did not prevent him from talking.

"I think you're bigger, old Cape!" he said, reaching up to pat his companion's chest.

"Yes, and in better condition!"

"So I felt when you embraced me."

"But how is the play getting on we were talking about?"

"Oh, the drama? Oh, it's going on, going on! But you see the action is getting complicated."

"Complicated?"

"Yes! It isn't a comedy, it's a drama, and there'll be a big fight before the curtain drops..."

Point Pescade stopped suddenly.

A carriage drove up rapidly to Toronthal's house. The gate opened immediately and as it shut Pescade recognized Sarcany in the carriage.

"Yes – lots of fighting," he continued, "and it looks as though it's going to be a great success."

"And the villain?" asked Matifou, who seemed to be more particularly concerned with that personage.

"Well – the villain is triumphant at the present moment, as he always is in a well-built piece! But, patience! Wait for the end!"

"At Cattaro," said Matifou, "I thought I was coming on."

"Coming on the scene?"

"Yes, Point Pescade, yes!"

And Matifou related what had passed at the bazaar at Cattaro, and how his two arms had been requisitioned for a kidnapping which did not take place.

"Good! That was too soon!" replied Point Pescade, who spoke for the sake of speaking, so to speak, keeping a keen lookout right and left of him. "You won't be wanted till the fourth or fifth act! Perhaps you may only have to appear in the last scene! But don't be uneasy! You'll make a great success when you do begin! You can reckon on that!"

At this moment a distant murmur was heard in the Stradone where the Rue Marinella ran in.

Point Pescade broke off the conversation abruptly and hurried to the right of Toronthal's house.

A procession was coming along the road to enter the Stradone on its way to the church of the Franciscans, where the funeral service was to be held.

There were few followers at the funeral, and nothing to attract much attention – merely a coffin carried under a black pall.

The procession slowly advanced, when suddenly Point Pescade, stifling an exclamation, seized Cape Matifou's arm.

"What's the matter?"

"Nothing! It'd take too long to tell you now!"

He had just recognized Madame Bathory, who had resolved to be present at her son's burial.

The Church had not refused its ministrations; and the priest was waiting in the Franciscan chapel to lead the procession to the grave.

Madame Bathory walked behind the coffin, looking into vacancy. She had no longer strength to cry. Her eyes were almost haggard and sometimes wandered from side to side then plunged for a time beneath the pall, which hid the coffin of her son.

Borik dragged himself along after her – a piteous sight to see.

Point Pescade felt the tears come into his eyes. Yes! If he had not had to remain on duty at his post he would not have hesitated to join the few friends and neighbours that were following all that was left on earth of Pierre Bathory.

Suddenly as the procession was about to pass Toronthal's mansion, the main gates opened. In the courtyard before the steps two carriages stood ready to start. The first came through the gate and turned down the Stradone.

In this carriage Point Pescade saw Silas Toronthal, his wife, and his daughter.

Madame Toronthal, overwhelmed with grief, was seated next to Sava, who looked whiter than her nuptial veil.

Sarcany, accompanied by some relatives or friends, occupied the second carriage.

The wedding and the funeral equally destitute of show! In both the same grief! It was frightful!

Suddenly as the first carriage turned out of the gate there was a piercing shriek.

Madame Bathory had stopped, and with her hand pointed to Sava was cursing her!

It was Sava who had shrieked! She had seen the mother in mourning! She had understood all they had hidden from her! Pierre was dead, dead

An hour afterwards they brought him home – dying

by her and for her, and it was his funeral that was passing as they were taking her to be married!

She fell back fainting. Madame Toronthal, distracted, tried to bring her back to consciousness. In vain! She scarcely breathed!

Toronthal could not restrain a gesture of anger. But Sarcany, who had hurried to her side, gave no sign of his annoyance.

Under these circumstances it was impossible to attend before the registrar, and the order was given to return to the house, of which the big gates shut with a clang.

Sava, carried to her room, was laid on her bed without having moved. Her mother knelt by her side, and a physician was summoned in all haste. During this time the funeral continued its progress to the Franciscan church, and then after the service it went on to the cemetery.

Point Pescade saw that the doctor ought at once to know what had happened.

Saying to Matifou, "Stop here and watch," – he ran off to the Plocce.

While Pescade told his story the doctor remained silent. "Have I exceeded my right?" he said to himself. "No! Have I struck one who is innocent? Yes, certainly! But she's the daughter of Silas Toronthal!"

Then he turned to Pescade.

"Where's Cape Matifou?"

"In front of Toronthal's house."

"I want you both this evening."

"At what time?"

"Nine o'clock."

"Where shall we be?"

"At the cemetery gates."

Point Pescade instantly returned to Matifou, who had not left his post.

That evening about eight o'clock the doctor, enveloped in an ample cloak, went for a walk towards the harbour of Ragusa. At the angle of the wall on the left he reached a small creek running up among the rocks a little above the harbour.

The place was quite deserted. Neither houses nor boats were near. The fishing craft never came there to anchor for fear of the numerous reefs, which lay round the creek.

The doctor halted, looked round him, and uttered a peculiar cry, which had doubtless been agreed upon beforehand. Almost immediately a sailor appeared, and approaching him, said:

"At your orders, sir!"

"The boat's ready, Pazzer?"

233

"Yes, behind the rock."

'With all the men?"

"All."

"And the *Electric*?"

"Farther north, about three cables outside the creek."

And the sailor pointed to a long grey tube just visible in the gloom, but without a light of any kind to indicate its presence.

"When did she arrive from Cattaro?"

"Hardly an hour ago."

"And she wasn't seen?"

"No! She came along by the reefs."

"Pazzer, see that no one leaves his post, and wait for me here all night if necessary."

"Ay, ay, sir!"

The seaman returned to the boat, which was indistinguishable among the rocks.

Dr. Antekirtt remained for some time on the beach, waiting probably for the darkness to increase. Sometimes he would stride along for a minute. Then he would stop. And then with folded arms, silent and motionless, he would look out over the Adriatic as if telling it his secrets.

The night was moonless and starless. The land breeze that rises with the evening and lasts but an hour or two had now lulled until it could scarcely be felt. A few thick clouds almost covered the sky except in the west where the last streaks of the sunset gave a feeble light that was swiftly fading.

"Now!" said the doctor.

And returning towards the town he kept outside the wall all the way to the cemetery.

There before the gate were Point Pescade and Cape Matifou hidden under a tree so as not to be seen in the shadow.

The cemetery was closed at this time of night. A light had just been extinguished in the gatekeeper's lodge. No one was expected there again before the morning.

The doctor seemed to know the plan of the cemetery. And it also appeared that he had no intention of entering by the gate. What he was going to do was to be done in secret.

"Follow me!" he said to Point Pescade and his companion as they came to meet him.

And the three silently crept along the slope that runs at the foot of the exterior wall.

After some ten minutes of this work the doctor stopped, and pointing to a breach caused by a recent fall of the wall said:

"Through here."

He glided through the breach. Point Pescade and Matifou followed him.

The darkness was profound beneath the large trees that overshadowed the tombs. But without hesitation the doctor went down one path and then turned off into another leading to the upper part of the cemetery. Some birds of the night disturbed by his presence flew backwards and forwards overhead, but not another living thing lurked round the gravestones scattered on the turf.

Soon the three stood in front of what looked like a small chapel, with the gate left unfastened.

The doctor pushed back the gate; and then pressing the button of a small electric lantern he threw on the light, but so that it could not be seen from without.

"Enter," said he to Matifou.

Cape Matifou entered and found himself facing a wall on which were three marble tablets.

On one of these tablets, the centre one, he read:

STEPHEN BATHORY

1867

The tablet to the left bore no inscription; that to the right was soon to have one.

"Take away that slab," said the doctor.

Cape Matifou easily removed the slab, which had not yet been fixed down. He laid it on the ground, and a bier was seen at the bottom of a cavity in the wall.

There was the coffin containing the body of Pierre Bathory.

"Bring out that coffin," said the doctor.

Cape Matifou pulled out the coffin without any help from Point Pescade, heavy though it was, and after lifting it outside the chapel he placed it on the ground.

"Take this," said the doctor, handing Pescade a screwdriver, "and get the lid off that coffin."

In a few minutes it was done.

The doctor moved aside the white garments with his hand, and placing his head to the body seemed to listen for the beating of the heart.

Her mother knelt by her side, and a physician was summoned in all haste

Then he rose.

"Lift out that body," said he to Cape Matifou.

Matifou obeyed, and neither he nor Pescade made the slightest objection, although such an exhumation was against the law.

When the body of Pierre Bathory was laid on the grass Cape Matifou wrapped it up again in its winding-sheet, and over it the doctor threw his mantle. The coffin was then screwed down, and returned to the cavity, and the tablet placed over it as before.

The doctor broke the current of his electric lantern and the darkness became profound again.

"Take up that body," said he to Cape Matifou.

Matifou lifted it in his arms as if it had been the body of a child. Then led by the doctor and followed by Point Pescade he regained the cross path leading to the breach in the wall.

Five minutes later they were through the breach and on their way to the shore.

Not a word was spoken; but if the obedient Cape Matifou thought no more than a machine, what a succession of ideas crowded through the active brain of Point Pescade!

In their journey from the cemetery to the shore they had met nobody. But as they approached the creek where the *Electric*'s boat was waiting for them, they saw a coastguardsman walking about the rocks.

They continued on their way without troubling themselves about his presence.

Again the doctor uttered his peculiar cry, and the sailor came up from the boat, which remained invisible.

At a sign Cape Matifou went down behind the rocks and was about to step into the boat.

At this moment the coastguardsman hurried up, and just as they were entering the boat he asked:

"Who are you?"

"People who can give you your choice between twenty florins, cash down, and a slap in the face from that gentleman," – pointing to Matifou – "also cash down!"

The coastguardsman did not hesitate: he took the twenty florins.

A moment afterwards the boat had vanished in the darkness. Five minutes later it was alongside the *Electric*. It was hoisted on board. The silent engines were started, and the launch was off to sea.

Matifou bore the body below and laid it on a couch in the saloon, from which not a light port allowed a ray to escape through the hull.

The doctor was left alone with the corpse. He bent over it, kissed the pallid forehead, and said:

"And now, Pierre, awake!"

Immediately, as if he had only been asleep, Pierre opened his eyes.

A look of aversion stole over his face when he recognized the doctor.

"You!" he murmured. "You who abandoned me!"

"I! Pierre!"

"But who are you then?"

"A dead man – like you!"

"A dead man?..."

"I am Count Mathias Sandorf!"

PART III

CHAPTER I

THE MEDITERRANEAN

'The Mediterranean,' wrote Michelet, 'is beautiful. Its harmonious setting, its pure, transparent air and light renew the human spirit. It moulds those living along its shores, imbuing them with strength, creating the heartiest of races.'

Fortunately for humanity, Nature, failing Hercules, has separated the rock of Calpe from the rock of Abyla to form the Straits of Gibraltar. Notwithstanding the opinion of many geologists it would seem that these straits are of no recent formation. Without them there would have been no Mediterranean. Evaporation robs it of more than three times the water its rivers bring in, and were it not for the Atlantic current which pours in through the straits it would in a few centuries become a kind of Dead Sea instead of the Living Sea that it is.

It was in one of its obscurest retreats, in one of the most unknown spots in this vast inland lake, that Count Mathias Sandorf – who intended to remain Dr. Antekirtt until he had finished his work – had concealed himself so as to make the best of all the advantages that his supposed death had given him.

There are two Mediterraneans on the terrestrial globe, one in the Old World, the other in the New. The American Mediterranean is the Gulf of Mexico; it has an area of about 500,000 square miles. The Mediterranean has an area of about 1,150,000 square miles, and is more varied in general outline and richer in basins and distinct gulfs and large hydrographical subdivisions which have even the name of seas – such as the Greek Archipelago and the Cretan Sea above the island of that name, the Libyan Sea below it, the Adriatic between Italy, Austria, and Turkey, the Ionian Sea round the islands of Corfu, Zante, Cephalonia and the other islands, the Tyrrhenian Sea on the west of Italy, the Aeolian Sea round the Liparis, the Gulf of Lyons running up into Provence, the Gulf of Genoa in the north of Italy, the Gulf of Khabs off the coast of Tunis, and the two Syrtes off the coast of Tripoli.

In what secret spot in this well-known sea had Dr. Antekirtt taken up his abode? There are islands in hundreds and islets in thousands within its bounds. To attempt to count its capes and creeks would be labour in vain. Many nations differing in race, in manners, in government, dwell on its coasts, where the history of humanity has been leaving its mark for the last twenty centuries: French, Italians, Spaniards, Austrians, Turks, Greeks, Arabs, Egyptians, Tripolitans, Tunisians, Algerians, Moors, even Britons at Gibraltar, Malta, and Cyprus. Three huge continents form its shores – Europe, Asia, Africa. Where then had Count Mathias Sandorf, otherwise Dr. Antekirtt – a name dear to the Orientals – taken up his residence to work out the programme of his new life? Pierre Bathory was soon to know.

After opening his eyes for an instant he had fallen back completely exhausted, as insensible as when the doctor had left him for dead in the house at Ragusa. It was then that the doctor had succeeded in one of those physiologic experiments in which the will plays so important a part, and of which the phenomena are no longer open to doubt. Gifted with a singular power of suggestion he had been able without the aid of magnesium light or even a brilliant point of metal, simply by the penetration of his look, to cast the dying man into hypnotic state and take command of his will. Pierre, enfeebled by the loss of blood, had lost the very look of life and had fallen asleep to awake when the doctor wished. But his life was almost gone, and now it had to be saved. It was a difficult task and required the most minute care and all the resources of the medical art. The doctor must not fail.

"He will live! I must have him live!" he repeated. "Ah, why at Cattaro did I not act on my first idea? Why did the arrival of Sarcany at Ragusa prevent my snatching him from that accursed town? But I'll save him! In the time to come Pierre Bathory will be Mathias Sandorf's right hand!"

And for fifteen years to punish and reward had been the constant thought of Dr. Antekirtt. He had never forgotten what he owed to his companions, Stephen Bathory and Ladislas Zathmar. The time had now come to act, and that was why the *Savarena* had gone to Ragusa.

During these long years the doctor had so altered in appearance that it was impossible to recognize him. His hair, worn short, had become white, and his complexion had turned deadly pale. He was one of those men of fifty who have kept the strength of their youth and acquired the coolness and calm of ripe old age. The bushy hair, full complexion, and

Venetian beard of the young Count Sandorf would never recur to those who looked at Dr. Antekirtt. But more rigidly refined and more highly tempered, he remained one of those natures of iron of whom it can be said that with them the magnet swings only as they near it. Of Stephen Bathory's son he wished to make what he had made of himself.

For a long time Dr. Antekirtt had been the sole representative of the great family of Sandorf. It will be remembered that he had a child, a daughter who after his arrest had been entrusted to the care of the wife of Landeck, the steward of the castle of Artenak. This little daughter, then only two years old, had been the count's sole heiress. To her when she reached eighteen was to come the half of her father's goods in accordance with the sentence, which enjoined the confiscation and the death penalty. The steward Landeck had been retained as manager of that part of the Transylvanian domain put under sequestration, and he and his wife remained at the castle with the child, intending to devote their lives to her. But it seemed as though some fate pursued the Sandorf family, now reduced to this one small individual. A few months after the conviction of the Trieste conspirators and the events, which succeeded, the child had disappeared, and it had proved impossible to find her. Her hat had been found on the bank of one of the numerous rivulets that ran through the park. It was only too obvious that the little girl had fallen into one of the ravines into which run the torrents of the Carpathians, and not a vestige of her could be found. Rosena Landeck, the steward's wife, took the loss so much to heart that she died a few weeks afterwards. The Government made no change in the arrangements ordered at the time of the sentence. The sequestration was maintained, and the possessions of Count Sandorf would return to the State if the heiress, whose death had not been legally proved, did not reappear to claim them.

Such was the last blow that had reached the Sandorf race, now doomed to extinction by the disappearance of the last representative of the family. Time was gradually accomplishing its work, and oblivion was throwing its shadow over the event as over all the other facts of the conspiracy of Trieste.

It was at Otranto, where he was living in the strictest incognito that Sandorf heard of his child's death. With his little daughter there disappeared all that remained to him of the Countess Rena who had died so soon and whom he loved so much. Then he left Otranto, as unknown as when he arrived there, and no one could tell where his life began anew.

"Through here."

Fifteen years later when Sandorf had reappeared on the scene no one suspected that he was playing the part of Dr. Antekirtt. Thenceforth Sandorf devoted himself entirely to his work. Now he was alone in the world with a task to perform – a task he regarded as sacred. Many years after he had left Otranto, grown powerful by all the power that a large fortune gives, acquired under circumstances we shall soon ascertain, forgotten and concealed by his incognito he had put himself on the track of those he had sworn to punish and reward. Already in his thoughts Pierre Bathory had been associated in the work of justice. Agents were stationed in the different coast towns of the Mediterranean. Well paid and sworn to secrecy they corresponded only with the doctor either by the swift launches we know of or by the submarine cable, which joined Antekirtta to Malta and Malta to Europe.

It was in verifying the statements of his agents that the doctor had discovered the traces of all those who directly or indirectly had been mixed up in Sandorf's conspiracy. He could then watch them from afar, and let them have their run as it were, uninterfered with for four or five years. Silas Toronthal he knew had left Trieste and settled at Ragusa with his wife and daughter. Sarcany he traced to the principal cities of Europe where he wasted his fortune, and then to Sicily, to the eastern provinces, where he and his companion Zirone were meditating some new scheme to again put them in funds. Carpena he learnt had left Rovigno and Istria to do nothing in Italy and Austria – the florins he had gained by his information permitting him to live in idleness.

Andrea Ferrato he would have helped to escape from the prison of Stein in the Tyrol – where he was expiating his generous conduct towards the fugitives of Pisino – had not death delivered the honest fisherman from his fetters a few months after he was sent there. His children Maria and Luigi had left Rovigno, and were now probably having a hard struggle for life. But they had disappeared and he had not yet been able to come upon any trace of them. Of Madame Bathory at Ragusa with her son Pierre, and Borik the old servant of Ladislas Zathmar, the doctor had never lost sight, and we know how he had sent them a considerable sum of money, which was not accepted by the proud courageous woman.

But the hour had come for the doctor to begin his difficult campaign. Assuring himself that he would never be recognized after his fifteen years' absence and his being supposed to be dead he arrived at Ragusa, and found Stephen Bathory's son in love with Silas Toronthal's daughter. It will be remembered how Sarcany had intervened and thrust them apart, how Pierre had been taken to his mother's house, how Dr. Antekirtt had acted when he was on the point of death, and how he had called him back to life to reveal himself to him under his real name of Mathias Sandorf. Now his task was to cure him, to tell him what he did not know, to tell him how treachery had delivered over his father and his companions, to acquaint him with the names of the traitors, to win over his help in the work the doctor had set himself of dealing out justice far beyond that ordinary justice of which he had been the victim.

In the first place then Pierre had to be restored to health, and it was to the restoration that he entirely devoted himself. In the first eight days after his arrival in the island Pierre literally hung between life and death. Not only was his wound very serious, but his mental state was even more so. The thought of Sava being now Sarcany's wife, the thought of his mother grieving for him, the resurrection of Count Mathias Sandorf as Dr. Antekirtt – Sandorf the most devoted of his fathers friends – all was enough to unsettle a mind already sorely shaken. Day and night the doctor did not leave him. He heard him in his delirium repeat the name of Sava Toronthal. He learned how deep and true was his love for her, and how her marriage was torturing him. He asked if this love would not prove resistless even when he learnt that Sava was the daughter of the man who had sold and killed his father. The doctor would tell him nevertheless. He had made up his mind to do so. It was his duty.

Again and again Pierre almost succumbed. Doubly injured, in mind and body, he was so near to death that he did not recognize Sandorf at his bedside. He had not even strength to whisper Sava's name.

But skilful care prevailed and the reaction began.

Youth gained the mastery. The sick man was cured in body before he was cured in mind. His wound began to heal, his lungs regained their normal powers, and on the 17th of July the doctor knew that Pierre was saved.

That day the young man recognized him. In a voice still weak, however, he called him by his true name.

"To you, my son, I am Mathias Sandorf," was the reply, "but to you alone!"

And as Pierre by his looks seemed to ask for explanations which he was naturally anxious to hear:

"Later on," added the doctor. "Later on."

It was in a beautiful room with the windows opening to the fresh sea breezes beneath the shade of lovely trees, which the running streams kept evergreen, that Pierre speedily and surely grew convalescent. The doctor was untiring in his attention, he was with him every moment, but as the recovery became assured there was nothing strange in his calling in an assistant in whose intelligence and kindness he had absolute confidence.

This was Point Pescade, who was as devoted to Pierre as he was to the doctor. We need hardly say that he and Cape Matifou had kept profoundly secret what had taken place at the cemetery of Ragusa, and that they had revealed to none that the young man had been snatched alive from his tomb.

Point Pescade had been intimately concerned in all that had passed during the last few weeks, and consequently he took a lively interest in the patient. The love affair of Pierre, the intervention of Sarcany – a scoundrel who inspired him with well-founded antipathy – the meeting of the funeral and marriage processions in the Stradone, the exhumation in the cemetery, had deeply moved him, and although he could not understand the object he felt him more closely associated in the schemes of Dr. Antekirtt. He therefore readily accepted the task of nursing the invalid. His instructions were to distract his patient's attention as much as possible by his wit and humour. And he did his best. Since the holiday at Gravosa he had looked upon Pierre as his creditor and on every occasion made every effort to pay off something on account of the debt. And so Point Pescade took up his quarters with the convalescent, and endeavoured all he could to keep his thoughts from running in the old groove by talking and joking incessantly and giving him the least possible time to reflect.

One day when thus occupied Pierre asked him how he had made Dr. Antekirtt's acquaintance.

"At the launch of the trabacolo," he answered. "You ought to remember it! The launch of the trabacolo that made a hero out of Cape Matifou!"

Pierre had not forgotten the important event, but he did not know that at the doctor's request the acrobats had abandoned their profession to enter his service.

"Yes, Mr. Bathory," answered Point Pescade. "Yes! That was it, and Cape Matifou's devotion was a stroke of fortune for us! But what we owe to the doctor does not make us forget what we owe to you!"

"To me?"

"To you, Mr. Pierre, to you who on that day gave us a couple of florins we had not earned; for our audience ran away although he had paid for his seat."

Five minutes later the boat was alongside the *Electric*

And Point Pescade reminded Pierre how, just as he was about to enter the arena and had put down his money, he had disappeared.

Pierre had forgotten all about it, but he answered Pescade with a smile – a sad smile, for he remembered that he had disappeared in the crowd to find Sava Toronthal.

His eyes closed. He thought of all that had happened since that day. As he thought of Sava whom he believed to be married he was wrung with grievous anguish and tempted even to curse those who had snatched him from death!

Point Pescade saw at once that the remembrance of Gravosa had thrown Pierre into a sorrowful reverie. He said no more for a minute or two, and then he whispered as if to himself:

"Half a teaspoon of cheerfulness to be taken every five minutes – those are the doctor's orders, but they are rather difficult to follow."

Pierre opened his eyes a few minutes afterwards and said:

"And so, Point Pescade, until the launch of the trabacolo you did not know Dr. Antekirtt?"

"No, we'd never seen him, and we'd never heard his name."

"And you've never left him since then?"

"Never, except on a few errands he's required of us."

"And in what country are we now? Can you tell me, Point Pescade?"

"I believe we're on an island, for the sea surrounds us."

"Doubtless, but in what part of the Mediterranean?"

"Ah! There you are! Whether it's south or north, or east or west I really do not know. After all what does it matter? One thing is certain, we're with the doctor, well fed, well clothed, well housed and..."

"But don't you know the island's name if you don't know its position?"

"Its name?" asked Pierre. "Oh, quite well! Its name is Antekirtta!"

Pierre vainly racked his memory for some island of the Mediterranean bearing the name, and then he looked at Pescade.

"Yes, Mr. Pierre. Yes! Antekirtta. Latitude – nought and longitude less! It is to that address my uncle ought to write if I had an uncle, but unfortunately I have not yet been favoured with that pleasure! After all there is nothing wonderful in its being called Antekirtta seeing it belongs to Dr. Antekirtt! Whether the doctor has taken his name from the island or the island has taken its name from him I should find it impossible to say even if I were the Secretary of the Royal Geographical Society."

Pierre's convalescence took the ordinary course. None of the anticipated complications showed themselves. With substantial nourishment the invalid from day to day visibly regained his strength. The doctor visited him often and talked about many things except those, which would appeal more directly to his mind. And Pierre thought it best not to provoke any premature confidences and waited till they were offered him.

Point Pescade always reported to the doctor the subjects of the conversations interchanged between him and his invalid. Evidently the incognito which enshrouded not only Count Sandorf but also the island in which he lived was a knotty point with Pierre. Nonetheless obvious was it that he was always thinking of Sava Toronthal, far away from him as she then seemed, for all communication appeared to be broken off between Antekirtta and the rest of Europe. But the time was coming when he would be strong enough to listen.

Yes! To hear everything! And on that day the doctor, like the operating surgeon, would be deaf to the patient's cries!

Many days went by. The young man's wound completely healed. Already he could leave his bed and take his place near the window. The lovely Mediterranean sun could caress him, and the life-giving breeze from the sea could inflate his lungs and yield him health and vigour. Against his will he felt himself restored to life. And his eyes dwelt on the distant horizon beyond which he would look in search of her who – in short he was still an invalid in his mind. The vast extent of water round the island was almost deserted. A few coasters, xebecs, or tartans, polaccas or speronares appeared on the horizon, and passed the island. Never came a merchant ship, never a mail steamer to plough its silent waters. Antekirtta seemed to be quite out of the world.

On the 24th of July the doctor told Pierre that he might go out the next afternoon, and offered to accompany him on his walk.

"Doctor," he replied, "if I'm strong enough to go out, I'm strong enough to listen!"

"To listen? What do you mean?"

"You know my history. I do not know yours."

The doctor eyed him attentively, not more as a friend than as a physician seeking to find if he could bear the knife or the fire that was coming.

Then he sat down beside him.

"You wish to know my history, Pierre? Then listen."

CHAPTER II

THE PAST AND THE PRESENT

"And first for the history of Dr. Antekirtt, which begins when Mathias Sandorf threw himself into the waves of the Adriatic.

"From the last shower of bullets rained round me by the police I escaped safe and sound. The night was very dark. No one could see me. The current bore me out to sea, and I could not have returned to the shore even if I would. And I would not. It was better to die than to be recaptured, taken back and shot in the donjon of Pisino. If I fell all was over. If I managed to save myself I could at the least pass for dead. Nothing would hinder me then in the work of justice I had sworn to Count Zathmar, to your father, and to myself to accomplish – and which I will accomplish."

"A work of justice?" answered Pierre, whose eyes kindled at the word so unexpected by him.

"Yes, Pierre, and this work you'll soon know, for it was to associate you in it that I brought you – a dead man, as I am, but a living man, as I am – from the cemetery of Ragusa."

At these words Pierre felt himself carried back fifteen years to the time when his father fell dead in the fortress of Pisino.

"Before me," continued the doctor, "was the open sea of the Italian shore. Good swimmer though I was I could not hope to cross it. Unless I was providentially rescued, unless I met with a raft, unless some foreign vessel took me on board, I was doomed to perish. But when you've risked your life you are strong enough to defend it if defence is possible.

"At first I dived once or twice to escape from the bullets. Then when I was sure I was not seen I kept at the surface and swam out to sea. My clothes were not much in my way as they were very light and tight fitting.

"It was then about half-past nine at night. I reckon that I swam away from the shore for about an hour; and I saw the lights of Rovigno vanish one after the other.

"Where was I going and what was my hope? I had no hope, Pierre, but I felt within me a strength of resistance, a tenacity, a superhuman will which sustained me. It was no longer my life I sought to save, but my future work I sought to do. At that moment had a fishing boat passed by I would have dived to avoid her! On that Austrian coast how many traitors might I not still find ready to hand me over for a reward as Carpena had done Andrea Ferrato!

"And this very thing happened at the end of the first hour. A boat did appear in the gloom. She came from the offing and was beating up to the coast. As I was getting tired I'd just slipped on my back, but instinctively I turned over again ready to disappear A fishing boat bound for an Istrian port could hardly be otherwise than suspicious.

"I was soon confirmed in this opinion. I heard one of the sailors say in Dalmatian that it was time to go about. Instantly I dived, and the boat passed over my head before those on board of it could see me.

"Almost breathless I came to the surface and struck out towards the west. The breeze fell lighter, the waves fell with the wind, and I was carried out to sea on the wide sweeping surge.

"Sometimes swimming, sometimes floating, I kept on farther and farther for about another hour. I saw but the object to attain and not the road to reach it. Fifty miles to cross the Adriatic! Yes! And I was willing to swim them! Yes! I would swim them. Ah! Pierre, you must go through such trials before you know of what man is capable, before you know what the human machine can do when all its mental and physical forces are combined!

"For the second hour I thus kept afloat. The Adriatic seemed absolutely deserted. The last birds had left it to regain the ledges in the rocks. Overhead the gulls and mews no longer circled, giving forth their plaintive screams.

"Although I felt no fatigue my arms became heavy, my legs seemed like lead. My fingers began to open, and I found it most difficult to keep my hands together. My head felt as if it were a shot on my shoulders, and I began to lose the ability of keeping myself afloat.

"A kind of hallucination seized on me. The guidance of my thoughts escaped me. Strange associations of ideas arose in my troubled brain. I felt I could no longer hear or see properly, but I fancied that some distance away from me a noise was being produced, and a light was approaching, and I was right in its path. And that proved to be the case.

"It must have been about midnight when a dull, distant booming arose in the east – a booming that I could not explain. A light flashed through my eyelids, which had shut in spite of all I could do. I tried to raise my head, and I could not do so without letting myself almost sink. Then I looked.

"I give you all these details, Pierre, because it is necessary you should know them, and through them know me as well!"

"There is no need of that, doctor – none!" answered the young man. "Do you think my mother has never told me what sort of a man was Mathias Sandorf?"

"She may have known Mathias Sandorf, Pierre, but Dr. Antekirtt she does not know! And he it is you must know! Listen then! Hear me out!

"The noise I had heard was made by a vessel coming from the east and bound for the Italian coast. The light was her white light hanging on her forestay – which showed her to be a steamer. Her side-lights I also saw, red at port and green at starboard, and as I saw them both together the steamer must have been bearing straight down on me.

"That moment was a critical one. In fact, the chances were that the steamer was an Austrian bound outwards from Trieste. To ask help from her was to put myself again in the power of the gendarmes of Rovigno. I resolved to do nothing of the kind, but to take advantage of another means of safety that I had thought of.

"The steamer was a fast one. She grew rapidly larger as she neared me, and I saw the foam furrowed off white from her bows. In less than two minutes she would cut through the place where I lay motionless.

"That the steamer was an Austrian I had no doubt. But there was nothing impossible in her destination being Brindisi and Otranto, or at least she might call there. If so she would arrive in less than twenty-four hours.

"My decision was taken, and I waited. Sure of being unseen in the darkness I kept myself in the steamer's path, and fortunately she slowed slightly as she gently rose and fell with the surge.

"At length the steamer reached me; her bow some twenty feet from the sea towered above me. I was wrapped in foam as she cleft the wave, but I was not struck. I was grazed by the long iron hull, and I pushed myself away from it with my hands as it passed me. That only lasted for a second or so. Then I found her lines begin to curve in for the run, and at the risk of being cut by the screw I caught hold of the rudder.

And so Point Pescade took up his quarters with the convalescent

"Fortunately the steamer had a full cargo, and her screw was deep down and did not strike above the water, else I should not have been able to get out of the eddy or retain my hold of the support to which I had clung. Like all steamships she had a pair of chains hanging from her stern and fixed on to the rudder and I had seized one of these chains pulled myself up to the ring to which it hung, and there I sat on the chain close to the sternpost and just a few inches above the sea. I was in comparative safety.

"Three hours elapsed and day broke. I reckoned I would have to remain where I was for another twenty hours if the steamer was going to call at Brindisi or Otranto. What I should have to suffer most from would be hunger and thirst. The important thing for me was that I could not be seen from the deck nor even from the boat hung by the stern davits. Some vessel meeting us might, it is true, see me and signal me. But very few ships met us that day, and they passed too far off for them to notice a man hanging to the rudder chains.

"A scorching sun soon dried my clothes. Andrea Ferrato's three hundred florins were in my belt; they made me feel safe once I got to land. There I should have nothing to fear. In a foreign country Count Mathias Sandorf would have nothing to fear from the Austrian police.

"There is no extradition for political refugees. But it was not enough that they should think my life was saved. I wished them to think I was dead. No one should know that the last fugitive from the donjon of Pisino had set foot on Italian soil.

"What I wished happened. The day passed without adventure. Night came. About ten o'clock in the evening I saw a light at regular intervals away to the southwest. It was the lighthouse at Brindisi. Two hours afterwards the steamer was just outside the harbour.

"But then before the pilot came on board, when we were about a mile from the land, after making a parcel of my clothes and tying them to my neck, I slipped off the rudder chains into the sea.

"A minute afterwards I had lost sight of the steamer whose steam whistle had begun its shrieking. In half an hour I had reached the shore, hidden among the rock, resumed my clothes, and on a bed of seaweed had fallen asleep. In the morning I entered Brindisi, found one of the humblest hotels in the place, and there awaited events before settling on the plan of an entirely new life.

"Two days afterwards, Pierre, the newspapers informed me that the conspiracy of Trieste was at an end. They said that the search for Count Sandorf's body had been fruitless. I was held to be dead – as dead as if I had fallen with my two companions, Ladislas Zathmar and your father Stephen Bathory, in the donjon of Pisino.

"I, dead! No, Pierre – and they shall see that I am living!"

Pierre had listened, greedily to the doctor's story. He was as deeply moved by it as if the story had been told him from the tomb. Yes! It was Count Mathias Sandorf who thus had spoken. In the presence of him, the living portrait of his father, the doctor's habitual coldness had gradually abandoned him, he had revealed his real character, he had shown himself as he really was, after years of disguise. What he had said about his audacious voyage across the Adriatic was true in the minutest detail. It was thus that he arrived at Brindisi, where Mathias Sandorf remained dead to the world.

But he had to leave Brindisi without delay. The town is only a transfer station. People come to it merely to embark for India or land for Europe. It is generally empty except on the two days of the week when ships from the Peninsular and Oriental Company come in.

The doctor had no further fear for his life, but it was important that his death should be believed in. Thus ran his thoughts on the morning after his arrival as he was walking at the foot of the terrace, which overlooks the column of Cleopatra at the very spot where the old Apian Way begins. Already he had formed his plans. He would go to the East in search of wealth and power. But to embark on one of the steamboats trading to Asia Minor among a crowd of passengers of all nations would not be wise. He wanted some in more secret means of transport than he could find in Brindisi. And that evening he took the train for Otranto.

In an hour and a half the train reached that town, which is situated almost at the end of the heel of the Italian boot. There in the almost abandoned port the doctor agreed with the captain of a xebec departing for Smyrna. In the morning the xebec sailed and the doctor saw the lighthouse of Punta di Luca, the extreme point of Italy, sink beneath the horizon, while on the opposite coast the Acroceraunian mountains were hidden in the mist. A few days afterwards, alter a voyage without incident, Cape Matapan, at the extremity of Southern Greece, was doubled and Smyrna safely reached.

The doctor had succinctly related to Pierre this part of his voyage and also how he had learnt from the newspapers of the unexpected death of his daughter, leaving him alone in the world.

"At last," he said, "I was in the land of Asia Minor where for so many years I was to live unknown. It was in studies of medicine, chemistry, natural science, that I had delighted during my youth at the schools and universities of Hungary – where your father gained his renown: and it was to these studies that I was to trust for my means of livelihood.

"I was fortunate enough to succeed and more promptly than I had hoped. I settled first at Smyrna, where for seven or eight years I obtained great reputation as a physician. Some unexpected cures brought me into connection with the richest people of those countries in which the medical art is still in a rudimentary state. I then made up my mind to leave the town. And like the doctors of the days gone by, healing at the same time as I taught the art of healing, studying the almost unknown therapeutics of the talebs of Asia Minor and the pundits of India, I travelled through the whole of those provinces, stopping here a few weeks, there a few months, called to Karahissar, Binder, Adana, Haleb, Tripoli, Damascus, ever preceded by a renown which increased without ceasing and brought me a fortune that increased with my renown.

"But that was not enough. What I wanted was unbounded power, such as that possessed by the rajahs of India, whose knowledge is equal to their wealth.

"My opportunity came.

"There was at Homs, in Northern Syria, a man dying of a slow disease. No physician had been able to tell what was the matter with him. Hence none of them knew how to treat him. The man was Faz-Rhât, and he had occupied very high posts in the Turkish Empire. He was then forty-five years of age, and an immense fortune allowed him to enjoy all the pleasures of life.

"Faz-Rhât had heard of me, for at the time my reputation was at its height he invited me to Homs, and I accepted the invitation.

"'Doctor,' said he, 'half of my fortune is yours if you'll give me back my life!'

"'Keep the half of your fortune,' I said, 'I will take care of you and cure you if Heaven permits.'

"I carefully studied the malady the physicians had abandoned. A few months at the outside was all they had given him to live. But I was lucky enough to discover what ailed him. For three weeks I remained with Faz-Rhât so as to follow the effects of the treatment I had prescribed. His cure was complete. When he wished to pay me I would accept only what seemed to me to be reasonable. And then I left Homs.

"Three years later Faz-Rhât lost his life in a hunting accident. He had no relatives whatever and his will made me the sole heir of all his possessions. Their value was certainly not less than fifty million florins.

"The steamer was a fast one. She grew rapidly larger as she neared me..."

"Thirteen years had then elapsed since the fugitive of Pisino had taken refuge in Asia Minor. The name of Dr. Antekirtt, although somewhat legendary, was known throughout Europe. I had obtained the result I wished. And now I was ready to set to work at the object of my life.

"I had resolved to return to Europe, or at least to some point of the Mediterranean. I visited the African coast and for a considerable sum I became the owner of an important island, rich, fertile and suitable in every way for a small colony – this isle of Antekirtta. Here, Pierre, I am sovereign, absolute master, king without subjects, but with a people devoted to me body and soul with means of defence that will be very formidable when I've finished them, with means of communication that link me to different points of the Mediterranean border, with a flotilla of such speed that I may almost say I've made this sea my dominion!"

"Where is Antekirtta situated?" asked Pierre.

"In the neighbourhood of the Syrtis Magna, which has had an evil reputation from the remotest antiquity, in the south of the sea which the north wind makes so dangerous even to modern ships, in the deepest bend of the Gulf of Sidra which cuts back into the African coast between Tripoli and Barca."

There at the north of the group of the Syrtic Islands is the island of Antekirtta. A few years before the doctor had travelled through the Tripolitan coasts, and visited Souza the old Port of Cyrene, the Barca country, the towns that have replaced the old Ptolemais, Berenice, Adrianopolis, and in a word that old Pentapolis, formerly Greek, Macedonian, Roman, Persian, Saracenic, and now Arabic and belonging to the Pachalik of Tripoli. The chances of his voyage – for he went to a certain extent where he was called – took him among the numerous archipelagos off the Libyan sea board, Pharos and Anthiroda, the Plinthine twins, Enesipte, and the Tyndaric rocks, Pyrgos, Platea, Ilos, the Hyphales, the Pontians, the White Islands, and last of all the Syrtics.

In the Gulf of Sidra, about thirty miles southwest of the vilayet of Ben Ghazi, the nearest point on the mainland, he found the isle of Antekirtta. It was large enough – eighteen miles in circumference – to accommodate all those he thought necessary for his plans; sufficiently elevated, consisting chiefly of a conical hill, towering up some eight hundred feet from the sea, and commanding the whole sweep of the gulf; and sufficiently varied in its productions, and watered by its streams, to satisfy the wants of several thousand inhabitants. Besides it was in that sea, terrible on account of its storms, which in prehistoric times had been fatal to the Argonauts, whose perils were sung by Apollonius of Rhodes, Horace, Virgil, Propertius, Valerius Flaccus, Lucan, and by so many others who were more geographers than poets, such as Polybius, Sallust, Strabo, Mela, Pliny and Procopius.

The doctor was the island's absolute owner. He had obtained the freehold for a considerable sum, clear of every feudal and other obligation; and the deed of cession, which made him sovereign proprietor, had been fully ratified by the Sultan.

For three years the doctor had lived in this island. About 300 European and Arabic families attracted by his offers and the guarantee of a happy life formed a small colony of some 2000 souls. They were not slaves, nor were they subjects; they were companions devoted to their chief, and none the less so because that small corner of the terrestrial globe had become their new home.

Gradually a regular administration had been organized, with a militia for the defence of the island, and a magistrate chosen from among the notables, who very seldom found his services required. Then according to plans sent by the doctor to the leading builders of England, France, and America, he had had constructed his wonderful fleet of steamers, schooners, and *"Electrics"* for his rapid passages across the Mediterranean. At the same time fortifications began to be thrown up round Antekirtta, but they were not yet finished, although the doctor for serious reasons was urging on the works.

Had then Antekirtta some enemy to fear in the vicinity of the Gulf of Sidra? Yes. A formidable sect or rather a society of pirates, who had not seen without envy and hatred a foreigner founding a colony off the Libyan coast.

This sect was the Mussulman Brotherhood of Sidi Mohammed Ben All Es Senoussi. In this year (1300 of the Hegira) it had become much more menacing than formerly, and its geographical dominion embraced some 3,000,000 adherents. His zaouiyas, his vilayets, his centers of activity established in Egypt, in the Turkish Empire, in Europe and Asia, in Eastern Nigritia, Tunis, Algeria, Morocco and the independent Sahara up to the frontiers of Western Nigritia, existed in still greater numbers in Barca and Tripoli. They were a source of serious danger to the European establishments of Northern Africa, including Algeria destined to become hereafter the richest country in the world, and especially to Antekirtta, and hence the doctor was only acting with ordinary prudence in availing himself of every modern means of protection and defence.

So Pierre learnt from the conversation which followed and which taught him many other things as well. It was to the isle of Antekirtta that he had been brought, to the Syrtic Sea, as to one of the most forsaken corners of the Ancient World, many hundreds of miles form Ragusa, where he had left behind two whose memory would never leave him – his mother and Sava Toronthal.

In a few words the doctor completed the details concerning the second half of his existence. While he was making his arrangements for assuring the security of his island, while he was developing the riches of the soil, and providing for the material and mental wants of the little colony, he had kept himself acquainted with all that was going on respecting his former friends, of whom he had never lost sight, and among whom were Madame Bathory, her son and Borik.

Pierre then learnt why the *Savarena* had arrived at Gravosa under conditions that so greatly excited the curiosity of the public, why the doctor had visited Madame Bathory, how and why her son had not been informed of his visit, how the money put at his mother's disposal had been refused by her, and how the doctor had arrived in time to snatch Pierre from the tomb to which he had been carried when in his magnetic sleep.

"You, my son," he added. "Yes! You lost your head entirely and did not recoil from suicide..."

At this word Pierre in a movement of anger found strength enough to sit up.

"Suicide!" he exclaimed. "Do you then think I stabbed myself?"

"Pierre – in a moment of despair..."

"Despair? Yes! I was! I thought I'd been abandoned even by you, my father's friend, after the promises you'd made! In despair? Yes! And I am now! But Heaven does not give death to those in despair! It says live – and be avenged!"

"No – punish!" answered the doctor. "But, Pierre, who stabbed you then?"

"A man I hate," replied Pierre, "a man who on that night I met by chance in a deserted road by the side of the walls of Ragusa! Perhaps he thought I was going to quarrel with him! But he prevented me! He stabbed me! This man, this Sarcany is..."

Pierre could not finish the sentence. At the thought of the wretch in whom he saw the husband of Sava, his brain seemed to fail him, his eyes closed and life seemed to leave him as if his wound had been reopened.

In a moment the doctor had restored him to consciousness and looking at him fixedly:

"Sarcany! Sarcany!" he whispered to himself.

"I seized one of the chains and pulled myself up..."

It was advisable for Pierre to take some rest after the shock he had just received. He declined to do so.

"No," said he. "You told me to begin with – 'and first for the story of Dr. Antekirtt, which begins when Mathias Sandorf threw himself into the waves of the Adriatic'..."

"Yes, Pierre."

"Then there is something else I ought to know about Count Mathias Sandorf."

"Are you strong enough to hear it?"

"Speak."

"Be it so," replied the doctor. "It's better to finish with the secrets that you have a right to know, with all the terrible past that'll never return. Pierre, you thought I'd abandoned you because I'd left Gravosa! Listen then and judge for yourself.

"You know, Pierre, that on the evening of the day fixed for our execution my companions and I attempted to escape from the fortress of Pisino; but Ladislas Zathmar was caught by the warders just as he was going to join us at the foot of the donjon. Your father and I, swept away by the torrent of the Buco, were already out of their reach.

"After miraculously escaping from the whirlpools of the Foiba, when we set foot on the Leme Canal we were noticed by a scoundrel who did not hesitate to sell our heads to the Government that had just put a price on them. Discovered in the house of a Rovigno fisherman just as he was about to take us across the Adriatic your father was arrested and returned to Pisino. I was more fortunate and escaped! You know that! But this you do not know.

"Before the information given to the police by this Spaniard named Carpena – information which cost Ferrato the fisherman his liberty and, a few months afterwards, his life – two men had sold the secret of the conspirators of Trieste..."

"Their names?" interrupted Pierre.

"First, ask me how their treachery was discovered," said the doctor.

And he hurriedly told what had passed in the cell of the donjon, and explained the acoustic phenomenon, which had revealed the names of the traitors.

"Their names, doctor!" exclaimed Pierre. "You won't refuse to give me their names!"

"I'll tell you."

"Who were they?"

"In half an hour I had reached the shore, hidden among the rock…"

"One of them was the accountant who had introduced himself as a spy into Zathmar's house! The man who tried to assassinate you! Sarcany!"

"Sarcany!" exclaimed Pierre, who found sufficient strength to rise and walk towards the doctor. "Sarcany! That scoundrel! And you knew it! And you, the companion of Stephen Bathory, you who offered his son your protection, you to whom I'd entrusted the secret of my love, you who had encouraged me, you allowed him to introduce himself into Silas Toronthal's house when you could have kept him out with a word! And by your silence you've authorized this crime – yes! This crime – which has delivered over that unfortunate girl to Sarcany!"

"Yes, Pierre, I did all that!"

"But why?"

"Because she can never be your wife!"

"She can never be my wife!"

"Because if Pierre Bathory marries Miss Toronthal he'll be guilty of an even more abominable crime!"

"But why? Why?" asked Pierre in a paroxysm of anguish.

"Because Sarcany had an accomplice! Yes, an accomplice in the horrible scheme, which sent your father to his death! And that accomplice – it's necessary you should know – was a banker from Trieste, Silas Toronthal!"

Pierre heard and understood! He could make no reply. A spasm contracted his lips, he sank, crushed to the earth, paralyzed with horror. His pupils dilated and his look seemed to be plunged into unfathomable darkness.

The paroxysm lasted but a few seconds, during which the doctor asked himself if the patient were about to succumb to the dreadful operation he had made him undergo.

But Pierre's nature was as energetic as his own. He gained the mastery over his tortured feelings. Tears welled up into his eyes. Then he fell back into his chair and held out his hand to the doctor, who said to him in a gentle, serious voice:

"Pierre, to the whole world you and I are dead! Now I'm alone in the world, with no friend, no child! Will you be my son?"

"Yes! Father!" answered Pierre.

And the father and son sat clasped in each other's arms.

Brindisi

CHAPTER III

EVENTS AT RAGUSA

Meanwhile what was taking place at Ragusa?

Madame Bathory no longer lived there. After her son's death, Borik and a few of her friends had persuaded her to shut up the house in the Rue Marinella. At first it seemed as though the unhappy mother had been driven mad; and strong-minded though she was, she had really given signs of derangement that alarmed her physicians. Under their advice she was removed to the little village of Vinticello, where a friend of her family was living. There she would receive every attention, but what consolation could they offer to the mother and wife who had suffered twice over in her love for her husband and her son?

Her old servant would not leave her, and the house in the Rue Marinella having been shut up, he had followed to Vinticello to become her humble and assiduous confidant in sorrow.

They had ceased to trouble themselves about Sava Toronthal, and were even unaware that the marriage had been put off for some time. And in fact the young lady's health necessitated her keeping to her bed. She had received a blow as unexpected as it was terrible to her. He whom she loved was dead – dead of despair probably! And it was his corpse they were taking to the grave at the very moment she was leaving the house on her way to her hateful wedding! For ten days, until the 16th of July, Sava was in a most alarming state. Her mother would not leave her. Moreover, that care and attention was the last her mother could give, for she herself had received a fatal shock.

During these long hours what thoughts were exchanged between mother and daughter? We can imagine, and we need not enlarge on them. Two names were of constant recurrence amid their sobs and tears – one, that of Sarcany, to be cursed, the other, that of Pierre, to be wept over.

From these conversations, in which Silas Toronthal refrained from taking part – for he even avoided seeing his daughter – it resulted that Madame Toronthal made one more appeal to her husband. She asked him to consent to break off the marriage, which Sava regarded only with fear and horror.

The banker remained unmoved in his resolution. Had he been left to himself he might perhaps have yielded, but he was in the power of his accomplice, more even than may be imagined, and he refused to listen to his wife. The marriage of Sava and Sarcany was decided on, and it would take place as soon as the state of her health would allow.

It is easy to imagine what was Sarcany's irritation when this unexpected incident intervened, with what ill-dissembled anger he saw his game interfered with, and with what persistency he attacked Toronthal. It was only a delay, doubtless, but the delay if prolonged would lead to the collapse of the whole scheme on which he had arranged his future. And, besides, he knew that Sava felt for him nothing but insurmountable aversion.

And what would this aversion become if the young lady suspected that Pierre Bathory had been stabbed by the man who was forced upon her as her husband? For his part he was only too pleased at having had the chance of getting rid of his rival. Not a shade of remorse did he feel, so dead was he to every human sentiment.

"It's lucky," said he one day to Toronthal, "that that fellow thought of killing himself! There might have been too many Bathorys! Heaven does indeed protect us!"

And who was there left of these three families of Sandorf, Zathmar and Bathory? An old woman whose days were numbered! Yes! Heaven did seem to protect the scoundrels, and assuredly would carry its protection to its extreme limits the day Sarcany became the husband of Sava Toronthal!

Nevertheless, it appeared as though Heaven were trying people's patience, for the delay of the marriage grew more and more prolonged. No sooner had Sava recovered – physically that is – and Sarcany was again thinking of realizing his projects, than Madame Toronthal fell ill. She had indeed lived out her life. After all that had occurred at Trieste when she learnt to what a scoundrel she was bound, after all her troubles about Pierre in whom she had tried to repair the wrong done to his family, after all she had suffered since Sarcany's unwelcome return, her illness could hardly be wondered at.

From the first it was evident her malady would be fatal. A few days of life were all her doctors could promise her. She was dying of exhaustion. Nothing could save her, even if Pierre Bathory were to rise from his grave to become her daughter's husband.

Sava could now return with interest the care and attention she had received from her, and she never left her bedside by night or day.

What Sarcany felt at this new delay can be imagined. Daily he came to abuse the banker, who like him was powerless. All they could do was to wait for the end.

On the 29th of July, Madame Toronthal seemed to have recovered a little of her strength, but she then fell into a burning fever, which threatened to carry her off in forty-eight hours.

In this fever she was seized with delirium; and as her mind began to wander many unintelligible phrases escaped her.

One word – one name repeated incessantly – came as a surprise to Sava. It was that of Bathory, not the name of the young man, but that of his mother, that the sick woman appealed to, prayed to, and returned to again and again as if she were assailed with remorse.

"Forgive me!... Madame!... Forgive me!..."

And when during a lull in the fever Madame Toronthal was interrogated by her daughter:

"Hush!... Sava!... Hush!... I said nothing!..." she exclaimed in terror.

The night between the 30th and 31st of July arrived. For a time the doctors might think that the fever having reached its maximum was about to subside. During the day she had been better, there had been no mental troubles, and the change in the patient seemed somewhat surprising. The night promised to be as calm as the day.

Buy if so, it was because Madame Toronthal on the point of death discovered an energy of which she had previously thought herself incapable. She had made her peace with God, and taken a resolution, which she only waited for the opportunity to carry out.

That night she insisted that Sava should go to bed for a few hours. Although she strongly objected to leave her, yet she did not think it right to disobey her mother's commands; and about eleven o'clock she went to her own room.

Madame Toronthal was then alone. All in the house were asleep, and the silence reigned which has been aptly named the silence of death.

Madame Toronthal rose from her bed, and this sick woman whom all thought too feeble to make even the slightest movement, dressed herself, and sat down in front of her writing table.

Madame Toronthal descended the main staircase...

There she took a sheet of letter paper and with trembling hand wrote a few lines and signed them. Then she slipped the letter into an envelope, which she sealed and which she thus addressed:

"Madame Bathory, Rue Marinella, Stradone, Ragusa."

Madame Toronthal then making a great effort to overcome the fatigue she had thus caused herself, opened the door of her room, descended the main staircase, crossed the courtyard, and by the small side gate let herself out into the Stradone.

The Stradone was then dark and deserted, for it was nearly midnight.

With tottering steps Madame Toronthal went along the pavement to the left for some fifty yards or so and stopped before a post-box. Into it she threw her letter. And then she returned to the hotel.

But all her strength was now exhausted; and she fell helpless and motionless on the step of the side gate. There an hour afterwards she was found. There Toronthal and Sava were brought to recognize her, and from there they took her back to her room before she had recovered her consciousness.

The next day Toronthal informed Sarcany of what had happened. Neither one nor the other suspected that Madame Toronthal had gone that night to post a letter in the Stradone. But why had she gone out of the house? They were unable to explain, and it proved to them a subject of great anxiety.

The sick woman lingered for another twenty-four hours.

She gave no sign of life except an occasional convulsive sob that showed her end was near. Sava held her hand as if to hold her back to the world where she had found herself so cast away. But her mother was now silent, and the name of Bathory no longer escaped from her lips. Doubtless her conscience had been quieted, her last wish had been accomplished, and she had neither prayer to make nor pardon to ask.

The following morning about three o'clock, while Sava was bending over her, the dying woman moved, and her hand seemed to feel for her daughter's hand.

As the hands touched her eyes half opened. Then she looked at Sava. The look could not be misunderstood.

"Mother," said Sava, "what do you want?"

Madame Toronthal gave a slight nod.

"To speak to me?"

"Yes!" said she distinctly.

Sava bent down over her pillow; and another gesture from her mother showed that she wished her to come still closer.

Sava laid her head beside her mother's.

"My child I am going to die!"

"Mother – mother!"

"Not so loud!" whispered Madame Toronthal. "Not so loud! No one must hear us!"

Then, with an effort:

"Sava," she said, "I have to ask your forgiveness for the injury I've done you – the injury I had not the courage to prevent."

"You – mother! You do me injury! Ask my forgiveness?"

"Kiss me, Sava! Yes! The last kiss of forgiveness."

The girl gently pressed her lips on the pallid forehead. And the dying woman folded her arms round her neck, and raising herself slightly looked at her with terrible earnestness.

"Sava!" she said, "Sava – you're not Silas Toronthal's daughter! You are not my daughter! Your father..."

She was unable to finish the sentence. A final convulsion threw her back into Sava's arms, and she died with the last word on her lips.

The girl was bending over a corpse! She tried to bring it back to life – in vain.

Then she called for help; and Silas Toronthal was one of the first to reach his wife's room.

As she saw him, Sava, seized with an irresistible feeling of repulsion, recoiled before the man whom she had now the right to despise and hate – for he was no longer her father! The dying woman had said so, and people do not die with a lie on their lips. And then she fled, terrified at what she had been told by the unhappy woman who had loved her as a daughter – still more terrified perhaps at her not having had time to tell her more.

The next day but one the funeral of Madame Toronthal took place with much ostentation. The crowd of friends that all rich men have swarmed round the banker. Near him walked Sarcany, affirming by his presence that nothing had changed his plans of becoming one of the Toronthal family. Such was his hope, but if he were ever to realize it he had many more obstacles to surmount, even though he believed that now Sava was more completely at his mercy and that circumstances were more favourable to the accomplishment of his schemes.

The delay caused by Madame Toronthal's illness was still further pro-longed by her death. While the family was in mourning there could be no question of marriage. Etiquette required that at least several months should elapse before anything of the sort could take place.

This was of course very galling to Sarcany, who was in haste to attain his object; but he was forced to respect the usages of society, although many lively explanations were exchanged between him and Toronthal. And these interviews always ended with a remark by the banker to the effect that:

"I can do nothing more, and besides if the marriage comes off within five months you have no reason to be anxious."

Evidently the two men understood each other, although Sarcany constantly showed an amount of irritation that often led to a violent scene. One thing puzzled them both, and that was the action of Madame Toronthal just before she died. The idea even occurred to Sarcany that she had gone out to post a letter whose destination she did not wish to be known.

"If that is so," repeated Sarcany, "that letter is a serious threat to us. Your wife always upheld Sava against me; she even helped my rival, and who knows but that in her death agony she did not find strength, for which we did not give her credit, to betray our secrets? In that case had we not better take the initiative and leave the place where you and I have more to lose than gain?"

"If that letter threatened us," said Toronthal, a few days later, "the threat would have produced its effect before now, and yet nothing has happened."

To this argument Sarcany had no reply. If Madame Toronthal's letter referred to his future plans, there had as yet been no result from it, and there seemed to be no danger. When the danger showed itself would be time enough to act.

But a fortnight after the death something did happen very different to what they had expected.

Sava had kept herself to her room, and no longer appeared at mealtimes. The banker, who was very angry with her, did not care for an interview, which might prove embarrassing. He therefore let her do as she pleased and kept away from her side of the house.

More than once Sarcany had blamed him for allowing such a state of things to continue. He had now no opportunity of meeting the girl, and that did not at all agree with his ulterior plans, as he very clearly explained to the banker. Although there could be no question of the wedding taking place in the early months of mourning, yet he did not wish

Sava to become accustomed to the idea that the match had been broken off.

At last Sarcany became so imperious and exacting, that on the 16th of August Toronthal informed Sava that he wished to see her during the evening. As he also told her that Sarcany desired to be present at the interview he expected a refusal, he did not get one; Sava replied that she would obey his orders.

The evening came. Toronthal and Sarcany impatiently awaited her in the drawing room; the latter intending to listen rather than to speak, to find out if possible what were the young lady's secret thoughts, for he could not help fearing she knew more of certain matters than they supposed.

Sava entered the room at the appointed time. Sarcany rose when she appeared, but she merely greeted him with a slight inclination of her head. She did not appear to have seen him or rather she did not wish to see him.

At a sign from Toronthal Sava sat down. Her pale face looked even paler in her deep black dress, as with every sign of indifference she waited for the banker to begin.

"Sava," said he, "I respect the grief your mother's death has caused you, and I have not troubled your solitude. But these sad events have necessarily had a certain influence on matters of interest to you, and although you have not yet attained your majority, it is well that you should now know what portion of the inheritance..."

"If it's only the money," answered Sava, "there's no need for us to say anything more about it! I claim no part of the inheritance you mention."

Sarcany gave a start, which indicated a good deal of disappointment, and also, perhaps, a certain surprise not unmixed with anxiety.

"I think, Sava," continued Toronthal, "that you misunderstand me. Whether you wish it or not, you are the heiress of Madame Toronthal, your mother, and the law obliges me to give you an account of it when you come of age..."

"Not if I renounce the succession!" was the tranquil reply.

"And why?"

"Because I have no right to it."

The banker rose from his armchair. The reply was quite unexpected by him.

Sarcany said nothing. In his eyes Sava was merely playing a game, and he was devoting himself entirely to seeing what that game was.

"I do not know, Sava," said Toronthal, angry at the girl's coolness, "I do not know what your words mean, nor who has dictated them to you. I am only discussing what is right and legal. You are under my guardianship, and you are not in a position to refuse or accept. You would do well then to submit to the authority of your father. You do not dispute it, I believe?"

"Perhaps I do."

"Indeed," exclaimed Toronthal, who began to lose the little coolness he had left. "Indeed! But you speak three years too soon, Sava! When you attain your majority you can do what you like with your fortune! At present your interests are entrusted to me, and I'll look after them as I think fit."

"Well," answered Sava, "I'm waiting."

"Waiting for what?" replied the banker. "You forget that the position will change as soon as propriety admits. You'll then have less right to manage your fortune when you're not the only one interested in the business..."

"Yes! – The business!" answered Sava with contempt.

"Believe me," said Sarcany, aroused by the word, which had been pronounced in a tone of the most scathing disdain, "believe me that a more honourable sentiment..."

Sava did not seem to hear him, and kept her eyes fixed on the banker, who continued angrily:

"Not the only one – for your mother's death in no way has altered our plans."

"What plans?" asked the girl.

"The marriage you pretend to forget, which is to make Mr. Sarcany my son-in-law."

"Are you sure that this marriage will make Mr. Sarcany your son-in-law?"

The insinuation this time was so direct that Toronthal would have left the room to hide his confusion. But Sarcany with a gesture kept him back. He wished to find out all he could, to know what it all meant.

"Listen, my father," said Sava, "for this is the last time I give you the title. It's not I Mr. Sarcany wants to marry; he wants to marry the fortune I abandon from today! Great as may be his impudence he won't dare deny it! You remind me that I had consented to this marriage, and my reply is easy. Yes! I'd have sacrificed myself, when I thought my father's honour was at stake; but my father you know well is in no way

"You – sir! – You are not my father!"

concerned with this hateful scheme! If you wish to enrich Mr. Sarcany give him your money! That's all he wants!"

The girl rose, and walked towards the door.

"Sava," said Toronthal, barring the way, "there is in your words such incoherence that I do not understand them – and you probably do not understand them yourself. Has the death of your mother?..."

"My mother! – Yes, she was my mother – my mother in her feelings towards me!"

"If grief has not deprived you of reason," continued Toronthal, who heard only himself, "Yes! if you're not mad..."

"Mad!"

"But what I have resolved on shall take place and before six months have elapsed you shall be Sarcany's wife!"

"Never!"

"I know how to compel you."

"And by what right?" answered the girl indignantly.

"The right given me by my paternal authority."

"You – sir! – You are not my father, and my name is not Sava Toronthal!"

At these words the banker stepped back speechless, and the girl without even turning her head walked out of the room.

Sarcany, who had been carefully watching Sava during the interview, was not surprised at the way it ended. He had suspected it. What he feared had taken place. Sava knew that she was bound by no tie to the Toronthals.

The banker was overwhelmed at the unexpected blow. He was hardly master of himself. Sarcany therefore began to sum up the case as it stood, while he simply listened. Besides he could have nothing but approval for what his old accomplice proposed with so much indisputable logic.

"We can no longer reckon on Sava voluntarily consenting to this marriage," he said. "But for reasons we know it's more than ever necessary the marriage should take place! What does she know of our past life? Nothing! For she told you nothing! What she knows is that she's not your daughter, that's all! Does she know her father? Not likely! His would have been the first name she'd have thrown in your face! Has she known our position for long? No, probably since the moment of Madame Toronthal's death!"

Toronthal nodded his approval of Sarcany' argument. He was right, as we know, in his suspicions as to how the girl had gained her information, as to how long she had known it, and as to what she had learnt of the secret of her birth.

"Now to conclude," continued Sarcany. "Little as she knows of what concerns her, and although she's ignorant of our proceedings in the past, we're both in danger – you in the position you hold at Ragusa, I in what I should gain by the marriage and which I have no intention of giving up! What we must do then is this, and we must do it as soon as possible. Leave Ragusa, you and I, and take Sava with us, without a word to anyone, either today or tomorrow, then return here after the marriage has been performed, and when she's my wife Sava will have to keep her mouth shut. Once we get her away she'll be so removed from outside influences that we shall have nothing to fear from her. I'll make her consent to this marriage, which will bring me in so much, and if I don't succeed, why then..."

Toronthal agreed; the position was the same as it had been with the cryptogram. He did not see how to resist. He was in his accomplice's power, and could not do otherwise. And why should he?

That evening it was agreed that the plan should be put into execution before Sava could leave the house. Then Toronthal and Sarcany separated and set to work as we shall soon see.

The next day but one Madame Bathory, accompanied by Borik, had left the village of Vinticello to return to the house in the Rue Marinella for the first time since her son's death. She had resolved to leave Ragusa forever, and had come to prepare for her departure.

When Borik opened the door, he found a letter, which had been slipped into the letterbox.

It was the letter Madame Toronthal had posted the day before her death.

Madame Bathory took the letter, opened it, looked first at the signature and then read the few lines that had been traced by the dying hand and revealed the secret of Sava's birth.

What sudden connection was there between the name of Sava and Pierre in Madame Bathory's mind?

"She! He!" she exclaimed.

And without another, word – without answering her old servant, whom she thrust aside as he tried to hold her, she rushed out, ran down the Rue Marinella into the Stradone, and did not stop till she reached Toronthal's house.

Did she know what she was doing? Did she know that in Sava's interest it would be better for her to act with less precipitation and more prudence? No! She was irresistibly urged towards the girl as if her husband and her son had come from the grave and sent her to the rescue.

She knocked at the door. The door opened. A domestic inquired her business.

Madame Bathory wished to see Sava.

Miss Toronthal was not in.

Madame Bathory would speak with Mr. Toronthal.

The banker had gone away the day before without saying where he was going, and had taken his daughter with him.

Madame Bathory staggered and fell into the arms of Borik, who had just come up to her.

And when the old man had taken her back to the house in the Rue Marinella:

"Tomorrow, Borik," she said, "tomorrow, we'll attend a wedding! Sava and Pierre are going to be married!"

Madame Bathory had gone mad.

Antekirtta: the port

CHAPTER IV

OFF MALTA

During these events, which concerned Pierre so intimately, he grew better from day to day. Soon there was no reason for anxiety about his wound. It had almost completely healed. But great were Pierre's sufferings as he thought of his mother and of Sava – whom he believed to be lost to him.

His mother? She could not be left under the supposition of her son's fictitious death. It had been agreed that she should be cautiously informed of the real state of things and brought to Antekirtta. One of the doctor's agents at Ragusa had orders not to lose sight of her until Pierre was completely restored to health – and that would be very soon.

As far as Sava was concerned Pierre was doomed never to speak of her to Dr. Antekirtt! But although he thought she was now Sarcany's wife, how could he forget her? Had he ceased to love her because she was the daughter of Silas Toronthal? No! After all was Sava responsible for her father's crime? But it was that crime that brought Stephen Bathory to his death! Hence a continual struggle within him, of which Pierre alone could tell the innumerable vicissitudes.

The doctor felt this. And to give the young man's thoughts another direction, he constantly spoke to him of the act of justice they were to work out together. The traitors must be punished, and they should be. How they were to reach them they did not yet know, but they would reach them.

"A thousand roads, one end!" said the doctor.

And if need be he would follow the thousand roads to reach that end.

During the last days of his convalescence Pierre went about the island, sometimes on foot, sometimes in a carriage. And he was astonished at what the little colony had become under the administration of Dr. Antekirtt.

Work was going on at the fortifications destined to protect the town, the harbour, and in short the whole island from attack. When the works were finished they were to be armed with long-range guns, which from their position would cross their fires and thus render the approach of an enemy's ship impossible.

Electricity was to play an important part in the defensive system, not only in firing the torpedoes with which the channel was armed, but even in discharging the guns in the batteries. The doctor had learnt how to obtain the most marvellous results from this agent to which the future belongs. The central station, provided with steam motors and boilers, contained twenty dynamo machines on a new and greatly improved system, and there the currents were produced which special accumulators of extraordinary intensity stored up in convenient form for the general use of Antekirtta – the water supply, the lighting of the town, telegraphs, telephones, and the circular and other railways on the island. In a word the doctor had applied the studies of his youth to practical purposes, and realized one of the desiderata of modern science – the transmission of power to a distance by electric agency. Having succeeded in this he had had vessels built as we have seen, and the *Electrics* with their excessive speed enabled him to move with the rapidity of an express from one end of the Mediterranean to the other. As coal was indispensable for the steam engines, which were required to produce the electricity, there was always a considerable stock in store at Antekirtta, and this stock was continually renewed by a ship that traded backwards and forwards to Wales.

The harbour, from which the little town rose in the form of an amphitheatre, was a natural one, and had been greatly improved. Two jetties, a mole, and a breakwater made it safe in all weathers. And there was always a good depth of water even alongside the wharves, so that at all times the flotilla of Antekirtta was in perfect security. This flotilla comprised the schooner *Savarena*, the steam collier working to Swansea and Cardiff, a steam yacht of between seven and eight hundred tons named the *Ferrato*, and three *Electrics*, of which two were fitted as torpedo boats which could usefully contribute to the defence of the island.

Under the doctor's directions Antekirtta saw its means of resistance improve from day to day; and of this the pirates of Tripoli were well aware. Great was their desire to capture it, for its possession would be of great advantage to the Grand Master of Senousism, Sidi Mohammed El Mahdi. But knowing the difficulties of the undertaking they waited their opportunity with that patience which is one of the chief characteristics of the Arab. The doctor knew all this, and actively pushed on his defensive works. To reduce them when they were finished the most modern engines of destruction would be required, and these the Senousists did not yet possess. All the inhabitants of the island between eighteen and forty were formed into companies of militia, provided with the newest arms of precision, drilled in artillery manoeuvres, and commanded by officers of their own election; and this militia made up a force of from five to six hundred trustworthy men.

Although there were a few farms in the country, by far the greater number of colonists lived in the town, which had received the Transylvanian name of Artenak in remembrance of Count Sandorf's estate on the Carpathian slopes. A picturesque place was Artenak with its few hundred houses! Instead of being built like a chessboard in the American style, with roads and avenues running at right angles, it was arranged irregularly. The houses clustered on the smaller hills, shaded with orange-trees and standing amid beautiful gardens, some of European, some of Arab design, and past them flowed the pleasant, cooling streams from the waterworks. It was a city in which the inhabitants were members of the same family, and could live their lives in common, without forfeiting the quiet and independence of home. Happy were the people of Antekirtta. *Ubi bene, ibi patria* is perhaps not a very patriotic motto, but it was appropriate enough for those who had gathered to the doctor's invitation and left their old country, in which they had been miserable, to find happiness and comfort in this hospitable island.

Dr. Antekirtt lived in what was known as the Stadthaus – not as their master, but as the first among them. This was one of those beautiful Moorish dwellings, with miradores and moucharabys, interior court, galleries, porticoes, fountains, saloons and rooms decorated by clever ornamentists from the Arabic provinces. In its construction the most precious materials had been employed – marble and onyx from the rich mountain of Filfila on the Numidian Gulf, a few miles from Philippeville – worked and introduced with as much knowledge as taste. These carbonates lend themselves marvellously to an architect's fancies, and under the powerful climate of Africa soon clothe themselves with that golden tone that the sun bestows on the buildings of the East. At the back of the city rose the tower of the small church built of the black and white marble from the same quarry, which served, indeed, for all the requirements of architecture and statuary, and which with its blue and yellow veins was curiously similar to the ancient products of Paros and Carrara.

They started that evening

Outside the town on the neighbouring hills were a few houses, a villa or two, a small hospital at the highest point, where the doctor intended to send his patients – when he had them. On the hillsides sloping to the sea there were groups of houses forming a bathing station. Among the other houses one of the most comfortable – a low blockhouse looking building near the entrance on to the mole – was called "Villa Pescade and Matifou," and there the two inseparables had taken up their quarters with a servant of their own. Never had they dreamt of such affluence!

"This is good!" remarked Cape Matifou over and over again.

"Too good!" answered Point Pescade. "It's much too good for us! Look here, Cape Matifou, we must educate ourselves, go to college, get the grammar prize, obtain our certificates of proficiency."

"But you are educated, Point Pescade," replied the Hercules. "You know how to read, to write, to cipher..."

In fact by the side of his comrade Point Pescade would have passed for a man of science! But he knew well enough how deficient he was. All the schooling he had had was at the "Lycée des Carpes de Fontaine-bleau," as he called it. And so he was an assiduous student in the library of Artenak, and in his attempt to educate himself he read and worked, while Cape Matifou with the doctor's permission cleared away the sand and rock on the shore, so as to form a small fishing harbour.

Pierre gave Pescade every encouragement, for he had recognized his more than ordinary intelligence, which only required cultivation. He constituted himself his professor and directed his studies so as to give him very complete elementary instruction, and his pupil made rapid progress. There were other reasons why Pierre should interest himself in Point Pescade. Was he not acquainted with his past life? Had he not been entrusted with the task of watching Toronthal's house? Had he not been in the Stradone during the procession when Sava had swooned! More than once Point Pescade had had to tell the story of the sad events in which he had indirectly taken part. It was to him alone that Pierre could talk when his heart was too full for him to be silent. But the time was approaching when the doctor could put his double plan into execution – first to reward, then to punish.

That which he could not do for Andrea Ferrato, who had died a few months after his sentence he wished to do for his children. Unfortunately his agents had as yet been unable to discover what had become of them. After their fathers death Luigi and his sister had left Rovigno and Istria, but where had they gone? No one knew, no one could say. The doctor was much concerned at this, but he did not give up the hope of finding the children of the man who had sacrificed himself for him, and by his orders the search was continued.

Pierre's wish was that his mother should be brought to Antekirtta, but the doctor thinking of taking advantage of Pierre's pretended death, as he had of his own, made him understand the necessity of proceeding with extreme prudence. Besides he wished to wait till the convalescent had regained sufficient strength to accompany him in his campaign, and as he knew that Sava's marriage had been postponed by the death of Madame Toronthal, he had decided to do nothing until the wedding had taken place.

One of his agents at Ragusa kept him informed of all that took place, and watched Madame Bathory's house with as much care as he did Toronthal's. Such was the state of affairs, and the doctor waited with impatience for the delay as to the wedding to come to an end. If he did not know what had become of Carpena whose track he had lost after his departure from Rovigno, Toronthal and Sarcany at Ragusa could not escape him. Suddenly, on the 20th of August, there arrived a telegram informing him of the disappearance of Silas Toronthal, Sava, and Sarcany, and also of Madame Bathory and Borik, who had just left Ragusa without giving any clue to their destination.

The doctor could delay no longer. He told Pierre what had happened, and hid nothing from him. Another terrible blow for him! His mother disappeared, Sava dragged off they knew not where by Silas Toronthal, and, there was no reason to doubt, still in Sarcany's hands.

"We shall start tomorrow," said the doctor.

"Today!" exclaimed Pierre. "But where shall we look for my mother? Where shall we look for?..."

He did not finish the sentence. The doctor interrupted him:

"I do not know if it's only a coincidence! Perhaps Toronthal and Sarcany have something to do with Madame Bathory's disappearance! We shall see! But we must be after the two scoundrels first!"

"Where shall we find them?"

"In Sicily – perhaps!"

It will be remembered that in the conversation between Sarcany and Zirone, that the doctor overheard in the donjon of Pisino, Zirone had spoken of Sicily as the usual scene of his exploits, and proposed that his companion should join him there if circumstances required it. The doctor had not forgotten this, nor had he forgotten the name of Zirone. It was a feeble clue perhaps, but in default of any other it might set them again on the trail of Sarcany and Toronthal.

The start was immediately decided on. Point Pescade and Cape Matifou were informed that they would be wanted to go with the doctor. Point Pescade at the same time was told who Toronthal, Sarcany, and Carpena were.

"Three scoundrels!" he said. "And no mistake!" Then he told Cape Matifou:

"You'll come on the scene soon."

"Now!"

"Yes, but you must wait for the cue."

They started that evening. The *Ferrato*, always ready for sea, with provisions on board, bunkers coaled, and compasses regulated, was ordered to sail at eight o'clock.

It is nine hundred and fifty miles from the Syrtis Magna to the south of Sicily, near Portio di Palo. The swift steam yacht whose mean speed exceeded eighteen knots would take about a day and a half to accomplish the distance. She was a wonderful vessel. She had been built at one of the best yards on the Loire. Her engines could develop nearly fifteen hundred horsepower effective. Her boilers were on the Belleville system – in which the tubes contain the flame and not the water – and possessed the advantage of consuming little coal, producing rapid vaporization, and easily raising the tension of the steam to nearly thirty pounds without danger of explosion. The steam, used over again by the reheaters, became a mechanical agent of prodigious power, and enabled the yacht, although she was not as long as the dispatch boats of the European squadrons, to more than equal them in speed.

It need scarcely be said that the *Ferrato* was fitted so as to insure every possible comfort to her passengers. She carried four steel breech-loaders mounted on the barbette principle, two revolving Hotchkiss guns, two Gatlings, and, in the bow, a long chaser which could send a five-inch conical shot a distance of four miles.

The captain was a Dalmatian named Kostrik, and he had under him a mate and second and third officers. For the machinery there was a chief engineer, a second engineer, and six firemen; the crew consisted of thirty men, with a boatswain and two quartermasters; and there was a steward, a cook, and three native servants. During the first hour or two the passage out of the gulf was made under favourable conditions. Although the wind was contrary – a brisk breeze from the northwest – the captain took the *Ferrato* along with remarkable speed; but he did not set either of the headsails or the square sails on the foremast, or the lateens on the main and mizzen.

More than a hundred and twenty miles had been run in the twelve hours since
they had left Antekirtta

During the night the doctor and Pierre in their rooms aft, and Point Pescade and Matifou in their cabin forward, could sleep without being inconvenienced by the movement of the vessel, which rolled a little like all fast boats. But although sleep did not fail the two friends, the doctor and Pierre had too much anxiety to take any rest. In the morning when the passengers went on deck more than a hundred and twenty miles had been run in the twelve hours since they had left Antekirtta. The wind was in the same direction with a tendency to freshen. The sun had risen on a stormy horizon, and everything betokened a roughish day.

Point Pescade and Cape Matifou wished the doctor and Pierre good morning.

"Thank you, my friends," said the doctor. "Did you sleep well in your bunks?"

"Like dormice with an easy conscience!" answered Point Pescade.

"And has Cape Matifou had his first breakfast?"

"Yes, doctor, a tureen of black coffee and four pounds of sea biscuit."

"Hum! A little hard, that biscuit!"

"Bah! For a man that used to chew pebbles – between meals!"

Cape Matifou slowly nodded his huge head in sign of approval of his friend's replies.

The *Ferrato* by the doctor's orders was now driving along at her utmost speed, and sending off from her prow two long paths of foam. To hurry on was only prudent. Already Captain Kostrik, after consulting the doctor, had begun to think of putting for shelter into Malta, whose lights were sighted about eight o'clock in the evening. The state of the weather was most threatening. Notwithstanding the westerly breeze, which freshened as the sun went down, the clouds mounted higher and higher, and gradually overspread three-quarters of the sky. Along the sea-line was a band of livid grey, deepening in its density and becoming black as ink when the sun's rays shot from behind its jagged edges. Now and then the silent flashes tore asunder the cloudbank whose upper edge rounded off into heavy volutes and joined on to the masses above. At the same time, as if they were struggling with the wind from the west and the wind from the east that they had not yet felt, but whose existence was shown by the disturbed state of the sea, the waves increased as they met, and breaking up confusedly began to come rolling on to the deck. About six o'clock the darkness had completely covered the cloudy vault, and the thunder growled, and the lightning vividly flashed in the gloom.

"Better keep outside!" said the doctor to the captain.

"Yes!" answered Captain Kostrik, "In the Mediterranean it's either one thing or another! East and west strive, which shall have us, and the storm coming in to help, I'm afraid the first will get the worst of it. The sea will become very rough off Gozo or Malta, and it may hinder us a good deal. I don't propose to run in to Valetta, but to find a shelter till daylight under the western coast of either of the islands."

"Do as you think best," was the reply.

The yacht was then about thirty miles to the westward of Malta. On the island of Gozo a little to the northwest of Malta, and separated from it only by two narrow channels formed by a central islet, there is a large lighthouse with a range of twenty-seven miles.

In less than an hour notwithstanding the roughness of the sea the *Ferrato* was within range of the light. After carefully taking its bearings and running towards the land for some time the captain considered he was sufficiently near to remain in shelter for a few hours. He therefore reduced his speed so as to avoid all chance of accident to the hull or machinery. About half an hour afterwards, however, the Gozo light suddenly vanished.

The storm was then at its height. A warm rain fell in sheets. The mass of cloud on the horizon, now driven into ribbons by the wind, flew overhead at a terrible pace. Between the rifts the stars peeped forth for a second or two, and then as suddenly disappeared, and the ends of the tatters dragging in the sea swept over its surface like streamers of crape. The triple flashes struck the waves at their three points, sometimes completely enveloping the yacht, as claps of thunder ceaselessly shook the air. The state of affairs had been dangerous; it rapidly became alarming.

Captain Kostrik, knowing that he ought to be at least twenty miles within the range of the Gozo light, dared not approach the land. He feared it was the height of the cliffs that had shut out the light, and if so he was extremely near. To run aground on the isolated rocks at the foot of the cliffs was to risk immediate destruction.

About half-past nine the captain resolved to lay-to and keep the screw at half-speed. He did not stop entirely, for he wanted to keep the ship under the control of her rudder.

For three hours she lay head to wind. About midnight things grew worse. As often happens in storms, the strife between the opposing winds from the east and west suddenly ceased. The wind went round to the point from which it had been blowing during the day.

"A light on the starboard bow!" shouted one of the quartermasters who was on the lookout by the bowsprit.

"Put the helm hard down!" shouted Captain Kostrik, who wished to keep off the shore.

He also had seen the light. Its intermittent flashes showed him it was Gozo. There was only just time for him to come round in the opposite direction, the wind sweeping down with intense fury. The *Ferrato* was not ten miles from the point on which the light had so suddenly appeared.

Orders to go full speed were telegraphed to the engineer, but suddenly the engine slowed, and then ceased to work.

The doctor, Pierre, and all those on deck feared some serious complication. An accident had in fact happened. The valve of the air pump ceased to act, the condenser failed, and after two or three loud reports, as if an explosion had taken place in the stern, the screw stopped dead.

Under such circumstances the accident was irreparable. The pump would have to be dismantled, and that would take many hours. In less than twenty minutes the yacht, driven to leeward by the squalls, would be onshore.

"Up with the forestaysail! Up with the jib! Set the mizzen!"

Such were the orders of Captain Kostrik, whose only chance was to get under sail at once. The orders were rapidly executed. That Point Pescade with his agility and Cape Matifou with his prodigious strength rendered efficient service we need hardly stop to say. The halyards would have soon broken if they had not yielded to the weight of Cape Matifou.

But the position of the *Ferrato* was still very serious. A steamer with her long hull, her want of beam, her slight draught, and her insufficient canvas is not made for working against the wind. If she is laid too near and the sea is rough she is driven back in irons; or she is blown off altogether. That is what happened to the *Ferrato*. She found it impossible to beat off the lee shore. Slowly she drifted towards the foot of the cliffs, and it seemed as though all that could be done was to select a suitable place to beach her. Unfortunately the night was so dark that the captain could not make out the coast. He knew that the two channels separated Gozo from Malta on each side of the central islet, one the North Comino, the other the South Comino. But how was it possible for him to find the entrances in the pitch darkness, or to take his ship across the angry sea to seek shelter on the eastern coast of the island, and perhaps get into Valetta harbour? A pilot might perhaps attempt the dangerous

The storm was then at its height

manoeuvre but in this dense atmosphere, in this night of rain and fog, what fisherman would venture out even to a vessel in distress? There was perhaps a chance that one might come, and so the steam whistle was set going, and three cannon shots were fired one after the other as a signal.

Suddenly from the landward side a black point appeared in the fog. A boat was bearing down on the *Ferrato* under close-reeled sail. Probably it was some fisherman who had been obliged by the storm to take shelter in the little creek of Melleah, where his boat run in behind the rocks had found safety in that admirable grotto of Calypso which bears favourable comparison with the grotto of Fingal in the Hebrides. He had evidently heard the whistle and the signal of distress and at the risk of his life had come to the help of the half-disabled yacht. If the *Ferrato* was to be saved it could only be by him.

Slowly his boat came up. A rope was got ready to be thrown to him as soon as he came alongside. A few minutes elapsed which seemed interminable. The steamer was not above half a cable's length from the reefs. The rope was thrown, but a huge wave caught the boat on its crest, and dashed it against the side of the *Ferrato*. It was smashed to pieces, and the fisherman would have certainly perished had not Matifou snatched at him, lifted him at arm's length, and laid him on the deck as if he had been a child.

Then without a word – would there have been time? – the man ran to the bridge, seized the wheel, and as the bows of the *Ferrato* fell off towards the rocks, he sent the wheel spokes spinning round, headed her straight for the narrow channel of the North Comino, took her down it with the wind dead aft, and in less than twenty minutes was off the east shore of Malta in a much calmer sea. Then with sheets hauled in he ran along about half a mile from the coast, and about four o'clock in the morning, when the first streaks of dawn began to tinge the horizon, he ran down the Valetta channel, and brought up the steamer off Senglea Point.

Doctor Antekirtt then mounted the bridge, and said to the young sailor:

"You saved us, my friend."

"I only did my duty."

"Are you a pilot?"

"No, just a fisherman."

"And your name?"

"Luigi Ferrato!"

The fisherman would have certainly perished

CHAPTER V

MALTA

And so it was the son of the Rovigno fisherman who had just told his name to Dr. Antekirtt. By a providential chance it was Luigi Ferrato whose courage and ability had saved the yacht and her passengers and crew from certain destruction!

The doctor was going to seize Luigi and clasp him in his arms. He checked himself. It would have been Count Sandorf who would have thus shown his gratitude; and Count Sandorf was dead to everybody, even to the son of Andrea Ferrato.

But if Pierre Bathory was obliged to keep the same reserve, and for the same reasons, he was about to forget it when the doctor stopped him by a look. The two went into the saloon and Luigi was asked to follow.

"My friend," asked the doctor, "are you the son of an Istrian fisherman whose name was Andrea Ferrato?"

"Yes, sir."

"Have you not a sister?"

"Yes, we live together at Valetta, but..." he added with a certain amount of hesitation, "Did you know my father?"

"Your father!" answered the doctor. "Fifteen years ago your father gave shelter to two fugitives in his house at Rovigno! Those fugitives were friends of mine whom his devotion was unable to save. But that devotion cost Andrea Ferrato his liberty and his life, for on account of it he was sent to Stein, where he died."

"Yes, died, but he did not regret what he had done," said Luigi.

The doctor took the young man's hand.

"Luigi," said he, "my friends gave me the task of paying the debt of gratitude they owed your father. For many years I have been searching to discover what had become of you and your sister, but all trace had been lost when you left Rovigno. Thank Heaven you were sent to our assistance! The ship you saved I named the *Ferrato* in remembrance of your father Andrea! Come to my arms, my child!"

While the doctor clasped him to his breast Luigi felt the tears start to well in his eyes. At this affecting scene Pierre could not remain unmoved. He felt his whole soul go forth towards this young man of his own age, the brave son of the fisherman of Rovigno.

"And I! I!" exclaimed he with outstretched arms.

"You, sir?"

"I am the son of Stephen Bathory!"

Did the doctor regret the avowal? No! Luigi Ferrato could keep the secret as well as Pescade and Matifou.

Luigi was then informed how matters stood, and learnt Dr. Antekirtt's objects. One thing he was not told: that he was in the presence of Count Mathias Sandorf.

The doctor wished to be taken at once to Maria Ferrato. He was impatient to see her again; impatient above all to hear how she had lived a life of work and misery since Andrea's death had left her alone with her brother to look after.

"Yes, doctor," answered Luigi, "we must go ashore at once! Maria will be very anxious about me! It's been forty-eight hours since I left to go fishing in Melleah creek, she may fear I drowned in last night's storm!"

"You're fond of your sister?" asked the doctor.

"She's my mother and my sister combined!" answered Luigi.

Does the Isle of Malta, situated about sixty-two miles from Sicily, belong to Europe or to Africa from which it is separated by one hundred and sixty miles? This is a question which has much exercised geographers; but in any case, having been given by Charles V. to the Hospitallers whom Suleiman drove out of Rhodes and who then took the name of Knights of Malta, it now belongs to England – and it would take some trouble to get it away from her. It is about eighteen miles long and ten across. It has Valetta and its suburbs for its capital, besides other towns and villages, such as Citta Vecchia – a sort of sacred town which was the seat of the bishop at the time of the Knights – Dingzi, Zebbug, Birchircara, etc. Rather fertile in its eastern half, and very barren in its western half, the density of its population towards the east is in striking contrast to that towards the west. In all it contains about a hundred thousand inhabitants. What Nature has done for this island in cutting out of its coast its four or five harbours, the most beautiful in the world, surpasses all that can be imagined. Everywhere water; everywhere points, capes and heights ready to receive fortifications and batteries.

The Knights had already made it a difficult place to take, and the English have made it impregnable. No ironclad could hope to force her way in against such an array of guns, which among others includes two at the water's edge, each of a hundred tons, fully equipped with hydraulic apparatus, and capable of sending a shot weighing seventeen and a half hundredweight to a distance of nine and a half miles! A piece of information that may be profitably noted by the powers who regret to see in England's hands this admirable station commanding the Central Mediterranean and which could hold the whole British fleet.

Assuredly there are English at Malta. There is a Governor lodged in the ancient palace of the Grand Master, there is an admiral to look after the fleet and the harbours, and a garrison of from four to five thousand men; but there are Italians who wish to be considered at home, a floating cosmopolitan population as at Gibraltar, and there are, of course, Maltese.

The Maltese are Africans. In the harbours they work their brightly-coloured boats, in the streets they drive their vehicles down the wildest slopes, in the markets they deal in fruits, vegetables, meats, fish, making a deafening uproar under the lamp of some small sacred daub. It is said that all the men are alike, copper in colour, with black slightly woolly hair, piercing eyes, robust and of medium height. It seems as though all the women were of the same family, with large eyes and long lashes, dark hair, charming hands, supple figures, and skin of a whiteness that the sun cannot touch beneath the "falzetta," a sort of black silk mantle worn in Tunisian fashion, common to all classes, and which answers at the same time for headdress, mantle, and even fan.

The Maltese have the mercantile instinct. Everywhere they are found doing a trade. Hardworking, thrifty, economic, industrious, sober, but violent, vindictive and jealous, it is among the lower classes that they are best worth studying. They speak a dialect of which the base is Arabic, the result of the conquest, which followed the fall of the Roman Empire, a language animated and picturesque, lending itself easily to metaphor and to poetry. They are good sailors when you can keep them, and bold fishermen familiarized with danger by their frequent storms.

It was in this island that Luigi pursued his calling with as much audacity as if he had been a Maltese, and here he had lived for nearly fifteen years with his sister Maria.

Valetta and its suburbs, we said. There are really six towns on the Grand and Quarantine harbours – Floriana, Senglea, Bighi, Burmola, Vittoriosa, Sliema, are hardly suburbs, nor even mere assemblages of

Between the high houses with their greenish miradores

houses inhabited by the poorer classes; they are regular cities with sumptuous mansions, hotels and churches, worthy of a capital which boasts some twenty-five thousand inhabitants.

It was at Valetta that the brother and sister lived. It would perhaps be more correct to say "under Valetta," for it was in a kind of subterranean quarter known as the Manderaggio, the entrance to which is on the Strada San Marco, that they had found a lodging suitable for their slender means; and it was into this hypogeum that Luigi led the doctor as soon as the yacht was moored.

After declining the services of the hundreds of boats that surrounded them they landed on the quay. Entering by the Marine Gate, and deafened by the pealing and ringing of the bells, which hover like a sonorous atmosphere over the Maltese capital, they passed beneath the double casemated fort, and mounted first a steep slope and then a narrow staircase. Between the high houses with their greenish miradores and niches with lighted lamps they arrived before the cathedral of St. John, and mingled with a crowd of the noisiest people in the world.

When they had reached the back of this hill, a little lower than the cathedral, they began their descent towards the Quarantine harbour; there in the Strada San Marco they stopped midway before a staircase which went off to the right down into the depths.

The Manderaggio runs along under the ramparts with narrow streets where the sun never shines, and high yellow walls irregularly pierced with innumerable holes, which do duty as windows, some of them grated and most of them free. Everywhere round about are flights of steps leading to veritable sewers; low gateways, humid, sordid, like the houses of a Kasbah; miserable courtyards, and gloomy tunnels, hardly worthy of the name of lanes. And at every opening, every breathing-place, on the ruined landings and crumbling footpaths, there gathers a repulsive crowd of old women with faces like sorceresses, mothers dirty and pallid and worn, daughters of all ages in rags and tatters, boys half-naked, sickly, wallowing in the filth, beggars with every variety of disease and deformity, men, porters, or fisher-folk, of savage look capable of everything evil and among this human swarm a few phlegmatic policemen, accustomed to the hopeless throng, and not only familiarized but familiar with it! A true Court of Miracles, but transported into a strange underworld, the last passageways of which open on to the curtain walls on the level of the Quarantine harbour, and are swept by the sun and the sea breeze.

It was in one of the houses in this Manderaggio, but in the upper portion of it, that Maria and Luigi Ferrato lived in two rooms.

The doctor was struck with the poverty of the miserable lodging and also with its neatness. The hand of the careful housekeeper again showed itself, as it had done in the house of the fisherman of Rovigno.

As the doctor entered Maria rose, saying to her brother, "My child! My Luigi!"

Luigi embraced his sister, and introduced his friends.

The doctor related in a few words how Luigi had risked his life to save a ship in distress, and at the same time he mentioned Pierre as the son of Stephen Bathory.

While he spoke, Maria looked at him with so much attention and even, emotion that he feared for a moment she had recognized him. But it was only a flash that vanished from her eyes almost immediately. After fifteen years how was it possible for her to recognize a man who had only been in her father's house for a few hours?

Andrea Ferrato's daughter was then thirty-three years old. She had always been beautiful owing to the purity of her features and the bright look of her splendid eyes. The white streaks here and there in her raven hair showed that she had suffered less from the length than from the severity of her life. Age had nothing to do with this precocious greyness, which was due entirely to the fatigues and troubles and griefs she had been through since the death of the fisherman of Rovigno.

"Your future and that of Luigi now belong to us," said Dr. Antekirtt as he finished his story. "Were not my friends deeply indebted to Andrea Ferrato? You won't object, Maria, to Luigi remaining with us."

"Sirs!" said Maria, "my brother has only acted as he should have done in going to your aid last night, and I thank Heaven he was inspired with the thought to do so. He's the son of a man who always strived to do his duty."

"As do we," replied the doctor, "and it's our duty to pay a debt of gratitude to the children of the man who..."

He stopped. Maria looked at him again, and the look seemed to pierce through him. He was afraid he had said too much.

"Maria," broke in Pierre, "will you prevent Luigi from being my brother?"

"And you won't refuse to be my daughter?" added the doctor, holding out his hand.

And then Maria told the story of her life since she left Rovigno, how the espionage of the Austrian police rendered her existence insupportable, and how they had come to Malta for Luigi to perfect himself in his trade of a seaman by continuing that of a fisherman; and how for many years they had struggled against misery, their feeble resources being soon exhausted.

But Luigi soon equalled the Maltese in boldness and ability. A wonderful swimmer, he could almost be compared to that famous Nicolo Pescei, a native of Valetta, who carried dispatches from Naples to Palermo by swimming across the Aeolian Sea. He was an adept at hunting the curlews and wild pigeons, whose nests have to be sought for among the almost inaccessible caves that border on the sea. He was the boldest of fishermen, and never had the wind kept him ashore when it had been necessary for him to go out to his nets and lines. And it was owing to this that he had been in Melleah creek when he heard the signals of the yacht in distress.

But at Malta the sea birds, the fish, the mollusks are so abundant that the moderation of their price makes fishing anything but a lucrative trade. Do all he could, Luigi could hardly manage to supply the wants of the humble home, although Maria contributed something towards it by what she earned from her needlework. And so they had been obliged to reduce their expenses and take this lodging in the Manderaggio. While Maria was telling her story, Luigi went into the other room and came back with a letter in his hand. It was the one Andrea Ferrato had written just before he died:

> "Maria," he said, "take care of your brother! He will soon have only you in the world! For what I have done, my children, I have no regret, unless it is for not having succeeded in saving those who trusted in me even at the sacrifice of my liberty and my life. What I did I would do again! Never forget your father, who is dying as he sends you this – his last love.
>
> ANDREA FERRATO

As he read this Pierre Bathory made no attempt to conceal his emotion, and Dr. Antekirtt turned away his head to avoid Maria's searching look.

"Luigi," he said abruptly, "last night your boat was smashed against my yacht..."

The doctor conversed with Maria

"She was an old one, doctor," answered Luigi, "and for any one but me the loss would not be much."

"Perhaps so, but you'll allow me to give you another for her. I'll give you the boat you saved."

"What?"

"Will you be the mate of the *Ferrato*? I want a man who's young, active, and a good sailor."

"Accept, Luigi," said Pierre, "accept!"

"But my sister?"

"Your sister shall become one of the family that lives on my island of Antekirtta!" replied the doctor. "Your lives henceforth belong to me, and I'll do all I can to make you happy, and that the only regret for your past life shall be that of having lost your father."

Luigi seized the doctor's hands; he clasped them, he kissed them, while Maria could find no other way of showing her gratitude than by bursting into tears.

"Tomorrow I expect you on board!" said the doctor.

And as if he could no longer master his emotion he hurriedly left, after beckoning Pierre to follow him.

"Ah!" he said, "it's good – it's good to make amends..."

"Yes, better than to punish!" answered Pierre.

"Yes, but we must punish as well!"

The next morning the doctor was waiting, ready to receive Maria and Luigi Ferrato. Already Captain Kostrik had taken steps to have the engine repaired. Thanks to the efforts of Messrs. Samuel Grech and Co., shipping agents of the Strada Levante, to which the ship had been consigned, the work advanced rapidly. But they required five or six days, for they had to unship the air pump and the condenser, several tubes of which were working badly. The delay was very serious to Doctor Antekirtt, who was most anxious to get to the Sicilian coast. And he even thought of sending for the *Savarena*, but it seemed better to wait a few days longer and start for Sicily in a fast and well-armed ship.

However, as a matter of precaution, and in view of eventualities that might arise, he sent a message by submarine cable to Antekirtta, and ordered *Electric No. 2* to cruise off the coast of Sicily near Cape Passaro.

About nine o'clock in the morning a boat came on board with Maria Ferrato and her brother. Both were received by the doctor with marks of the liveliest affection. Luigi was introduced to the captain and crew as the mate, the officer he replaced being transferred to *Electric No. 2*.

With regard to Luigi, there could be no mistake; he was a thorough sailor. His courage and boldness were known from the way in which thirty-six hours before he had acted in the creek of Melleah. He was received with acclamation. Then his friend Pierre and Captain Kostrik did the honours of the ship, which he went round to examine in all her details, while the doctor conversed with Maria and spoke of her brother in a way that deeply affected her.

"Yes!" she said, "he's just like his father!"

To the doctor's proposal either for her to remain on board until the end of the projected expedition, or to return direct to Antekirtta, where he offered to take her, Maria asked to be allowed to go with him to Sicily; and it was agreed that she should profit by the stay of the *Ferrato* at Valetta to put her affairs in order, to sell certain things which were only valuable as remembrances, and realize the little she possessed, so as to take up her quarters the day before the yacht left.

The doctor had told her of his plans, and how he was going to persist until he had accomplished them. Part of his plan had been realized, for the children of Andrea Ferrato need now have no anxiety for the future. But to get hold of Toronthal and Sarcany on the one hand, and Carpena on the other, remained to be done, and it would be done. The two former he thought he should meet with in Sicily, the latter he had still to seek.

Thus he told Maria, and when he had finished she asked to speak with him in private.

"What I am going to tell you I have hitherto thought it my duty to keep hidden from my brother. He would not have been able to contain himself; and probably new misfortunes would have come upon us."

"Luigi is at this moment among the crew forward," answered the doctor. "Let us go into the saloon, and there you can speak without fear of being overheard."

When the door of the saloon was shut, they sat down on one of the benches, and Maria said:

"Carpena is here, doctor!"

"In Malta?"

"Yes, and has been for some days."

"At Valetta?"

"In the Manderaggio, where we live."

The doctor was much surprised and pleased.

"You're not mistaken, Maria?"

"No, I'm not mistaken! The man's face remains burned in my memory, a hundred years might pass, but I should recognize him! He is here!"

"Luigi doesn't know this?"

"No, doctor; and you understand why I didn't tell him. He would have found Carpena and provoked him..."

"You've done well, Maria! The man belongs to me alone! Do you think he's recognized you?"

"I don't know," answered Maria. "I've met him in the Manderaggio two or three times, and he's turned round to look after me with a certain suspicious attention. If he's followed me, if he's asked my name, he ought to know who I am."

"He's never spoken to you?"

"Never."

"And do you know why he's come to Valetta, and what he's been doing since his arrival?"

"All I can say is that he lives with the most hateful men in the Manderaggio. He hangs about the most suspicious drinking houses, and associates with the worst of the scoundrels. Money seems to be plentiful with him, and I fancy he's busy enlisting bandits like himself to take part in some villainous scheme..."

"Here?"

"I don't know."

"I must find out!"

At this moment Pierre entered the saloon followed by the young fisherman, and the interview was at an end.

"Well, Luigi," asked the doctor, "are you content with what you've seen?"

"The *Ferrato* is a splendid ship."

"I'm glad you like her," answered the doctor, "for you'll act as her mate until circumstances take place to make you her captain."

"Oh, sir!"

"My dear Luigi," said Pierre, "with Dr. Antekirtt do not forget that all things will come."

"Yes, all things come, Pierre, but say rather with the help of God."

Maria and Luigi then took their leave to return back to their small lodging. It was arranged that Luigi should commence his duties as soon as his sister had come on board. It would not do for Maria to remain alone in the Manderaggio, for it was possible that Carpena had recognized the daughter of Andrea Ferrato.

When the brother and sister had gone, the doctor sent for Point Pescade, to whom he wished to speak in Pierre's presence.

Pescade immediately came in, and stood in the attitude of a man ever ready to receive an order and ever ready to execute it.

"Point Pescade," said the doctor, "I have need of you."

"Of me and Cape Matifou?"

"Of you alone at present."

"What am I to do?"

"Go ashore at once to the Manderaggio, and get a lodging in the dirtiest public house you can find."

"Yes, sir."

"I need you to keep an eye on a man, it's very important you do not lose sight of him. Above all, no one must suspect you're connected to me! Disguise yourself if you must."

"Leave it to me."

"This man I'm told is trying to buy over some of the chief scoundrels in the Manderaggio. What his object is I do not know, and that's what I want you to find out as soon as possible."

"I understand."

"Once you've found out, do not return on board, as you may be followed. Put a letter in the post, and meet me in the evening at the other end of Senglea. You'll find me there."

"Agreed," answered Point Pescade, "but how am I to know the man?"

"Oh, that won't be very difficult! You're intelligent, my friend, and I trust to your intelligence."

"May I know the gentleman's name?"

"Carpena."

As he heard the name Pierre exclaimed:

"What! The Spaniard here?"

"Yes," replied the doctor, "and he's living in the very street where we found the children of Andrea Ferrato whom he sent to prison and to death."

The doctor told them all he had heard from Maria. Point Pescade saw how urgent it was for them to understand the Spaniard's game, for he was evidently at work at some dark scheme in the slums of Valetta.

An hour afterwards Point Pescade left the yacht. To throw any spy off the track in case he was followed, he began by a stroll along the Strada Reale, which runs from Fort Saint Elmo to Floriana; and it was only when evening closed in that he reached the Manderaggio.

To get together a band of ruffians ready for either murder or robbery no better place could be chosen than this sink of corruption. Here were scoundrels of every nation from the rising to the setting of the sun, runaways from merchant ships, deserters from warships, and Maltese of the lowest class, cutthroats in whose veins ran the blood of their pirate ancestors who made themselves so terrible in the razzias of the past.

Carpena was endeavouring to enlist a dozen of these determined villains – who would stick at nothing – and was quite embarrassed in his choice. Since his arrival he had hardly been outside the taverns in the lower streets of the Manderaggio, and Pescade had no difficulty in recognizing him, though he could not easily find out on whose behalf he was acting.

Evidently his money was not his own. The reward of five thousand florins for his share in the Rovigno matter must have been exhausted long ago. Carpena, driven from Istria by public reprobation, and warned off from all the salt works along the coast, had set out to see the world. His money soon disappeared, and rascal as he was before, he had become still more of a rascal.

No one would be astonished to find him in the service of a notorious band of malefactors for whom he recruited to fill the vacancies that the halter had caused. It was in this way that he was employed at Malta, and more particularly in the Manderaggio. The place to which he took his recruits Carpena was too mistrustful of his companions to reveal. And they never asked him. Provided he paid cash down, provided he guaranteed them a future of successful robbery, they would have gone to the world's end – in confidence.

It should be noted that Carpena had been considerably surprised at meeting Maria in the Manderaggio. After an interval of fifteen years he had recognized her at once, as she had recognized him. And he was very anxious to keep her from knowing what he was doing in Valetta.

Point Pescade had therefore to act warily if he wished to discover what the doctor had such interest in learning, and the Spaniard so jealously guarded. However, Carpena was completely circumvented by him. The precocious young bandit who became so intimate with him, who took the lead of all the rascality in the Manderaggio, and boasted to have already such a history that every page of it would bring him the rope in Malta, the guillotine in Italy, and the garrote in Spain, who looked with the deepest contempt at the poltroons whom the very sight of a policeman rendered uneasy, was just the man whom Carpena, a judge in such matters, could fully appreciate!

Catania

In this adroit way Point Pescade succeeded in gaining what he wanted, and on the 26th of August the doctor received a word making an appointment for that evening at the end of Senglea.

During the last few days the work had been pushed ahead on board the *Ferrato*. In three days or more the repairs would be finished, and she would be coaled up and ready for sea.

That evening the doctor went to the place named by Pescade. It was a sort of arcade near a circular road at the end of the suburb.

It was eight o'clock. There were about fifty people gathered about in the market, which was still in progress.

Dr. Antekirtt was walking up and down among these people – nearly all of them men and women of Maltese birth – when he felt a hand touch his arm.

A frightful scamp, very shabbily dressed, and wearing a battered old hat presented him with a handkerchief, saying:

"See here what I've just stolen – from your Excellency! Another time you'd better look after your pockets."

It was Point Pescade, absolutely unrecognizable under his disguise.

"You funny rascal!" said the doctor.

"Funny, yes! Rascal, no!" said Pescade as the doctor recognized him; and immediately came to the point with:

"Carpena?"

"He's at work collecting a dozen of the biggest ruffians in the Manderaggio."

What for?"

"On behalf of a certain Zirone."

The Sicilian Zirone, the companion of Sarcany? What connection was there between those scoundrels and Carpena?

As he thought thus the following explanation presented itself to him, and it was the correct one:

The Spaniard's treachery, which had brought about the arrest of the fugitives from Pisino, had not been unknown to Sarcany, who had doubtless sought him out, and finding him in want had easily gained him over to be an agent of Zirone's band. Carpena would therefore be the first link in the chain, which the doctor could now follow up.

"Do you know what his object is?" he asked of Pescade.

"The gang is in Sicily."

"In Sicily? Yes! That is it! And particularly?"

"In the eastern provinces between Syracuse and Catania!"

The trail was evidently recovered.

307

"How did you obtain that information?"

"From Carpena himself, who has taken me into his friendship, and whom I recommend to your Excellency!"

A nod was the doctor's reply.

"You can now return on board and resume more proper attire!"

"No, this suits me fine."

"And why?"

"Because I've had the honour of being recruited into Zirone's gang of bandits!"

"My friend," answered the doctor, "be careful! You'll risk your life among them..."

"At your service, doctor," said Pescade, "I owe you so much more."

"You're a brave lad, my friend."

"Boasting aside, I fancy myself rather clever, and I've made up my mind to trap these beggars!"

The doctor saw that in this way the help of Point Pescade might prove very useful. It was in playing this game that the intelligent fellow had gained Carpena's confidence and wormed out his secrets. He had better leave him to go on.

After five minutes the doctor and Point Pescade, not wishing to be surprised together, left each other. Point Pescade, following the wharves of Senglea, took a boat at the end and returned to the Manderaggio.

Before he arrived Doctor Antekirtt was already on board the yacht. There he told Pierre of what had taken place. At the same time he thought it his duty to tell Cape Matifou that his friend had started on a very dangerous enterprise for the common good.

Hercules lifted his head and three times opened and shut his huge hands. Then he was heard to repeat to himself:

"If he's lost a hair of his head when he comes back – yes! A hair of his head – I'll..."

To finish the phrase was too much for Cape Matifou. He had not the gift of making long sentences.

CHAPTER VI

THE ENVIRONS OF CATANIA

The coast of Sicily between Acireale and Catania abounds in capes, reefs, caves, cliffs, and mountains. It faces the Tyrrhenian Sea just where the Straits of Messina begin, and is immediately opposite the hills of Calabria. Such as the Straits with the hills round Etna were in the days of Homer so they are today – superb! If the forest in which Aeneas received Achemenides has disappeared, the grotto of Galatea, the cave of Polyphemus, the isles of the Cyclops, and a little to the north Scylla and Charybdis are still in their historic places, and we can set foot on the very spot where the Trojan hero landed when he came to found his new kingdom.

That the giant Polyphemus is credited with exploits to which our Herculean Cape Matifou could not pretend it may perhaps be as well to remember. But Cape Matifou had the advantage of being alive, while Polyphemus has been dead some three thousand years – if he ever existed, notwithstanding the story of Ulysses. Reclus has remarked that it is not unlikely that the celebrated Cyclops was simply Etna, "the crater of which during eruption glares like an immense eye at the summit of the mountain, and sends down from the top of the cliffs the rocky fringes which become islets and reefs like the Faraglioni.

These Faraglioni, situated a few hundred yards from the shore by the road to Catania, now doubled by the railway from Syracuse to Messina, are the ancient islands of the Cyclops. The cave of Polyphemus is not far off and along the whole coast there is heard that peculiar roar which the sea always makes when it beats against basaltic rocks.

Half-way along these rocks on the evening of the 29th of August two men were to be seen quite indifferent to the charms of historic associations, but conversing of certain matters that the Sicilian gendarmes would not have been sorry to hear.

One of these men was Zirone. The other, who had just come by the Catania road, was Carpena.

"You're late," exclaimed Zirone. "I began to think that Malta had vanished like Julia, her old neighbour, and that you'd become food for the tunnies and bonicous at the bottom of the Mediterranean."

It was obvious that although fifteen years had passed over the head of Sarcany's companion, neither his loquacity nor his natural effrontery had left him. With his hat over his ear, a brownish cape over his shoulders, leggings laced up to the knee, he looked what he was, and what he had never ceased to be – a bandit.

"I couldn't come any sooner," answered Carpena, "and it was only this morning I landed at Catania."

"You and your men?"

"Yes."

"How many have you?"

"Twelve."

"Is that all?"

"Yes, but good ones!"

"Manderaggio fellows?"

"A few, chiefly Maltese."

"Good recruits, but not enough of them; the last few months times have been rough and costly! The gendarmes have begun to swarm in Sicily, and they'll soon get as thick as – well, if your goods are good..."

"I think so, Zirone; you'll see when you try them. Besides, I've brought with me a jolly fellow, an old acrobat from the shows, active and artful, whom you can disguise as a girl if need be, and who'll be of great use, I fancy."

"What was he doing in Malta?"

"Watches when he had an opportunity, handkerchiefs when he could not get watches..."

"And his name?"

"Pescador."

"Good!" said Zirone. "We'll put his talents and intelligence to good use. Where have you put your men?"

"At the inn at Santa Grotta above Nicolosi."

"Where you'll resume your role as innkeeper?"

"Tomorrow."

"No, tonight," answered Zirone, "after I've received my new orders. I'm waiting here for the train from Messina. I'm going to get a message from its last carriage."

"A message from – him?"

"Yes – from him – with his marriage that never comes off he obliges me to work for my living! Bah! What wouldn't a fellow do for such a friend?"

At this moment a distant roar that could not be mistaken for the roar of the surf was heard along the Catanian shore. It was the train Zirone was waiting for. Carpena and he climbed up the rocks, and in a few moments were alongside the line.

Two whistles, as the train entered a short tunnel, told them it was near. Its speed was not very great. Soon the puffing of the engine became louder, the lamps showed their two white lights in the darkness, the rails in front were rendered visible by the long projecting glare.

Zirone attentively watched the train as it rolled past some three yards away from him.

A moment before the last carriage reached him, a window was put down and a woman put her head out of the window. As soon as she saw the Sicilian at his post she threw him an orange, which rolled on the ground about a dozen yards from Zirone.

The woman was Namir, Sarcany's spy. A few seconds afterwards she had disappeared with the train in the direction of Aci Reale.

Zirone picked up the orange, or rather the two halves of orange-skin that were sewn together. The Spaniard and he then hurried behind a lofty rock; Zirone lit a small lantern, broke open the orange skin, and drew out a letter which contained the following message:

"I hope to join you at Nicolosi in five or six days. Be particularly careful of a Doctor Antekirtt!"

Evidently Sarcany had learnt at Ragusa that this mysterious personage, who had so much exercised public curiosity, had twice visited Madame Bathory's house. Hence a certain uneasiness on his part, although he had hitherto defied everybody and everything, and hence also his sending this message to Zirone, not through the post, but by Namir.

Zirone put the letter in his pocket, extinguished his lantern, and, addressing Carpena, said:

"Have you ever heard of a Dr. Antekirtt?"

"No," answered the Spaniard, "but perhaps Pescador has. That little beggar knows everything."

"We'll see about it then," said Zirone. "There's no danger in going out at night, is there?"

"Less than in going out during the day!"

Zirone lit a small lantern

"Yes – in the day there are the gendarmes who are so thoughtless! Come on! In three hours we must be inside your place at Santa Grotta!"

And, crossing the railway, they took to the footpaths well known to Zirone, and were soon lost to sight as they crossed the lower buttresses of Etna.

For eighteen years there had existed in Sicily, and principally at Palermo its capital, a formidable association of malefactors. Bound together by a sort of freemasonry, their adherents were to be counted in thousands. Theft and fraud by every possible means were the objects of the Society of Mafia, to which a number of shopkeepers and working people paid a sort of annual tithe to be allowed to carry on their trade without molestation.

At this time Sarcany and Zirone – this was before the Trieste conspiracy – were amongst the chiefs of the Mafia, and none were more zealous than they.

However, with the general progress, with a better administration of the towns if not of the country round them, the association became somewhat interfered with in its proceedings. The tithes and blackmail fell off; and most of the members separated and tried to get a more lucrative means of existence by brigandage. The government of Italy then underwent a change owing to the unification, and Sicily like the other provinces had to submit to the common lot, to accept other laws, and especially to receive the yoke of conscription. Rebels who would not conform to the new laws, and fugitives who refused to serve in the army, then betook themselves to the "mafias!" and other unscrupulous ruffians, and formed themselves into gangs to scour the country.

Zirone was at the head of one of these gangs, and when the share of Count Sandorf's possessions, which had fallen to Sarcany, had been run through, he and his friend had returned to their old life and waited till another opportunity offered to acquire a fortune. The opportunity came – the marriage of Sarcany with Toronthal's daughter. We know how that had failed up to the present, and the reasons for the failure.

Sicily at the time in question was singularly favourable for the pursuit of brigandage. The ancient Trinacria in its circuit of 450 miles round the points of the triangle, Cape Faro on the northeast Cape Marsala on the west, and Cape Passaro on the southeast, includes the mountains of Pelores and Nebrocles, the independent volcanic group of Etna, the streams of Giarella, Cantara, and Platani, and torrents, valleys, plains, and towns communicating with each other with difficulty, villages perched on almost inaccessible rocks, convents isolated in the gorges or on the slopes, a number of refuges in which retreat was possible, and an infinity of creeks by which the sea offered innumerable means of flight. This slip of Sicilian ground is the world in miniature; in it everything that is met with on the globe can be found – mountains, volcanoes, valleys, meadows, rivers, rivulets, lakes, torrents, towns, villages, hamlets, harbours, creeks, promontories, capes, reefs, breakers – all ready for the use of a population of nearly 3,000,000 of inhabitants scattered over a surface of 16,000 square miles.

Where could there be found a better region for the operations of banditti? And so although they tended to decrease, although the Sicilian brigand like his cousin of Calabria seemed to have had his day, although they are proscribed – at least in modern literature – although they have begun to find work more profitable than robbery, yet travellers do well to take every precaution when they venture into the country so dear to Cacus, and so blessed by Mercury.

However, in the last few years the Sicilian gendarmerie always on the alert, had made many successful forays into the eastern provinces and many bands had fallen into ambuscades and been partly destroyed. One of these bands was Zirone's, which had thus been reduced to thirty men; and on account of this he had conceived the idea of infusing some foreign blood into his troop, and Maltese blood more particularly. He knew that in the Manderaggio, which he used to frequent, bandits out of work could be picked up in hundreds; and that was why Carpena had gone to Valetta, and if he had only brought back a dozen men, they were, at least, hand picked men.

There was nothing surprising in the Spaniard showing himself so devoted to Zirone. The trade suited him; but as he was a coward by nature he put himself as little as possible within range of the rifles. It pleased him best to prepare matters, to draw up plans, to keep this tavern at Santa Grotta, situated in a frightful gorge on the lower slopes of the volcano.

Although Sarcany and Zirone knew all about Carpena's share in the matter of Andrea Ferrato, Carpena knew nothing of the Trieste affair. He thought he had become connected with honest brigands who had been carrying on their "trade" for many years in the mountains of Sicily.

Zirone and Carpena in the course of their walk of eight Italian miles from the rocks of Polyphemus to Nicolosi met with no mishap, in the sense that not a single gendarme was seen on the road. They went along the rough footpaths among the vineyards, olive trees, orange trees, and cedars, and through the clumps of ash trees, cork trees, and fig trees.

Now and then they went up one of the dry torrent beds, which seem from a distance to resemble macadamized roads in which the roller has left the pebbles unbroken. The Sicilian and the Spaniard passed through the villages of San Giovanni and Tramestieri at a considerable height above the level of the Mediterranean. About half-past ten they reached Nicolosi, situated as in the middle of an open plain flanking on the north and west the eruptive cones of Monpilieri, Monte Rossi, and Serra Pizzuta.

The town has six churches, a convent dedicated to San Nicolo d'Arena, and two taverns – a significant token of its importance. But with these taverns Carpena and Zirone had nothing to do. Santa Grotta was an hour farther on in one of the deepest gorges of the volcanic range, and they arrived there before midnight.

The men were not asleep at Santa Grotta. They were at supper with an accompaniment of shouts and curses. Carpena's recruits were there, and the honours were being done by an old fellow named Benito. The rest of the gang, some forty in number, were then about twenty miles off to the westward on the other side of Etna. There were therefore at Santa Grotta only the dozen Maltese recruited by the Spaniard, and among these Pescador – otherwise Point Pescade – was playing quite a prominent part, at the same time as he heard, saw, and noted every thing so as to forget nothing that might prove useful.

And one of the things he had made a mental note of was Benito's shout to his comrades just before Carpena and Zirone arrived.

"Be quiet, you Maltese, be quiet! They'll hear you at Cassone, where the central commissary, the amiable quaestor of the province, has sent a detachment of carabinieri!"

A playful threat, considering how far Cassone was from Santa Grotta. But the newcomers supposed that their vociferations might possibly reach the ears of the soldiers, and moderated them considerably as they drank off large flasks of the Etna vine that Benito himself poured out for them. In short they were more or less intoxicated when the door opened.

"Jolly fellows!" exclaimed Zirone as he entered. "Carpena has been lucky, and I see that Benito has done his work well."

"These gallant fellows were dying of thirst!" answered Benito.

"And from that worst of deaths," said Zirone with a grin, "you thought to save them! Good! Now let them go to sleep! We'll make their acquaintance tomorrow!"

"Why wait till tomorrow?" said one of the recruits.

The men were not asleep at Santa Grotta

"Because you're too drunk to understand and obey orders."

"Drunk! Drunk! After drinking a bottle or two of this table wine when we're accustomed to gin and whiskey in the Manderaggio!"

"And who are you?" asked Zirone.

"That's little Pescador!" answered Carpena.

"And who are you?" asked Pescador.

"That's Zirone!" answered the Spaniard.

Zirone looked attentively at the young bandit whom Carpena had praised so much, and who introduced himself in such a free and easy manner. Doubtless he thought he looked intelligent and daring, for he gave an approving nod. Then he spoke to Pescador:

"You've been drinking like the others?"

"More than the others."

"And you've kept your senses?"

"Bah! It hasn't hurt me in the least."

"Then perhaps you can answer some questions. Carpena says you may have some information for me!"

"Gratis?"

"Catch!"

And Zirone threw him a half piastre, which Pescador instantly slipped into his waistcoat pocket as a professional juggler would a ball.

"He's obliging!" said Zirone.

"Very obliging!" replied Pescador. "And now what do you wish to know?"

"You know Malta?"

"Malta, Italy, Istria, Dalmatia, and the Adriatic," answered Pescador.

"You've travelled?"

"Much, but always at my own expense."

"I'll see that you never travel otherwise, for when it's the Government that pays..."

"It costs too much!" interrupted Pescador.

"Exactly," replied Zirone, who was delighted to have found a new companion with whom he could talk.

"And now?" asked Pescador.

"And now, Pescador, in your numerous voyages did you ever hear of a certain Dr. Antekirtt?"

In spite of all his cleverness Point Pescade had never expected that; but he was sufficiently master of himself not to betray his surprise.

How Zirone, who was not at Ragusa during the stay of the *Savarena*, nor at Malta while the *Ferrato* was there, could have heard of the doctor was a puzzler. But with his decision of character he saw that his reply might be of use to him, and he did not hesitate to say at once:

"Dr. Antekirtt! Oh! Perfectly! People talk of nothing else throughout the Mediterranean!"

"Have you seen him?"

"Never."

"But do you know who he is?"

"A poor fellow, a hundred times a millionaire, who never goes about without a million in each pocket, and he has at least half a dozen! An unfortunate who's reduced to practice medicine as an amusement, sometimes on a schooner, sometimes on a steam yacht, a man who has a cure for every one of the 22,000 maladies with which nature has gratified the human species."

The mountebank of former days was again in his glory, and the fluency of his patter astonished Zirone, and none the less Carpena, who muttered:

"What a recruit!"

Pescador was silent, and lighted a cigarette from which the smoke seemed to come out of his eyes, his nose, and his ears as he pleased.

"You say the doctor's rich?" asked Zirone.

"Rich enough to buy Sicily and turn it into an English garden," replied Pescador.

Then thinking the moment had come for him to inspire Zirone with the idea of the scheme he had resolved to put into execution, he continued:

"And look here, Captain Zirone, though I haven't seen Dr. Antekirtt, I've seen one of his yachts, for they say he has quite a fleet to sail about the sea in!"

"One of his yachts!"

"Yes, the *Ferrato*, which would suit me nicely to go for a sail in the Bay of Naples with a princess or two."

"Where did you see the yacht?"

"At Malta."

"And when?"

"The day before yesterday at Valetta as we were going on board with Sergeant Carpena. She was then at her moorings in the military port, but they said she was going out four and twenty hours after us."

"Where to?"

"To Sicily, to Catania!"

"Catania?" asked Zirone.

The coincidence between the departure of Dr. Antekirtt and the warning he had received from Sarcany to beware of him could not but awake Zirone's suspicions.

Point Pescade saw that some secret thought was working in Zirone's brain, but what was it? Not being able to guess he resolved to press the captain more directly.

"What business could the doctor have in Sicily and Catania?" asked Zirone.

"Eh! By Saint Agatha," replied Point Pescade, "he's coming to visit the town! He's going to ascend Mount Etna! He'll travel like the rich traveller that he is!"

"Pescador," said Zirone, with a certain amount of suspicion, "you seem to have known this man some time."

"Not so long as I'd like to if I had an opportunity."

"What do you mean?"

"That if Dr. Antekirtt, as is probable, comes for a walk in our ground we might as well make his Excellency pay his footing."

"Indeed!" said Zirone.

"And if that only comes to a million or two it'll be good business."

"You're right."

"And in that case Zirone and his friends would not have been fools."

"Good," said Zirone with a smile. "After that compliment you can go to sleep."

"That'll suit me, for I know what I shall get dreaming about."

"What?"

"The millions of Dr. Antekirtt – dreams of gold!" And then Pescador, having given his cigarette its last puff, went off to rejoin his companions in the barn of the inn, while Carpena retired to his room.

And then he set to work to piece together all that he had said and heard. From the time that Zirone to his great astonishment had spoken to him of Dr. Antekirtt, had he done the best for the interests entrusted to him? Let us see.

In coming to Sicily the doctor hoped to again meet with Sarcany, and perhaps Toronthal, in case he accompanied him, which was not improbable, considering that they had left Ragusa together. Failing Sarcany, he reckoned on capturing Zirone, and by bribe or threat making him reveal where Sarcany and Toronthal could be found. That was his plan, and this was how he intended executing it.

In his youth the doctor had several times visited Sicily, particularly the district round Etna. He knew the different roads by which the ascent is made; the most used being that which passes by a house built at the commencement of the central cone, and which is known as the "Casa degli Inglesi."

Zirone's gang, for which Carpena had been recruiting at Malta was then at work on the Etna slopes, and it was certain that the arrival of a personage as famous as Dr. Antekirtt would produce the usual effect at Catania. If the doctor were to put it about that he was going to make the ascent of Etna, Zirone would be sure to hear of it – especially with the help of Point Pescade. The scheme had begun well, for Zirone himself had introduced the subject of the doctor to Pescade.

The trap which was to be laid for Zirone, and in which there was a good chance of his being caught, was the following:

The night before the doctor was to make the ascent of the volcano a dozen well-armed men from the *Ferrato* were to make their way secretly to the Casa degli Inglesi. In the morning the doctor, accompanied by Luigi, Pierre, and a guide, would leave Catania and follow the usual road so as to reach the Casa degli Inglesi about eight in the evening, and then pass the night like all the tourists do who wish to see the sun rise over the mountains of Calabria.

Zirone, urged by Point Pescade, would doubtless endeavour to capture the doctor, thinking he had only to do with him and his two companions; but when he reached the Casa degli Inglesi he would be received by the sailors of the *Ferrato*, and resistance would be impossible.

Point Pescade, knowing this scheme, had happily profited by the circumstances that presented themselves to put this idea of capturing the doctor into Zirone's head. It meant a heavy ransom, and would also work in with the message he had received. If he was to be careful of this man, would it not be better for him to seize him even if he lost the ransom? And Zirone decided to do so and wait for further instructions from Sarcany. But to be certain of success, as he had not his whole gang with him, he resolved to make the attempt with Carpena's Maltese – much to the comfort of Pescade, as the dozen ruffians would be no match for the *Ferrato* men.

But Zirone trusted nothing to chance. As Pescador had told him that the steam yacht was to arrive in the morning he left Santa Grotta early, and walked down to Catania. Not being known he could go there without danger.

In a few hours the steam yacht arrived at her moorings, not near the quay, which is always crowded with ships, but at a sort of entrance harbour between the north jetty and a huge mass of blackish lava which the eruption of 1669 sent down into the sea.

Already at daybreak Cape Matifou and eleven men of the *Ferrato* crew under Luigi had been landed at Catania, and separately had started on the road to the Casa degli Inglesi. Zirone knew nothing of this landing, and as the *Ferrato* was moored a cable length from the shore he could not even see what was passing on board.

About six o'clock in the evening the gig brought ashore two passengers. These were the doctor and Pierre Bathory. They went up the Via Stesicoro and the Strada Etnea towards the Villa Bellini, a public garden perhaps one of the most beautiful in Europe, with its masses of flowers, its varied slopes, its terraces shaded with large trees, its running streams, and the superb volcano plumed with mist rising in the background.

Zirone had followed the two passengers, doubting not that one of them was this famous Dr. Antekirtt. He even managed to get rather near them in the crowd that the music had attracted to the Villa Bellini, but he did not do this without being noticed by the doctor and Pierre. If this suspicious fellow were the Zirone they were looking for, here was a fine opportunity for enticing him still further into the snare that they had laid!

And so about eleven o'clock in the evening, when they were leaving the garden to return on board, the doctor replying to Pierre in a loud tone said:

"Yes, it's understood! We start tomorrow, and we'll sleep at the Casa degli Inglesi."

Doubtless the spy had learnt what he wanted, for a moment afterwards he had disappeared.

The Faraglionis, otherwise known as the rocks of Polyphemus

CHAPTER VII

THE CASA DEGLI INGLESI

Next day about one o'clock in the afternoon the doctor and Pierre Bathory completed their preparation to go ashore.

The gig received its passengers; but, before he left, the doctor ordered Captain Kostrik to watch for the arrival of *Electric No. 2*, then expected at any moment, and to send her out beyond the Faraglionis, otherwise known as the rocks of Polyphemus. If the plan succeeded, if Sarcany or even Zirone and Carpena were taken prisoners, the launch would be ready to convey them to Antekirtta, where he would have them in his power.

The gig put off. In a few minutes she reached the steps at the wharf. Doctor Antekirtt and Pierre had assumed the usual dress of tourists ascending the mountain who may have to endure a temperature of fourteen degrees below freezing, while at the sea level it stands at fifty degrees above that point. A guide was in waiting with the horses, which at Nicolosi were to be replaced by mules as more untiring and surer of foot.

The town of Catania is of little width compared to its length and was soon crossed. Nothing occurred to show that the doctor was watched and followed. Pierre and he, after taking the Belvidere road, began to ascend the earlier slopes of the mountain to which the Sicilians give the name of Mongibello, and of which the diameter is not less than twenty-five miles.

The road is uneven and winding. It turns aside frequently to avoid the lava streams and basaltic rocks solidified millions of years ago, the dry ravines filled in the spring time with impetuous torrents, and on its way it cuts through a well-wooded region of olive trees, orange trees, carob trees, ash trees, and long-branched vines. This is the first of the three zones, which gird the volcano, the "mountain of the smithy," the Phoenician translation of the word Etna – "the spike of the earth and the pillar of the sky" for the geologists of an age when geological science did not exist.

After a couple of hours' climbing, during a halt of some minutes, more needed by the horses than the riders, the doctor and Pierre beheld at their feet the town of Catania, the superb rival of Palermo. They could look down on the lines of its chief streets running parallel to the quays, the towers and domes of its hundred churches, the numerous and picturesque convents, and the houses in the pretentious style of the seventeenth century – all enclosed in the belt of green that encircles the city. In the foreground was the harbour, of which Etna itself formed the walls in the frightful eruption of 1669 which destroyed fourteen towns and villages, claimed 18,000 victims, and poured out over the country more than a million cubic yards of lava.

Etna is quieter now, and it has well earned the right to rest. In fact there have been more than thirty eruptions since the Christian era. That Sicily has not been overwhelmed is sufficient proof of the solidity of its foundation. It should be noted, however, that the volcano has not formed a permanent crater. It changes it as it pleases. The mountain falls in where one of the fire-vomiting abysses opens, and from the gap there spreads the lavic matter accumulated on the flanks. Hence the numerous small volcanoes – the Monte Rossi, a double mountain piled up in three months to a height of four hundred feet by the sands and scoria of 1669, Frumento, Simoni, Stornello, Crisinco, arranged like the turrets round a cathedral dome, to say nothing of the craters of 1809, 1811, 1819, 1838, 1852, 1865, 1875, whose funnels perforate the flanks of the central cone like the cells of a beehive.

After crossing the hamlet of Belvidere the guide took a short cut so as to reach the Tramestieri road near that from Nicolosi. The first cultivated zone extends almost from this town to two thousand one hundred and twenty feet above. It was nearly four o'clock in the afternoon when Nicolosi appeared, and the travellers had not met with a single adventure along the nine miles from Catania, and had seen neither boars nor wolves. They had still twelve and a half miles to go before they reached the Casa degli Inglesi.

"How long will your Excellency stop here?" asked the guide.

"No longer than necessary," answered the doctor, "let's get in tonight about nine o'clock."

"Forty minutes, then?"

"Forty minutes be it!"

And that was enough to procure a hasty meal in one of the two inns of the town, which – be it said to the honour of the three thousand inhabitants of Nicolosi, including the beggars who swarm in it – has rather a better culinary reputation than most Sicilian inns. A piece of kid, some fruit, raisins, oranges, and pomegranates, and San Placido wine from the environs of Catania – there are very few important towns in Italy in which an innkeeper would offer as much.

Before five o'clock the doctor, Pierre, and the guide, mounted on their mules, were climbing the second stage of the ascent – the forest zone. Not that the trees there are numerous, for the woodcutters, as everywhere else, are at work destroying the ancient forests which will soon be no more than a mythological remembrance. Here and there, however, in clumps and groups along the sides of the lava streams and on the edges of the abysses grow beeches and oaks, and almost black-leaved figs, and then, still higher, firs and pines and birches. Even the cinders mixed with a little mould give birth to large masses of ferns, fraxinellas, and mallows, rising from a carpet of moss.

About eight o'clock in the evening the doctor and Pierre had already reached the 3280 feet almost marking the limit of perpetual snow, which on the flanks of Etna is abundant enough to supply all Italy and Sicily. They were then in the region of black lavas, cinders, and scoria which stretches away beyond an immense crevasse, the vast elliptic amphitheatre of the Valle del Bove, forming cliffs of from 1000 to 3000 feet high, at whose base lie the strata of trachyte and basalt which the elements have not yet destroyed.

In front rose the cone of the volcano, on which, here and there, a few phanerogams formed hemispheres of verdure. This central hump, which is quite a mountain in itself – a Pelion on Ossa – rises till it reaches an altitude of 10,874 feet above the level of the sea.

Already the ground trembled under foot. Vibrations caused by the plutonic labouring ever present in the mountain ran beneath the patches of snow. The cloud of sulphurous vapours driven down by the wind from the mouth of the crater occasionally reached to the base of the cone, and a shower of scoria like incandescent coke fell on the whitish carpet, where it hissed as it suddenly cooled.

The temperature was then very low – many degrees below freezing – and respiration had become difficult owing to the rarefaction of the air. The travellers wrapped their cloaks more closely round them. A biting wind cut across the shoulder of the mountain, whirling along the snow-flakes it had swept from the ground. From the height there could be

On the edges of the abysses grow beeches and oaks, and almost black-leaved figs, and then, still higher, firs and pines and birches

seen the mouth where issued the faintly flickering flame and many other secondary craters, narrow solfataras or gloomy depths, at the bottom of which could be heard the roaring of the subterranean fire – a continuous roaring rising occasionally into a storm, as if it were due to an immense boiler from which the steam had forced up the valves. No eruption was anticipated, however, and all this internal rage was due to the rumblings of the higher crater and the eructations from the volcanic throats that opened out on to the cone.

It was then nine o'clock. The sky was resplendent with thousands of stars that the feeble density of the atmosphere at this altitude rendered still more sparkling. The moon's crescent was dipping in the west in the waters of the Aeolian Sea. On a mountain that was not an active volcano the calm of the night would have been sublime.

"We ought to have arrived," said the doctor.

"There's the Casa degli Inglesi," answered the guide.

And he pointed to a short wall having two windows and a door, which its position had protected from the snow, and which was about fifty paces away to the left, and nearly 1400 feet below the summit of the central zone. This was the house constructed in 1811 by the English officers then stationed in Sicily. It is built on a plateau at the base of the lava mass named Piano del Lago.

Works have now been commenced by the Italian Government and the municipality of Catania for transforming the Casa degli Inglesi into an observatory. It is sometimes called the Casa Etnea, and was kept up for some years by M. Gemellaro, the brother of the geologist of that name. A few months previous to the doctor's arrival it had been restored by the Alpine Club.

Not very far away there loomed in the darkness the Roman ruins which are known as the Tower of the Philosopher. From it legend states that Empedocles was precipitated into the crater; in fact it would require a singular dose of philosophy to spend eight hours of solitude in such a spot, and we can quite understand the act of the celebrated philosopher of Agrigentum.

However, Dr. Antekirtt, Pierre Bathory, and the guide came up to the Casa degli Inglesi, and as soon as they reached it they knocked at the door, which was opened immediately. A moment afterwards they were among their men.

The Casa degli Inglesi consisted of only three rooms, with table, chairs, and cooking utensils; but that was enough for the climbers of Etna, after reaching a height of 9469 ft. Till then Luigi, fearing the presence of his little detachment might be suspected, had not lighted a fire, although the cold was extreme. But now there was no need to continue the precaution, for Zirone knew that the doctor was to spend the night at the Casa degli Inglesi. Some wood found in reserve in the shed was therefore piled on the hearth, and soon a crackling flame gave the needed warmth and light.

The doctor took Luigi apart, and asked him if anything had happened since he arrived.

"Nothing," answered Luigi. "But I'm afraid our presence here is not as secret as we wished."

"And why?"

"Because, after we left Nicolosi, if I'm not mistaken, we were followed by a man who disappeared just before we reached the base of the cone."

"That is a pity, Luigi! That may prevent Zirone from having the honour to surprise me! Since sundown no one has been lurking round the Casa degli Inglesi?"

"No one, sir," answered Luigi, "I even took the precaution to search the ruins of the Philosopher's Tower; there's nobody there."

"See that a man is always on guard at the door! You can see a good way tonight, for it's so clear, and it's important we're not surprised."

The doctor's orders were executed, and when he had taken his place on a stool by the fire the men lay down on the bundles of straw around him. Cape Matifou, however, came up to the doctor. He looked at him without daring to speak. But it was easy to understand what made him anxious.

"You wish to know what has become of Point Pescade?" asked the doctor. "Patience! He'll return soon, although he's now playing a game that might cost him his neck."

An hour elapsed, and nothing occurred to trouble the solitude round the central cone. Not a shadow appeared on the shining slope in front of the Piano del Lago. Both the doctor and Pierre experienced an impatience and even an anxiety that they could not restrain. If unfortunately Zirone had been warned of the presence of the little detachment, he would never dare to attack the Casa degli Ingesi. The scheme had failed. And yet, somehow, it was necessary to get hold of this accomplice of Sarcany, failing Sarcany himself.

A little before ten o'clock the report of a gun was heard about half a mile below the Casa degli Inglesi.

They all went out and looked about, but saw nothing suspicious.

"It was unmistakably a gun!" said Pierre.

"Perhaps someone out after an eagle or a boar!" answered Luigi.

"Come in," said the doctor, "and keep yourselves out of sight."

They went back into the house.

But ten minutes afterwards the sailor on guard without rushed in hurriedly.

"All hands!" he said. "I think I can see..."

"Many of them?" asked Pierre.

"No, only one!"

The doctor, Pierre, Luigi, and Cape Matifou went to the door, taking care to keep out of the light.

They saw a man bounding along like a chamois and crossing the lines of old lava, which ran alongside the plateau. He was alone, and in a few bounds he fell into the arms held open for him – the arms of Cape Matifou.

It was Point Pescade.

"Quick! Quick! Under cover, doctor!" he exclaimed.

In an instant all were inside the Casa degli Inglesi, and the door was immediately shut.

"And Zirone?" asked the doctor, "What's become of him? You've had to leave him?"

"Yes, to warn you!"

"Is he not coming?"

"In twenty minutes he'll be here."

"So much the better."

"No! So much the worse! I don't know how he was told that you had first sent up a dozen men."

"Probably by the mountaineer that followed us!" said Luigi.

"Anyhow he knows it," answered Pescade, "and he saw that you were trying to get him in a trap."

"He'll come then!" said Pierre.

"He's coming, Mr. Pierre! But to the dozen recruits he had from Malta there's been added the rest of the band, come in this very morning to Santa Grotta."

"And how many bands are there?"

"Fifty," replied Pescade.

The position of the doctor and his little band, consisting of the eleven sailors, Luigi, Pierre, Cape Matifou, and Point Pescade – sixteen against fifty was rather alarming; and if anything was to be done, it should be done immediately.

"Quick! Quick! Under cover, doctor!" he exclaimed

But in the first place the doctor wished to know from Pescade what had happened, and this is what he was told:

That morning Zirone had returned from Catania, where he had passed the night, and he it was whom the doctor had noticed prowling about the gardens of the Villa Bellini. When he returned to Santa Grotta he found a mountaineer who gave him the information that a dozen men coming from different directions had occupied the Casa degli Inglesi.

Zirone immediately understood how matters lay. It was no longer he who was trapping the doctor, but the doctor who was trapping him. Point Pescade, however, insisted that Zirone ought to attack the Casa degli Inglesi, assuring him that the Maltese would soon settle the doctor's little band. But Zirone remained none the less undecided what he should do, and the urgency of Point Pescade appeared so suspicious, that Zirone gave orders that he should be watched – which Pescade easily and immediately discovered. It is probable that Zirone would have given up his idea of carrying off the doctor had not his band been reinforced about three o'clock in the afternoon. Then with fifty men under his orders he no longer hesitated, and leaving Santa Grotta with all his followers he advanced on the Casa degli Inglesi.

Point Pescade saw that the doctor and his people were lost if he did not warn them in time, so as to let them escape, or at least put them on their guard. He waited until the gang was in sight of the Casa degli Inglesi, the position of which he did not know. The light shining in the windows rendered it visible about nine o'clock, when he was less than two miles off on the slopes of the cone. As soon as he saw it Point Pescade set off at a run. A gun was fired at him by Zirone – the one heard up at the Casa – but it missed him. With his acrobatic agility he was soon out of range. And that is how he had arrived at the house only about twenty minutes in advance of Zirone.

When Point Pescade had told his story a clasp from the doctor's hand thanked him for what he had done. The next question was how to foil the brigands. To leave the Casa degli Inglesi and retreat in the middle of the night down the flanks of the volcano with Zirone and his people knowing every footpath and every refuge was to expose themselves to complete destruction. To wait for daylight to entrench themselves and defend themselves in the house would be a far more advantageous plan. When the day came, if they had to retreat, they could at least do so in broad daylight and would not go out like blind men down the precipices and solfataras. The decision was therefore to remain and fight. The preparations for the defence immediately commenced.

Zirone and his men advanced slowly and cautiously

And first the two windows of the Casa degli Inglesi had to be closed and their shutters firmly fastened down. As embrasures there were the openings between where the rafters of the roof rested on the front wall. Each man was provided with a repeating rifle and twenty cartridges. The doctor, Pierre and Luigi could assist with their revolvers, but Cape Matifou had only his arms and Point Pescade had only his hands. Perhaps they were not the worst armed.

Nearly forty minutes passed and no attempt at attack was made. Zirone, knowing that Dr. Antekirtt had been warned by Point Pescade and could not be surprised, had possibly abandoned his idea? With fifty men under his command and all the advantages that a thorough knowledge of the ground could give him, success was certainly in his favour.

Suddenly about eleven o'clock the sentry reported a number of men approaching in skirmishing order so as to attack the hut on three sides – the fourth side, backing on to the slope, afforded no possible retreat. The manoeuvre having been discovered, the door was shut and barricaded, and the men took their posts near the rafters with orders not to fire unless they were sure of their object.

Zirone and his men advanced slowly and cautiously, taking advantage of the cover of the rocks to reach the crest of the Piano del Lago. Enormous masses of trachyte and basalt were heaped up on the edge, intended probably to protect the Casa degli Inglesi from being destroyed by the snow during the winter. Having reached the plateau the assailants could more easily charge up to the house, break through the door or windows, and by means of their superior numbers carry off the doctor and his people.

Suddenly there was a report. A light smoke drifted in between the rafters. A man fell mortally wounded. The bandits at once rushed back and disappeared behind the rocks. Profiting by the unevenness of the ground, Zirone gradually brought his men to the foot of the Piano del Lago; but he did not do so until a dozen shots had been fired from the caves of the Casa degli Inglesi – and two more of his associates were stretched dead on the snow.

Zirone then gave the word to storm, and at the cost of several wounded the whole band rushed on the Casa degli Inglesi. The door was riddled with bullets, and two sailors were slightly hurt, and had to stand aside while the struggle grew brisker. With their pikes and hatchets the assailants attempted to break through the door and one of the windows, and a sortie had to be undertaken to repel them under an incessant fusillade from all sides. Luigi had his hand pierced by a bullet, and

Pierre, without the assistance of Cape Matifou, would have been killed by a pike thrust, had not Hercules seized the pike and settled its possessor at one blow.

During this sortie Cape Matifou was quite a terror. Twenty times was he shot at, and not a bullet reached him. If Zirone won, Point Pescade was a dead man, and the thought of this redoubled his rage. Against such resistance the assailants had again to retreat; and the doctor and his friends returned into the Casa and reviewed their position.

"What ammunition have you left?" asked he.

"Ten or a dozen cartridges per man," said Luigi.

"And what time is it?"

"Hardly midnight."

Four hours still to daybreak! The men must be more careful with the ammunition, for some of it would be wanted to protect the retreat at the earliest streak of dawn.

But how could they defend the approaches, or prevent the capture of the Casa degli Inglesi, if Zirone and his band again tried an assault? And that is what he did in a quarter of an hour's time, after taking all the wounded to the rear under shelter of a line of lava that did duty for an entrenchment, when the bandits enraged at the resistance, and drunk with fury at the sight of five or six of their injured comrades, mounted the ridge and appeared on the edge of the plateau.

Not a shot was fired as they crossed the open, and hence Zirone concluded that the besieged were running short of ammunition. The idea of carrying off a millionaire was just the thing to excite the cupidity of the scoundrels that followed him. Such was their fury during this attack that they forced the door and the window, and would have taken the house by assault, had not a volley point blank killed five or six of them. They had therefore to return to the foot of the plateau, not without wounding two of the sailors, who could take no further part in the fray.

Four or five rounds were all that remained to the defenders of the Casa degli Inglesi. Under these circumstances retreat even during daylight had almost become impossible. They felt that they were lost if help did not come. But where could help come from? Unfortunately they could not expect that Zirone and his companions would give up their enterprise while they were still nearly forty in number, unhurt, and well armed.

They knew that the besieged would soon be unable to reply to their fire, and they returned to the charge. Suddenly enormous blocks like the rocks of an avalanche came rolling down the slope, and crushed three between them before they had time to step aside.

Cape Matifou had started the rocks in order to hurl them over the crest of the Piano del Lago. But this means of defence was not enough. The heap of rocks would soon be used up, and the besieged would have to surrender or seek help from outside.

And now an idea occurred to Point Pescade, which he did not care to mention to the doctor for fear that he would not give his consent. But he went and whispered it to Cape Matifou.

He knew from what he had heard at Santa Grotta that a detachment of gendarmes was at Cassone.

To reach Cassone would only take an hour, and it would take another hour to get back. Could he not fetch this detachment? Yes, but only by passing through the besiegers, and making off to the westward.

"It's necessary for me to get through, and I will get through!" he said. "Otherwise I wouldn't be much of an acrobat!"

And he told Cape Matifou what he proposed to do.

"But," said Matifou, "you risk..."

"I'm going!"

Cape Matifou never dared to resist Point Pescade.

Both then went to the right of the Casa degli Inglesi, where the snow had accumulated to a considerable depth.

Ten minutes afterwards, while the struggle continued along the front, Cape Matifou appeared pushing before him a huge snowball, and among the rocks that the sailors continued to hurl on to their assailants he started this ball, which rolled down the slope past Zirone's men, and stopped fifty yards in the rear at the bottom of a gentle hollow. It half broke with the shock; it opened, and from it emerged a living man, active, and "a little malicious," as he said of himself.

It was Point Pescade. Enclosed in the carapace of hardened snow he had dared being started on the slope of the mountain at the risk of being rolled into the depths of some abyss!

And now he was free, he made the best haste he could along the footpaths to Cassone.

It was then half-past twelve.

At this moment the doctor not seeing Pescade thought he was wounded. He called him.

"Gone!" said Cape Matifou.

"Gone?"

"Yes! To get some help!"

Enormous blocks came rolling down the slope

"And how?"

"In a snowball!"

And Cape Matifou told him what Pescade had done.

"Ah! Brave fellow!" exclaimed the doctor. "Courage, my friends! The scoundrels will not have us after all."

And the masses of rock continued to roll clown on the assailants, although the means of defence were rapidly disappearing.

About three o'clock in the morning the doctor, Pierre, Luigi, Cape Matifou and the sailors, carrying their wounded, would have to evacuate the house and allow it to fall into the possession of Zirone, twenty of whose companions had been killed. The retreat would have to be up the central cone — that heap of lava, scoriae, and cinders whose summit, the crater, was an abyss of fire — and all were to ascend it and carry their wounded with them. Of the 1000 feet they would have to climb, over 700 feet would be through the sulphurous fumes that the winds beat down from the top.

The day began to break, and already the crests of the Calabrian Mountains above the eastern coast of the Straits of Messina were tipped with the coming light. But in the position in which the doctor and his men found themselves the day had no chance of being welcomed. They would have to fight as they retreated up the slope, using their last cartridges and hurling down the last masses of rock that Matifou sent flying along with such superhuman strength. They had almost given themselves up for lost when the sound of guns was heard below them. A moment of indecision was observed among the bandits. They hesitated, and then they broke into full flight down the mountainside. They had sighted the gendarmes who had arrived from Cassone, Point Pescade at their head.

He had not had to go as far as the village. The gendarmes had heard the firing and were already on the road. All he had to do was to lead them to the Casa degli Inglesi.

Then the doctor and his men took the offensive. Cape Matifou, as if he were an avalanche himself, bounded on the nearest and knocked down two before they had time to get away; and then he rushed at Zirone.

"Bravo, old Cape! Bravo!" shouted Pescade, running up. "Down with him! Lay him flat! The contest, gentlemen, the desperate contest between Zirone and Cape Matifou!"

Zirone heard him, and with the hand that remained free he fired his revolver at Pescade — who fell to the ground.

And then there was a terrible scene. Cape Matifou had seized Zirone and was dragging him along by the neck. The wretch, half strangled, could do nothing to help himself.

In vain the doctor, who wished to have him alive shouted out for him to be spared. In vain Pierre and Luigi rushed up to stop him. Cape Matifou thought of one thing only: Zirone had mortally wounded Point Pescade! He heard nothing, he saw nothing, he gave one last leap on to the edge of the gaping crater of a solfatara, and hurled the bandit into the abyss of fire!

Point Pescade, seriously wounded, was lifted on to the doctor's knee. He examined and bathed the wound, and when Cape Matifou returned to him, with great tears rolling down his cheeks:

"Never fear, old Cape, never fear!" murmured Pescade. "It's nothing!"

Cape Matifou took him in his arms like a child, and followed by all went down the side of the cone; while the gendarmes gave chase to the last fugitives of Zirone's band.

Six hours afterwards the doctor and his men had returned to Catania and were on board the *Ferrato*. Point Pescade was laid in the cabin. With Doctor Antekirtt for surgeon and Cape Matifou for nurse he was well looked alter! His wound – a bullet in the shoulder – was not of a serious kind. His cure was only a question of time. When he wanted sleep Cape Matifou told him tales – always the same tales – and Point Pescade was soon in sound slumber!

However, the doctor's campaign had opened unsuccessfully. After nearly falling into Zirone's hands, he had not been able to get hold of Sarcany's companion and obtain the information from him that he wanted – and all owing to Cape Matifou! Although the doctor stayed at Catania for eight days, he could obtain no news of Sarcany. If Sarcany had intended to rejoin Zirone in Sicily, his plans had been changed probably when he heard the result of the attempt on Dr. Antekirtt.

The *Ferrato* put to sea on the 8th of September, bound for Antekirtta, and she arrived after a rapid passage.

There the doctor, Pierre and Luigi conferred as to their future plans. The first thing to do was obviously to get hold of Carpena, who ought to know what had become of Sarcany and Silas Toronthal.

Unfortunately for the Spaniard, although he escaped the destruction of Zirone's band, he remained at Santa Grotta, and his good fortune was of short duration. In fact ten days afterwards one of the doctor's agents informed him that Carpena had been arrested at Syracuse – not as an accomplice of Zirone, but for a crime committed more than fifteen years ago, a murder at Alrnayate in the province of Malaga, which had caused his flight to Rovigno.

Three weeks later, Carpena, whose extradition was obtained, was convicted, and sent to the coast of Morocco, to Ceuta – one of the chief penal colonies of Spain.

"At last," said Pierre, "there is one of the scoundrels settled for life!"

"For life? No!" answered the doctor. "If Andrea Ferrato died in prison, it is not in prison that Carpena ought to die."

Cape Matifou hurled the bandit into the abyss of fire!

PART IV

CHAPTER I

CEUTA

On the 21st of September, three weeks after the doctor left Catania, a swift steam yacht – the *Ferrato* – could have been seen running before a north easterly breeze between the European cape the English hold on Spanish ground and the African cape the Spaniards hold on Moorish ground. If we are to believe mythology, the twelve miles that separate these capes from each other were cleared away by Hercules – a predecessor of De Lesseps – who let in the Atlantic by knocking a hole with his club in the border of the Mediterranean.

Point Pescade would not have forgotten to tell this to his friend Cape Matifou as he showed him to the north the rock of Gibraltar, and to the south Mount Hacho. And Cape Matifou would have appreciated at its true value this wonderful feat, and not a shade of envy would have overshadowed his simple, modest soul. The Provencal Hercules would have bowed low before the son of Jupiter and Alcmena.

But Cape Matifou was not among the yacht's passengers, and neither was Point Pescade. One taking care of the other, both had remained at Antekirtta. If, later on, their assistance became necessary, they could be summoned by telegram and brought from the island by one of the *Electrics*.

On the *Ferrato* were the doctor and Pierre Bathory, and in command were Kostrik and Luigi. The last expedition to Sicily in search of Sarcany and Toronthal had resulted in nothing beyond the death of Zirone. They had therefore decided to resume the chase by obtaining from Carpena all the information he possessed as to Sarcany and his accomplice; and as the Spaniard had been sent to the galleys and shipped to Ceuta, they were on their way there to find him.

Ceuta is a small, fortified town, a sort of Spanish Gibraltar, built on the eastern slopes of Mount Hacho; and it was in sight of its harbour

341

that the yacht was now steaming some three miles from the coast. No more animated spot exists than this famous strait. It is the mouth of the Mediterranean. Through it come the thousands of vessels from Northern Europe and the two Americas bound for the hundreds of ports on the coast of the inland sea. Through it come the powerful mail boats and warships, for which the genius of a Frenchman has opened a way to the Indian Ocean and the Southern Seas.

Nothing can be more picturesque than this narrow channel through the mountains. To the north are the sierras of Andalusia. To the south, along the strangely varied coastline, from Cape Spartel to Almina, are the black summits of the Bullones, the Apes' Hill, and the Seven Brothers. To the right and left are picturesque towns crouching in the curves of the bays, straggling on the flanks of the lower hills, and stretching along the beaches at the base of the mountainous background – such as Tarifa, Algesiras, Tangier, and Ceuta. Between the two shores, cut by the prows of the rapid steamers that stop not for wind or wave, and the sailing vessels that the westerly winds keep back at times in hundreds, there stretches the expanse of ever-moving water, ever-changing, here grey and streaked with foam, there blue and calm, and broken into restless hills that mark the zigzagged current line. No one can remain insensible to the sublime beauties that the two continents, Europe and Africa, bring face to face along the double panorama of the Straits of Gibraltar.

Swiftly does the *Ferrato* approach the African coast. The bay at the back of which Tangier is hidden begins to close, while the rock of Ceuta becomes more visible as the shore beyond trends away to the south. Above towards the top of Mount Hacho, there appears a fort, built on the site of a Roman citadel, in which the sentries keep constant watch over the straits and the Moorish territory of which Ceuta is but a slip.

At ten o'clock the *Ferrato* dropped anchor in the harbour, or rather about two cable lengths from the pier, which receives the full strength of the sea, for there is nothing but an open roadstead exposed to the surf of the Mediterranean waves. Fortunately when vessels cannot anchor to the west of Ceuta they find a second anchorage on the other side of the rock, in which they are sheltered from the easterly winds.

At about one o'clock in the afternoon, once the health officer had been on board and the clean bill duly passed, the doctor accompanied by Pierre went ashore, and landed at the little quay at the foot of the town walls.

That he was fully determined to carry off Carpena there was no doubt. But how would he do so? Nothing could be done until he had seen the place, and made himself acquainted with the circumstances, and then he would be able to decide if it were best to carry off the Spaniard by force, or help him to escape.

This time the doctor did not attempt to remain incognito. Quite the contrary. Already his correspondents had been on board, and gone off again to announce the arrival of so famous an individual. Who throughout that Arab country from Suez to Cape Spartel had not heard of the reputation of the learned taleb who now lived in retirement at Antekirtta in the Syrtic Sea? And so the Spaniards like the Moors gave him a hearty welcome, and as there were no restrictions on visiting the *Ferrato*, very many boats came off to her.

All this excitement was evidently part of the doctor's plan. His celebrity was to be brought in to help his enterprise. Pierre and he did nothing to restrain the public enthusiasm. An open carriage obtained from the chief hotel enabled them to visit the town with its narrow streets of gloomy houses destitute of character and colour, and its little squares with sickly, dusty trees shading some miserable inn or one or two official buildings. In a word there was nothing original to be seen except perhaps in the Moorish quarter, where colour had not entirely disappeared.

About three o'clock the doctor requested to be taken to the Governor of Ceuta, whom he wished to visit – an act of courtesy quite natural on the part of a stranger of distinction.

It need scarcely be said that the governor was not a civil functionary. Ceuta is above all things a military colony. It contains about 10,000 people, officers and soldiers, merchants, fishermen or coasting sailors housed in the town and along the strip of land whose prolongation towards the east completes the Spanish possession.

Ceuta was then administered by Colonel Guyarre. He had under his orders three battalions of infantry detached from the continental army to serve their time in Africa, one regiment permanently quartered in the colony, two batteries of artillery, a company of engineers, and a company of Moors whose families occupied special quarters. The convicts amounted to nearly 2000.

To reach the governor's house the carriage had to traverse a macadamized road outside the town, which ran through the colony to its eastern end. On each side of the road a narrow band between the foot of the hills and the waste along the beach is well tilled, thanks to the assiduous labour of the inhabitants, who have a hard struggle against the poverty of the soil. Vegetables of all sorts and even trees are there to be found – and the labourers are many.

The doctor and Pierre Bathory

For the convicts are sentenced to various periods ranging from twenty years to detention for life, and are set to work in various ways under conditions determined by the Government. They are not only employed by the State in special workshops, on the fortifications, and the roads, which require constant repair, but fulfil the duties of urban police when their good conduct permits.

During his visit to Ceuta the doctor met several of these moving about freely in the streets of the town, and even engaged in domestic work, but he saw a much larger number outside the fortifications, employed on the roads and in the fields. To which class Carpena belonged it was important he should know, as his scheme would have to be modified to suit the man's being at work, guarded or unguarded, either for the State or a private individual.

"But," said he to Pierre, "as his conviction is so recent, it's unlikely he would have obtained the advantages accorded to old stagers for good conduct."

"But if he's under lock and key?" asked Pierre.

"Then his capture will be more difficult, but it must be managed."

The carriage rolled slowly along. At a couple of hundred yards beyond the fortifications a number of convicts under a guard were working at macadamizing the road. They were about fifty, some breaking the stones, others scattering them, and some rolling them in. The carriage had to proceed slowly along the side where the repairs had not been commenced.

Suddenly the doctor touched Pierre's arm.

"There he is!" said he in a low voice.

A man was resting on the handle of his pickaxe, about twenty paces in front of his companions.

It was Carpena.

The doctor, after fifteen years, recognized the salt-marsh worker of Istria in his convict garb, as Maria Ferrato had recognized him in his Maltese dress in the lanes of the Manderaggio. He was even then only pretending to work. Unfit for any trade, he could not be employed in any of the workshops, and he was not really able to break stones on the road.

Although the doctor had recognized him, Carpena had not recognized Count Mathias Sandorf. He had only seen him for so short a time on the banks of the canal and in the house of Ferrato the fisherman when he brought in the police. But like everybody else he had heard that Dr. Antekirtt had arrived at Ceuta, and Dr. Antekirtt he remembered was the personage of whom Zirone had spoken during their interview near the grotto of Polyphemus on the coast of Sicily. He was the man whom Sarcany had warned them to beware of; he was the millionaire over whom Zirone's band had met their destruction at the Casa degli Inglesi.

What passed in Carpena's brain when he found himself so unexpectedly in the doctor's presence? Did he receive an impression with that instantaneousness which characterizes certain photographic processes? It would be difficult to say. But he did feel that the doctor had taken possession of him by a sort of moral ascendancy, that his personality had been annihilated, that a strange will had taken the place of his own will. In vain he would have resisted; he had to yield to the domination.

The carriage stopped and the doctor continued to gaze into his eyes with penetrating fixity. The brilliancy of those eyes produced in Carpena's brain a strange and irresistible effect. Gradually the Spaniards senses faded. His eyelids closed, and blinked, and retained only a flickering vibration. Then the anaesthesia became complete, and he fell by the side of the road without his companions seeing anything of what had passed; and there he slept in a magnetic sleep from which not one of them could rouse him.

Then the doctor gave orders for the coachman to drive on to the governor's house. The scene had not occupied more than half a minute. No one had noticed what had passed between the Spaniard and the doctor – no one except Pierre Bathory.

"Now, that man is mine," said the doctor, "and I can do what I like with him."

"Shall we find out all he knows?" asked Pierre.

"No, but he'll do all that I require and that unconsciously. At the first glance I gave at the scoundrel I saw I could become his master and substitute my will for his."

"But the man was not ill."

"Eh! Do you think these effects of hypnosis can only be produced on neuropaths? No, Pierre, the most refractory are not safe from them. On the contrary, it is necessary that the subject should have a will of his own, and I was favoured by circumstances in finding in Carpena a nature entirely disposed to submit to my influence. And so he will remain asleep until I choose to wake him."

"Exactly," said Pierre, "but what's the good of it, seeing that even in the state he now finds himself it's impossible to make him tell us what we are so anxious to know."

"Doubtless," answered the doctor, "and it's obvious I cannot make him say what I do not know myself. But he's in my power. I can make him do what I please and when I think fit I shall make him do it and he'll be powerless to prevent it. For example, tomorrow, or the day after, or a week after, or six months after, even if he has awoke, if I desire him to leave Ceuta, he will leave Ceuta!"

"Leave Ceuta!" said Pierre. "Gain his liberty! But will the warders let him? The influence of the suggestion cannot make him break his chain, nor open the prison gate, nor scale an unscalable wall..."

"No Pierre," replied the doctor. "I cannot compel him to do what I could not do myself, and it's for that reason that I'm now on my way to visit the Governor of Ceuta."

The doctor was not exaggerating. The fact of the influence of suggestion in the hypnotic state is now admitted. The works and observations of Charcot, Brown-Séquard, Azam, Richet, Dumontpallier, Maudslay, Bernheim, Hack Tuke, Rieger, and many others leave no doubt on the subject. During his travels in the East the doctor had studied some of the more curious cases, and had added to that branch of physiology a rich contingent of new observations. He was thoroughly well informed as to the phenomena and the results that could be obtained from them. Gifted himself with great suggestive power which he had often exercised in Asia Minor, it was on it that he relied to carry off Carpena – if chance had not made the Spaniard insensible to its influence.

But if the doctor was henceforth master of Carpena, if he could make him do what he liked in suggesting to him his own will, it was still necessary that the prisoner should be free to move when the time came for him to accomplish whatever might be his work. And this permission the doctor hoped to obtain from Colonel Guyarre in such a form as to render it possible for the Spaniard to escape.

Ten minutes later the carriage arrived at the entrance to the large barracks just inside the Spanish boundary, and drew up before the governor's house.

Colonel Guyarre had already been informed that Dr. Antekirtt was in Ceuta. Thanks to the reputation he had gained by his talents and fortune, this famous individual was a sort of monarch on his travels, and as soon as he entered the reception room the colonel gave a hearty welcome to him and his young companion Pierre Bathory, and at the outset offered to put at their entire disposal the "little piece of Spain so fortunately cut off from the Moorish territory."

"We thank you for your offer," was the doctor's reply in Spanish, a language that, like him, Pierre understood and spoke fluently. "But I'm not sure we shall be able to take advantage of your kindness."

"What is the matter?" asked the governor

"Oh! The colony is not a large one, Dr. Antekirtt," answered the governor. "In half a day you could get round it! Are you going to stay here any time?"

"Four or five hours at the most," said the doctor. "I must leave to-night for Gibraltar, where I have an appointment tomorrow morning."

"Leave this evening!" exclaimed the governor. "Allow me to insist! I assure you, Dr. Antekirtt that our military colony is worth studying thoroughly! You've doubtless seen much and observed much during your travels, but perhaps have not paid much attention to the question of prison discipline; and I assure you that Ceuta is worth study, not only by scientific men, but by economists."

Naturally the governor was not without some conceit in singing the praises of his colony, but he did not exaggerate in the least. The administrative system of Ceuta is considered one of the best in the world, both as affecting the material well being of the convicts and their moral amelioration. The governor insisted that a man in Dr. Antekirtt's position should delay his departure so as to honour by a visit the different departments of the penitentiary.

"That would be impossible, but today I'm at your service, and if you like..."

"It's four o'clock," said Colonel Guyarre, "and you see there's so little time."

"Quite so," said the doctor, "and I'm in a similar fix, for just as you wish to do me the honours of your colony, I'm anxious to do you the honours of my yacht."

"Cannot you postpone for today your departure to Gibraltar?"

"I would do so if an appointment had not been arranged for me for tomorrow, and which, as I say, compels me to sail."

"That is really annoying!" replied the governor, "and I shall never console myself for not having kept you longer! But take care! I've got your vessel under the guns of my forts, and I can sink her if I give the word!"

"And the reprisals?" answered the doctor with a laugh. "Are you prepared for a war with the mighty kingdom of Antekirtta?"

"I know that would be serious!" replied the governor, in the same tone. "But what would we not risk to keep you here twenty-four hours longer?"

Pierre did not take part in this conversation. He contented himself with wondering if the doctor were making any progress towards the object he had in view. The decision to leave Ceuta that evening astonished him not a little.

How in so short a time could he take the indispensable steps for bringing about Carpena's escape? In a few hours the convicts would be sent back to gaol and shut up for the night, and then to get the Spaniard away was a very doubtful undertaking indeed.

But Pierre saw that the doctor was acting on a quickly formed plan when he heard the reply:

"Really, I'm deeply grieved I cannot accept your invitation – today at least! But we might perhaps arrange it in some way?"

"Say on, doctor, say on!"

"As I must be at Gibraltar tomorrow morning, I must leave here to-night. But I do not think my stay on the rock will last more than two or three days. It's now Thursday, and instead of continuing my voyage up the north of the Mediterranean, nothing could be easier than for me to call at Ceuta on Sunday morning..."

"Nothing could be easier," interrupted the governor, "and nothing would give me greater pleasure. Of course my vanity has something to do with it, but who has not some vanity in this world? So it's agreed, Dr. Antekirtt, Sunday?"

"Yes, on one condition!"

"Whatever it be, I accept!"

"That you and your aide-de-camp come to breakfast with me on the *Ferrato*."

"With pleasure, but on one condition also!"

"Likewise, whatever it be, I accept the invitation."

"That M. Bathory and you come and dine with me!"

"Very good, and we'll go the rounds between breakfast and dinner."

"And I'll abuse my authority to make you admire all the splendours of my kingdom!" replied Colonel Guyarre, shaking hands with the doctor.

Pierre also accepted the invitation, and bowed respectfully to the very obliging and very much satisfied Governor of Ceuta.

The doctor then prepared to take his leave, and Pierre read in his eyes that he had gained his object. But the governor would not allow them to leave alone, and accompanied them to the town. The three therefore took their seats in the carriage and drove along the only road, which put the residence in communication with Ceuta.

The governor would not have been a Spaniard if he had not enlarged on the more or less contestable beauties of the little colony, on the im-provements he proposed to introduce in both military and civil matters, on the superiority of the situation of the ancient Abyla to that of Calpe, on the fact of its being possible to make of it a Gibraltar as impregnable as that belonging to Britain, and of course he protested against the insolence of Mr. Ford in saying that "Ceuta ought to belong to England, for Spain does nothing, and hardly knows how to keep it," and showed great irritation against the English, "who never put their foot on a piece of ground without the foot taking root."

"Yes," he remarked, "before they think of taking Ceuta, let them take care of Gibraltar! There's a mountain there that Spain will one day shake down on their heads!"

The doctor, without inquiring how the Spaniards were to bring about such a geological commotion, did not contest the statement, which was made with all the loftiness of a hidalgo. And besides the conversation was interrupted by the sudden stoppage of the vehicle. The driver had to pull in his horses before a crowd of some fifty convicts that barred the road.

The governor beckoned to one of the sergeants to approach. The sergeant immediately advanced to the carriage with military step, and with his heels together and his hand at his peak waited to be spoken to.

The other prisoners and warders were drawn up on each side of the road.

"What is the matter?" asked the governor.

"Excellency," replied the sergeant, "we've found a convict on the bank who seems to be asleep, and we cannot wake him."

"How long has he been in that state?"

"About an hour."

"Has he been asleep all the time?"

"He has, your Excellency. He's as insensible as if he were dead. We've shaken him, and prodded him, and even fired a pistol close to his ear. But he feels nothing and hears nothing."

"Why did you not send for the surgeon?" asked the governor.

"I did send for him, your Excellency, but he wasn't at home, and until he comes we do not know what to do with this man."

"Well, take him to the hospital."

The sergeant was about to execute the order when the doctor intervened.

"Will your Excellency allow me, as a physician, to examine this recalcitrant sleeper? I shall not be sorry to have a closer look at him.'

"And it's really your trade, is it not?" answered the governor. "A lucky rascal to be a patient of Dr. Antekirtt! He'll not have much cause to complain."

The three left the carriage, and the doctor walked up to the convict who was stretched at full length by the side of the road. In the man's heavy sleep the only signs of life were the panting respiration and the beating of the pulse.

The doctor signalled for the crowd to stand away from him. Then he bent over the inert body, spoke to it in a low voice, looked at it for some time, as if he wished to penetrate its brain with his will.

Then he arose.

"It's nothing," said he. "The man has simply fallen into a magnetic sleep!"

"Indeed!" said the governor. "That is very curious! Can you wake him?"

"Nothing can be easier!" answered the doctor. And after touching Carpena's forehead he gently lifted his eyelids and said:

"Awake! I will, it so!"

Carpena shook himself and opened his eyes, though he still remained in a certain state of somnolence. The doctor made several passes across the Spaniard's face so as to stir the cushion of air, and gradually the torpor left him. He sat up; and unconscious of all that had happened, took his place among his companions.

The governor, the doctor and Pierre Bathory stepped into the carriage and resumed their road to the town.

"Had not that rascal had something to drink?" asked the governor.

"I do not think so," replied the doctor. "It was only a simple effect of somnambulism."

"How is it produced?"

"That I cannot say. Perhaps the man is subject to such attacks? But now he's on his legs again and none the worse for it."

Soon the carriage reached the fortifications, entered the town, crossed it obliquely, and stopped in the little square above the wharf.

The doctor and the governor took leave of each other with great cordiality.

"There's the *Ferrato*," said the doctor, pointing to the yacht, which was gracefully riding at her anchor. "You won't forget that you've accepted my invitation to breakfast aboard her on Sunday?"

"No more than you'll forget, Dr. Antekirtt, that you're to dine with me on Sunday evening."

"I shall not fail to be with you!"

They separated; and the governor did not leave the wharf until the gig had started.

And when as they were on their way back Pierre asked the doctor if all had gone as he wished, the reply was, "Yes! On Sunday evening, with the permission of the governor of Ceuta, Carpena will be on board the *Ferrato.*"

At eight o'clock, the steam yacht left her anchorage, proceeded to the north, towards Mount Hacho, the prominent height of this part of the Moorish coast, and soon vanished in the mists of the night.

It was Sarcany and Namir

CHAPTER II

THE DOCTOR'S EXPERIMENT

The passenger who had not been told whither the ship was bound that carried him would hardly guess in what part of the world he had set foot if he landed at Gibraltar.

First there is a quay cut up into little docks for ships to be moored along, then a bastion and a wall with an insignificant gate, then an irregular square bordered by high barracks which rise one behind the other up a hill, then the long narrow, winding thoroughfare known as Main Street.

At the end of this road, which is always sloppy and dirty, among the porters, smugglers, boot-blacks, and sellers of cigar-lights, among the trucks, trolleys, and carts of vegetables and fruits, all on the move there crowds a cosmopolitan mixture of Maltese and Moors, Spaniards and Italians, Arabs and Frenchmen, Portuguese and Germans – a little of everything, in fact, even of citizens of the United Kingdom, who are specially represented by infantrymen in red coats, and artillerymen in blue tunics, with their caps only kept above their ears by a miracle of equilibrium.

Main Street runs right through the town from the Sea Gate to the Alameda Gate. Thence it runs on towards Europe, by the side of many coloured villas and verdant squares, shaded by large trees, through beds of flowers, green parks, batteries of cannons of all designs, and masses of plants of all countries, for a length of four miles and three hundred yards. Such is the rock of Gibraltar, a sort of headless dromedary that crouches on the sands of San Roque, with its tail dragging in the Mediterranean Sea.

This enormous rock is nearly 1400 ft. above the shore of the continent that it menaces with its guns – "the teeth of the old woman," as the Spaniards call them – more than 700 pieces of artillery whose throats stretch forth from the embrasures of its casemates. Twenty thousand inhabitants and 6000 men of the garrison are housed on the lower spurs of the hill, without counting the quadrumana, the famous "monos," the tailless apes, the descendants of the earlier families of the place, the real proprietors of the soil who now occupy the heights of the ancient Calpe. From the summit of the rock the view extends across the straits; the Moorish coast can be seen; the Mediterranean is looked down upon from one side, the Atlantic from the other; and the English telescopes have a range of 124 miles, of which they can keep watch over every foot – and they do keep watch.

If happily the *Ferrato* had arrived two days sooner in the roadstead of Gibraltar, if between the rising and setting of the sun Dr. Antekirtt and Pierre Bathory had landed on the little quay, entered by the Sea Gate, walked along Main Street, passed the Alameda Gate and reached the lovely gardens planted halfway up the hill to the left, perhaps the events reported in this narrative would have advanced more rapidly, and had a different result. For on the afternoon of the 19th of September, on one of the wooden benches under the shade of the trees with their backs turned to the batteries commanding the roadstead, two persons were talking together, and carefully avoiding being overheard by the people around: Sarcany and Namir.

It may be remembered that Sarcany was to rejoin Namir in Sicily when the expedition took place against the Casa degli Inglesi that resulted in Zirone's death. Warned in time, Sarcany changed his plan of campaign, and consequently the doctor waited a week in vain at his moorings off Catania. Acting on the orders she received, Namir immediately left Sicily to return to Tetuan, where she then lived. From Tetuan she returned to Gibraltar, where Sarcany had appointed to meet her. He had arrived the night before, and intended to leave next day.

Sarcany's companion was devoted to him body and soul. She it was who had brought him up in the douars of Tripoli, as if she had been his mother. She had never left him even when he was living as a broker in the Regency, where through his secret acquaintances he became one of the formidable sectaries of Senousism, whose schemes, as we have said above, were being directed against Antekirtta.

Namir in thought and deed treated Sarcany with almost maternal affection, and was even more attached to him than Zirone, the companion of his pleasures and miseries. At a sign from him she would have committed any crime; at a sign from him she would have walked to death without hesitation. Sarcany could thus have absolute confidence in

Namir, and when he sent for her to Gibraltar, it was to talk to her about Carpena, from whom he had now much to fear.

This interview was the first that had taken place between them since Sarcany's arrival at Gibraltar; it was to be the only one, and the conversation was carried on in Arabic.

Sarcany began with a question, and received an answer which both probably regarded as of the utmost importance for their future depended on it.

"Sava?" asked Sarcany.

"She's safe at Tetuan," replied Namir, "and you can feel quite easy concerning her."

"But during your absence?"

"During my absence the house is in the charge of an old Jewess, who won't leave it for an instant! It's like a prison to which nobody goes or can go! Sava doesn't know she's at Tetuan, she doesn't know who I am, and she doesn't even know that she's in your power."

"You always talk to her of the wedding?"

"Yes, Sarcany," replied Namir. "I never allow her to be free from the idea that she's to be your wife – and she will be!"

"She must, Namir, she must; and all the more because Toronthal's money has nearly gone! Gambling does not agree with poor Silas!"

"You've no need of him, Sarcany; without him you can become richer than you've ever been."

"I know it, Namir, but the latest date at which my marriage with Sava must take place is approaching! I must have a voluntary consent on her part, and if she refuses..."

"I'll make her!" replied Namir. "Yes! I'll tear her consent from her! You can trust me, Sarcany!"

And it would be difficult to imagine a more savage, determined looking face than that of the Moor as she thus expressed herself.

"Good, Namir!" answered Sarcany. "Continue to watch her, and I'll soon be with you."

"Do you intend us to leave Tetuan soon?" asked the Moor.

"No, not till I'm obliged, for no one there knows, or can know, Sava! If events oblige me to send you away, you'll get notice in time."

"And now, Sarcany," continued Namir, "Tell me why you've sent for me to Gibraltar?"

"Because I have certain things to say to you that are better said than written."

"Say on, then, Sarcany, and if it's an order I will obey it."

"This is now the position," answered Sarcany. "Madame Bathory has disappeared, and her son is dead. From that family I have nothing further to fear. Madame Toronthal is dead, and Sava is in my power! On that side I'm also safe! Of the others who know my secret, one, Silas Toronthal, my accomplice, is under my thumb, the other, Zirone, died in Sicily. Of all those I've mentioned none can speak, and none will speak."

"What are you afraid of, then?"

"I'm afraid only of the interference of two individuals; one knows a part of my past life, and the other seems to mix himself up with my present more than is convenient."

"One is Carpena?" asked Namir.

"Yes," answered Sarcany, "and the other is that Dr. Antekirtt, whose communications with the Bathory family at Ragusa always seemed to me to be suspicious! Besides, I've heard from Benito, the innkeeper at Santa Grotta, that this personage, who is a millionaire, laid a trap for Zirone by introducing a certain Pescador into his service. If that is so, it was certainly to get possession of him – in default of me – and get my secret out of him!"

"Nothing can be clearer," answered Namir, "than that you should be more careful than ever of Dr. Antekirtt."

"And as much as possible we should know what he's doing, and above all things where he is."

"That isn't easy, Sarcany," answered Namir, "for when I was at Ragusa, for instance, I heard that today he would be at one end of the Mediterranean, and tomorrow at the other."

"Yes! The man seems to have the gift of ubiquity," growled Sarcany. "But it shall not be said that I let him interfere with my game without making a fight for it, and when I go to his home in his island of Antekirtta, I know well..."

"That the wedding will have taken place," answered Namir, "and you'll have nothing to fear from him or anyone."

"That is so, Namir, and till then..."

"Till then we must mind what we're about! One way we shall always have the best of it, for we shall know where he is without his knowing where we are! Now about Carpena, Sarcany; what have you to fear from him?"

"Carpena knows my connection with Zirone! For many years he took part in expeditions in which I had a hand, and he might talk..."

"Agreed, but Carpena is now imprisoned for life at Ceuta."

"And that's what makes me anxious, Namir! Carpena, to improve his position, may say something. If we know he has been sent to Ceuta, others know it as well; others know him personally. There's that Pescador who found him out at Malta. And through that man Dr. Antekirtt may be able to get at him. He can buy his secrets from him! He may even try to help him escape. In fact, Namir, it's all so very obvious that I wonder why it hasn't yet happened."

Sarcany, wide-awake and keen sighted, had thus guessed at the doctor's plans with regard to the Spaniard, and perceived the danger. Namir agreed that there was considerable cause for anxiety.

"Why," said Sarcany, "why didn't we lose him instead of Zirone!"

"But what did not happen in Sicily might happen in Ceuta," said Namir coolly.

That, in short, was what the interview meant. Namir then explained to Sarcany that nothing could be easier than for her to go from Tetuan to Ceuta as often as she liked. It was only twenty miles from one town to the other. Tetuan was a little to the south of the penitentiary colony. As the convicts worked on the roads leading to the town, it would be easy to enter into communication with Carpena, whom she knew, to make him think that Sarcany was anxious for him to escape, and to give him a little money, or even a little extra food. And if it did happen that one of the pieces of bread or fruit was poisoned, who would trouble himself about the death of the convict Carpena? Who would make any inquiries? One scoundrel the less would not seriously inconvenience the Governor of Ceuta! And Sarcany would have nothing further to fear from the Spaniard, nor from the attempts of Dr. Antekirtt to fathom his secrets.

And from this interview it resulted that while one side was busy scheming the escape of Carpena, the other was endeavouring to render it impossible by sending him prematurely to the penal colony in the other world from which there is no escape!

Having agreed on their plans, Sarcany and Namir returned to the town, and separated. That evening Sarcany left Spain to join Silas Toronthal, and the next morning Namir, after crossing the Bay of Gibraltar, embarked at Algesiras on the steamer that runs regularly between Europe and Africa. As she left the harbour the steamer ran past a yacht steaming into the bay.

It was the *Ferrato*. Namir, who had seen her while she lay at Catania, recognized her immediately.

"Dr. Antekirtt here!" she muttered. "Sarcany was right. There is danger, and the danger is close at hand!"

Narnir was on the watch, and had followed all the yacht's manoeuvres

A few hours afterwards the Moor landed at Ceuta. But before returning to Tetuan she had taken steps to enter into communication with the
Spaniard. Her plan was simple and it was almost sure to succeed if she
had sufficient time.

But a complication had arisen which Namir did not expect. Carpena,
owing to the doctor's intervention at his first visit to Ceuta, had been
put on the sick list, and been obliged to go into hospital for some days.
Namir could only loiter round the hospital without being able to get at
him. One thing she contented herself with, and that was that if she
could not see Carpena, neither could the doctor nor his agents. There
was therefore no danger, she thought, and no fear of escape until the
convict got back to his work on the roads. Namir was mistaken. Carpena's entrance into the hospital favoured the doctor's plans, and would
probably bring about their success.

The *Ferrato* anchored on the evening of the 22nd of September in the
Bay of Gibraltar, which is so frequently swept by the easterly and south-
easterly winds. But she was only to remain there during the 23rd. The
doctor and Pierre landed on the Saturday morning, and went for their
letters to the post office in Main Street.

One of these, addressed to the doctor from his Sicilian agent, informed him that since the departure of the *Ferrato* Sarcany had not appeared at Catania, Syracuse, or Messina. Another, addressed to Pierre,
was from Point Pescade, and informed him that he was much better,
and felt none the worse for his wound; that Dr. Antekirtt could command his services as soon as he pleased, in addition to those of Cape
Matifou, who also presented his respects. There was a third letter to
Luigi from Maria. It was more than the letter of a sister – it was the letter of a mother.

If the doctor and Pierre had taken their walk in the gardens of Gibraltar thirty-six hours before, they would have come across Sarcany and
Namir.

The day was spent in coaling the *Ferrato* from the lighters, which carry
the coals from the floating stores moored in the harbour. Freshwater
tanks were also replenished, and everything was in trim when the doctor
and Pierre, who had dined at the hotel in Commercial Square, returned
on board at gunfire.

The *Ferrato* did not weigh anchor that evening. As it would only take
her a couple of hours to cross the Straits, she did not start till eight
o'clock the next morning. Then passing the English batteries, she went
out under full steam towards Ceuta. At half past nine she was under

Mount Hacho, but as the breeze was blowing form the northwest, she could not bring up in the same position she had occupied three days before. The captain therefore took her the other side of the town, and anchored about two cable lengths from the shore in a small well-sheltered creek.

A quarter of an hour later the doctor landed at the wharf. Narnir was on the watch, and had followed all the yacht's manoeuvres. The doctor did not recognize the Moor, whom he had only seen in the shadow of the bazaar at Cattaro. But she had often met him at Gravosa and Ragusa, and recognized him immediately; and she resolved to be more on her guard than ever during his stay at Ceuta.

As he landed, the doctor found the governor and an aide-de-camp waiting for him on the wharf.

"Good morning, my dear friend, and welcome!" said the governor. "You're a man of your word! And now you belong to me for the rest of the day at least..."

"I do not belong to your Excellency until you've been my guest! Don't forget that breakfast is waiting for you on board the *Ferrato*."

"And if it's waiting, Dr. Antekirtt, it would not be polite to keep it waiting any longer."

The gig took the doctor and his guests out to the yacht. The breakfast was luxuriously served, and all did it honour.

During the meal, the conversation chiefly dwelt on the administration of the colony, on the manners and customs of the inhabitants, on the relations which had been established between the Spanish and native populations. Incidentally the doctor was led to speak of the convict whom he had awakened from the magnetic sleep two or three days before on the road into the town.

"He remembers nothing about it, probably?" asked the doctor.

"Nothing," replied the governor, "but he isn't now at work on the roads."

"Where is he, then?" asked the doctor with a certain feeling of anxiety that Pierre was the only one to remark.

"He's in the hospital," answered the governor. "It seems the shock upset his precious health."

"Who is he?"

"A Spaniard named Carpena, a vulgar murderer, not at all interesting, Dr. Antekirtt; and if he happened to die, I can assure you he would be no loss to us!"

Then the conversation took another turn. Doubtless it did not suit the doctor to lay too much stress on the case of the convict, who would be quite recovered after a day or two in hospital.

Breakfast over, coffee was served on deck, and cigars and cigarettes vanished in smoke beneath the awning. Then the doctor suggested going ashore without delay. He now belonged to the governor, and was ready to visit the Spanish colony in all its branches.

The suggestion was accepted, and up to dinnertime the governor devoted himself to doing the honours of the colony to his illustrious visitor. The doctor and Pierre were conscientiously taken all over the place, and did not miss a single detail either in the prisons or the barracks. The day being Sunday, the convicts were not at their ordinary tasks, and the doctor could observe them under different circumstances. Carpena he only saw as they passed through one of the wards in the hospital, and he did not appear to attract his attention.

The doctor intended to leave for Antekirtta that night, but not until he had given the greater part of the evening to the governor, and about six o'clock he returned to the house, where an elegantly served dinner awaited them – the reply to the morning's breakfast.

We need hardly say that during this walk through the colony the doctor was followed by Namir, and was quite unaware that he was so closely watched.

The dinner was a pleasant one. A few of the chief people in the colony, officers and their wives, and two or three rich merchants had been invited, and did not conceal the pleasure they experienced at seeing and hearing Dr. Antekirtt. The doctor spoke of his travels in the East, in Syria, in Arabia, in the north of Africa. Then leading the conversation round to Ceuta, he complimented the governor who administered the Spanish colony with so much ability.

"But," added he, "looking after the convicts must give you a great deal of trouble."

"And why, my dear doctor?"

"Because they must try to escape. And as the prisoner must think more of getting away than the warders think of stopping him, it follows that the advantage is on the side of the prisoner, and I should not be surprised if one is sometimes missing at roll call."

"Never," answered the governor. "Never! Where would the fugitives go? By sea escape is impossible! By land among the savage people of Morocco flight would be dangerous! And so the convicts remain here, if not from pleasure, from prudence!"

Gibraltar

"Well," answered the doctor, "I must congratulate you! For it's to be feared that guarding prisoners will become more and more difficult in the future."

"And why, if you please?" asked one of the guests who was much interested in the conversation owing to his being the director of the penitentiary.

"Because, sir," replied the doctor, "the study of magnetic phenomena has made great progress, because their action can be applied to everything in the world, because the effects of suggestion are becoming more and more frequent and tend so much towards substituting one personality for another."

"And so?" asked the governor.

"And so I think that if it's wise to watch your prisoners, it's just as wise to watch your warders. During my travels I've witnessed some extraordinary things that I would not have believed possible, with regard to these phenomena. And in your own interest do not forget that if a prisoner can unconsciously escape under the influence of a stranger's will, a warder subject to the same influence can none the less unconsciously allow him to escape."

"Will you explain these phenomena to us?" asked the director of the penitentiary.

"Yes, sir, and I'll give an example to make them clear to you. Suppose a warder has a natural disposition to submit to magnetic or hypnotic influence; and admit that a prisoner can exercise such influence over him. Well, from that moment the prisoner has become the warder's master and can do what he likes with him. He can make him go where he pleases, and can make him open the prison doors whenever he likes to suggest the idea to him."

"Doubtless," replied the director, "but on condition that he has first sent him to sleep..."

"That's where you're mistaken," said the doctor. "He can do all these things when he's awake, and yet he'll know nothing about them."

"What, do you mean to say?"

"I mean to say, and I affirm, that under the influence the prisoner can say to the warder, 'On such a day at such an hour you'll do such a thing,' and he will do it. 'On such a day you'll bring me the keys of my cell,' and he'll bring them. 'On such a day you'll open the gate of the prison, and he'll open it. 'On such a day I'll pass by you,' and he won't see him pass."

"Not when he is awake?"

"Quite wide awake!"

At the doctor's affirmation a shrug of incredulity passed round the company.

"Nothing can be truer, nevertheless," said Pierre, "for I myself have seen such things."

"And so," said the governor, "the materiality of one person can be suppressed at the look of another?"

"Entirely," said the doctor, "and in some people in such a way as to cause such changes in their senses that they'll take salt for sugar, milk for vinegar, and wine for physic. Nothing is impossible in the way of illusion or hallucination while the brain is under the influence."

"It seems to me, Dr. Antekirtt," said the governor, "that the general feeling of the company is that those things must be seen to be believed!"

"And more than once!" said one of the guests.

"It's a pity," said the governor, "that the short time you have to give us won't allow you to convince us by an experiment."

"But I can!" replied the doctor.

"Now?"

"Yes, now, if you like!"

"How?"

"Your Excellency has not forgotten that three days ago one of the convicts was found asleep on the road, and I told you that it was a magnetic sleep?"

"Yes," said the director of the penitentiary, "and the man is now in the hospital."

"You remember I awakened him, for none of your warders could."

"Quite so."

"Well, that was enough to create between me and this convict – what is his name?"

"Carpena."

"Between me and Carpena, a bond of suggestion putting him completely in my power."

"When he's in your presence."

"And when we are apart."

"Between you here and him in the hospital?" asked the governor.

"Yes; and if you'll give orders for them to leave the doors open, do you know what he'll do?"

"Run away!" said the governor with a laugh in which all joined.

"No, gentlemen," replied the doctor very seriously, "Carpena won't run away until I wish him to run away, and he'll only do what I want him to do."

"And what's that, if you please?"

"For example, when he gets out of the prison, I can order him to take the road here."

"And will he come here?"

"Into this very room, if I please, and he'll insist on speaking to you."

"To me?"

"To you. And if you like, as he'll have to obey all my suggestions, I'll suggest the idea to him to take you for somebody else – say – for his Majesty Alfonso XII!"

"For his Majesty the King of Spain!"

"Yes, your Excellency, and he'll ask you..."

"To pardon him?"

"Yes, to pardon him, and, if you like, to give him the cross of Isabella into the bargain!"

Shouts of laughter greeted this last assertion.

"And the man wide awake all the time?" asked the director of the penitentiary.

"As wide awake as we are."

"No! No! It's not credible, it's not possible," exclaimed the governor.

"Then try the experiment! Give orders for Carpena to be allowed to do what he likes, and for security have one or two warders follow him at a distance. He shall do all I have just told you."

"Very well, when would you like to begin?"

"It's now eight o'clock," said the doctor, consulting his watch. "At nine o'clock?"

"Be it so; and after the experiment?"

"After the experiment Carpena will go quietly back to the hospital without the slightest remembrance of what has passed. I repeat – and it's the only explanation I can give you of the phenomenon – that Carpena will be under a suggestive influence coming from me, and in reality I shall be doing these things, not Carpena."

The governor, whose incredulity was manifest, wrote a note to the chief warder, directing him to allow Carpena full liberty of action and to follow him from a distance; and the note was immediately dispatched to the hospital.

The dinner at an end, the company at the governor's invitation adjourned to the drawing room.

Naturally the conversation still dwelt on the different phenomena of magnetism or hypnotism, and controversy between the believers and unbelievers grew animated. Dr. Antekirtt, while the cups of coffee circulated amid the smoke of the cigars and cigarettes, which even the Spanish ladies did not despise, related a score of facts of which he had been the witness or the author during the practice of his profession, all to the point, all indisputable, but none of them, seemingly, convincing.

He added also that this faculty of suggestion would give serious trouble to legislators and magistrates, for it could be used for criminal purposes; and cases could arise in which crime could be committed without its being possible to discover its author.

Suddenly, at twenty-seven minutes to nine, the doctor interrupted himself, and said:

"Carpena is now leaving the hospital!"

And a minute afterwards he added:

"He's just passed through the gate of the penitentiary!"

The tone with which the words were pronounced had a strange effect on those around him. The governor alone continued to shake his head.

Then the conversation for and against began again, each one saying but little at a time, until – at five minutes to nine – the doctor interrupted them for the last time:

"Carpena is at the front door."

Almost immediately afterwards one of the servants entered the drawing room and told the governor that a man dressed like a convict was waiting below and insisted on seeing him.

"Let him come in!" replied the governor, whose incredulity began to vanish in face of the facts.

As nine o'clock struck, Carpena appeared at the door of the drawing room. Without appearing to see any of those present, although his eyes were wide open, he walked up to the governor, and, kneeling before him, said:

"Sire, I ask you to pardon me."

The governor, absolutely dumfounded, as if he himself was under an hallucination, knew not what to say.

"You can pardon him," said the doctor with a smile, "he'll have no recollection of all this!"

"I grant you your pardon!" said the governor with all the dignity of the King of all the Spains.

"And to that pardon, sire," said Carpena, still bending low, "will you add the cross of Isabella?"

"I give it you!"

And then Carpena made as though to take something from the governor's hand and attach the imaginary cross to his breast. Then he rose, and walking backwards quitted the room.

This time the whole company followed him to the front door.

"I'll go with him, I'll see him go back to the hospital," said the governor, struggling with himself as if loath to yield to the evidence of his senses.

"Come, then!" said the doctor.

And the governor, Pierre Bathory, Dr. Antekirtt, and the rest followed after Carpena as he went along the road towards the town. Namir, who had watched him since he left the penitentiary, glided along in the shadow and continued to watch.

The night was rather dark. The Spaniard walked along at a regular pace with no hesitation in his stride. The governor and his guests were twenty paces behind him with the two warders who had received orders to keep him in sight.

The road as it approaches the town bends round a small creek, forming the second harbour on that side of the rock. The reflections of two or three lights flickered on the black motionless water. They came from the ports and lanterns of the *Ferrato*, whose hull loomed large in the darkness.

As he reached this spot Carpena left the road and inclined to the right towards a heap of rocks which rose from the shore a dozen feet away. Doubtless a gesture from the doctor, unseen by anyone – perhaps a simple suggestion of his will – had obliged the Spaniard to leave the path.

The warders prepared to close up so as to send him back; but the governor, knowing that no escape from that side was possible, ordered them to leave him to himself.

However, Carpena halted on one of the rocks as if he had been struck motionless and fixed there by some irresistible power. He tried to lift his feet, to move his arms, but he could not. The doctor's will within him nailed him to the ground.

The governor looked at him for a minute or so. Then he said to his guest:

"Well, doctor, whether he's awake or not, we must give in to the evidence!"

"You're convinced, quite convinced?"

Carpena kneeled before the governor

"Yes, quite convinced that there are things we must believe in like the brutes! Now, Dr. Antekirtt, suggest to him to go back to the penitentiary! Alfonso XII commands it!"

The governor had hardly finished the sentence before Carpena, without uttering a sound, threw himself into the water. Was it an accident? Was it a voluntary act on his part? Had some fortuitous circumstance intervened to snatch him out of the doctor's power? No one could say.

Immediately there was a general rush to the rocks, and the warders ran on to the beach. There was no trace of Carpena. Some fishing boats came up, as did the boats from the yacht. All was useless. They did not even find the corpse, which the current would carry out to sea.

"I'm very sorry, your Excellency," said the doctor, "that our experiment has had so tragically an end, which it was impossible to anticipate."

"But how do you account for it?" asked the governor.

"The exercise of this suggestive power, of which you cannot deny the effects, there are intermittences. That man escaped me for an instant, and either from his being seized with vertigo or some other cause he fell off the rocks! It's a great pity, for we've lost such a splendid specimen!"

"We've lost a scamp – nothing more!" said the governor philosophically.

And that was Carpena's funeral oration!

The doctor and Pierre then took leave of the governor. They had to start before daybreak for Antekirtta, and they were profuse in their thanks to their host for the hospitable welcome he had given them in the Spanish colony.

The governor shook the doctor's hand, wished him a pleasant journey, and after promising to come and see him, returned to his house.

Perhaps it may be said that Dr. Antekirtt had somewhat abused the good faith of the Governor of Ceuta. His conduct under the circumstances is certainly open to criticism. But we should not forget the work to which Count Sandorf had consecrated his life. "A thousand roads – one end!" And this was one of the thousand roads he had to travel.

A few minutes afterwards one of the boats of the *Ferrato* had taken them on board. Luigi was waiting for them as they came up the side.

"That man?" asked the doctor.

"According to your orders," said Luigi, "our boat was near the rocks and picked him up after his fall, he's under lock and key in the fore cabin."

"He's said nothing?" asked Pierre.

"How could he say anything? He seems asleep and unconscious of his acts."

"Good," answered the doctor. "I willed that Carpena should fall from those rocks, and he fell! I willed that he should sleep, and he sleeps! When I will that he wakes, he shall wake! And now, Luigi, up anchor and away!"

The steam was up, and a few minutes afterwards the *Ferrato* was off, heading out to sea straight for Antekirtta.

CHAPTER III

SEVENTEEN TIMES

"Seventeen times?"

"Seventeen times!"

"Yes, the red has passed seventeen times!"

"Is it possible?"

"It may be impossible, but it is!"

"And the players are mad against it?"

"More than 900,000 francs won by the bank!"

"Seventeen times! Seventeen times!"

"At roulette or trente-et-quarante?"

"At trente-et-quarante."

"It's fifteen years since anything like it!"

"Fifteen years, three months, and fourteen hours," coolly replied an old gambler belonging to the honourable class of the ruined. "Yes, sir, and a very strange thing – it was in the height of summer on the 16th of June, 1867 – I know something about it!"

Such was the conversation, or rather the chorus of exclamation heard in the vestibule and peristyle of the Cercle des Etrangers at Monte Carlo, on the evening of the 3rd of October, eight days after the escape of Carpena from the Spanish penitentiary.

Among the crowd of gamblers – men and women of all nations, ages, and classes – there was quite an uproar of enthusiasm. They would willingly have greeted the red as the equal of the horse that had carried off the Epsom Derby or the Longchamps Grand Prix. In fact, for the people that the Old and New Worlds daily pour into the little principality of Monaco, this series of seventeen had quite the importance of a political event affecting the laws and equilibrium of Europe.

It will easily be believed that the red in its somewhat extraordinary obstinacy had made a good many victims, and that the winnings of the bank had been considerable. Nearly a million francs, said some – which meant that nearly the whole of the players had become infuriated at the extraordinary series of passes.

Between them, two foreigners had paid a large part of what these gentlemen of the board of green cloth the "déveine" – one, very cool, very self-restrained, although the emotions within him were traceable in his pallid face; the other with his features distorted, his hair in disorder, his look that of a madman or a desperado – and these had just descended the steps of the peristyle, and were strolling out under the trees on the terrace.

"That makes more than 400,000 francs that the cursed series has cost us," said the eldest.

"You may as well say 413,000," said the younger in the tone of a cashier casting a column.

"And now I've only got 200,000 – and hardly that," said the first gambler.

"One hundred and ninety-seven thousand," said the other in the same tone.

"Yes! Of nearly two millions that I once had, when you made me come with you!"

"One million seven hundred and seventy-five thousand francs!"

"And that in less than two months!"

"In one month and sixteen days!"

"Sarcany!" exclaimed the eldest, whom his companion's coolness seemed to exasperate as much as the ironical precision with which he rolled out the ciphers.

"Well, Silas?"

Toronthal and Sarcany were the speakers. Since leaving Ragusa, in the short space of three months they had reached the verge of ruin. After dissipating all that they had received as the reward of their abominable treachery, Sarcany had hunted his accomplice out of Ragusa, taking Sava with them, and then had enticed him into gambling and every dissipation in which he could squander his wealth. It is only just, however, to say that the old banker, daring speculator as he was, had in times gone by more than once risked his fortune in hazardous adventures in which luck was his only guide.

How could Toronthal resist? Was he not more than ever in the power of the Tripolitan broker? Sometimes he revolted, but Sarcany had obtained an irresistible ascendancy over him, and the wretched man fell so heavily that strength almost failed him to rise again, so that Sarcany was not at all uneasy about the occasional fancies that Toronthal had to withdraw himself from his influence. The brutality of his retorts and the implacability of his logic soon brought Toronthal back beneath the yoke.

In leaving Ragusa under circumstances, which will not have been forgotten, their first care had been to put Sava in some safe place under the charge of Namir. And now in this retreat at Tetuan, on the borders of Morocco, it would have been difficult, if not impossible, to find her. There Sarcany's pitiless companion undertook to break down the girl's resolution, and tear from her her consent to the marriage. Unshaken in her repulsion and strengthened by the recollection of Pierre, Sava hitherto had obstinately resisted. But could she always do so?

In the meantime Sarcany never ceased from exciting his companion to plunge into the follies of the gaming table, although he had lost his own fortune in a similar way. In France, in Italy, in Germany, in the great centres where chance keeps house in all its forms, on the Exchange, on the race course, in the clubs of the great capitals, in the watering places as in the seaside towns, Silas Toronthal had followed as Sarcany led, and had soon been reduced to a few hundred thousands of francs. While the banker risked his own money, Sarcany risked the banker's, and down this double slope both went to ruin at double quick time. What gamblers call the "déveine" had been dead against them, and it was not for want of trying every chance that offered. In short their amusement cost them the best part of the millions received from the possessions of Count Sandorf, and it had even become necessary to offer for sale the house in the Stradone at Ragusa.

And so they had been at Monte Carlo for the last three weeks, never leaving the tables of the club, trying the most infallible dodges, working out schemes that always went awry, studying the rotation of the cylinder of the roulette when the croupier's hand was tiring during his last quarter hour of duty, loading to the maximum numbers which obstinately refused to come, combining simple combinations with multiple combinations, listening to the advice of ruined old stagers and becoming professional gamblers, trying in fact every imbecile device, and employing every stupid fetish that could class the gambler between the child who has no reason and the idiot who has forever lost it. And not only did they risk their money, but they enfeebled their intelligence by imagining absurd combinations; and they compromised their personal dignity by the familiarity which the frequenting of the very mixed assembly imposed upon all. In short at the close of this evening, which would hereafter be celebrated in the annals of Monte Carlo, owing to their obsti-

Carpena halted on one of the rocks as if he had been struck motionless

nacy in struggling against a series of seventeen rouges at trente-et-quarante, they had left off with less than 200,000 francs between them.

But if they had nearly lost their fortunes, they had not yet lost their senses, like the gambler who had become suddenly deranged while they were talking on the terrace, and who was running through the gardens shouting: "It turns! It turns!"

The unfortunate man imagined that he had just put his money on the coming number, and that the cylinder in a movement of fantastic gyration was turning, and doomed to turn for ages! He had gone mad for the rest of his life!

"Have you become calmer, Silas?" asked Sarcany of his companion. "Doesn't that lunatic teach you to keep cool? We haven't won, it's true, but our luck will turn, it must turn, and without our doing anything to make it. Why try to better it? It's dangerous, and besides, it's useless! You cannot change the 'veine' if it's bad, and you would not change it when it's good! Wait then, and when the luck turns, let us be bold and make our game while the 'veine' lasts."

Did Toronthal listen to this advice – absurd as is all advice connected with games of chance? No! He was overwhelmed, and he had then but one idea – to escape from this domination of Sarcany, to get away, and to get away so far that his conscience could not reproach him! But such a fit of resolution could not last long in his enervated, helpless nature. Besides, he was watched by his accomplice. Sarcany would not leave him until the marriage to Sava had taken place. Then he would get rid of Silas Toronthal, he would forget him, and he would not even remember that that feeble individual had ever existed, or that he had ever been associated with him in any enterprise whatever! Until then it was necessary for the banker to remain under his thumb!

"Silas," continued Sarcany, "we've been unfortunate today; chance was against us. Tomorrow, it will be for us!"

"And if I lose the little that's left?" answered Toronthal, who struggled in vain against these deplorable suggestions.

"There's still Sava, Toronthal!" answered Sarcany quickly. "She's our ace of trumps, and you cannot overtrump her!"

"Yes! Tomorrow! Tomorrow!" said the banker, who was just in that mental condition in which a gambler would risk his head.

The two then entered their hotel, which was situated halfway down the road from Monte Carlo to La Condamine.

The port of Monaco lies between Point Focinana and Fort Antoine, and is an open bay exposed to the northeast and southeast winds. It rounds off between the rock on which stands the capital and the plateau on which are the hotels and villas, at the foot of the superb Mont Agel whose summit rising to 3600 feet towers boldly above the picturesque panorama of the Ligurian coast. The town has a population of some 1200 inhabitants, and is situated on the rock of Monaco, surrounded on three of its sides by the sea. It lies hidden beneath the never fading verdure of palms, pomegranates, sycamores, pear trees, orange trees, citron trees, eucalyptuses, and arborescent bushes of geraniums, aloes, myrtles, lentisks, and palma christies, heaped all over the place in marvellous confusion.

At the other side of the harbour Monte Carlo faces the tiny capital with its curious pile of houses built on all the ledges, and its zigzags of narrow climbing roads running up to the Corniche suspending in mid-mountain its chessboard of gardens in perpetual bloom, its panorama of cottages of every shape, its villas of every style, of which some seem actually to hang over the limpid waters of this Mediterranean bay.

Between Monaco and Monte Carlo, at the back of the harbour from the beach up to the throat of the winding valley which divides the group of mountains is a third city – La Condamine.

Above to the right rises a large mountain, whose profile turned towards the sea has gained it the name of the Dog's Head. On this head there is now a fort, which is said to be impregnable, and which has the honour to be French, for it marks the limit on that side of the Principality of Monaco.

From La Condamine to Monte Carlo vehicles have to ascend a superb hill, at the upper end of which are the private houses and the hotels in one of which Toronthal and Sarcany were now staying. From the windows of their apartment the view extended from La Condamine to beyond Monaco, and was only shut in by the Dog's Head, which seemed to be interrogating the Mediterranean as the Sphinx does the Libyan Desert.

Sarcany and Toronthal had retired to their rooms. There they examined the situation, each from his own point of view. Had the vicissitudes of fortune broken the community of interests, which for fifteen years had bound them so closely together?

Sarcany when he entered had found a letter addressed to him. It came from Tetuan, and he hastily tore it open.

In a few lines Namir told him of two things that interested him deeply. The first was the death of Carpena, drowned in the harbour of Ceuta under such extraordinary circumstances; the second was the ap-

378

pearance of Dr. Antekirtt on the Moorish coast, the way in which he had dealt with the Spaniard, and then his immediate disappearance.

Having read the letter, Sarcany opened the window. Leaning on the balcony he looked out into space and set himself to think.

"Carpena dead? Nothing could be more opportune! Now his secrets are drowned with him! Nothing more to fear there!"

Then coming to the second passage of his letter, "As to the appearance of Dr. Antekirtt at Ceuta that's more serious! Who is this man? It wouldn't matter much after all, if I hadn't found him for some time more or less mixed up in my concerns! At Ragusa his interviews with the Bathory family! At Catania, the trap he laid for Zirone! At Ceuta, this interference which has cost the life of Carpena! Then he's very near Tetuan, but it doesn't seem that he's gone there, nor that he's discovered Sava's retreat. That would be the most terrible blow, and it may yet come! We shall see if we cannot keep him off, not only in the future, but in the present. The Senousists will soon be masters of all the Cyrenaic, and there's only an arm of the sea to cross to get at Antekirtta! If they must be urged on – I know well..."

It was evident Sarcany's horizon was not without its black spots. In the dark schemes, which he followed out step by step in pursuit of the object he had set himself and which he had almost attained, he might stumble over the very smallest stone in his path and perhaps never get up again. Not only was this intervention of Dr. Antekirtt enough to unsettle him, but Toronthal's position was also beginning to cause him anxiety.

"Yes," he said to himself, "we're in a corner! Tomorrow we must stake everything! Either the bank goes, or we go! If I'm ruined by his ruin I know how to recoup myself! But for Silas it's different! He may become dangerous, he may talk, he may let out the secret on which all my future rests! I've been his master up to now, but he may become my master!"

The position was exactly as Sarcany had described it. He was under no mistake as to the moral courage of his accomplice. He had had his lesson before: Silas Toronthal, when he had nothing to lose, would only use him to make money out of him.

Sarcany pondered over what was best to be done. Absorbed in his reflections, he did not see what was happening at the entrance to the harbour of Monaco a few hundred feet beneath him

About half a cable-length away a long hull without mast or funnel came gliding through the waves. Altogether, it did not show for more

And now I've only got 200,000 francs

than three feet above the water level. Soon after, gradually nearing Point Focinana, it slipped into smoother water near the beach. Then there shot off from it a little boat, which had appeared like an incrustation on the side of the almost invisible hull. Three men were in the boat. In a few strokes of the sculls they reached the shore, two of them landed, and the third took back the boat. A few minutes afterwards the mysterious craft, which had not betrayed its presence, either by light or sound, was lost in the darkness and had left no trace of its passage.

The two men as soon as they had left the beach went along by the edge of the rocks towards the railway station, and then up the Avenue des Spelugues, which runs round the gardens of Monte Carlo.

Sarcany had seen nothing of this. His thoughts were far away from Monaco – at Tetuan. But he would not go there alone; he would compel his accomplice to go with him.

"Silas, my master!" he repeated. "Silas being able to checkmate me with a word! Never! If tomorrow luck does not give us back what it's taken away from us, I shall be obliged to make him follow me to Tetuan, and there on the coast of Morocco if Silas Toronthal gives trouble, Silas Toronthal will disappear!"

As we know, Sarcany was not the man to recoil at one crime more, particularly when circumstances, the distance of the country, the wildness of the inhabitants, and the impossibility of seeking and finding the criminal, rendered its accomplishment so easy.

Having decided on his plans, Sarcany shut the window, went to bed, and was soon asleep without being in the least troubled by his conscience.

It was not so with Toronthal. He passed a horrible night. Of his former fortune what had he left? Hardly 200,000 francs – and these were to be squandered in play. It was the last throw! So his accomplice wished, and so he himself wished. His enfeebled brain, filled with chimerical calculations, was no longer able to reason coolly nor justly. He was even incapable – at this moment at least – of understanding his real position with regard to Sarcany. He could not see that the parts had shifted, and that he who held him in his power was now in his power. He only saw the present with its immediate ruin, and only dreamt of the morrow, which might float him again or plunge him into the depths of misery.

Thus passed the night for the two associates. One was permitted to spend it in repose, the other to struggle with all the anguish of insomnia.

In the morning about ten o'clock Sarcany joined Toronthal. The banker was seated before a table, covering the pages of his notebook with figures and formulae.

"Well, Silas," said he in a careless tone – the tone of a man who would not assign more importance to the world's miseries than he could help: "well, Silas, did you give preference to red or black in your dreams?"

"I did not sleep a wink!" replied the banker.

"So much the worse, Silas, so much the worse. Today you must be cool, and a few hours of repose were what you wanted. Look at me! I've had a little, and I'm in capital condition to struggle with fortune! She's a woman after all, and she loves best the men who can command her."

"She's betrayed us all the same!"

"Bah! Merely caprice! The caprice will pass, and she'll soon smile upon us!"

Toronthal made no reply. Did he even understand what Sarcany had said to him, while his eyes were fixed on the pages of his notebook and the useless combinations?

"What are you doing there?" asked Sarcany. "Tips? Diddles? Tut-tut! You're ill, Silas! You can't mix luck with mathematics, it's luck alone we want today!"

"Be it so!" said Toronthal, shutting up his book. "Eh! Of course, Silas! I only know one way to go to work," said Sarcany ironically. "But to do that we must have made special studies – and our education has been neglected on that point! Then stick to chance! She stuck to the bank yesterday! She may desert it today! And if she does, she'll give back all she took!"

"All!"

"Yes, all, Silas! But don't be cast down! Cheer up and keep cool!"

"And tonight if we're ruined?" asked the banker, looking straight at Sarcany.

"Well, we'll clear out of Monaco!"

"Where to?" exclaimed Toronthal. "Cursed be the day I knew you, Sarcany! Cursed be the day I employed you! I should never have been where I am if it had not been for you!"

"It's too late to abuse me, my dear fellow, and it's not quite the thing to quarrel with people who are going to help you!"

"Be careful!" said the banker.

"I am careful!" said Sarcany.

And Toronthal's threat confirmed him in his scheme.

"My dear Silas," he continued, "do not worry yourself! Why should you? It excites your nerves, and you must not be nervous today! Have confidence, and don't despair about me! If unfortunately the déveine goes against us, think of the other millions waiting for me, in which you'll share."

"Yes! Yes! I must have my revenge!" said Toronthal with the gambler's instinct. "The bank was too lucky yesterday – and tonight..."

"Tonight we shall be rich, very rich," said Sarcany. "And I engage that we shall get back all we've lost! And then we shall leave Monte Carlo! And start for..."

"For where?"

"For Tetuan, where we've another part to play! And that a far better one!"

Monte Carlo: The Casino

CHAPTER IV

THE LAST GAME

The saloon of the Cercle des Etrangers otherwise the Casino – had been open since eleven o'clock. The number of players was still few, but some of the roulette tables were already in operation.

The equilibrium of these tables had previously been rectified, it being important that their horizontality should be perfect. In fact the slightest flaw affecting the movement of the ball thrown into the turning cylinder would be remarked and utilized to the detriment of the bank.

At each of the six tables of roulette 16,000 francs in gold, silver, and notes had been placed; on each of the two tables of trente-et-quarante, 10,000. This is the usual stake of the bank during the season, and it is very seldom that the administration has to replenish the starting fund. Except with a drawn game or a zero the bank must win – and it always wins. The game is immoral in itself, but it is more than that, it is stupid, for its conditions are unfair.

Round each of the roulette tables are eight croupiers, rake in hand, occupying the places reserved for them. By their side, sitting or standing, are the players and spectators. In the saloons the inspectors stroll to and fro, watching the croupiers and the players, while the waiters move about for the service of the public and the administration, which employs not less than 150 people to look after the tables.

About half-past twelve the train from Nice brings its customary contingent. Today they were perhaps rather numerous. The series of seventeen for the rouge had produced its natural result. It was a new attraction, and all who worshipped chance came to follow its vicissitudes with increased ardour.

An hour afterwards the rooms had filled. The talk was chiefly of that extraordinary run, but it was carried on in subdued voices. In these immense rooms with their prodigality of gilding, their wealth of ornamentation, the luxury of their furniture, the profusion of the lustres that poured forth their floods of gaslight, to say nothing of the long suspenders from which the green-shaded oil lamps more specially illuminated the gaming tables, the dominating sound, notwithstanding the crowd of visitors, was not that of conversation; it was the clatter and chinking of the gold and silver pieces as they were counted or thrown on the table, the rustling of the bank-notes, and the incessant "Rouge gagne et couleur," or "Dixsept, noir, impair et manque," in the indifferent voices of the chiefs of the parties – and a very sad sound it was!

Two of the losers who had been amongst the most prominent the evening before had not yet appeared in the saloons. Already some of the players were following the different chances endeavouring to tap the veine of luck, some at roulette, others at trente-et-quarante. But the alternations of gain and loss seemed to be pretty equal, and it did not look as though the phenomenon of the night before would be repeated.

It was not till three o'clock that Sarcany and Toronthal entered the Casino. Before entering the gaming room they took a stroll in the hall, where they were the object of a little public curiosity. The crowd looked at them and watched them, and wondered if they would again try a struggle with this chance that had cost them so dear. Several of the profession would willingly have taken advantage of the occasion to favour them with infallible dodges – for a consideration – had they been more accessible. The banker with a wild look in his eyes did not seem to notice what was passing around him. Sarcany was cooler and firmer than ever. Both shrank for a time from trying their last stake.

Among the people who were watching them with that special curiosity accorded chiefly to patients or convicts, there was one stranger who seemed resolved never to lose sight of them. He was a knowing looking young man of about three-and-twenty with a thin face and pointed nose – one of those noses that seem to look at you. His eyes, of singular vivacity, were sheltered behind spectacles merely of preserver glass. As if he had live money in his veins, he kept his hands in his coat pockets to prevent their gesticulating, and he kept his feet close together in the first position, to make sure of remaining in his place. He was fashionably dressed, without any sacrifices to the latest exigencies of dandyism, and he gave himself no airs – but probably felt very ill at ease in his well-fitting clothes. For the young man – there could be no doubt – was nobody else but Point Pescade!

Outside, in the gardens, Cape Matifou was in attendance. The person on whose behalf these two had come on a special mission to this heaven or hell of Monte Carlo was Dr. Antekirtt.

The vessel that had dropped them the night before at Monte Carlo point was *Electric No. 2*, of the flotilla of Antekirtta, and this was their object:

Two days after the kidnapping on board the *Ferrato*, Carpena had been brought ashore, and in spite of his protests, imprisoned in one of the casemates on the island. There he found that he had only changed one prison for another. Instead of being in the penitentiary of Ceuta, he was, although he knew it not, in the power of Dr. Antekirtt. Where was he? He could not tell. Had he gained by the change? He wondered much and not without anxiety. He resolved at any rate to do all he could to improve his position.

And to the first question propounded by the doctor he replied with the utmost frankness.

Did he know Silas Toronthal and Sarcany?

Toronthal, no, Sarcany, yes — but he had only seen him at rare intervals.

Had Sarcany been in communication with Zirone and his band while they were in the neighbourhood of Catania?

Yes, Sarcany was expected in Sicily, and he would certainly have come, if it had not been for the unfortunate expedition, which ended in the death of Zirone.

Where was he now?

At Monte Carlo, at least unless he had left that town, where he had been living for some time, and very likely with Silas Toronthal.

Carpena knew no more. But what he had just told the doctor was sufficient information for a fresh campaign.

Of course the Spaniard did not know what object the doctor had in helping him to escape from Ceuta and carrying him off; he did not know that his treachery to Andrea Ferrato was known to him who interrogated him; and he did not know that Luigi was the son of the fisherman of Rovigno. In his casemate he was as strictly guarded as he had been in the penitentiary at Ceuta without being able to communicate with any one until his fate had been decided.

One, then, of the three traitors who had brought about the sanguinary collapse of the conspiracy of Trieste was in the hands of the doctor. There were the other two still to be seized, and Carpena had just told where they could be found.

As the doctor was known to Toronthal, and Pierre was known to Toronthal and Sarcany, it seemed best for them not to appear until they could do so with some chance of success. But now they were on the

Monte Carlo

track of the accomplices it was important not to lose sight of them until circumstances favoured the attack. And so Point Pescade, to follow them wherever they went, and Cape Matifou, to lend the strong hand when needed, were sent to Monaco, where the doctor, Pierre and Luigi would come in the *Ferrato* as soon as they were wanted.

As soon as they arrived they set to work. They had no difficulty in discovering the hotel in which Toronthal and Sarcany had taken up their quarters. While Cape Matifou walked about the neighbourhood till the evening, Point Pescade kept watch. He saw the two friends come out at about one o'clock in the afternoon. It seemed that the banker was much depressed and spoke little, while Sarcany was particularly lively. During the morning Pescade had heard what had happened the previous evening in the saloons of the Cercle, that is to say, of that extraordinary series which had made so many victims, among the chief of whom were Toronthal and Sarcany. He therefore assumed that their conversation was about that curious piece of bad luck. In addition he had learnt how these two men had been heavy losers for some time, and he also assumed that they had almost exhausted their funds, and that the time was coming when the doctor could usefully intervene.

This information was contained in a telegram, which Pescade, without mentioning names, sent off during the morning to Malta, whence it was forwarded by the private wire to Antekirtta.

When Sarcany and Toronthal entered the hall of the Casino, Pescade followed them; and when they entered the gaming saloons he was close behind.

It was then three o'clock in the afternoon. The play was growing animated. The banker and his companion first strolled round the rooms. For a minute or so they stopped at different tables and watched the game but took no part in it.

Point Pescade strolled about among the spectators, but did not lose sight of them. He even thought it best, so as to disarm suspicion, to risk a few five franc pieces on the columns and dozens of roulette, and, as was proper, he lost them – with the most exemplary coolness. But he did not avail himself of the excellent advice given him in confidence by a professor of great merit.

"To succeed, sir, you should study to lose the small stakes and win the big ones! That's the secret!"

Four o'clock struck, Sarcany and Toronthal thought the time had come for them to try their luck. There were several vacant places at one of the roulette tables. They seated themselves facing each other, and the chief of the table soon saw himself surrounded not only by players, but by spectators eager to assist at the revenge of the famous losers of the previous night. Quite naturally Pescade found himself in the front rank of the spectators, and he was not one of those least interested in the vicissitudes of the battle.

For the first hour the chances seemed about equal. To divide them better Toronthal and Sarcany played independently of each other. They staked separately, and won a few large amounts, sometimes on simple combinations, sometimes on multiple combinations, and sometimes on many combinations at once. Luck decided neither for or against them. But between four and six o'clock it seemed to be running in their favour. At roulette the maximum is 6000 francs, and this they gained several times on full numbers.

Toronthal's hands shook as he stretched them across the table to stake his money, or as he snatched from under the rake the gold and notes of the croupiers. Sarcany was quite at his ease, and his countenance gave no sign of his emotions. He contented himself with encouraging his companion with his looks, and it was Toronthal whom chance then followed with most constancy.

Point Pescade, although rather dazzled by the constant movement of the gold and notes, kept close watch on them, and wondered if they would be prudent enough to keep the wealth, which was growing under their hands, and if they would stop in time. Then the thought occurred to him that if they had that good sense – which he doubted – they would leave Monte Carlo and fly to some other corner of Europe, where he would have to follow them. If money did not fail them they would not fall so easily into the power of Dr. Antekirtt.

"Certainly," he thought, "in every way it'll be better for them to get ruined, and I'm very much mistaken if that scoundrel Sarcany is the man to stop once he's in the swim!"

Whatever were Pescade's thoughts and fears luck did not abandon the two friends. Three times in fact they would have broken the bank, if the chief of the table had not thrown in an additional 20,000 francs.

The strife was quite an event among the spectators, the majority of whom were in favour of the players. Was not this in revenge for the insolent series of rouge by which the administration had so largely profited during the previous evening?

At half-past six, when they suspended their play, Toronthal and Sarcany had realized more than 20,000 louis. They rose and left the roulette table. Toronthal walked with uncertain step, as if he were slightly intoxicated, intoxicated with emotion and cerebral fatigue. His companion, impassable as ever, watched him, thinking if he would be tempted to escape with the money he had won, and withdraw himself from his influence.

Without a word they passed through the hall, descended the peristyle, and walked towards their hotel.

Pescade followed them at a distance.

As he came out he saw Cape Matifou seated on a bench near one of the kiosks in the garden.

Point Pescade stepped up to him.

"Has the time come?" asked Matifou.

"What time?"

"To – to..."

"To come on the stage? No! Not yet! You must wait at the wings! Have you had your dinner?"

"My compliments to you! My stomach is in my heels – and that's not the place for a stomach! But I'll get it up again if I have time! Do not move from here till I get back!"

And Pescade rushed off down the hill after Toronthal and Sarcany.

When he found that they were at dinner in their rooms he sat down at the table d'hôte. He was only just in time and in half an hour, as he said, he had brought his stomach back to the normal place that that organ occupies in the human machine.

Then he went out with a capital cigar in his mouth and took up his position opposite the hotel.

"Assuredly," he said to himself, "I must have been made to be a policeman! I've mistaken my profession!"

The question he then asked himself was: Were these gentlemen going back to the Casino this evening?

About eight o'clock they appeared at the hotel door. Pescade saw and heard that they were in eager discussion.

Apparently the banker was trying to resist once more the entreaties and injunctions of his accomplice, for Sarcany in an imperious voice was heard to say:

"You must, Silas! I will have it so!"

They walked up the hill to the gardens of Monte Carlo. Point Pescade followed them, without being able to overhear the rest of their conversation – much to his regret.

But this is what Sarcany was saying, in a tone, which admitted of no reply, to the banker whose resistance was growing feebler every minute.

Point Pescade followed them at a distance

"To stop, Silas, when luck is with us is madness! You must have lost your head! In the 'déveine' we faced our game like fools, and in the 'veine' we must face it like wise men. We have an opportunity, the only one perhaps, an opportunity that may never occur again, to be masters of our fate, masters of fortune, and by our own fault we shall let it escape us! Silas, do you not feel that luck..."

"If it's not exhausted," said Toronthal.

"No! A hundred times, no!" replied Sarcany. "It cannot be explained, but it can be felt, and it thrills the bones! A million is waiting for us tonight on the Casino tables. Yes, a million, and I will not let it slip!"

"You play, then, Sarcany."

"Me! Play alone? No?! Play with you, Silas? Yes! And if we have to choose between us I'll yield my place to you. The 'veine' is personal, and it is manifest that to you it has returned. Play on then and win!"

In fact what Sarcany wished was that Toronthal should not be content with the few hundred thousand francs that would allow him to escape from his power; but that he would either become the millionaire he had been or be reduced to nothing. Rich, he would continue his former life. Ruined, he would have to follow Sarcany where he pleased. In either case, he would be unable to injure him.

Resist as he might Toronthal felt all the passions of the gambler rising within him. In the miserable abasement into which he had fallen he felt afraid to go, and at the same time longed to go back to the tables. Sarcany's words set his blood on fire. Visibly luck had declared in his favour, and during the last few hours with such constancy that it would be unpardonable to stop.

The madman! Like all gamblers he spoke in the present when he should have spoken only in the past! In stead of saying, "I've been lucky" – which was true – he said, "I am lucky" – which was false. And in his brain, as in that of all who trust to chance, there was no other reasoning! They forget what was recently said by one of the greatest mathematicians of France, "Chance has its caprices; it has not its customs."

Sarcany and Toronthal walked on to the Casino followed by Pescade. There they stopped for a moment.

"Silas!" said Sarcany, "no hesitation! You've resolved to play, have you not?"

"Yes! Resolved to risk everything for everything!" replied the banker in whom all hesitation had ceased when he found himself on the steps of the peristyle.

"It's not for me to influence you!" continued Sarcany. "Trust to your own inspiration, not to mine! It won't lead you astray. Are you going for roulette?"

"No – trente-et-quarante!" said Toronthal as he entered the hall.

"You're right, Silas! Listen only to yourself. Roulette has almost given you a fortune! Trente-et-quarante will do the rest!"

They entered the saloons, and walked round them. Ten minutes afterwards Pescade saw them seat themselves at one of the trente-et-quarante tables.

There in fact they could play more boldly, for if the chances of the game are simple, the maximum is 12,000 francs, and a few passes can give considerable differences in gain or loss. Hence it is the favourite game with desperate players, and at it wealth and poverty can be made with a vertiginous rapidity sufficient to raise the envy of all the Stock Exchanges of the world.

Toronthal lost his fear as soon as he was seated at the trente-et-quarante table. There was no timidity now about his play; he staked his money like a madman. And Sarcany watched his every movement, deeply interested in this supreme crisis, deeply interested in the issue.

For the first hour the alternations of loss and gain almost balanced each other, the advantage being on Toronthal's side. Sarcany and he imagined they were sure of success. They grew excited, and staked higher and higher until they staked only the maximum. But soon the luck returned to the imperturbable bank which by this maximum protects its interests in no inconsiderable measure, and which knows no transports of folly.

Then came blow after blow. The winnings during the afternoon went heap by heap. Toronthal was an awful spectacle; his face became congested, his eyes grew haggard, he clung with the twitchings and convulsions of a drowning man to the table, to his chair, to the rolls of notes, and the rouleaux of gold that his hand would hardly yield over! And no one was there to stop him on the brink of the chasm! Not a hand was stretched out to help him! Not an effort from Sarcany to tear him from the place before he was lost, before he finally sank beneath the wave of ruin!

At ten o'clock Toronthal had risked his last stake, his last maximum. He won! Then he staked again — and again – and lost. And when he rose, dazed and scared and fiercely wishing that the very walls would crumble and crush the crowd around him, he had nothing left – nothing of all the millions that had been left in the bank when the millions of Count Sandorf had poured in to its aid.

Toronthal, accompanied by Sarcany, who acted as his gaoler, left the gaming-room, crossed the hall, and hurried out of the Casino. Then they fled across the square to the footpaths leading to La Turbie.

Point Pescade was already on their traces, and as he passed had shaken Cape Matifou as he lay half-asleep on his bench with a shout of:

"Wake up! Eyes and legs!"

And Cape Matifou had come along with him on a trail it would not do to lose.

Sarcany and Toronthal continued to hurry on side by side, and gradually mounted the paths which twist and wind on the flank of the mountain among the olive and orange gardens. The capricious zigzags allowed Pescade and Matifou to keep them in view, although they could not get near enough to hear them.

"Come back to the hotel, Silas!" Sarcany continued to repeat in an imperious tone. "Come back, and be cool again!"

"No! We're ruined! Let us part! I do not want to see you again! I do not want..."

"Part? And why? You'll follow me, Silas! Tomorrow we'll leave Monaco! We have enough to take us to Tetuan, and there we'll finish our work!"

"No! No! Leave me, Sarcany, leave me!" said Toronthal.

And he pushed him violently aside as he tried to catch hold. Then he darted off at such speed that Sarcany had some trouble in keeping up. Unconscious of his acts, Toronthal at every step risked falling into the steep ravines, above which, the winding footpaths lay unrolled. Only one idea possessed him; to escape from Monte Carlo where he had consummated his ruin, to escape from Sarcany whose counsels had led him to misery, to escape without caring where he went or what became of him.

Sarcany felt that his accomplice was at last beyond him, that he was going to escape him! Ah! If the banker had not known those secrets, which might ruin him, or at least irretrievably compromise the third game he wished to play, how little anxiety he would have felt for the man he had dragged to the brink of destruction! But, before he fell, Toronthal might give a last cry, and that cry he must stifle at all costs!

Then from the thought of the crime on which he had resolved to its immediate execution was only a step, and this step Sarcany did not hesitate to take. That which he had intended to do on the road to Tetuan in the solitudes of Morocco might be done here, this very night, on this very spot, which would soon be deserted!

But just at present between Monte Carlo and La Turbie a few belated wayfarers were along the slopes. A cry from Silas might bring them to his help, and the murderer intended the murder to be committed in such a way that it would never be suspected. And so he had to wait. Higher up, beyond La Turbie and the frontier of Monaco, along the Corniche clinging to the lower buttresses of the Alps, 2000 feet above the sea, Sarcany could strike a far surer blow. Who could then come to his victim's help? How at the foot of such precipices as border that road could Toronthal's corpse be found?

But, for the last time, Sarcany tried to stop his accomplice and tempt him back to Monte Carlo.

"Come, Silas, come," said he, seizing him by the arm. "Tomorrow we'll begin again! I have some money left."

"No! Leave me! Leave me!" exclaimed Toronthal with an angry gesture.

And if he had been strong enough to struggle with Sarcany, if he had been armed, he might not even have hesitated to take vengeance on his old Tripolitan agent for all the evil he had done him.

With a hand strengthened by anger Toronthal thrust him aside. Then he rushed towards the last turn of the path and ran up a few steps roughly cut in the rock between the little gardens. Soon he reached the main road of La Turbie along the narrow neck, which divides the Dog's Head from Mont Agel, the old frontier line between Italy and France.

"Go, then, Silas!" exclaimed Sarcany. "Go! But you won't go far!"

Then turning off to the right he scrambled over a stone hedge, scaled a garden wall, and ran on in front so as to precede Toronthal along the road.

Pescade and Matifou, although they had not heard what had passed, had seen the banker thrust Sarcany away and watched him disappear in the shade.

"Eh!" exclaimed Pescade. "Perhaps the best of them has gone! Anyhow Toronthal is worth something! And we have no choice! Come on, Cape; forward away!"

And in a few rapid strides they were close to Toronthal, who was hurrying up the road. Leaving to the left the little knoll with the tower of Augustus, he passed the houses at a run, and at length came out on the Corniche. Point Pescade and Cape Matifou followed him, less than fifty yards behind.

But of Sarcany they thought no more. He had either taken the crest of the slope to the right, or abandoned his accomplice to return to Monte Carlo.

The Corniche is an old Roman road. When it leaves La Turbie, it drops towards Nice, running in mid-mountain by magnificent rocks, isolated cones, and profound precipices that cleave their ravines down to the railway line along the shore. Beyond, on this starry night by the light of the moon then rising in the east, there showed forth confusedly the six gulfs, the isle of Sainte Hospice, the mouth of the Var, the peninsula of Garoupe, the Cape of Antibes, the Juan Gulf, the Lerins Islands, the Gulf of Napoli, and the Gulf of Cannes, with the mountains of Esterel in the background. Here shone the harbour lights of Beaulieu at the base of the escarpments of Petite-Afrique, there of Villefranche in front of Mont Leuza, and yonder the lamps of the fishing boats reflected on the calm waters of the open sea.

It was just after midnight. Toronthal, as soon as he had got out of La Turbie, left the Corniche, and dashed down a little road leading directly to Eza, a sort of eagle's nest with a half-savage population, boldly placed on a rock above a mass of pines and carob trees.

The road was quite deserted. The madman kept on for some time without slackening his pace or turning his head; suddenly he threw himself off to the left, down a narrow footpath running close to the high cliff along the shore, under which the railway and carriage-road pass by the tunnel.

Point Pescade and Cape Matifou hurried after him. A hundred paces further on Toronthal stopped. He had jumped on to a rock which overhung a precipice whose base, hundreds of feet below, dropped deep into the sea.

What was he going to do? Had the idea of suicide crossed his brain? Would he then end his miserable existence by hurling himself into the waves?

"A thousand devils!" exclaimed Pescade, "We must have him alive! Catch him, Cape Matifou, and hold him tight!"

But they had not gone twenty yards before they saw a man appear to the right of the path, glide along the slope among the myrtles and lentisks, and clamber up so as to reach the rock on which Toronthal stood.

It was Sarcany.

"Hello!" exclaimed Point Pescade. "He's going to speed his friend's journey into the next life! Hurry, Matifou! You take one – I'll take the other!"

But Sarcany stopped. He risked being recognized. A curse escaped his lips. Then springing off to the right before Pescade could reach him, he vanished among the bushes.

An instant afterward, as Toronthal had gathered himself together to jump from the rock, he was seized by Cape Matifou, and pulled back on to the road.

"Let me go! Let me go!"

"Let you make a mistake, Mr. Toronthal? Oh, dear no!" answered Point Pescade.

He was quite unprepared for this incident, which his instructions had not foreseen. But although Sarcany had escaped, Toronthal was captured, and all that could now be done was to take him to Antekirtta, where he would be received with all the honour that was his due.

"Will you forward this gentleman – at a reduced rate?" asked Point Pescade.

"With pleasure," said Matifou.

Toronthal, hardly knowing what had happened, made but very slight resistance. Pescade found a rough footpath leading to the beach, and down it he was followed by Cape Matifou, who sometimes carried and sometimes dragged his passive prisoner.

The descent was extremely difficult, and without Pescade's extraordinary activity and his friend's extraordinary strength, they would certainly have had a fatal fall. However, after risking their lives a score of times, they gained the rocks on the beach. There the shore is formed of a succession of small creeks, capriciously cut back into the sandstone, shut in by high reddish walls, and bordered by ferruginous reefs tinting the waves a bright blood-colour as they curl over them.

Day had begun to break when Point Pescade found shelter at the back of a deep ravine that had been cut down into the cliff in geologic ages. Here he left Toronthal in charge of Cape Matifou.

The banker, having been carried there by the giant, did not show the least apprehension, nor the slightest concern with what was to become of him.

"You'll guard him here!" said Point Pescade.

"For as long as you like."

"It may be twelve hours, what if I'm twelve hours away?"

"Twelve hours will pass."

"Without eating?"

"If I don't eat breakfast this morning, I'll have lunch this evening – and for both of us!"

"And if you don't have lunch for two, you shall have dinner for four!"

And then Cape Matifou sat down on a rock so as not to lose sight of his prisoner; and Point Pescade made his way along the shore from creek to creek towards Monaco. He was not away as long as he expected. In less than two hours he came upon the *Electric* moored in one of the deserted creeks. And an hour later that swift vessel had arrived off the ravine in which Cape Matifou seen from the sea looked like a mythological Proteus herding the sheep of Neptune.

A minute or two afterwards he and his prisoner were on board, and without having been noticed by the coastguard or the fishermen the *Electric* was off, under full power, for Antekirtta.

Eza

CHAPTER V

TO THE MERCIFUL CARE OF GOD

And now we must return to the island.

Toronthal and Carpena were in the doctor's power, and the pursuit of Sarcany would be resumed as soon as opportunity offered. The agents entrusted with the discovery of Madame Bathory's retreat were still unresting in their endeavours – but with no result. Since his mother had disappeared with only old Borik to help her, Pierre's anxiety had been constant. What consolation could the doctor give to that twice-broken heart? When Pierre spoke of his mother how could he help thinking of Sava Toronthal whose name was never mentioned between them?

Maria Ferrato occupied one of the prettiest houses in Artenak. It was close to the Stadthaus. There the doctor's gratitude had endeavoured to ensure her all the comforts of life. Her brother lived near her, when he was not at sea occupied on some service of transport or surveillance. Not a day elapsed without her visiting the doctor, or his going to see her. His affection for the children of the fishermen of Rovigno increased as he knew them better.

"How happy we are!" said Maria very often. "If Pierre could only be so!"

"He cannot be so," Luigi would answer, "Until he finds his mother! But I haven't lost all hope of that. Maria! With the doctor's means we ought to discover where Borik took Madame Bathory after they left Ragusa!"

"I also have that hope, Luigi! But if he got back his mother, would he be happy?"

"No, Maria, that would be impossible until Sava Toronthal is his wife!"

"Luigi," answered Maria, "is that which seems impossible to man impossible to God?"

When Pierre had told Luigi that they were brothers he did not then know Maria Ferrato, he did not know what a sister, tender and devoted, he would find in her! And when he had become able to appreciate her, he had confided to her all his troubles! It soothed him a little to talk them over with her. What he could not say to the doctor, what he had been forbidden to say to him, he could say to Maria. He found there a loving heart, open to all compassion, a heart that understood him, that consoled him, a soul that trusted in God and did not know despair.

In the casemates of Antekirtta there was now a prisoner who knew what had become of Sava, and if she were still in Sarcany's power. This was the man who had passed her off as his daughter – Silas Toronthal. But out of respect to his father's memory Pierre would never speak to him on the subject.

Ever since his capture Toronthal had been in such a state of mind, in such physical and mental prostration that he could have told nothing even if it had been his interest to do so. But he would gain no advantage in revealing what he knew of Sava, for he did not know on the one hand that he was Dr. Antekirtt's prisoner, and on the other that Pierre Bathory was alive on this island of Antekirtta, of which the name even was unknown to him.

So that, as Maria Ferrato said, God alone could unravel the mystery!

No sketch of the state of the colony would be complete without mention of Point Pescade and Cape Matifou.

Although Sarcany had managed to escape, although his track was lost, the capture of Toronthal had been of such importance that Point Pescade was overwhelmed with thanks. And when the doctor was satisfied, the two friends were quite satisfied with themselves. They had again taken up their quarters in their cottage, and waited ready for any services that might be required, hoping that they would still be of use to the good cause.

Since their return to Antekirtta they had visited Maria and Luigi Ferrato, and then they had called on several of the notables of Artenak. Everywhere they were warmly welcomed, for everywhere they were esteemed. It was worth a journey to see Cape Matifou under such solemn circumstances, always very much embarrassed at his enormous figure taking up nearly all the room.

"But I'm so small that that makes up for it!" said Point Pescade.

His constant good-humour made him the delight of the colony. His intelligence and skill were at everyone's disposal. And when everything had been settled to the general satisfaction, what entertainments he would organize, what a programme of gaiety and attractions would he keep going in the town and its neighbourhood! Yes! If necessary Cape Matifou and Point Pescade would not hesitate to resume their old profession and astonish their Antekirttian audience with their acrobatic wonders!

Till that happy day arrived Point Pescade and Cape Matifou improved their garden under the shade of the huge trees, and their cottage was hidden beneath its masses of bloom. The work at the little dock began to grow into shape. To see Cape Matifou lifting and carrying the huge masses of rock was convincing enough that the Provencal Hercules had lost none of his prodigious strength.

The doctor's correspondents had found no trace of Madame Bathory, and they were equally unsuccessful with regard to Sarcany. They could find no trace of his movements since he left Monte Carlo.

Did Toronthal know what had become of him? It was at the least doubtful, considering the circumstances under which they had separated on the road to Nice. And admitting that he knew, would he consent to say? Impatiently did the doctor wait until the banker was in a fit state to be questioned.

It was in a fort at the northwest angle of Artenak that Toronthal and Carpena had been secured in the most rigorous secrecy. They were known to each other but by name only, for the banker had never been mixed up with Sarcany's Sicilian affairs. And so there was a formal order against their being allowed to suspect each other's presence in this fort. They occupied two casemates far apart from each other, and they came out for exercise at different hours in different courts. Sure of the fidelity of those who had charge of them – two of the militia sergeants of Antekirtta – the doctor could be certain that no communication could take place between them.

And there was no indiscretion to fear, for none of the questions from Toronthal and Carpena as to where they were had been replied to or would be replied to. And there was nothing to lead them to suppose that they had fallen into the hands of the mysterious Dr. Antekirtt, whom Toronthal had once or twice met at Ragusa.

But to find Sarcany, to carry him off like his accomplices, was now the doctor's object. And on the 16th of October having learnt that Toronthal was now strong enough to reply to any questions that might be put to him, he resolved to proceed with his examination.

To begin with, the subject was talked over by the doctor, Pierre, and Luigi, and Point Pescade, whose advice was not to be despised.

Cape Matifou sat down on a rock

The doctor informed them of his intentions.

"But," said Luigi, "but to ask Toronthal if he knows anything about Sarcany is enough to make him suspect that we want to get hold of him."

"Well," replied the doctor, "what does it matter if Toronthal learns he cannot escape us?"

"One thing," answered Luigi, "is that Toronthal might think it in his interest to say nothing that might damage Sarcany."

"And why is that?"

"Because it might damage him."

"May I make an observation?" asked Pescade, who was seated a little apart.

"Certainly, my friend!" said the doctor.

"Owing," said Point Pescade, "to the peculiar circumstances under which these gentlemen parted I have reason to believe that they're not likely to care very much for each other. Mr. Toronthal must very cordially hate Mr. Sarcany for leading him to his ruin. If then Mr. Toronthal knows where Mr. Sarcany is to be found he'll have no hesitation in telling you – at least I think not. If he says nothing, it's because he has nothing to say."

The reasoning was at least plausible. It was very likely that if the banker did know where Sarcany had gone to, he would willingly reveal the secret, for his true interest was to break with him.

"We shall know today," said the doctor. "And if Toronthal knows nothing, or will tell us nothing, I'll see what next to do. But as he must be kept ignorant that he's in the power of Dr. Antekirtt, and that Pierre Bathory is alive, it must be Luigi's task to examine him."

"I'm at your orders, doctor," said the sailor.

Luigi then went to the fort, and was admitted into the Casemate, which served as Toronthal's prison.

The banker was seated in a corner at a table. He had just left his bed. There could be no doubt that he was in much better health. It was not of his ruin that he was now thinking, nor of Sarcany. What was troubling him was why and where he was in prison, and who was the powerful individual that had carried him off.

When he saw Luigi Ferrato enter, he rose; but at a sign he resumed his seat. The following dialogue then ensued:

"You're Silas Toronthal, formerly a banker at Trieste, and lately living at Ragusa?"

"I have no reply to that question. It's for those that keep me prisoner to know who I am."

"They do know."

"Who are they?"

"You'll learn in due time."

"And who are you?"

"A man who has been sent to interrogate you."

"By whom?"

"By those with whom you have accounts to settle."

"Once more, who are they?"

"I shall not tell you."

"In that case, I shall not reply."

"Be it so! You were at Monte Carlo with a man you've known for many years, and who has not left you since your departure from Ragusa. This man is a Tripolitan by birth and his name is Sarcany. He escaped at the moment you were arrested on the road to Nice. Now this is what I've been sent to ask you: Do you know where that man now is, and if you know, will you tell me?"

Toronthal paused before replying. If they want to know, he thought, where Sarcany is, it is obvious that they want to get hold of him as they got hold of me. Why? Is it for something we have both been concerned in during the years gone by and particularly for our schemes in the Trieste conspiracy? But how can these things have been found out? Who could be interested in avenging Mathias Sandorf and his two friends who died fifteen years ago? These were the banker's first thoughts. Then he went on to himself, it cannot be any properly constituted authority that threatens me and my companion — and that is serious. And so, although he had no doubt that Sarcany had fled to Tetuan to Namir, where he was trying his third game and forcing it as much as he could, he resolved to say nothing about it. If later on he could gain anything by speaking, he would speak. Now he would be as reserved as possible.

"Well?" asked Luigi, after giving him time to reflect.

"Sir," answered Toronthal, "I could tell you that I know where Sarcany is, and that I will not say. But in reality, I do not know."

"That's your reply?"

"My only reply and the truth."

Then Luigi returned to inform the doctor of what had passed. As there was nothing inadmissible in the reply, they had to be content with it. And to discover Sarcany's retreat, all that could be done was to press on the search, no matter the cost, no matter the risk.

While waiting for some clue to Sarcany's whereabouts the doctor was busy with questions seriously affecting the general safety of Antekirtta.

He had recently had secret information from the Cyrenaic provinces, and had been advised to keep a sharp look out towards the Gulf of Sidra. The formidable association of the Senousists seemed to be collecting their forces on the Tripolitan frontier. A general movement was taking them gradually towards the Syrtic coast. An exchange of messages was going on between the different zaouiyas of Northern Africa. Arms from foreign parts had been delivered to and received by the Brotherhood. And a concentration was evidently taking place in the vilayet of Ben Ghazi, and consequently close to Antekirtta.

In preparation for the danger, which seemed imminent the doctor took all possible precautions. During the last three weeks of October, Pierre and Luigi were busy helping him, and the whole of the colonists placed their services at his disposal. Several times Point Pescade was secretly dispatched to the coast, and returned with the news that the danger was not imaginary. The pirates of Ben Ghazi had been reinforced by quite a mobilization of the confederates in the province, and were preparing an expedition of which Antekirtta was the objective. Was it to take place soon? That could not yet be discovered. In any case the chiefs of the Senousists were still in the southern vilayets, and it was not likely that any enterprise would be undertaken without their being present to direct it. The result of this was that the *Electrics* were ordered to cruise in the Syrtic Sea and reconnoitre the coast of the Cyrenaic and Tripoli, and that of Tunis up to Cape Bon.

The defences of the island, as we know, were still incomplete. But if it was not possible to finish them in time, at least provisions and stores of all sorts abounded in the arsenal.

Antekirtta was about twenty miles from the Cyrenaic coast, and would have been quite isolated in the gulf, if it had not been for an islet known under the name of Kencraf, which measured about three hundred yards round, and emerged from the sea about a couple of miles to the southwest. The doctor's idea was that this islet would do for the prison if any of the colonists were sentenced to be imprisoned after conviction by the regular judicial authority of the island – and which event had not yet happened. And a few buildings had been erected for this purpose.

But Kencraf was not fortified, and in case a hostile flotilla came to attack Antekirtta, its very position constituted a danger. In fact the islet would easily become a solid base of operations. With the facility of landing munitions and food, with the possibility of establishing a battery, it

The *Electrics* were ordered to cruise in the Syrtic Sea

would afford an assailant an excellent centre, and all the more because there was now no time to put it into a proper state of defence.

The position of this island and the advantages it would give to an enemy of Antekirtta made the doctor uneasy. Thinking matters over he resolved to destroy it, but at the same time to make its destruction serve for the complete annihilation of the pirates who risked its capture. The project was immediately put in execution. Galleries were driven in the ground, and Kencraf became an immense mine united to Antekirtta by a submarine cable. All that was wanted was a current through the wire, and not a trace of the island would remain on the surface of the sea.

For this formidable effort of destruction the doctor had not used ordinary powder, nor gun cotton, nor even dynamite. He knew the composition of a recently discovered explosive whose destructive power is so considerable that it may be said it is to dynamite what dynamite is to gunpowder. More manageable than nitroglycerine and more portable, for it only requires two isolated liquids whose mixture does not take place until the moment of using them, it is refractory to congelation down to six below zero, while dynamite turns to jelly at ten below freezing, and it is only liable to explode from a violent shock, such as that from a fulminating capsule. How is it obtained? Quite simply by the action of protoxide of nitrogen, pure and anhydrous, in a liquid state on different carburets, mineral oils, vegetable oils, or animal oils derived from fatty bodies. Of these two liquids, which are harmless when apart and are soluble in each other, the explosive can be produced in the desired proportion as easily a mixture of water and wine, without any danger in manipulation. Such is panclastite, a word meaning smashing everything – and it does smash everything.

This panclastite was buried in the islet in the form of several fougasses. By means of the cable from Antekirtta, which led the spark into the charges of fulminate with which each fougasse was furnished, the explosion would take place instantaneously. As it might happen that the cable could be cut and put out of action, by excess of precaution a certain number of electric batteries were buried in the ground and joined by surface wires, so that they had only to be trod upon accidentally to bring the wires in contact, make the current, and cause the explosion. If many assailants landed on Kencraf it would thus be difficult for them to avoid utter destruction.

These different works were well advanced by the early days of November, when something occurred to take the doctor away from the island for some days.

On the 3rd of November, in the morning, the steamer engaged in bringing coals from Cardiff dropped anchor in the harbour of Antekirtta. During the voyage she had had to put in at Gibraltar. There at the post office, waiting "to be called for," the captain found a letter addressed to the doctor, a letter the coast offices had been sending after him from time to time without being able to find him.

The doctor took the letter, the envelope of which was crowded with postmarks – Malta, Catania, Ragusa, Ceuta, Otranto, Malaga, Gibraltar.

The superscription – in a large shaky hand – was evidently that of somebody who was not accustomed or perhaps had not the strength to write many words. The envelope bore but the name – that of the doctor – with the following touching recommendation:

> Dr. Antekirtt
> To the merciful care of God

The doctor tore open the envelope, opened the letter – a sheet of paper now yellow with age – and read as follows:

> Doctor:
>
> May God bring this letter to your hands! I am very old! I am going to die! She will be alone in the world in the last days of a life that has been so sorrowful; have pity on Madame Bathory! Come and help her! Come!
>
> Your humble servant,
>
> BORIK

In a corner was the word "Carthage," and below it "Regency of Tunis."

The doctor was alone in the saloon in the Stadthaus when he received this letter. A cry of joy and of despair escaped him – of joy at having come on the track of Madame Bathory – of despair, or rather of fear, for the marks on the envelope showed that the letter was nearly a month old.

Luigi was summoned immediately.

"Luigi," said the doctor, "tell Captain Kostrik to get the *Ferrato* under steam in two hours."

410

"In two hours she'll be ready to take to the sea," answered Luigi. "Is she for you, doctor?"

"Yes."

"Is it to be a long voyage?"

"Three or four days only."

"Are you going alone?"

"No! Find Pierre and tell him to be ready to go with me."

"Pierre's away, but he'll be back in an hour from the works at Ken-craf."

"I also want your sister to come with us. Have her prepare to do so at once."

"At once."

And Luigi immediately went out to execute the orders he had just received.

An hour afterwards Pierre arrived at the Stadthaus. "Read," said the doctor.

And he showed him Borik's letter.

But Kencraf was not fortified, and its very position constituted a danger

CHAPTER VI

THE APPARITION

The steam yacht went out a little before noon. Her passengers were the doctor, Pierre and Maria, who had come to look after Madame Bathory in the event of its being impossible to take her back immediately from Carthage to Antekirtta.

There is no need to say much about what Pierre felt when he knew he was on his way to meet his mother. But why had Borik hurried her off so precipitately from Ragusa to this out-of-the-way spot in Tunis? In what state of misery would they be found? To the anxieties Pierre confided to her Maria did not cease to respond with words of sympathy and hope.

The *Ferrato* was driven at her utmost speed, and attained a mean of at least fifteen knots. The distance between the Gulf of Sidra and Cape Bon, the northeast point of Tunis, is about 620 miles; from Cape Bon to La Goulette, which is the port of Tunis, is only about an hour and a half's run for a steamer. In thirty hours, therefore, barring accidents, the *Ferrato* would reach her destination.

The sea was smooth outside the gulf; the wind blew from the northwest, but with no signs of increasing. Captain Kostrik steered for a little below Cape Bon, so as to get the shelter of the land, in case the breeze freshened. He did not, therefore, sight the island of Pantellaria halfway between Cape Bon and Malta, for he intended to round the cape as closely as possible.

As it bends out of the Gulf of Sidra, the shoreline is much cut into towards the west, and describes a wide curve. This is the coast of Tripoli running up to the Gulf of Gabes, between the Island of Dscherba and the town of Sfax; then the line trends a little to the east towards Cape Dinias, to form the Gulf of Hammamet; and it thence develops south and north to Cape Bon.

It was towards the Gulf of Hammamet that the *Ferrato* headed. There it was she would make the land and hug it till she got to La Goulette.

During the 3rd of November and the following night the size of the waves increased considerably. It takes but little wind to raise the Syrtic Sea, and through it flow the most capricious currents in the Mediterranean. In the morning at eight o'clock land was sighted at Cape Dinias, and under the shelter of the high shore the progress became rapid and easy.

The *Ferrato* ran along two miles away from the beach. Beyond the Gulf of Hammamet, in the latitude of Kelibia, there lies the little creek of Sidi Yussuf, sheltered on the north by a long ridge of rocks. Round the curve is a magnificent sandy beach with a background of low hills covered with stunted bushes that grow in a soil far richer in stones than in vegetable mould. This range of hills joins on to the "djebels," which form the mountains in the interior. Here and there, like white spots in the distant verdure, are a few abandoned marabouts. In front is a small ruined fort, and higher up there is one in better repair built on the hill that shuts in the creek towards the north.

The place was not deserted. Close to the rocks were several Levantine vessels, xebecs and polaccas, anchored in about five or six fathoms; but such was the transparency of the green water that the black rocks and streaked sand beneath them on which the anchors lay and to which refraction gave the most fantastic forms, could be plainly seen.

Along the beach at the foot of the small sand hills with their lentisks and tamarinds, a "douar," composed of some twenty huts, displayed its yellow-striped roofs, and looked like a large Arab mantle thrown in a heap on the shore. Outside the folds of the mantle were a few sheep and goats, seeming at the distance like large black crows that a gunshot would frighten into noisy flight. A dozen camels, some stretched on the sand, others motionless as if turned to stone, ruminated near a narrow strip of rock that served as a landing stage.

As the *Ferrato* steamed past Sidi Yussuf, the doctor noticed that arms, ammunition, and a few field pieces were being taken ashore; and owing to its remote position on the confines of Tunis, the creek is well fitted for such contraband trade. Luigi pointed out to the doctor what was going on.

"Yes, Luigi," he said, "and if I'm not mistaken, the Arabs are the destined owners of those weapons. Are they for the use of the mountaineers against the French troops landed at Tunis? I doubt it. I'm sure they must be for the Senousists, those pirates now gathering in the Cyrenaic!

414

Those Arabs don't appear to be the type you'd find in the Tunisian province, they're more like the kind you'd find in the interior."

"But," asked Luigi, "why doesn't the regency or the French authorities stop that landing of arms and ammunition?"

At Tunis they hardly know what passes on the other side of Cape Bon, and when the French become masters of Tunisia it will take them a long time to reduce the coast to the east of the djebels into order! At any rate, the shipment looks very suspicious, and if it were not that the speed of the *Ferrato* prevents their making an attempt, I expect the flotilla would have come out to attack us."

If the Arabs had any notion of doing so, there was nothing to fear from them. In less than half an hour the *Ferrato* had passed Sidi Yussuf. Then having reached the extremity of Cape Bon, standing out in bold outline from the Tunisian range, she swiftly steamed by the lighthouse, which rises on the point with the superbly rugged pile of rocks around it.

The *Ferrato* then at full speed shot across the gulf of Tunis between Cape Bon and Cape Carthage. On the left runs the series of escarpments of the "djebels," Bon Karnin, Rossas and Zaghouan, with a few villages half hidden in their gorges. On the right, in all the splendour of the Arab Kasbah, in the full glare of the sun shone the sacred city of Sibi-Bou-Saïd, which was perhaps one of the suburbs of ancient Carthage. In the background not far from Lake Bahira, lay Tunis, a mere mass of white, a little behind the arm with which La Goulette welcomes its visitors from Europe. Two or three miles from the port lay a squadron of French vessels; then, more in the offing, a few merchant ships were riding at anchor, and with their fluttering flags giving life to the roadstead.

In an hour the *Ferrato* had dropped anchor at about three cable lengths from the wharf. As soon as the necessary formalities were complied with pratique was given to her passengers. The doctor, Pierre, Luigi and his sister took their places in the gig, which immediately bore them ashore. After rounding the mole they glided into that narrow canal crowded with vessels ranged along both wharves, and reached that irregular square planted with trees, and bordered with villas, shops, and cafes, swarming with Maltese Jews, Arabs, and French and native soldiers, into which runs the main street of La Goulette.

Borik's letter was dated from Carthage, and the name, with a few ruins scattered on the ground, is about all that remains of the old city of Hannibal.

The chapel of Saint Louis

To reach the shore at Carthage there is no need to take the little Italian railway that runs between La Goulette and Tunis, skirting the Lake of Bahira. The hard, fine sand affords excellent walking, or the dusty road across the plain a little behind it gives easy access to the base of the hill on which stand the chapel of Saint Louis and the convent of the Algerian missionaries.

At the time the doctor and his companions landed, several carriages, drawn by pigmy horses, were waiting in the square. To hail one and order it to drive rapidly to Carthage was the work of a minute. The carriage after traversing the main road of La Goulette at a trot passed by the sumptuous villas that the rich Tunisians inhabit during the hot season, and the palaces of Keredin and Mustapha that rise on the shore, close to the outskirts of the Carthaginian city. Two thousand years ago the rival of Rome covered the whole extent between the point of La Goulette and the cape that still bears its name.

The chapel of Saint Louis is built on a knoll about two hundred feet high, on which the King of France died in 1270. It occupies the middle of a small enclosure containing many more remains of ancient architecture and broken statuary, vases, columns, capitals, and stele than trees or shrubs. Behind it is the missionary convent, of which Père Delathe, the archaeologist, is now the prior. The top of this enclosure commands the stretch of sand from Cape Carthage up to the first houses of La Goulette.

At the foot of the hill are a few palaces of Arab design, with piers in English style, which run out into the sea for the vessels of the roadstead to unload alongside. Beyond is the superb gulf of which every promontory, point and mountain has historic interest.

But if there are palaces and villas on the site of the old harbours, there are on the slopes of the hill among the ruins a few wretched houses inhabited by the poor of the place. Most of these have no other trade beyond searching for more or less precious Carthaginian relics, bronzes, stones, pottery, medals, and coins, which the convent buys for its archaeological museum — rather for pity's sake than because they are wanted.

Some of these refuges are merely two or three fragments of wall, such as the ruins of the marabouts, which lie whitening in the broiling sun.

The doctor and his companions journeyed from one to the other in search of Madame Bathory, hardly believing she could have been reduced to such misery. Suddenly the carriage stopped before a dilapidated building, with a door that was merely a hole in a wall almost overgrown with bushes.

An old woman in a black cloak was seated before this door. Pierre had recognized her! He uttered a cry! It was his mother! He rushed towards her, he knelt to her, he clasped her in his arms! But she replied not to his caresses, and did not even seem to recognize him!

"Mother! Mother!" he exclaimed, while the doctor, Luigi and his sister crowded around her.

At the same moment an old man appeared at the angle of the ruin.

It was Borik.

At first sight he recognized Dr. Antekirtt, and his knees shook. Then he caught sight of Pierre – Pierre, whose body he had followed to the cemetery of Ragusa! The shock was too much for him! He fell motionless to the ground, and as he did so these words escaped from his lips:

"She's lost her reason!"

And so when the son recovered his mother all that was left to him was an inert body. And the sudden appearance of her son, whom she thought to be dead, had not been enough to restore her to any recollection of the past.

Madame Bathory rose; her eyes were haggard, but still there was in them the light of life. Then, without seeing anything, without uttering a single word, she entered the marabout, and Maria, at a sign from the doctor, followed her in.

Pierre remained at the door without daring to move, without being able to do so.

With the doctor's help Borik began to regain his consciousness.

"You, Mr. Pierre! You! Alive!"

"Yes!" answered Pierre. "Yes! Alive! Though it would be better if I were dead!"

In a few words the doctor informed Borik of what had taken place at Ragusa. Then the old servant told him the story of those two months of misery.

"But," asked the doctor at the outset, "was it her son's death that caused Madame Bathory to lose her reason?"

"No, sir, no!" answered Borik.

And this is what he told them.

Madame Bathory, being alone in the world, had left Ragusa and gone to live at the little village of Vinticello, where she had a few relatives.

While there she had been planning how to dispose of her house, as she had no further intention of inhabiting it.

Six weeks afterwards, accompanied by Borik, she had returned to Ragusa to arrange all these matters, and when she reached the house in the Rue Marinella she found that a letter had been dropped into the box.

Having read the letter – and the reading seemed to have given her mind its first shock – Madame Bathory screamed and ran into the road, and down into the Stradone, and knocked at Toronthal's door, which opened immediately.

"Toronthal's?" exclaimed Pierre.

"Yes," answered Borik, "and when I came up to Madame Bathory she did not recognize me. She was..."

"But why did my mother go to Toronthal's? Yes! Why?" asked Pierre, looking at the old servant as if he were quite mystified.

"She probably desired to speak with Mr. Toronthal," answered Borik, "and two days before Mr. Toronthal had left his house with his daughter, and no one knew where he had gone."

"And this letter? This letter?"

"I haven't been able to find it, Mr. Pierre," answered the old man. "Madame Bathory must have lost it or destroyed it, or had it taken from her; and I do not know what it was about."

There was some mystery here. The doctor, who had listened without saying a word, could see no reason for this act of Madame Bathory's. What imperious motive had urged her to the house in the Stradone, which everything would have made her avoid; and why, when she learnt that Toronthal had disappeared, had she received so violent a shock as to drive her mad?

Borik's story only took a few minutes. He succeeded in keeping Madame Bathory's mental state secret, and busied himself in realizing her property. The calm, gentle, mania of the unhappy widow allowed him to act without suspicion. His only object, then, was to leave Ragusa, and obtain shelter in some distant town; it mattered not where, provided it was far away from that accursed place. A few days afterwards, he took Madame Bathory on board one of the steamers that trade with the Mediterranean coast, and arrived at Tunis, or rather La Goulette. There he resolved to stop.

And then, in this deserted marabout, he devoted himself entirely to the care of Madame Bathory, who seemed to have lost her speech as well as her senses. But his resources were so slight that he could see the time coming when they would both be reduced to the last misery.

An old woman in a black cloak was seated before this door

It was then that the old servant thought of Dr. Antekirtt, of the interest he had always taken in the Bathory family. But Borik did not know his usual residence. He, however, wrote, and the letter he trusted, in despair, to Providence, and it appeared that Providence had brought the letter into the doctor's hands.

There could be no doubt what was next to be done. Madame Bathory, without any resistance on her part, was placed in the carriage with Borik and Pierre and Maria. And then the doctor and Luigi walked back by way of the beach, while the carriage returned along the road to La Goulette.

An hour afterwards they all embarked on the yacht, which was under steam. The anchor was immediately weighed, and as soon as she had doubled Cape Bon the *Ferrato* steered so as to sight the lights of Pantellaria. The day after the next, in the early morning, she ran into harbour at Antekirtta.

Madame Bathory was taken ashore at once, led to Artenak, and installed in one of the rooms at the Stadthaus.

Another sorrow for Pierre Bathory! His mother deprived of reason, become mad under circumstances, which would probably remain inexplicable! If the cause of this madness could be ascertained, some salutary reaction might have been provoked, but nothing about it was known and nothing could be known.

"She must be cured! Yes! She must!" said the doctor, who devoted himself to the task.

And the task was a difficult one, for Madame Bathory remained quite unconscious of her actions, and not a remembrance of her past life did she display.

Could the power of suggestion that the doctor possessed in so high a degree be employed to change the mental state of the patient? Could she by magnetic influence be recalled to reason and kept in that state until the reaction took place?

Pierre adjured the doctor to try even the impossible to cure his mother.

"No!" answered the doctor. "That would not do. Mad people are the most refractory subjects for the purpose! For the influence to act, your mother must have a will of her own, for which I can substitute mine! And I assure you I should have no influence over her."

"No! I won't admit it," said Pierre, who would not be convinced. "I won't admit that we shall not see the day when my mother will recognize me – her son she believes to be dead."

"Yes! That she believes to be dead," answered the doctor. "But perhaps if she believed you to be alive or if she saw you coming out of the grave. If she saw you appear..."

The doctor paused at the thought. Why should not a sudden shock, provoked under favourable conditions, have some effect on Madame Bathory?

"I'll try it!" he exclaimed.

And when he explained the experiment on which he based his hope of curing his mother, Pierre threw himself into the doctor's arms.

From that day the scenery and surroundings to bring about the success of the attempt were the object of anxious care. The idea was to revive in Madame Bathory the effects of memory, of which her derangement had deprived her, and to revive it under such striking circumstances that a reaction would be caused in her brain.

The doctor appealed to Borik, to Point Pescade, so as to reproduce with sufficient exactness the appearance of the cemetery at Ragusa and the monument, which served as the tomb of the Bathory family. And in the cemetery of the island, about a mile from Artenak, under a group of trees they built a small chapel as much as possible like that at Ragusa. Everything was done to produce the most striking resemblance between the two monuments; and on the wall there was placed a slab of black marble bearing the name of Stephen Bathory, with the date of his death, 1867.

On the 13th of November the time seemed come for beginning the preparatory attempt to revive Madame Bathory's reason.

About seven o'clock in the evening, Maria and Borik took the widow's arm, and leading her from the Stadthaus, walked out to the cemetery. There Madame Bathory remained before the threshold of the little chapel motionless and silent as always, although by the light of the lamp, which burnt within, she could read the name of Stephen Bathory engraved on the marble slab. Only when Maria and the old man knelt as they went along did she have a faint look of intelligence in her eyes, which almost instantly vanished.

An hour afterwards she was taken back to the Stadthaus followed by a crowd who had come to join the procession at this first experiment.

The next and succeeding mornings the experiments were continued, but without result. Pierre looked on with poignant emotion and despaired of their success, although the doctor told him that time would be his most useful ally. He did not intend to strike his last blow until Madame Bathory had been sufficiently prepared to feel its full force.

Each time she visited the cemetery a slight but unmistakable change took place in her; and one evening when Borik and Maria were kneeling at the chapel door she had slowly come forward, put her hand on the iron grating, looked at the wall beyond brightly illuminated by the lamp, and hurriedly run back.

Maria, returning to her, heard her murmur a name several times.

It was the first time for months that her lips had opened to speak!

But what was the astonishment – more than the astonishment – the stupefaction of those who heard her!

The name was not that of Pierre, her son, – it was the name of Sava!

If we can understand what Pierre felt, who can describe what passed in the doctor's soul when he heard this unexpected invocation of Sava Toronthal? But he made no observation; he gave no sign of what he felt.

Another evening the experiment was repeated. This time, as if she had been led by an invisible hand, Madame Bathory went and knelt on the chapel step. She bowed her head, a sigh escaped her, and tears fell from her eyes. But that evening not a name escaped her lips, and it seemed as though she had forgotten Sava.

She was taken back to the Stadthaus and there showed herself a prey to unusual nervous agitation. The calm hitherto characteristic of her mental state gave place to singular exaltation. Some work of vitality was evidently going on in her brain, and this looked hopeful.

The night proved troubled and restless. She several times muttered vague words which Maria could scarcely hear, but it was evident she was dreaming. And if she dreamt, reason was coming back, and she might be cured if her reason would only stay with her till she woke.

Then the doctor decided to make a fresh attempt on the morrow, of which the surroundings should be more striking.

During the whole of this 18th she continued under violent mental excitement. Maria was much struck with her state, and Pierre, who spent nearly all his time with his mother, felt a presentiment of happy augury.

The night arrived – a night dark and gloomy without a breath of wind, after a day that had been very warm in this low latitude of Antekirtta.

About half-past eight the patient, accompanied by Maria and Borik, left the Stadthaus. The doctor, with Luigi and Point Pescade, followed a few steps behind.

The whole of the little colony was anxiously expectant of the success of what was going to happen. A few torches beneath the trees threw a fuliginous light on the chapel and its surroundings. Afar at regular intervals the bell in Artenak church sounded a funeral knell.

Madame Bathory went and knelt on the chapel step

Pierre was the only one absent from the procession which advanced slowly towards the cemetery. But if he was not there, it was because he was to appear in the closing scene of this final experiment.

It was about nine o'clock when Madame Bathory reached the cemetery. Suddenly she shook herself free from Maria's arm, and walked towards the little chapel. She was allowed to do as she pleased under the influence of this new feeling, which seemed to have entire possession of her.

Amid a profound silence, broken only by the tolling of the bell, Madame Bathory stopped, and remained motionless. Then she knelt on the first step, and bent down, and then they heard her weep.

At this moment the railing of the chapel slowly opened. Wrapped in a white shroud, as if he had risen from his grave, Pierre appeared in the light.

"My son! My son!" exclaimed Madame Bathory, who stretched out her arms and fell senseless.

It mattered little. Memory and thought had returned to her! The mother was awakened! She had recognized her son!

The doctor soon revived her, and when she had recovered her consciousness, when her eyes rested on her son:

"Alive! My Pierre! Alive!" she exclaimed.

"Yes! Living for your sake, mother, living to love you."

"And to love her – her also!"

"Her?"

"Her! Sava!"

"Sava Toronthal?" exclaimed the doctor.

"No! Sava Sandorf!"

And Madame Bathory drew from her pocket a crumpled letter that contained the last words written by the hand of the dying Madame Toronthal, and held it out to the doctor.

The letter left no doubt as to Sava's birth. Sava was the child that had been carried away from the Castle of Artenak! Sava was the daughter of Count Mathias Sandorf!

"Where is Sava? Where is Sava?" said the doctor, his anger mounting

PART V

CHAPTER I

CAPE MATIFOU LENDS A HAND

Count Mathias, as we know, wished to remain Dr. Antekirtt to the whole colony except Pierre, until his work had been accomplished. When his daughter's name was suddenly pronounced by Madame Bathory, he had sufficient control over himself to suppress his emotion. But his heart for a moment ceased to beat, and he fell on the threshold of the chapel as if he had been struck by lightning!

And so his daughter was alive! And she loved Pierre, and she was loved! And it was Mathias Sandorf who had been doing everything to prevent the marriage! And the secret, which gave Sava back to him, would never have been discovered had not Madame Bathory's reason been restored to her as by a miracle!

But what had happened fifteen years ago at the Castle of Artenak? That was obvious enough! This child, the sole heiress of Count Sandorf's wealth, whose death had never been proved, had been stolen by Toronthal. And shortly afterwards when the banker settled at Ragusa, Madame Toronthal had had to bring up Sava Sandorf as her own daughter.

Such had been the scheme devised by Sarcany and executed by his accomplice Namir. Sarcany knew perfectly that Sava would come into possession of a considerable fortune when she reached eighteen; and when she had become his wife, he would then procure her acknowledgment as the heiress of Sandorf's estates. This was to be the crowning triumph of his abominable existence. He would become the master of Artenak!

Had he then foiled this odious scheme? Yes, undoubtedly. If the marriage had taken place Sarcany would already have availed himself of all its advantages.

427

And now how great was the doctor's grief! Was it not owing to him that there had been brought about this deplorable chain of events; at first in refusing his help to Pierre, then in allowing Sarcany to pursue his plans, then in not rendering him harmless at the meeting at Cattaro, then in not giving back to Madame Bathory the son he had snatched from death? In fact, what misfortunes would have been avoided had Pierre been with his mother when Madame Toronthal's letter had reached the house in the Rue Marinella! Knowing that Sava was Sandorf's daughter, would not Pierre have known how to get her away from the violence of Sarcany and Toronthal?

Where was Sava Sandorf now? In Sarcany's power, of course! But where was she hidden? How could they get her away? And besides, in a few weeks she would attain her eighteenth year — the limit fixed for the time during which she could be the heiress — and that fact would impel Sarcany to use every effort to make her consent to the marriage!

In an instant this succession of thoughts passed through Dr. Antekirtt's mind. As he built together the past, as Madame Bathory and Pierre were themselves doing, he felt the reproaches, unmerited assuredly, that Stephen Bathory's wife and son might be tempted to assail him with. And now as things had turned out, would he be able to bring together Pierre and her who for all and for himself he must still continue to call Sava Toronthal?

He must before everything find Sava, his daughter — whose name, added to that of the Countess Rena his wife, he had given to the schooner *Savarena*, as he had given that of Ferrato to his steam yacht! But there was not a day to lose.

Already Madame Bathory had been led back to the Stadthaus, when the doctor came to visit her accompanied by Pierre, whom he left to his alternations of joy and despair. Much enfeebled by the violent reaction whose effects had just been produced in her, but cured of her illness, Madame Bathory was sitting at the window when the doctor and her son entered.

Maria, seeing it would be better to leave them together retired to the large saloon.

Dr. Antekirtt then approached her, and laid his hand on Pierre's shoulder.

"Madame Bathory," he said, "I've already made your son my own! But what he is now through friendship I will do all the more to make him through paternal love when he marries my daughter Sava."

"Your daughter!" exclaimed Madame Bathory.

"I am Count Mathias Sandorf."

Madame Bathory jumped up and fell back into her son's arms. But though she could not speak she could still hear. In a few words Pierre told her what she did not know, how Mathias Sandorf had been saved by the devotion of the fisherman Andrea Ferrato, why for fifteen years he had passed as dead, and how he had reappeared at Ragusa as Dr. Antekirtt. He told her how Sarcany and Toronthal had betrayed the Trieste conspirators, and related the treachery of Carpena of which Ladislas Zathmar and his father had been the victims, and how the doctor had taken him from the cemetery of Ragusa to associate him in the work he had undertaken. He finished his story by stating that two of the scoundrels, the banker Toronthal and the Spaniard Carpena, were then in their power, but that the third, Sarcany, was still at large – the Sarcany who desired Sava Sandorf for his wife!

For an hour the doctor, Madame Bathory, and her son went over in detail the facts regarding the young lady. Evidently Sarcany would stick at nothing to bring about Sava's consent to the marriage, which would bring him the wealth of Count Sandorf; and this state of affairs was what principally exercised them during their interview. But if the plans of the past had now collapsed, those of the present promised to be even more formidable. Above everything it was necessary to move heaven and earth to recover Sava.

It was in the first place agreed that Madame Bathory and Pierre should alone know that Mathias Sandorf was concealed under the name of Dr. Antekirtt. To reveal the secret would be to say that Sava was his daughter, and in the interest of the new search to be undertaken it was necessary to keep this quiet.

"But where is Sava? Where are we to look for her?" asked Madame Bathory.

"We'll know!" answered Pierre, in whom despair had given place to an energy that nothing could quench.

"Yes! We'll know!" said the doctor. "In admitting that Silas Toronthal does not know where Sarcany is we cannot suppose that he does not know where my daughter..."

"And if he knows he must tell!" said Pierre.

"Yes! He must speak!" answered the doctor.

"Now!"

"Now!"

The doctor, Madame Bathory, and Pierre would remain in this state of uncertainty no longer.

Twice or thrice they had to pull up before isolated houses

Luigi, who was with Point Pescade and Cape Matifou, in the large saloon of the Stadthaus, where Maria had joined them, was immediately called in. He received orders to go with Cape Matifou to the fort, and bring back Silas Toronthal.

A quarter of an hour afterwards the banker left the casemate that served him for a prison, and with his hand grasped in the large hand of Cape Matifou, was brought along the main street of Artenak. Luigi, whom he had asked where he was going, had given him no reply, and the banker, who knew not into what powerful person's hands he had fallen, was extremely uneasy.

Toronthal entered the hall. He was preceded by Luigi, and held all the time by Cape Matifou. He just saw Point Pescade, but he did not see Madame Bathory and her son, who had stepped aside. Suddenly he found himself in the presence of the doctor, with whom he had vainly endeavoured to enter into communication at Ragusa.

"You! You!" he exclaimed. "Ah!" he said, collecting himself with an effort. "It's Dr. Antekirtt, who arrests me on French territory. It is he who keeps me prisoner against all law."

"But not against all justice!" interrupted the doctor.

"And what have I done to you?" asked the banker, to whom the doctor's presence had evidently given confidence. "Yes! What have I done to you?"

"To me? You'll know soon enough," answered the doctor. "But to start with, Silas Toronthal, ask what have you done to this unhappy woman..."

"Madame Bathory!" exclaimed the banker, recoiling before the widow who advanced towards him.

"And to her son!" added the doctor.

"Pierre! Pierre Bathory!" stammered Silas Toronthal.

And he would certainly have fallen if Cape Matifou had not held him upright.

And so Pierre, whom he thought dead, Pierre whose funeral he had seen, who had been buried in the cemetery at Ragusa, Pierre was there before him, like a spectre from the tomb! Toronthal grew frightened. He felt he could not escape the chastisement for his crimes. He felt he was lost.

"Where's Sava?" asked the doctor abruptly.

"My daughter?"

"Sava is not your daughter! Sava is the daughter of Count Mathias Sandorf, whom Sarcany and you sent to death after having treacherously denounced him and his companions, Stephen Bathory and Ladislas Zathmar!"

At this formal accusation, the banker was overwhelmed. Not only did Dr. Antekirtt know that Sava was not his daughter, but he knew that she was the daughter of Count Mathias Sandorf! He knew how and by whom the Trieste conspirators had been betrayed!

"Where is Sava?" said the doctor, restraining himself only by a violent effort of his will. "Where is Sava, whom Sarcany, your accomplice in all these crimes, stole fifteen years ago from Artenak? Where is Sava, whom that scoundrel is keeping in a place you know, to which you have sent her that her consent to this horrible marriage may be obtained! For the last time, where is Sava?"

So alarming had been the doctor's attitude, so threatening had been his words that Toronthal did not reply. He saw that the present position of the girl might prove his safety. He felt his life might be respected so long as he kept the secret.

"Listen," continued the doctor, beginning to recover his coolness, "Listen to me, Silas Toronthal. Perhaps you think you can assist your accomplice! Perhaps you think you may betray him. Well, know this: Sarcany, in order to ensure your silence after he had ruined you, tried to assassinate you as he assassinated Pierre Bathory at Ragusa! Yes! At the moment my people seized you on the road to Nice he was going to stab you! And now will you persist in your silence?"

Toronthal, obstinately imagining that his silence would compel them to make terms with him, said nothing.

"Where is Sava? Where is Sava?" said the doctor, his anger mounting.

"I do not know! I do not know!" replied Toronthal, resolved to keep his secret.

Suddenly he screamed, and writhing with pain he tried unsuccessfully to thrust Matifou away.

"Mercy! Mercy!" he cried.

Matifou, unconsciously perhaps, was squeezing the banker's hand in his own.

"Mercy!"

"Will you speak?"

"Yes! Yes! Sava – Sava..." said Toronthal, who could only speak in broken sentences – "Sava – in Namir's house: Sarcany's spy – at Tetuan!"

Cape Matifou let go Toronthal's arm, and the arm remained motionless.

"Take back the prisoner!" said the doctor. "We know what we wished to know!"

And Luigi took Toronthal back to his casemate.

Sava at Tetuan! Then when the doctor and Pierre, hardly two months before, were at Ceuta capturing the Spaniard only a few miles separated them from Sava!

"This very night, Pierre, we start for Tetuan."

In those days the railroad did not run from Tunis to the Moorish frontier; and to reach Tetuan as quickly as possible the doctor and his companions had to embark in one of the swiftest boats of the Antekirttian flotilla.

Before midnight, *Electric No. 2* had been got ready, and was on her way across the Syrtic Sea.

On board were the doctor, Pierre, Luigi, Point Pescade, and Cape Matifou. Pierre was known to Sarcany, the others were not. When they reached Tetuan they would consult as to their proceedings. Would it be better to act by stratagem or force? That would depend on Sarcany's position in this absolutely Moorish town, on his arrangements in Namir's house, and on the adherents he could command. Before everything they must get to Tetuan!

From the end of the Syrtis to the Moorish frontier is about two thousand five hundred kilometers – nearly thirteen hundred and fifty nautical miles. At full speed *Electric No. 2* could do her twenty-seven miles an hour. How many railway trains there are, that are not as fast! That long steel tube, offering no resistance to the wind, could slip through the waves without hindrance and would reach its destination in fifty hours.

Before daybreak the next morning the *Electric* had doubled Cape Bon. Then having crossed the Gulf of Tunis it only took her a few hours to lose sight of Point Bizerte, La Calle, Bone, the Iron Cape, whose metallic mass is said to disturb the compasses, the Algerian coast, Stora, Bougie, Dellys, Algiers, Cherchell, Mostaganem, Oran, Nemours, then the shores of Riff, the Point of Mellelah which, like Ceuta, is Spanish, and Cape Tres Forcas, whence the continent rounds off to Cape Negro: all this panorama of the African coastline was unrolled during the 20th and 21st of November without either incident or accident. Never had the machine worked by the currents from the accumulators had such a run. If the *Electric* had been perceived either along the shore or crossing the gulfs from cape to cape, there would have been telegrams as to the appearance of a phenomenal ship, or perhaps of a cetacean of extraor-

For an hour they traversed the motley crowd in search of Namir

dinary power that no steamer in the Mediterranean waters had yet exceeded in speed.

About eight o'clock in the evening the doctor, Pierre, Luigi, Point Pescade, and Cape Matifou landed at the mouth of the small river of Tetuan, in which their rapid vessel had dropped anchor. A hundred yards from the bank, in the centre of a small caravanserai, they found mules and a guide to take them into the town, which was about four miles distant. The price asked was agreed to instantly, and the party set off.

In this part of the Riff, Europeans have nothing to fear from the indigenous population, nor even from the nomads of the district. The country is thinly peopled and almost uncultivated. The road lies across a plain dotted with straggling shrubs – and it is a road made by the feet of the beasts rather than by the hand of man. On one side is the river with muddy banks, alive with the croak of frogs and the chirp of crickets, and bearing a few fishing boats moored in the centre or drawn up on the shore. On the other side, to the right, is the outline of the bare hills running off to join the mountain masses of the south.

The night was magnificent. The moon bathed the whole country in its light. Reflected by the mirror of the river the moonlight seemed to soften the sharp outline of the heights on the northern horizon. In the distance, white and gleaming, lay the town of Tetuan – a shining patch in the dark clouds of mist beyond.

The Arab did not waste much time on the road. Twice or thrice they had to pull up before isolated houses, where the windows on the side not lighted by the moon threw a yellow beam across the shadow, and out would come two or three Moors with a lantern, who, after a hurried conference with the guide, would let them pass.

Neither the doctor nor his companion spoke a word. Absorbed in their thoughts, they left the mules to follow the road, which here and there was cut through by gullies strewed with boulders, or cumbered with roots, which avoided with sure feet. The largest of the mules was, however, very often in the rear. This might have been expected, for it bore Cape Matifou.

Its difficulties led Point Pescade to reflect:

"Perhaps it would have been better for Cape Matifou to carry the mule instead of the mule carrying Cape Matifou!"

About half past nine the Arab stopped before a large blank wall, surmounted by towers and battlements, on that side defending the town. In this wall was a low door, decorated with arabesques in Moorish fashion.

Above, through the numerous entrances, pointed the throats of the cannons, looking like crocodiles carelessly sleeping in the light of the moon.

The gate was shut. Some conversation was needed, with cash in hand, before it could be opened. Then the party passed in down the winding, narrow, and often-vaulted streets, whose other gates, barred with iron, were successively opened by similar means. At length the doctor and his companions, in a quarter of an hour, reached an inn or "fonda" – the only one in the place – kept by a Jewess, with a one-eyed girl as servant.

The total want of comfort in this fonda, which had the rooms disposed round the central court, was sufficient explanation as to why strangers so very seldom ventured into Tetuan. There is actually only one representative of the European powers, among a population of several thousands, with whom the native element predominates – the Spanish consul.

Although Dr. Antekirtt wished exceedingly to ask for Namir's house, and to be taken there at once, he restrained himself. It was necessary to act with great prudence. To carry Sava away under such circumstances was a serious matter. Everything for and against it had been taken into account. Perhaps they might be able to get the girl set free for a consideration? But the doctor and Pierre would have to keep themselves out of sight – more especially from Sarcany, who might perhaps be in Tetuan. In his hands Sava would become a guarantee for the future that he would not easily part with. Here they were not in one of the civilized countries of Europe, where justice and police could easily interfere. In this country of slaves how could they prove that Sava was not Namir's legitimate slave? How could they prove that she was Count Sandorf's daughter, otherwise than by Madame Toronthal's letter, and the banker's confession? The houses in these Arab towns are carefully guarded, and not easily accessible. They are not entered easily. The intervention of a cadi even might be useless, supposing it could be obtained.

It had been decided that at the outset Namir's house should be carefully watched in a way to prevent suspicion. In the morning Point Pescade would go out with Luigi to pick up information. During his stay in Malta, Luigi had learnt a little Arabic, and the two would start to find out in what street Namir lived, to act accordingly. Meanwhile *Electric No. 2* would be concealed in one of the narrow creeks along the coast near the entrance of the Tetuan River, and kept ready for sea at a moment's notice.

The night, whose hours were so long for the doctor and Pierre, was thus passed in the fonda. If Point Pescade and Cape Matifou had any desire to be on beds encrusted with crockery ware, they were satisfied.

In the morning Luigi and Point Pescade began by visiting the bazaar, in which there had already gathered a large part of the Tetuan population. Pescade knew Namir whom he had a score of times noticed in the streets of Ragusa while she was acting as spy for Sarcany. There was a chance he could run into her, but as they had never met this would not be an inconvenience, quite the opposite, for then he could follow her.

The principal bazaar of Tetuan is a collection of sheds, shacks, and hovels, low, narrow, and miserable, arranged in sultry lanes. A few cloths of different colours are stretched on lines and protect it from the heat of the sun. Around are dull-looking shops with broidered silk, gorgeous trimmings, slippers, purses, cloaks, pottery, jewels, collars, bracelets, rings, and other common goods such as are found in the shops of the large towns of Europe.

It was already crowded. The people were taking advantage of the coolness of the morning. Moors veiled to the eyes, Jewesses with uncovered faces, Arabs, Kabyles, moved to and fro in the bazaar, elbowed by a certain number of strangers, so that the presence of Luigi Ferrato and Point Pescade did not attract special attention.

For an hour they traversed the motley crowd in search of Namir. In vain! The Moor did not appear, nor did Sarcany.

Luigi then asked one of the half-naked boys – hybrid products of all the African races from the Riff to the Sahara – who swarm in the bazaars of Morocco.

The first he spoke to made no reply. At last one of them, a Kabyle, about twelve years old, said that he knew the house, and offered to take the Europeans there – for a trifle.

The offer was accepted, and the three started through the tangled streets, which radiate towards the fortifications. In ten minutes they had reached a part that was almost deserted, in which the houses were few and far between, and had no windows on their outer sides.

During this time the doctor and Pierre were waiting the return of Luigi and Pescade with feverish impatience. Twenty times were they tempted to go out and look for themselves. But they were both known to Sarcany and the Moor. It would perhaps be risking everything to meet them and give them an alarm, which might enable them to escape. So they remained a prey to the keenest anxiety. It was nine o'clock when Luigi and Point Pescade returned to the fonda.

On the fragments of paper they read…

Their lugubrious faces proclaimed that they were the bearers of bad news.

In fact, Sarcany and Namir, accompanied by a girl whom nobody knew, had left Tetuan five weeks before and the house was now in the charge of an old woman.

The doctor and Pierre had not expected this; they were in despair.

"Their departure is easily accounted for!" said Luigi. "Sarcany was evidently afraid that Toronthal, for revenge or some other motive would reveal the place of his retreat."

While he was only in pursuit of his betrayers the doctor had never despaired of success. But he did not feel the same confidence now that it was his daughter he sought to rescue from Sarcany.

However, Pierre agreed with him that they had better go at once to Namir's house. Perhaps they might find some trace or remembrance of Sava. Perhaps the old Jewess who had been left in charge might give, or rather sell, some hint that might prove useful.

Luigi led them there immediately. The doctor, who spoke Arabic as if he had been born in the desert, introduced himself as a friend of Sarcany's. He was passing Tetuan, he said, and would have been glad to see him.

The old woman at first raised difficulties, but a handful of sequins made her much more obliging; and she willingly answered the questions the doctor asked with the appearance of the liveliest interest in her master.

The young lady who had been taken away by the Moor was Sarcany's intended wife. That had been arranged for some time, and probably the marriage would have taken place at Tetuan had it not been for the hurried departure. The young lady since her arrival three months before had not been outside the house. They said she was an Arab, but the Jewess thought she was a European. She had seen her very little, and only during the Moor's absence and she could not find out any more about her.

The old woman could not say where Sarcany had taken them. All she knew was that they went away about five weeks before with a caravan to the eastward, and that since then the house had been in her care and was to continue so until Sarcany found someone to buy it, which showed that he did not intend returning to Tetuan.

The doctor listened coldly to these replies, and as they passed translated them to Pierre.

From them it appeared that Sarcany had not thought it desirable to embark on one of the steamers calling at Tangiers, nor to go by the rail-

439

way, which has its terminus at Oran. He had joined a caravan that had left Tetuan – bound whither? To some oasis in the desert, or, still farther, to some half-savage country, where Sava would be entirely at his mercy? How could they know? On the roads of Northern Africa it is as difficult to recover the track of a caravan as the track of an individual.

And so the doctor persisted in his questions to the Jewess. He had received important news, which was of interest to Sarcany, he said, and they referred to this very house, which he wished to dispose of. But do what he could no other information did he get. It was evident that the woman did not know where Sarcany had gone.

The doctor, Pierre and Luigi then asked to be allowed to see the house, which was built in Arab fashion, with the different rooms lighted from a courtyard surrounded by a rectangular gallery,

They soon reached the room that Sava had occupied. It was quite a prison cell. There what hours the unhappy girl must have passed a prey to despair and without hope of help! The doctor and Pierre looked round the room seeking the least indication that might put them on the track.

Suddenly the doctor stepped up to a small brasero, which stood on a tripod in a corner of the room. In this brasero were a few fragments of paper that had been destroyed by fire, but the incineration of which had not been completed.

Had Sava written them? And surprised by the hurried departure had she burnt the letter before she left Tetuan? Or rather – and that was possible – had the letter been found on Sava and destroyed by Sarcany or Namir?

Pierre had watched the doctor's look as he bent over the brasero. What had he found?

On the fragments of paper that a breath would reduce to dust, a few words stood out in black. Among others were these, unfortunately incomplete:

Mad – Bath...

Had Sava attempted to write to her as the only person in the world to whom she could appeal for help, not knowing and not being able to know that she had disappeared from Ragusa?

Then after Madame Bathory's name another could be deciphered – that of her son.

Pierre held his breath, and tried to find some other word still legible! But his look was troubled. He could see no more.

But there was one word that might perhaps put them on the girl's track, a word, which the doctor found almost intact.

"Tripoli!" he exclaimed.

Was it in the Regency of Tripoli, his native country, where he might be absolutely safe, that Sarcany had sought refuge? Was it thither that the caravan was bound?

"To Tripoli!" said the doctor.

That evening they were again at sea. If Sarcany had already reached the capital of the Regency they were in hopes that they would be only a few days behind him.

Horsemen were leaping about discharging their long guns and saddle pistols

CHAPTER II

THE FEAST OF THE STORKS

On the 23rd of November the plain of Soung-Ettelate around the walls of Tripoli afforded a curious spectacle. On that day no one could tell if the plain were barren or fertile, for its surface was hidden beneath multi-coloured tents adorned with feathers and flags, miserable gourbis with their roofs so tattered and patched as to give very insufficient shelter from that bitter dry wind the "gibly," which sweeps across the desert from the south; here and there were groups of horses in rich oriental trappings, meharis stretched on the sand with their flat heads like half-empty goatskin bottles, small donkeys about as big as large dogs, large dogs as big as small donkeys, mules with the enormous Arab saddle that has the cantle and pommel as round as a camel hump; horsemen were there with guns across their shoulders and knees up to their stomachs, and feet in slipper-like stirrups, and having double sabres at their belt, galloping among a crowd of men, women, and children, careless of whom they might run down as they dashed along; and natives were there almost uniformly clothed in the Barbary "haouly," beneath which the women would be indistinguishable from the men, if the men did not fix the folds to their waist with brass pin, while the women let the upper part fall over their faces so that they can only see with the left eye – a costume which varies with the classes, the poor having nothing on but the simple linen mantle, the more affluent having the waistcoat and wide breeches of the Arabs, and the wealthy having splendid patterns in white and blue over a second haouly of gauze or glossy silk above the dead white of the gold-spangled shirt

Were they only Tripolitans that had gathered on the plain? No. The environs of the capital were crowded with merchants from Ghadames and Sokna, escorted by their black slaves; Jews and Jewesses of the province with uncovered faces; Africans from the neighbouring villages who had come from their cabins of rushes and palms to assist in the general gaiety, poorer in linen than in jewellery, with large brass bracelets, shell-work collars, strings of teeth, and rings of silver in their ears and their noses; and Benoulies and Awaguirs, from the shores of the Syrtes, to whom the date-palm of their country yielded its wine, its fruit, its bread, and its preserves. Among this agglomeration of Moors, Berbers, Turks, Bedouins, and Muzaffirs, or Europeans, were pashas, sheiks, cadis, all the lords in the land walking through the crowds of raayas which opened humbly and prudently before the drawn swords of the soldiers, or the truncheons of the police of the zapties as there passed in haughty indifference the Governor General of this African cyalet, of this province of the Turkish empire whose administration belongs to the Sultan.

If there are more than 1,500,000 in Tripoli, with 6000 soldiers – 1000 for the Djebel and 5000 for the Cyrenaic – the town of Tripoli itself has not more than from 20,000 to 24,000 souls. But on this occasion it appeared as though the population had been at least doubled by the crowd of spectators coming from all parts of the territory. These rurals had not, it is true, entered the capital of the Regency. Within the walls of the fortifications neither the houses, which through the worthlessness of their materials soon fall into ruins, nor the narrow, tortuous, unpaved streets, nor the neighbouring mole with its consulates, nor the western quarter inhabited by the Jews, nor the rest of the town inhabited by the Mussulmans were equal to such an invasion.

But the plain of Soung-Ettelate was large enough for the crowd of spectators attracted to this feast of the storks whose legend always receives due honour in the eastern countries of Africa. This plain – a small fragment of the Sahara, with its yellow sand often invaded by the sea during the violent winds from the east – surrounds the town on three sides and is about 1000 yards across. In strong contrast is the oasis of Menchie – with its white walled houses its gardens watered by the leather-chain pump worked by a skinny cow, its woods of orange trees, citrons, and dates, its green clumps of shrubs and flowers, its antelopes, gazelles, fennecs and flamingos – a huge patch of ground in which live not less than 30,000 people. Beyond is the desert, which in no part of Africa comes nearer to the Mediterranean, the desert and its shifting sand hills, and its immense carpet of sand on which, says Baron Krafft, "the wind raises the waves as easily as on the ocean," the Libyan ocean with its mists of impalpable dust.

Tripoli – a country almost as large as France – is bounded by Tunis and Egypt and to the south by the Sahara at a distance of 10 miles from the Mediterranean coast.

It was in this province, one of the least known in Northern Africa, and which will be perhaps one of the last to be thoroughly explored, that Sarcany had taken refuge after leaving Tetuan. A native of Tripoli, he had returned to the country, which had been the scene of his earliest exploits. Affiliated to the most formidable sect of Northern Africa, he had sought the powerful protection of the Senousists, whose agent for the acquisition of arms and ammunition in foreign parts he had never ceased to be. And when he arrived at Tripoli he had taken up his quarters in the house of the moqaddem, Sidi Hazam, the recognized chief of the sectaries of the district.

After the capture of Toronthal on the road to Nice – a capture that still remained inexplicable to him – Sarcany had left Monte Carlo. A few thousand francs that he had kept back from his earlier winnings had enabled him to pay his passage, and defray his expenses. He had good reason to fear that Toronthal would be reduced to despair, and urged to seek vengeance on him, either by revealing his past life, or giving information as to the whereabouts of Sava. The banker knew that the girl was at Tetuan in charge of Namir, and hence Sarcany's decision to leave Morocco as soon as possible.

He resolved to take refuge in Tripoli, where he could avail himself, not only of the means of action, but the means of defence. But to go there by steamer or the Algerian railway would have been too dangerous – as the doctor had suspected. And so he joined a caravan of Senousists, who were on their way to the Cyrenaic, recruiting as they went in the chief villages of Morocco, Algeria, and Tunis. This caravan, which would quickly travel the 500 leagues between Tetuan and Tripoli, following the northern edge of the desert, set out on the 12th of October.

And now Sava was entirely at the mercy of her captors. But her resolution was not shaken. Neither the threats of Namir nor the rage of Sarcany had had any effect on her.

At its departure from Tetuan the caravan already numbered fifty of the brethren, or Khouans, under the leadership of an imam, who had organized it in military fashion. There was no intention of crossing the provinces under French influence, or the journey might give rise to difficulties.

The coast of Algeria and Tunis forms an arc up to the western coast of the grand Syrtes, where it drops abruptly to the south. The most di-

The crowd roared in transports of delight

rect road from Tetuan to Tripoli is along the chord of this arc, and that does not run higher than Laghouat, one of the most distant French towns on the borders of the Sahara.

The caravan, on leaving the empire of Morocco, skirted the boundary of Algeria, and in Beni Matan, in Oulad Nail, in Charfat-el-Hamel, secured a goodly number of recruits, so that when it reached the Tunisian coast at the Syrtis Magna it numbered more than 300 men. Then it followed the coast, recruiting Khouans in the different villages and on the 20th of November, after a six weeks' journey, it reached the frontier of Tripoli. On the day, therefore, that this feast of the storks was taking place, Sarcany and Namir had only been the guests of Sidi Hazam for three days.

The moqaddem's house, which was now Sava's prison, was surrounded by a slender minaret, and with its white walls pierced with loopholes, its embattled terraces, its want of exterior windows, and its low, narrow doorway, had very much the appearance of a small fortress. It was in reality a regular zaouiya, situated beyond the town, on the skirt of the sandy plain and the plantations of Menchie with its gardens defended by the high wall running up on to the oasis.

The interior was of the ordinary Arab design but with three courtyards instead of one. Around each of these courtyards was a quadrilateral of galleries, columns and arcades, on to which opened the rooms of the house, which for the most part, were luxuriously furnished. In the second courtyard the visitor or guests found a vast "skifa," a sort of hall or vestibule, in which more than one conference had been held by Sidi Hazam.

The house was naturally defended by its high walls, and the defence was further assured by the number of servants who could be summoned in case of an attack from the wandering tribes, or even the recognized authorities of the province whose efforts were directed to keeping the Senousists in check. There were, in fact, fifty of the brethren, well armed and equally ready for the defensive or the offensive.

There was only one door to the zaouiya, but this door was very thick and solid, and bound with iron, and could not be easily forced, and once forced could not be easily entered. Sarcany had thus found a safe refuge in which he hoped to end his work successfully. His marriage with Sava would bring him considerable wealth, and if needed he could count on the assistance of the brotherhood who were directly interested in his success.

The brethren from Tetuan and the vilayets on the road had been dispersed in the oasis of Menchie, ready for action at the first signal. The feast of the storks, as the Tripolitan police knew well, would be most convenient for the Senousists. On the plain of Soung-Ettelate, the Khouans of Northern Africa could receive their orders from the muftis as to their concentration in the Cyrenaic, where they were to found a regular pirate kingdom under the all-powerful authority of a caliph. And the circumstances were highly favourable, for it was in the vilayet of Ben Ghazi in the Cyrenaic, that the association already had its greatest number of adherents.

On this day of the feast of storks, three strangers were strolling through the crowd on the plain of Soung-Ettelate. These strangers, these muzaffirs, would not have been recognized as Europeans under their Arab dress. The eldest of them wore his with that perfect ease which only long custom gives. He was Dr. Antekirtt, and his companions were Pierre Bathory and Luigi Ferrato. Point Pescade and Cape Matifou were stopping in the town where they were engaged in certain preparations, and probably would not appear on the scene until they were wanted.

The *Electric* had only come in the afternoon before and anchored under shelter of the long rocks, which act as a natural breakwater to the harbour of Tripoli. The passage had been as rapid as the voyage outwards. A three hours' stay at Philippevllle, in the little bay of Filfila, had been all that was necessary to procure the Arab dresses. Then the *Electric* had departed immediately, and its presence had not even been detected in the Numidian Gulf.

When the doctor and his companions came ashore, not at the quay, but on the rocks outside the harbour, they were no longer five Europeans entering Tripolitan territory, they were five Orientals whose garb would attract no attention. Pierre and Luigi dressed up in this way might betray themselves to the eyes of a close observer, but Pescade and Matifou, accustomed to the many dresses of the mountebank, were completely at their ease.

When night came the *Electric* moved round to one of the creeks on the other side of the harbour, where she ran little risk of being observed; and there she remained ready for sea at any moment. As soon as they had landed, the doctor and his companions ascended the rocks that skirt the coast until they reached the quay leading to Bab-el-Bahr, the marine gate, and entered the narrow streets of the town. The first hotel they came to seemed good enough for a few days – a few hours perhaps.

They seemed to be respectable people – Tunisian merchants, probably, taking advantage of their journey through Tripoli to be present at the feast of the storks! As the doctor spoke Arabic as correctly as he did all the other Mediterranean languages there was no danger that his speech would betray them.

The innkeeper with great cordiality received the five travellers who did him the great honour of selecting his house. He was a large man and very talkative. And so in encouraging him to talk, the doctor soon learnt certain things that interested him greatly. In the first place he heard that a caravan had recently arrived there from Morocco, that Sarcany, who was well known in the Regency, formed part of this caravan, and that he had availed himself of the hospitality of Sidi Hazam.

And hence that evening the doctor, Pierre, and Luigi, taking such precaution as ensured their not being observed, had mixed with the crowd of nomads encamped in the plain of Soung-Ettelate. As they strolled about they took careful notes of the moqaddem's house on the skirt of the oasis.

There, then, Sava Sandorf was a prisoner. Since the doctor had been at Ragusa, the father and daughter had never been so near together. But now an impassable wall lay between them. To get her away Pierre would have consented to everything, even to agree to Sarcany's terms. Count Sandorf and he were ready to abandon the fortune the scoundrel coveted! And this, although he did not forget that justice ought to be done on the betrayer of Stephen Bathory and Ladislas Zathmar.

Situated as they were, there would seem to be almost insurmountable difficulties in carrying off Sarcany or getting Sava away from Sidi Hazam's house. Force was not likely to succeed, would stratagem? Would tomorrow's festival in any way assist? Probably it would, and a plan had been suggested by Point Pescade, and had been under the consideration of the doctor, Pierre, and Luigi during the evening. In executing it Pescade would risk his life; but if he could enter the moqaddem's house he might succeed in managing Sava's escape. Nothing seemed impossible with his courage and cleverness.

It was, then, in execution of this plan that the next day the doctor, Pierre and Luigi were on the watch among the crowd on the plain of Soung-Ettelate, while Pescade and Matifou were preparing their parts. There was then no sign of the noise and excitement with which the plain would be full beneath the glare of innumerable torches when the evening arrived. In the compact crowd they had scarcely noticed the

Senousists who, in their simple costumes, communicated with each other only by Masonic signs.

But it is desirable that we should know the Oriental, or rather African, legend, of which the chief incidents were to be reproduced in the feast of the storks, which is the "great attraction" for the Mohammedans.

There was formerly on the African continent a race of Djins. Under the name of Bou-Chebris, these Djins occupied a vast territory situated on the borders of the desert of Hammada, between Tripoli and the kingdom of Fezzan. They were a powerful people, fearless and feared.

They were unjust, perfidious, aggressive, inhuman, and no African monarch had been able to suppress them.

There came a day when the prophet Suleiman attempted, not to attack, but to convert these Djins. And with this object he sent one of his apostles to preach to them the love of good and the hatred of evil. Vain effort! The ferocious horde seized the missionary and put him to death. The Djins showed so much audacity because their country was isolated and difficult of access, and they knew that no neighbouring ruler would dare to venture there with his armies. Besides, they thought that no messenger would carry to the prophet Suleiman the news of what they had done to his apostle. They were mistaken.

In the country were a great number of storks. As we know, storks are birds of good manners, of unusual intelligence, and above all things of great common sense, for the legend affirms that they never inhabit a country the name of which appears on a piece of money – for money is the source of all wickedness and the great power that draws all men to the abyss of their evil passions.

These storks, then, seeing the perverse way in which the Djins lived, mustered one day in deliberative assembly, and decided to dispatch one of their number to the prophet Suleiman, so as to procure his just vengeance on the missionary's assassins.

And so the prophet called the hoopoe, his favourite courier, and ordered him to collect in the upper zones of the African sky all the storks on earth. This was done, and when the innumerable flocks of these birds were gathered before the prophet Suleiman the legend says they formed a cloud which put in shadow all the land between Mezda and Mourzouk.

Then each one, taking a stone in its beak, flew towards the country of the Djins. And from above they stoned to death the unhappy race whose souls are now imprisoned for all eternity in the desert of Hammada.

Such is the fable, which has given rise to the festival of the day. Many hundreds of storks had been got together under huge nets stretched over the surface of the plain of Soung-Ettelate. And there, for the most part standing on one leg, they waited for the hour of their deliverance, and the clicking of their beaks caused a sound in the aims of the beating of a tambourine. At the given signal they would be set free to fly off, dropping harmless stones of clay among the crowd of the faithful, amid the cheers of the spectators, the uproar of the instruments, the reports of the musketry, and the light from the torches with coloured flames.

Pescade knew the programme of this festival, and it was from it that he received the suggestion as to the part he intended to play, and by the aid of which he was to obtain admission to Sidi Hazam's house.

As soon as the sun set a gun from the fortress of Tripoli gave the signal so impatiently expected by the people on Soung-Ettelate. The doctor, Pierre, and Luigi were at first almost deafened by the frightful noise which arose on every side, and were then nearly blinded by the thousands of lights that sprang up all over the plain.

When the gun was heard the crowd of nomads were still busy at their evening meal. Here the roast mutton, the pilaw of fowls for those who were Turks and wished it to be seen; there the couscousson for the well-to-do Arabs; farther off a simple bazina, a sort of barley-flour boiled in oil, for the poorer people, whose pockets contained more mahboubs of brass than mictals of gold; and everywhere the "lagby," the juice of the date palm, which, when taken as an alcoholic beer, can produce of the worst excesses of intoxication.

A few minutes after the gun had been heard, men, women, children, Turks, Arabs, and Africans had finished their meal. The instruments of the barbaric orchestras necessarily rejoiced in alarming sonorousness to make themselves heard above the human tumult. In places horsemen were leaping about discharging their long guns and their saddle pistols, while fireworks were thrown about amid an uproar it would be impossible to describe.

Here in the torchlight, to the rattling of the wooden drum and the intonation of a monotonous chant, an African chief, fantastically dressed, with a rattling belt of bones, and his face hidden beneath a diabolical mask, was exciting to the dance some thirty mens, grimacing in a circle of convulsionary women who beat them with their hands. And these savage Aissassouas, in the last stage of religious exaltation and alcoholic intoxication, with froth on their faces, and eyes from their orbits, were biting at wood, chewing iron, gashing their skins, juggling with live coals, and wrapping themselves with the long serpents which bit their hands, their cheeks, their lips and like them devoured their blood.

But soon the crowd hurried with extraordinary eagerness to the house of Sidi Hazam, as though some new spectacle had attracted them.

Two men were there, one large the other small – two acrobats whose curious feats of strength and agility amid a quadruple row of spectators were calling forth the most noisy cheers that could escape from Tripolitan throats.

They were Point Pescade and Cape Matifou. They had taken up their stand only a few paces from Sidi Hazam's house. Both on this occasion had resumed their characters as foreign artistes. With their dresses devised out of Arab materials, they were again in quest of success.

"You haven't gotten rusty?" Point Pescade had previously asked Cape Matifou.

"No!"

"And you won't shrink from anything that may amuse the imbeciles?"

"Me! Shrink!"

"Even if you have to chew pebbles with your teeth and swallow serpents!?!"

"Cooked?" asked Cape Matifou.

"Raw."

"Raw?"

"And living!"

Cape Matifou grimaced, but if necessary he resolved to eat a snake like a simple Aissassou.

The doctor, Pierre, and Luigi mingled in the crowd of spectators, and did not lose sight of the two friends.

No! Cape Matifou was not rusty; he had lost nothing of his prodigious strength. At first the shoulders of five or six robust Arabs, who had risked a fall with him, were laid on the ground.

Then followed the juggling, which astonished the Arabs, above all when the flaming torches were launched from Pescade to Matifou, coming and re-coming in their zigzags of fire.

And the public might well be critical. There were there a goodly number of the admirers of the Touaregs, those semi-savages "whose agility is equal to that of the most formidable animals in these latitudes" according to the astounding programme of the famous Bracco troupe. These connoisseurs had already applauded the intrepid Mustapha, the Samson of the Desert, the "man-cannon, to whom the Queen of England had sent her valet begging him not to continue his performance for fear of an accident."

But Cape Matifou was incomparable in his feats of strength, and feared no rivals.

At last came the final exercise, which was to raise to the highest pitch the enthusiasm of the cosmopolitan crowd that surrounded the European performers. Although it had done frequent duty in the circuses of Europe it seemed that it was still unknown to the loungers of Tripoli. And the crowd crushed more and more round the ring to look at the two acrobats.

Cape Matifou seized a pole nearly thirty feet long, and held it upright against his chest with his two hands. At the end of this pole Point Pescade, who had climbed up like a monkey, began to balance himself in attitudes of astonishing audacity, and he made it bend alarmingly.

But Cape Matifou remained undismayed, shifting about gradually so as to retain his equilibrium. Then, when he was close to the wall of Sidi Hazam's house, he summoned strength enough to lift the pole at arm's length, while Point Pescade assumed the attitude of a favourite actress throwing kisses to her admirers

The crowd roared in transports of delight, clapped their hands, and stamped their feet. Never had Samson of the Desert, the intrepid Mustapha, the boldest of the Touaregs, been raised to such a height!

At this moment the report of a gun echoed over the plain from the fortress of Tripoli. At the signal the hundreds of storks, suddenly delivered from the immense nets, which kept them prisoners, rose in the air, and a shower of sham stones began to fall on the plain, amid a deafening concert of aerial cries, to which the terrestrial concert gave back an equally noisy reply.

This was the paroxysm of the festival. It seemed as though all the madhouses in the old continent had been emptied on to Soung-Ettelate!

But, as if it were deaf and dumb, the moqaddem's house had remained obstinately closed during those hours of public rejoicing, and not one of Sidi Hazam's people had shown themselves at the gate, or on the terraces.

But, strange to relate! At the moment the torches were extinguished, after the flight of the storks, Point Pescade had suddenly disappeared, as if he had been borne upwards to the sky by the faithful birds of the prophet Suleiman.

What had become of him?

Cape Matifou did not seem to be at all concerned at the disappearance. He threw the pole into the air, caught it adroitly by the other end, and turned it as a drum major does his cane. Point Pescade's performance seemed to him to be the most natural thing in the world.

The astonishment of the spectators was unbounded, and their enthusiasm displayed itself in an immense hurrah, which extended far beyond the limits of the oasis. None of them doubted but what the active acrobat had jumped off into space, on his way to the kingdom of the storks.

What most charms the multitude? Is it not that which they are unable to explain?

CHAPTER III

THE HOUSE OF SIDI HAZAM

It was about nine o'clock. Musketry, music, shouting, all had suddenly ceased. The crowd had begun to disperse; some went back to Tripoli, others to the oasis of Menchie and the neighbouring villages. In an hour the plain of Soung-Ettelate would be silent and empty. Tents would be folded up, camps would be raised, Africans and Berbers were already on the road to the different Tripolitan districts, while the Senousists were off towards the Cyrenaic, and more especially towards the vilayet of Ben Ghazi to join the concentration of the Caliph's forces.

The doctor, Pierre, and Luigi were the only people that did not leave the place during the night. Ready for all that might happen since the disappearance of Point Pescade, each of them had chosen his post of observation at the base of the walls of Sidi Hazam's house.

Point Pescade had given a tremendous leap, as Matifou held the pole up at arm's length, and fallen on the parapet of one of the terraces at the foot of the minaret which commanded the different courtyards of the house.

On that dark night no one within or without had noticed him. He was not even observed from the skifa in the second courtyard, in which were a few Khouans, some of whom were asleep while others were on watch by order of the moqaddem.

Point Pescade, be it understood, had really no definite plan. The interior arrangement of the house was unknown to him, and he did not know in what part the girl was detained, nor if she was alone or kept out of sight, nor if he had sufficient strength to help her escape. Hence he must act a little at a venture; and this is what he thought:

"Anyhow, by force or stratagem, I must reach Sava Sandorf. If she cannot come with me immediately, if I cannot get her away tonight, she must be told that Pierre Bathory is alive, that he's here at the foot of these walls, that Dr. Antekirtt and his companions are ready to help her,

After waiting some minutes Point Pescade moved towards the minaret

and that if her escape must be delayed she must not yield to any threats! I may of course be found out before I reach her! But then I must take care of that."

Pescade's first care was to unwind a slender-knotted cord that he had hidden under his clown's dress; then he tied one end of this round the angle of one of the battlements and threw over the other so that it hung down to the ground. This was only a measure of precaution, a good one nevertheless. And when he had finished, Pescade, before going farther, lay clown on his stomach and remained motionless. If he had been seen, the terrace would soon be invaded by Sidi Hazam's people, and then he would have to use the cord on his own account, instead of that of Sava Sandorf, as he intended.

Complete silence reigned in the moqaddem's house. As neither Sidi Hazam nor Sarcany, nor any of their people, had taken part in the feast of the storks, the door of the zaouiya had not been opened since sunrise.

After waiting some minutes Point Pescade moved towards the angle from which arose the minaret. The staircase, which led to the upper part of this minaret, evidently ran down to the ground in the first courtyard. A door opening on to the terrace gave admission to the stairs leading to the rooms below.

This door was shut from the inside, not with a key, but with a bolt that it would be impossible to slip back from the outside unless a hole was made through the wood. This labour Point Pescade would have attempted, for he had in his pocket a many-bladed knife, a precious present from the doctor, of which he could make good use. But that would be a long, and perhaps noisy task.

It was unnecessary. Three feet above the terrace a window in the form of a loophole opened in the minaret wall. If the window was small, Point Pescade was not large. Besides, was he not like a cat that can elongate herself to pass through where there seems to be no passage? And so he tried, and after some squeezing of the shoulders he found himself in the minaret.

"Cape Matifou could not have done that!" he thought.

Then feeling his way round, he returned to the door, and unbolted it, so that it remained unfastened in case he had to return by the same road.

As he went down the winding stairs of the minaret, Point Pescade glided rather than stepped, so that his weight would not cause the wooden stairs to creak. At the bottom he found a second door. It was shut; but he had only to push it for it to open.

457

The door opened on to a gallery of little columns, by which access was given to a certain number of rooms. After the complete darkness of the minaret, the gallery seemed light to Pescade; but there was no light in the Interior, and not a sound.

In the centre of the courtyard was a basin of running water surrounded by large pots of shrubs, pepper trees, palms, laurel roses, and cacti, the thick foliage forming a clump of verdure round the edge.

Point Pescade stole round this gallery like a wolf, stopping before each room. It seemed they were inhabited. Not all of them however; but behind one of the doors he distinctly heard the murmur of a voice he knew.

He stepped back. It was Sarcany's voice! The voice he had often heard at Ragusa; but although he kept his ear to the door, he could hear nothing of what was going on.

At this moment there suddenly came a loud noise, and Point Pescade had only just time to slip behind one of the flowerpots round the water.

Sarcany came out of the room. An Arab of tall stature accompanied him. They continued their conversation, walking up and down the gallery of the courtyard.

Unfortunately Point Pescade could not understand what Sarcany and his companion were saying, for they were talking in that Arab tongue which he did not know. Two words he frequently heard, or rather two names. One of these was Sidi Hazam, for it was the moqaddem himself who was talking with Sarcany; the other was Antekirtta, which was mentioned several times during the conversation.

"That's strange," thought Pescade. "Why are they talking about Antekirtta? Are Sidi Hazam, Sarcany, and all the pirates of Tripoli thinking of a campaign against the island? Confound it! And not to know the lingo those two rascals are using!"

And Point Pescade, keeping himself well hid behind the flowerpots, tried hard to catch another suspicious word when Sarcany and Sidi Hazam came near. But the night was too dark for them to see him.

"And yet," said he to himself, "if Sarcany was alone in this courtyard I might have jumped at his throat and put it out of his power for him to damage us! But that would not help Sava Sandorf, and it was for her I made that risky jump! Patience! Sarcany's turn will come some day."

The conversation between Sidi Hazam and Sarcany lasted about twenty minutes. The name of Sava was mentioned several times, with the qualification "arroueh," and Point Pescade remembered that he had already heard the word, and that it meant "betrothed" in Arabic. Evidently the moqaddem knew of Sarcany's projects and was assisting him.

Then the two men retired through one of the doors in the angle of the courtyard, which put this gallery in communication with the other parts of the house.

As soon as they had disappeared Point Pescade glided along the gallery and stopped at this door. He had only to push it to find himself in a narrow corridor whose wall he felt his way along. At its end was a double arcade supported by a central column and giving access to the second courtyard. A few bright lights from between the bays by which the skifa obtained its light from the court were thrown in luminous sectors on the ground, and at the moment it would not be prudent to cross them, for a noise of many voices was heard behind the door of this room.

Point Pescade hesitated. What he sought was the room in which Sava was living, and he could only trust to chance to find it.

Suddenly a light appeared at the other end of the courtyard. A woman carrying an Arab lantern had just come out of the room in the far angle and turned along the gallery on to which the door of the skifa opened.

Point Pescade recognized her as Namir.

As it was possible that the moor was going to the room it was necessary to find the means of following her, and in order to follow her to let her go by without her seeing him. The moment was decisive of the audacious attempt of Point Pescade and the fate of Sava Sandorf.

Namir came on. Her lantern swinging almost on the ground left the upper part of the gallery in as deep a gloom as the lower part was brightly lighted. And as she passed along the arcade Point Pescade did not know what to do. A ray from the lantern, however, showed him that the upper part of the arcade was ornamented with open arabesques in Moorish fashion.

To climb the central column, seize hold of one of these arabesques, draw himself up, and crouch in the central oval, where he remained as motionless as a saint in a niche, was the work of a second.

Namir passed along the arcade without seeing him, and crossed to the opposite side of the gallery. When she reached the door of the skifa she opened it. A bright light shot across the courtyard, and was instantly extinguished as the door was shut.

Point Pescade set himself to reflect, and where could he find a better position for reflection?

It was the moqaddem himself who was talking with Sarcany

"That's Namir who has just gone into that room," he said to himself. "It's evident she's not going to Sava Sandorf! But perhaps she came from her, and in that case her room will be the one in the angle over there – I'll go and see!"

He waited a few minutes before he left his post. The light inside the skifa seemed to grow less, and the voices died out to nearly a murmur. Doubtless the hour had come when Sidi Hazam's household retired to rest. The circumstances were therefore more favourable for him, for that part of the habitation would be plunged in silence when the last light had gone out. And that was exactly what happened.

Pescade glided along the columns of the arcade, crept across the flags of the gallery, passed the door of the skifa, went round the end of the courtyard, and reached the angle near the room from which Namir had come. He opened the door, which was unlocked, and then by the light of an Arab lamp, placed like a nightlight beneath its shade, gave a rapid glance round the room.

A few hangings suspended from the walls here and there a stool of Moorish pattern, cushions piled in the angles, a double carpet on the mosaic floor, a low table with the fragments of a meal, a divan covered with linen cloth – that was what he first saw.

He entered, and shut the door.

A woman, dozing rather than sleeping, was reclining on the divan, half-covered in one of those burnouses with which the Arabs wrap themselves from head to feet.

It was Sava Sandorf.

Point Pescade had no hesitation in recognizing the young lady he had met so many times in the streets of Ragusa. How changed she seemed to be! Pale as she had been when in her wedding carriage she had met the funeral procession of Pierre Bathory, her attitude, and the expression of her face all told what she had had to suffer!

There was not an instant to lose.

And in fact, as the door had not been locked, was not Namir coming back? Perhaps the Moor guarded her night and day? And if the girl could leave her room, how could she escape without help from the outside? Sidi Hazam's house was walled like a prison!

Point Pescade bent over the divan. What was his astonishment at a resemblance, which had never struck him before – the resemblance between Sava Sandorf and Dr. Antekirtt!

The girl opened her eyes.

461

At seeing a stranger standing near her in the fantastic dress of an acrobat, with finger on his lips and an appealing look in his eyes, she was bewildered rather than frightened. But she arose, and had sufficient coolness to make no sound.

"Silence!" said Point Pescade. "You have nothing to fear from me! I've come here to save you! Behind those walls your friends are waiting for you, friends who'll give their lives to get you out of Sarcany's hands! Pierre Bathory is alive..."

"Pierre – alive?" exclaimed Sava, restraining the beatings of her heart.

"Read!"

And Point Pescade gave the girl a letter, which contained these words:

> Sava,
> Trust him who has risked his life to reach you! I am alive! I am here!
>
> > Pierre Bathory

Pierre was alive! He was at the foot of these walls! By what miracle? Sava would know later on! But Pierre was there.

"We must escape!" she said.

"Yes! We'll escape," answered Pescade. "But chance must be on our side! One question, is Namir accustomed to spending the night in this room?"

"No," answered Sava.

"Does she take the precaution of locking you in when she's away?"

"Yes."

"Then she'll come back?"

"Yes! We must go!"

"Now," answered Pescade.

And first they must reach the staircase of the minaret to gain the terrace. Once they got there the rope that hung down outside would render escape easy.

"Come!" said Point Pescade, taking Sava's hand.

And he was going to open the door when he heard steps coming along the gallery. At the same time a few words were pronounced in an imperious tone. Point Pescade recognized Sarcany's voice. He stopped at the threshold.

"It's him!" whispered the girl. "You're lost if he finds you here!"

"He won't find me!" answered Pescade.

And throwing himself to the ground he then, by one of those acrobatic contortions he had often performed in sight of an audience, wrapped himself up in one of the carpets on the floor and rolled himself into the darkest corner of the room.

At the same moment the door opened to admit Sarcany and Namir, who shut it behind them.

Sava resumed her seat on the divan. Why had Sarcany come to her at that hour? Was this a new attempt to overcome her refusal? But Sava was strong now! She knew that Pierre Bathory was alive – that he was waiting outside!

Beneath the carpet, which covered him, Point Pescade, although he could not see, could hear everything.

"Sava," said Sarcany, "tomorrow morning we're going to leave this for another place. But I do not wish to leave here until you've consented to our marriage, until it's been celebrated. All is ready, and it's necessary that now..."

"Neither now nor later!" replied the girl, in a voice as cold as it was resolute.

"Sava," continued Sarcany, as though he had not heard this reply, "in the interest of us both, it's necessary that your consent should be given freely. In the interest of us both, you understand?"

"We have not, and we never shall have, any interest in common!"

"Take care! I may remind you that you gave your consent at Ragusa."

"For reasons which no longer exist!"

"Listen to me, Sava," said Sarcany whose apparent calm hid the most violent irritation, "this is the last time I shall ask you for your consent."

"And I shall refuse it as long as I have strength to do so!"

"Well, that strength we'll take away from you," exclaimed Sarcany. "Do not drive me to extremes! Yes! The strength, which you use against me, Namir will take from you, and in spite of you, if necessary! Do not resist me, Sava! The imam is here; ready to celebrate our marriage according to the custom of my own country! Follow me then!"

Sarcany advanced towards the girl, who quickly rose and stepped back to the end of the room.

"Scoundrel!" she exclaimed.

"You'll come with me! You'll come with me!" exclaimed Sarcany.

"Never!"

"Ah! Take care!"

Pescade led the way along the gallery round the courtyard wall

And Sarcany, having seized the girl's arm, was, with Namir's help, violently dragging her towards the skifa, where Sidi Hazam and the imam were waiting.

"Help! Help!" screamed Sava. "Help me – Pierre Bathory!"

"Pierre Bathory!" exclaimed Sarcany. "You're calling a dead man!"

"No! He's alive! Help me – Pierre!"

The answer was so unexpected by Sarcany that he could not have been more frightened had he seen Pierre's ghost. But he was soon himself again. Pierre alive! Pierre, whom he had stabbed with his own hand, and seen buried in the cemetery at Ragusa! In truth, it could only be the idea of a mad woman, and it was possible that Sava in the excess of her despair had lost her reason.

Point Pescade had heard all that passed. In telling Sarcany that Pierre was alive, Sava had staked her life that was certain. And in case the scoundrel offered any violence, he so disposed his carpet as to be ready to appear on the scene instantly, knife in hand: and those who thought he would hesitate to strike did not know Point Pescade.

There was no necessity for him to do so. Sarcany abruptly dragged Namir out of the room. Then the key was turned in the lock while the girl's fate was being decided.

At a bound Pescade had thrown off the carpet, and was by her side.

"Come!" said he.

As the lock was inside the room, to unscrew it by means of his knife was not a long, difficult, or noisy job.

As soon as the door was opened, and then shut behind them, Pescade led the way along the gallery round the courtyard wall.

It was about half-past eleven. A few beams of light filtered through the skifa's bays. Pescade avoided crossing them on his way to the passage that led to the first courtyard.

They reached the passage, and went along it; but when they were only a few yards from the minaret staircase, Pescade suddenly stopped and held back Sava, whose hand his had never left.

Three men were talking in this first courtyard by the side of the water. One of them – it was Sidi Hazam – was giving orders to the others. Almost immediately they disappeared up the minaret staircase, while the moqaddern went into one of the lateral chambers. Pescade perceived that Sidi Hazam had sent the men to watch the neighbourhood. And that when he and the girl appeared on the terrace it would be occupied and guarded.

"We must risk it, however!" said Point Pescade.

"Yes. Everything!" replied Sava.

Then they crossed the gallery and reached the staircase, which they mounted with extreme care. Then when Point Pescade had reached the upper landing, he stopped.

No sound on the terrace, not even a sentry's step!

Point Pescade quietly opened the door, and followed by Sava he glided along the battlements.

Suddenly a shout came from the minaret above from one of the men on guard. At the same moment the other jumped on Pescade, while Namir rushed on to the terrace, and the whole household came hurrying out of their rooms.

Would Sava allow herself to be retaken? No! To be retaken by Sarcany was to be lost! A hundred times would she prefer death!

With a prayer to God the brave girl ran to the parapet and without hesitation leapt from the terrace.

Pescade had not even time to interfere; but throwing off the man that held him, he caught hold of the rope and a second later was at the foot of the wall.

"Sava! Sava!" he shouted.

"Here is the young lady!" said a familiar voice, "and no bones broken! I was just in the way..."

A shout of fury, followed by a heavy thud, cut short Cape Matifou's speech.

Namir in a moment of rage, unwilling to abandon the prey that was escaping her, had leapt and been smashed to pieces, as Sava would have been smashed if two strong arms had not caught her as she fell.

Doctor Antekirtt, Pierre, and Luigi, had rejoined Cape Matifou and Point Pescade who were running towards the shore. Although Sava had fainted she weighed almost nothing in the arms of her rescuer.

A few minutes afterwards Sarcany with a score of armed men came out in pursuit of the fugitives.

When he reached the creek where the *Electric* had been waiting, the doctor and his companions were already on board, and in a few turns of the screw the swift vessel was out of range.

Sava, alone with the doctor and Pierre, soon regained her consciousness. She learnt that she was the daughter of Count Mathias Sandorf! She was in her father's arms!

CHAPTER IV

ANTEKIRTTA

Fifteen hours after leaving the coast of Tripoli the *Electric* was signalled by the lookout at Antekirtta, and in the afternoon she came into harbour.

We can easily imagine the reception given to the doctor and his companions.

Now that Sava was out of danger it was decided to still keep secret her relationship to Dr. Antekirtt.

Count Mathias wished to remain unknown until the accomplishment of his work. But it was enough that Pierre, whom he had made his son, was the betrothed of Sava Sandorf for signs of rejoicing to be shown on all sides – in the Stadthaus as well as in the town of Artenak.

We may judge what were Madame Bathory's feelings when Sava was given back to her after so many trials. And Sava herself soon recovered her health – a few days of happiness were sufficient for her complete re-establishment.

That Point Pescade had risked his life there could be no doubt. But as he seemed to think it quite a natural thing to do there was no possibility of rewarding him – except with a few simple words. Pierre Bathory had clasped him to his breast, and the doctor had given him such a look of gratitude that he would hear of no other recompense. According to his custom he gave the whole credit of the adventure to Cape Matifou.

"He's the man that should be thanked," he said. "He did it all! If old Cape hadn't been so clever with that pole I should never have been able to jump into Sidi Hazam's house, and Sava Sandorf would have been killed by her fall if Cape Matifou hadn't been below to receive her in his arms!"

"Look here! Look here!" answered Cape Matifou. "You're going too far and the idea of..."

"Be quiet!" continued Pescade. "I'm not strong enough to receive compliments of that calibre, while you... Come, let's tend to the garden!"

And Cape Matifou held his peace, and returned to his pleasant villa, and finally accepted the felicitations that were thrust upon him so as not to disoblige his little Pescade.

It was arranged that the wedding of Pierre and Sava should take place on the 9th of December. When Pierre was Sava's husband he could claim his wife's rights in the inheritance of Count Sandorf. Madame Toronthal's letter left no doubt as to the girl's birth, and if necessary they could obtain a format statement from the banker.

And this statement would be obtained in time, for Sava had not yet reached the age at which she would enter into her rights. She would not be eighteen until six months later.

It should be added that in the fifteen years a political change had taken place favourable to the Hungarian question, and this had considerably modified the situation – particularly with regard to the conspiracy of Trieste.

It was not intended to come to any decision as to the fate of Carpena and Toronthal until Sarcany had joined them in the casemates of Antekirtta. Then, and not till then, would the work of justice be completed.

But while the doctor was still scheming how to attain his object, it was absolutely necessary that he should provide for the safety of the colony. His agents in the Cyrenaic and Tripoli had informed him that the Senousist movement was attaining great importance, particularly in the vilayet of Ben Ghazi, which is that nearest to the island. Special messengers were continually on the move to the minor chiefs of the province from Jerhboûb, the new pole of the Islamic world,' as Dr. Duveyrier calls it, the metropolitan Mecca where lived Sidi Mohammed El Mahedi, grandmaster of the order; and as the Senousists are the worthy descendants of the old Barbary pirates and bear a mortal hate to everything European, the doctor had to take steps to be very carefully on his guard.

In fact, is it not to the Senousists that we can attribute the massacres in African necrology during the last twenty years? The sanguinary brotherhood has put in practice the Senousistic doctrines against our explorers, and we have seen Beurman killed at Kanem in 1863, Von der Decken and his companions on the Djouba River in 1865, Madame Alexine Tinné and her people in Wady Abedjouch in 1865, Dournaux Dupeiré and Joubert at the wells of In-Azhar in 1874, Fathers Paulmier Bouchard and Menoret beyond the In-Calah in 1876, Fathers Richard

Morat and Pouplard of the Ghadames mission in the north of Azdjer, Colonel Flatters, Captains Masson and Dianous, Dr. Guiard, and Engineers Beringer and Roche on the road to Wargla in 1881.

On this subject the doctor often talked with Pierre Bathory, Luigi Ferrato, the captains of the flotilla, the chiefs of the militia and the principal notables of the island. Could Antekirtta resist an attack form the pirates? Yes, doubtless, although the fortifications were not complete, but on condition that the number of assailants was not too great. On the other hand, had the Senousists any interest in capturing it? Yes, for it commanded all the Gulf of Sidra, which formed the coast of Tripoli and the Cyrenaic.

It will not have been forgotten that southwest of Antekirtta, at a distance of some two miles, there lay the islet of Kencraf. This islet, which there was no time to fortify, would constitute a serious danger if a hostile flotilla made it its base of operation, and so the doctor had taken the precaution to mine it extensively. And now a terrible explosive agent filled the fougasses amid its rocks. It would suffice for an electric spark to be sent through the cable from Antekirtta, and the island of Kencraf would be annihilated with everything that was on it.

With regard to the other defences of the island this is what had been done. The flanking batteries had been completed, and only waited for the militia assigned to them to move to their stations. The fortress on the central cone was ready with its long-range pieces. Numerous torpedoes had been sunk in the channel, and defended the entrance to the harbour. The *Ferrato* and three *Electrics* were ready for all eventualities either in awaiting the attack or advancing on a hostile flotilla.

But in the southwest of the island there was a vulnerable spot. A landing might take place there sheltered from the guns of the fortress. There was the danger, and it might be too late to become sufficiently advanced with the works of defence.

After all, was it quite certain that the Senousists intended to attack Antekirtta? It was a big affair, a dangerous expedition that would require a good deal of material. Luigi still doubted, and he said so one day while the doctor and Pierre were inspecting the fortifications.

"That's not my opinion," said the doctor. "Antekirtta is rich, it commands the Syrtic Sea; and those are sufficient reasons for the Senousists sooner or later to attack it."

"Nothing can be more certain," added Pierre "and it's an eventuality against which we should be prepared."

The flanking batteries had been completed

"But what makes me fear an immediate attack is that Sarcany is one of the brotherhood of these Khouans, and I know that he has always been in their service as an agent in foreign parts. Do you not remember the conversation Pescade overheard in the moqaddem's house? Sidi Hazam and Sarcany mentioned Antekirtta several times; Sarcany knows this island belongs to Dr. Antekirtt, the man he fears, the man whom he made Zirone attack on the slopes of Etna. As he did not succeed in Sicily, there's little doubt he'll try to succeed here under better circumstances."

"Has he any personal hate against you?" asked Luigi. "Does he know you?"

"It's possible that he's seen me at Ragusa," replied the doctor. "In any case he would not be ignorant that in that town I was in communication with the Bathory family. Besides, the existence of Pierre was revealed to him when Sava was carried off by Pescade from the house of Sidi Hazam. In his mind he would see the association and would have no doubt but what Pierre and Sava had taken refuge in Antekirtta. He will therefore urge on against us the whole Senousitic horde, and we shall have no quarter if he succeeds in getting possession of our island."

The argument was quite plausible. That Sarcany did not know that the doctor was Count Sandorf was certain, but he knew enough to wish to get away from him the heiress of the Artenak estate; and there was nothing surprising in his attempt to excite the caliph to undertake an expedition against the Antekirttian colony.

However, they had reached the 3rd of December and there had been no sign of an imminent attack.

Besides, the thought of the approaching marriage of Pierre Bathory and Sava Sandorf occupied everybody. And the colonists tried to persuade themselves that the evil days had passed and would not return.

Point Pescade and Cape Matifou of course shared in the general sense of security. They were so happy in the happiness of others that they lived in a state of perpetual enchantment with everything.

"I can hardly believe it!" repeated Point Pescade.

"What can you hardly believe?" asked Cape Matifou.

"That you are to become a big fat annuitant, my Cape! I must think of marrying you."

"Marrying me?"

"Yes, to some nice little woman!"

"Why little?"

"That's only just! A large one would never do! Eh! We should have to look for Mrs. Cape Matifou among the Patagonians!"

471

But pending the marriage of Cape Matifou, which might end satisfactorily, if he could find only a companion worthy of him, Point Pescade busied himself about the marriage of Pierre and Sava. With the doctor's permission he was thinking of organizing a public festival, with foreign games, songs, and dances, discharges of artillery, a grand banquet in the open air, a serenade, and a torchlight procession and fireworks. That just suited him! He was in his element! It would be splendid! They would talk of it for long afterwards! They would talk of it forever!

All this excitement was nipped in the bud.

During the night of the 3rd and 4th of December – a calm night, but a very cloudy one – an electric bell sounded in Dr. Antekirtt's room in the Stadthaus.

It was ten o'clock.

At the call the doctor and Pierre left the saloon in which they had passed the evening with Madame Bathory and Sava Sandorf. On entering the room they saw that the call was from the lookout on the central cone. Questions and answers immediately passed by means of the telephone.

The lookouts signalled the approach of a flotilla to the southwest of the island, the vessels appearing very confusedly in the thick mist.

"We must summon the Council," said the doctor.

Less than ten minutes afterwards the doctor, Pierre, Luigi, Captains Narsos and Kostrik, and the chiefs of the militia were at the Stadthaus, considering the information sent down from the cone. A quarter of an hour afterwards they were all at the harbour, at the end of the main jetty, on which the bright light was burning.

From this point, which was very little above sea level, it would be impossible to distinguish the flotilla that the lookouts on the central cone could clearly see. But in brightly illuminating the horizon towards the southwest it would doubtless be possible to make out the number of ships, and their plan of attack.

Was it not unwise to thus disclose the position of the island? The doctor did not think so. If it was the enemy they expected that enemy was not coming as a blind man. He knew the position of Antekirtta and nothing could keep him away from it.

The machinery was put into action, and with the aid of the two electric beams projected into the offing, a vast stretch of the horizon was suddenly illuminated.

The lookouts had not been mistaken. Two hundred boats, at the least, were advancing in line, xebecs, polaccas, trabacolos, saccolevas, and others of less importance. There was no doubt that this was the flotilla of the Senousists, recruited by the pirates in every port along the coast. The wind failing, they had had recourse to their sweeps. The passage between Antekirtta and the Cyrenaic was not a long one. The calm night even helped them, for it would allow a landing to take place under favourable conditions.

At the moment the flotilla was about four or five miles off, in the southwest. It could not reach the coast before sunrise.

After the first reconnaissance the lights were extinguished. The only thing to do was to wait for day.

However, by the doctor's orders, the militia were mustered and sent to their stations.

It was necessary to be in a position to strike the first blow, on which perhaps the issue of the enterprise would depend.

It was now certain that the assailants could no longer hope to take the island by surprise, inasmuch as the projection of the light had allowed of their course and numbers to be known.

A most careful watch was kept during the last hours of the night. The horizon was illuminated again and again, to track the flotilla's exact position. That the assailants were numerous there could be no doubt. That they were sufficiently armed to have a chance against the Antekirtta batteries was doubtful. They were probably without artillery. But the number of men that the chief could land at once would make the Senousists really formidable.

Day at last began to break, and the first rays of the sun dissipated the mists on the horizon. Every eye was turned seaward towards the east and south of Antekirtta. The flotilla was advancing in a long curved line. There were over two hundred vessels, some of them of thirty or forty tons. Altogether they could carry from 1500 to 2000 men.

At five o'clock the flotilla was off Kencraf. Would the enemy stop there and take up their position before attacking the island? If they did so, it would indeed be fortunate. The mines laid by the doctor would seriously damage their attack, if they did not entirely settle it.

An anxious half-hour elapsed. It seemed as though the vessels, as they reached the islet, were about to land – but they did, nothing of the sort. Not one stopped. The line curved farther off to the south, leaving it to the right, and it became evident that Antekirtta would be directly attacked, or rather invaded, in an hour.

"The only thing now is to defend ourselves," said the doctor to the chief of the militia.

Two hundred boats, at the least, were advancing

The signal was given, and those on the island hastened into the town to take the posts that had been assigned them beforehand. By the doctor's orders Pierre Bathory took command of the fortifications to the south, Luigi of those to the east. The defenders – five hundred at the most – were posted so that they could face the enemy wherever he attempted to force the walls. The doctor held himself ready to go where his presence might be necessary. Madame Bathory, Sava Sandorf, Maria Ferrato remained in the hall of the Stadthaus. The other women, should the town be carried, were ordered to take shelter with their children in the casemates where they would have nothing to fear even if the assailants possessed a few landing guns.

The question of Kencraf being settled – unfortunately to the doctor's advantage – there remained the question of the harbour. If the flotilla attempted to force an entry, the forts on the two jetties, with their crossfire, the guns of the *Ferrato*, the torpedoes of the *Electrics*, and the torpedoes sunk in the channel would have something to say in the matter. It would, in short, be fortunate if the attack were made on that side.

But – as was only too evident – the chief of the Senousists was perfectly acquainted with Antekirtta's means of defence.

To attempt a direct attack on the harbour would have been to run to complete and immediate annihilation. A landing in the southern part of the island, where the operation would be an easy one, was the plan he adopted. And so having passed by the harbour, as he had passed by Kencraf, he took his flotilla, still rowing, towards the weak point of Antekirtta.

As soon as he saw this, the doctor took such measures as circumstances demanded. Captains Kostrik and Narsos each took command of a torpedo boat, and slipped out of harbour.

A quarter of an hour afterward the two *Electrics* had rushed into the midst of the flotilla, broken the line, sunk five or six of the vessels, and, stove in more than a dozen others. But the numbers of the enemy was so great that, to avoid being boarded, the *Electrics* had to retreat to the shelter of the jetties.

But the *Ferrato* had now come into position and begun firing on the flotilla. Her guns and those of the batteries that could be brought to bear were, however, insufficient to prevent the pirates landing. Although a great number had perished, although twenty of their vessels had been sunk, more than a thousand scrambled on to the rocks in the south, to which the calm sea rendered the approach so easy.

It was then found that the Senousists were not without artillery. The largest of the xebecs had several fieldpieces on wheeled carriages, and these were landed on the shore, which was out of range of the guns either of the town or the central cone.

The doctor, from his position on the nearest salient, had seen all this, and with his much fewer men could not attempt to stop it. But as they were sheltered by the walls, the assailants, numerous as they were, would find their task a difficult one.

The Senousists, dragging their light guns with them, formed up into two columns, and came marching along with all the careless bravery of the Arab and the audacity of the fanatics, who glory in their contempt of death, their hope of pillage, and their hate of the European.

When they were well within range the batteries opened on them. More than a hundred fell, but the others still kept on. Their fieldpieces were brought into position and they began to breach the wall in the angle of the unfinished curtain towards the south.

Their chief, calm amid those who were falling at his side, directed the operation. Sarcany, close by, was exciting him to deliver the assault, and hurl several hundred men at the falling wall.

From the distance, Dr. Antekirtt and Pierre had recognized him, and he had recognized them.

And now the mass of besiegers began their advance to the wall, which had been beaten in sufficiently to let them through. If they succeeded in clearing this breach, they would spread themselves over the town, and the besieged, too weak to resist, would have to abandon it, and, with the sanguinary temperament of the pirates, the victory would be followed by a general massacre.

The hand-to-hand struggle at this point was terrible. Under the doctor's orders, who stood as impassable in the danger as he was invulnerable amid the bullets, Pierre and his companions performed prodigies of valour, and Point Pescade and Cape Matifou lent their assistance, and displayed the most brilliant audacity.

The Hercules, with a knife in one hand, and an axe in the other, kept clear the space around him.

"Go to it, my Cape, go to it! Down with them!" shouted Point Pescade, whose revolver, incessantly recharging and discharging, was going like a Gatling.

But the foe would not yield. After being many times driven out of the breach, they had again swarmed on to the attack, and were slowly fighting their way through, when they suddenly found themselves attacked in the rear.

The *Ferrato* had managed to get into a commanding position within three cable lengths of the shore, and with her carronades all brought to the one side, her long chaser, her Hotchkiss cannons, and her Gatling machine guns, she opened such a fire on the assailants that they were mown down as the grass before the scythe. She attacked them in the rear and cannonaded them on the beach at the same time so as to destroy and sink the boats, which had been moored round the rocks.

The blow was a terrible one, and was quite unexpected by the Senousists. Not only were they taken in the rear, but all means of escape would be cut off if their vessels were knocked to pieces by the guns of the *Ferrato*. The assailants hesitated in the breach that the militia were defending so obstinately. Already more than five hundred had met their deaths, while the besieged had lost but few.

The leader of the expedition saw that he must immediately retreat to sea or expose his companions to certain and complete destruction. In vain Sarcany demanded that they might continue the attack on the town. The order was given to return to shore; and the Senousists drew off as if they would be killed to the last man, were the orders given them to die.

But it was necessary to give these pirates a lesson they would never forget.

"Forward! My friends! Forward!" shouted the doctor.

And under the orders of Pierre and Luigi, a hundred of the militia threw themselves on to the fugitives as they retreated to the beach. Between the fire from the *Ferrato* and the fire from the batteries, the Senousists had to give way. Their ranks broke in disorder, and they ran in a crowd to the seven or eight vessels that still were left to them.

Pierre and Luigi, amid the confusion, endeavoured above all things to take one man prisoner: Sarcany. But they wished to have him alive, and it was only by a miracle that they escaped the revolver shots the scoundrel fired at them.

It seemed, however, that fate would again withdraw him from their hands.

Sarcany and the leader of the Senousists, followed by a dozen of their companions, had managed to regain a small polacca, which they had cast off and were preparing to get under way. The *Ferrato* was too far off for them to signal her to pursue, and it looked as though she would escape.

At the moment Cape Matifou saw a field gun dismounted from its carriage and thrown on the beach.

Two *Electrics* had rushed into the midst of the flotilla

To hurl himself on the still loaded gun, to lift it with superhuman force on to one of the rocks, to steady it by the trunnions, and in a voice of thunder to shout, "Come here, Pescade! Here!" was the work of a moment.

Pescade heard Matifou's shout, and saw what he had done; instantly he understood, ran up, pointed the gun at the polacca, and fired.

The shot went clean through the hull. The recoil hardly shook the living gun carriage. The leader of the Senousists and his companions were pitched into the water and, for the most part drowned. Sarcany was struggling with the surf when Luigi threw himself into the sea.

A minute afterwards Sarcany was safe in the huge hands of Cape Matifou.

The victory was complete. Of the two thousand assailants who had landed on the island, only a few hundred escaped to the Cyrenaic to tell the story of the disaster.

Antekirtta would, it could be hoped, for many a year be free from another pirate attack.

Pescade pointed the gun at the polacca, and fired

CHAPTER V

JUSTICE

Count Mathias Sandorf had paid his debt of gratitude to Maria and Luigi Ferrato. Madame Bathory, Pierre, and Sava were at last reunited. After the reward came the punishment.

For some days following the defeat of the Senousists the colonists were actively employed in repairing damages. With the exception of a few trifling scars, Pierre, Luigi, Point Pescade and Cape Matifou – that is to say all those who had been most intimately connected with the events of this drama – were safe and sound. That they had not spared themselves, however, needs no affirmation.

Great, therefore, was the rejoicing when they met together in the Stadthaus with Sava Sandorf, Maria Ferrato, Madame Bathory, and her old servant Borik. After the funeral of those who had fallen in the battle, the little colony resumed its happy existence. Its future would be free from trouble. The defeat of the Senousists had been disastrous, and Sarcany, who had persuaded them to undertake this campaign against Antekirtta, would no longer be with them to fan the flame of hatred and vengeance.

The doctor proposed completing his system of defence without delay. Not only would Artenak be promptly rendered secure from a sudden surprise, but the island itself would nowhere afford a landing place. And it was intended to invite thither a few more colonists to whom the fertility of the soil would prove an attraction and a guarantee of prosperity.

Meanwhile no further obstacle existed to the marriage of Pierre and Sava. The ceremony had been fixed for the 9th of December; and it would take place on that date. And so Point Pescade was particularly busy with the preparations that had been interrupted by the invasion of the pirates from the Cyrenaic.

And now without delay the fate of Sarcany, Toronthal, and Carpena was to be decided.

On the 6th of December, two days after the retreat of the Senousists, the doctor ordered them to be brought to the Stadthaus. The prisoners were unaware of each other's presence in the island, and for the first time found themselves together, when under a guard of a detachment of militia, they came before the tribunal of Artenak, consisting of the chief magistrates of Antekirtta.

Carpena appeared uneasy; but having lost nothing of his devious look, he merely threw furtive glances to the right and left of him, and dared not lift his eyes to his judges.

Toronthal seemed quite cast down, and bowed his head, and instinctively avoided the touch of his old accomplice.

Sarcany had only one feeling – he was furious at having fallen into the hands of this Dr. Antekirtt.

Luigi advanced towards the judges, and began by addressing the Spaniard.

"Carpena," said he, "I am Luigi Ferrato, the son of the fisherman of Rovigno, whom you informed against and sent to prison at Stein, where he died."

Carpena drew himself up for an instant. A paroxysm of anger sent the blood to his eyes. Then it was indeed Maria whom he had recognized in the lanes of the Manderaggio, and it was her brother Luigi who thus accused him.

Pierre then advanced, and at first pointing to the banker he said:

"Silas Toronthal, I am Pierre Bathory, the son of Stephen Bathory, the Hungarian patriot, whom you, with your accomplice Sarcany, most shamefully betrayed to the Austrian police at Trieste, and sent to death!"

Then to Sarcany he said:

"I am Pierre Bathory, whom you tried to assassinate in the road at Ragusa. I am the intended husband of Sava, the daughter of Count Mathias Sandorf whom you stole fifteen years ago from the Castle of Artenak."

Neither Toronthal nor Sarcany said a word in reply. And what could they say to their victim, who seemed to have risen from the tomb to accuse them?

But it was quite another thing when Dr. Antekirtt rose in his turn, and said in a grave voice: "And I, I am the companion of Ladislas Zathmar and Stephen Bathory, whom your treachery caused to be shot in the donjon of Pisino! I am the father of Sava, whom you abducted to get possession of her fortune! I am Count Mathias Sandorf!"

This time the effect of the declaration was such that the knees of Silas Toronthal bent to the ground, while Sarcany crouched as if he would sink into himself. Then the three accused were examined one after the other. Their crimes they could not deny, and for their crimes no pardon was possible. The chief magistrate reminded Sarcany that the attack on the island, undertaken in his own personal interest, had made many victims whose blood cried out for vengeance. Then having given the accused full liberty to reply, he gave sentence conformably to the right given him by this regularly constituted jurisdiction.

"Silas Toronthal, Sarcany, and Carpena, you have caused the deaths of Stephen Bathory, Ladislas Zathmar, and Andrea Ferrato! You are sentenced to death!"

"Whenever you like!" replied Sarcany, whose impudence again asserted itself.

"Mercy!" cried Carpena.

Toronthal had not the strength to speak. The three were taken away to the casemates and there kept under guard.

How were these scoundrels to die? Were they to be shot in some corner of the island? That would be to defile the soil of Antekirtta with the blood of traitors! And it was decided that the execution should take place at Kencraf. That evening one of the *Electrics*, commanded by Luigi Ferrato, took the prisoners on board, and bore them off to the island, where they were to wait till sunrise for the firing party.

Sarcany, Toronthal, and Carpena saw that their time had come; and when they had been landed, Sarcany went up to Luigi, and asked him, "Is it to be this evening?"

Luigi made no reply. The three doomed men were left there alone, and night had fallen when the *Electric* returned to Antekirtta.

The island was now free from the presence of the traitors. That they could escape from Kencraf, which was twenty miles away from the mainland, was impossible.

"By tomorrow," said Point Pescade, "they'll have eaten each other!"

"Pouah!" said Cape Matifou in disgust.

That night Count Sandorf had not a moment's repose. Locked in his room, he did not leave it until four o'clock in the morning, when he descended to the hall to meet Pierre and Luigi, who were immediately summoned.

A file of militia was waiting in the courtyard of the Stadthaus under orders to embark for Kencraf.

"Pierre Bathory, Luigi Ferrato," said Count Sandorf, "have these traitors been justly condemned to die?"

"Yes, they deserve it," answered Pierre.

Not a trace was left of the islet of Kencraf

"Yes," replied Luigi, "the scoundrels deserve no mercy."

"Then let justice be done, and may God give the pardon that man cannot..."

He had scarcely finished speaking when a fearful explosion shook the Stadthaus, and the whole of the island, as if an earthquake had taken place. Count Sandorf and his companions rushed out, and the whole population in terror came streaming into the streets of Artenak.

An immense sheaf of flame, with enormous masses of rock and showers of stones, was blazing to a prodigious height towards the sky. Then the masses fell back round the islet, raining huge waves in the sea; and a thick cloud remained suspended in space. Not a trace was left of the islet of Kencraf, nor of the three men whom the explosion had annihilated. What, then, had happened?

It will not have been forgotten that the island had been mined in preparation for the landing of the Senousists, and that in case the submarine cable which united it to Antekirtta was put out of action, certain, electrical batteries had been buried in the ground, so that the wires had only to be pressed by the feet to be brought in contact and fire the fougasses of panclastite.

What had happened was this. By chance one of the doomed men had trodden on these wires. And hence the complete and instantaneous destruction of the islet.

"Heaven has spared us the horrors of an execution!" said Count Sandorf.

Three days afterwards the marriage of Pierre and Sava was duly celebrated at the church at Artenak. On that occasion Dr. Antekirtt signed his real name of Mathias Sandorf; which he would never again lay down now that justice had been done. A few words will suffice to finish our story.

Three weeks afterwards Sava Bathory was recognized as the heiress of the Sandorf property. The letter from Madame Toronthal and a declaration obtained from the banker in which the circumstances and the motive behind her abduction were duly set forth, proved sufficient to establish her identity. As Sava was not yet eighteen all that remained of the Carpathian estates in Transylvania came back to her.

Count Sandorf himself could, if he had chosen, have entered into possession of this property, under an amnesty, which had been issued in favour of political prisoners. But though he returned to public life as

Mathias Sandorf, he decided to remain as head of his great family of Antekirtta, for he wished to live his life among those who loved him.

The little colony, thanks to his renewed efforts, began to flourish rapidly. In less than a year, it had doubled its population. Scientists and inventors, invited thither by Count Sandorf, had come to make good use of discoveries that would have been forsaken without his advice and the wealth of which he was the master. And so Antekirtta would soon become the most important place in the Syrtic Sea and with the completion of its defensive system, its security would become absolute.

Of Madame Bathory, Maria, Luigi Ferrato, and of Pierre and Sava, we need say no more; who does not feel that their lives were happy? What more can be said of Point Pescade and Cape Matifou, who were now perhaps the most famous colonists of Antekirtta? If they regretted anything, it was that they had no further opportunity to show their gratitude to the man who had provided them with such an existence.

Count Mathias Sandorf had accomplished his task, and, had it not been for the remembrance of his two companions, Stephen Bathory and Ladislas Zathmar, he would have been as happy as a generous man can be on this earth when he spreads his wealth and joy about him.

In the whole Mediterranean, in all the distant seas of the globe – even in the Fortunate Islands – we may seek in vain for an island whose prosperity rivals that of Antekirtta!

And when Cape Matifou burdened by his good fortune found it necessary to say:

"Do you think we deserve such happiness?"

Point Pescade replied, "No, my, Cape! I don't! But what have you? Best we resign ourselves to our fate!"

Also from ROH Press

The Works of Emilio Salgari, "The Italian Jules Verne"

The Mystery of the Black Jungle

An apparition has been haunting Tremal-Naik, the renowned Hunter of the Black Jungle. Try as he may, he cannot shake the hold it has over him. But when one of his hunters is mysteriously murdered, Tremal-Naik must put his feelings aside and obtain vengeance. Accompanied by his faithful servant Kammamuri, he heads deep into the jungles of the Sundarbans and discovers an evil sect that threatens all of British India.

The Tigers of Mompracem

The Tigers of Mompracem are a band of rebel pirates fighting for the defence of tiny native kingdoms against the colonial powers of the Dutch and British empires. They are lead by Sandokan, the indomitable "Tiger of Malaysia", and his faithful friend Yanez De Gomera, a Portuguese wanderer and adventurer. Orphaned when the British murdered his family and stole his throne, Sandokan has been mercilessly leading his men in vengeance. But when the pirate learns of the extraordinary "Pearl of Labuan" his fortunes begin to change…perhaps forever….

The Pirates of Malaysia

Fortune has not smiled on Tremal-Naik. Wrongfully imprisoned, the great hunter has been banished from India; sentenced to life in a penal colony. Knowing his master is innocent, Kammamuri dashes off to the rescue, planning to free him at the first opportunity. When the ever-loyal servant is captured by the Tigers of Mompracem, he manages to enlist their help. But to succeed, Sandokan and Yanez must lead their men against the forces of James Brooke, "The Exterminator" the dreaded White Rajah of Sarawak.

For more information visit www.rohpress.com or contact us at:

info@rohpress.com